STEVEN PETERSEN

The Fall of Idunn

The Lightning Goddess Chronicles

Contents

Acknowledgement

Writing a book is not a simple undertaking. Between trying to sort through the tornado of ideas, tapping away on a keyboard, erasing pretty much everything that was just typed, typing it again because you realized you liked it, then re-reading what was typed dozens of times and trying to correct errors (including the spelling on names that sound a certain way in your head but don't translate to the page the same way), its easy to become distracted. So much so, that at times in the process it becomes very easy to forget to do something as important as expressing gratitude for all the people who don't get their names on the cover. In my excitement to write and publish my first book, I forgot to express thanks to those very important people. I hope that by doing it now, I can rectify my mistake adequately enough to make up for that omission.

There are so many people who have influenced me as a writer—many of whom probably didn't know it at the time and still don't. Teachers who graded poorly-thought out but hopefully passably written papers and encouraged me to dig deeper, to work harder. Family who sat through countless versions of my very animated stories without letting on that they felt like their time was being wasted. Friends who were willing to go along with me in the making of homemade movies based off of stories that I made up on the spot (sorry Jordan for making you lick that rubber pheasant all for the sake of getting a realistic shot). I even have to thank the editors, agents, and publishers that passed on my work. Rejection didn't define me—it fueled my hunger to chase this dream.

Now, for the specifics. My parents should be at the top of the list of people to thank. I'm sure they wondered about what was going on in my head with all my talk about elves, swords, magic, and epic adventures, but regardless of the fact that fantasy was not their thing, they always encouraged my creativity. I was blessed with siblings who fostered my interest in reading and storytelling, especially fantasy. Through them I was introduced to the works of Brooks, Salvatore, Tolkien, and Jordan. I'm thankful for each of them and the influence they had on me. I hope that you all see yourselves to some degree in my writing—you're in there!

I want to thank my beta readers for their time and feedback, including printing off copies and giving it a more thorough read than perhaps even I ever managed to achieve. You were all fantastic in helping me with the development of my story.

To my three little girls, thank you for listening to my crazy, often silly versions of bedtime stories. Even more, thank you for sharing your own stories with me. The mind of a child is magic, and if there's magic in my stories, a lot of it comes from seeing the world through your eyes.

Of course, none of this would have been possible without my wife, Kelly. She supported me in chasing this dream, reading countless drafts of these stories and many, many, MANY others. Thank you for being my sounding board and helping me develop my characters beyond what I was capable of doing alone. You didn't start out a fan of fantasy, but I'm grateful you've become a bigger one out of support for me. I love you!

Prologue

It felt like waking from a long, dreamless sleep.

When his gray-blue eyes opened, he couldn't help but feel confused by the blue of the sky visible through gently swaying tree branches. It felt wrong.

Sitting up slowly, he looked around at his surroundings. He was on a wicker bed near a lush garden ringed by mature trees. The moment his eyes touched the garden, an overwhelming sense of peace flooded into him and washed away some of the confusion he felt. He knew that he belonged and was safe as long as he was in this garden.

Rising to his feet, he took an awkward step forward. A sharp pain lanced up his left leg and he sucked in through his teeth. He reached down and rubbed at his thigh. To his surprise, he felt a half healed wound beneath the soft, woven pants he wore. He couldn't remember where it came from. In fact, he couldn't remember anything that had happened before he woke up. As hard as he tried, everything before a few moments ago was a blank.

He walked carefully into the garden and slowly wove his way between the lush bushes and trees. He looked for some sign that he wasn't alone, but didn't find any. He knew instinctively that a garden like this didn't just spring up by itself, which meant there had to be a caretaker somewhere nearby. With no direction in mind, he wandered aimlessly, breathing in the smells of the garden and enjoying a ripe, red apple he plucked from one of the trees.

He had just finished with the fruit when he noticed a woman in a flowing white dress watching him from the edge of the trees. Shocked by her sudden appearance, he stopped in place and stared at her. They remained locked in that silent exchange until she turned and strode deeper into the garden. Even though she had given him no sign, he felt confident that she wanted him to follow her. Still cautious, he matched her pace in order to keep some distance between them. He didn't know where he was or who she was, and he felt caution was better exercised and not needed rather than the contrary.

It wasn't long before the sound of people talking on the breeze reached his ears. They emerged into a clearing where a dozen other men and women dressed in a similar fashion to him were milling around the base of an enormous tree with a dark trunk. He could tell from their expressions and the way they milled about that they were just as confused as he was.

The woman he'd followed walked to the center of the clearing and turned to face him. He stopped a few steps shy of where she stood and waited for her to speak, taking the moment to get a better look at her. Her brown hair was swept over one shoulder and framed a face that he couldn't put an age to. Her vibrant green eyes sparkled with youthful exuberance, but she carried a maturity that made him think she was older than she appeared.

"You must have questions," she finally said in a voice so melodic that he had a sudden urge to ask to hear her sing.

Brushing aside the strange feeling, he asked the most obvious of his questions. "Who are you? And where am I?"

"You are in my garden," the woman replied.

"How did I get here?"

"I brought you here," the woman said. "You've been asleep for a long time. You were the last one to wake. The others have been waiting for you."

"We were all asleep?" he asked, scanning the faces around him.

She nodded. "My garden is a place of rest for those who need it. You, of all people, were in need of rest."

"Rest from what?"

"Life."

"That doesn't make sense."

"No," she said. She sighed softly. "I suppose it doesn't. Suffice it to say, you were very near death when I brought you here to heal."

His eyes narrowed. "Heal from what?"

Her eyes drifted to his left leg. "You will walk with a limp. I was never a gifted healer, and your leg was the least of my concerns. Time does mend wounds, though." Her eyes rose to meet his. "Perhaps with time, your leg will regain its strength."

"I don't understand," he said. "How was I wounded?"

"In battle," she said. "Not just any battle. *The* battle—Ragnarok. At least, what you thought was Ragnarok."

The sound of the name tugged at something deep inside, but it slipped through his fingers before he could grasp it.

"I don't remember a battle," he said.

"I had to shield your mind from the trauma your body experienced," she explained. "It was the only way to heal you. With time, your memories will return."

"How long have I been asleep?"

"Almost a thousand years."

The response made the hairs on his neck stand on end. How was that possible? He looked around the clearing at the faces gathered. The unease he felt was reflected on their expressions as well.

Turning back to the woman, he asked his first question again. "Who are you?"

She smiled. "My name is Idunn."

Again, the name tugged at something buried deep down, but he couldn't penetrate the fog that covered his mind. Grasping onto a sliver of hope, he asked the question he hoped would help push the fog away.

"Do you know who I am?"

Idunn nodded, a curious expression on her face. "Of course. You look different with both of your eyes."

"Both of my eyes?" he asked in surprise. "Was I missing one before?"

Idunn nodded slowly. "It was taken from you. It seems that it's been returned. I wonder what that means for you. Perhaps another has finally been chosen."

"What do you mean?" he asked. "How could it be missing and then be returned?"

She ignored his question and continued to study him. "Your time here has changed you. It's changed all of you."

"If you know something about me," he said, a twinge of impatience entering his voice, "please tell me."

"Are you sure you want to know?" Idunn asked. "The answer may be a burden."

"How could knowing who I am be a burden?"

"Knowledge always requires a sacrifice," she replied cryptically.

"Only because the sacrifice makes the knowledge all the more precious." While it was his voice that spoke, they didn't feel like his words. Taking a moment to gather himself, he continued. "I want to know who I am. Please tell me."

"What if you aren't the same as you were?" Idunn asked. "What if you can't be the man you were before? Would you still want to know, even if there was a chance that what was in the past might never be again?"

There was something dire in those words that made him pause. Finally, he nodded. "I want to know."

"Very well," Idunn said. She drew herself up, the underlying nobility in her bearing coming fully to the surface. "You are Odin, and you've been dead for almost a thousand years."

That name—his name—sent a bolt of energy through him. Odin, the Allfather, leader of the Norse Gods! Some of the fog that covered his mind retreated and he remembered sitting in a gilded throne with a strange orb ringed in blue flame hovering above a pedestal at his side. It wasn't much, but he clung to the memory with everything he had.

"I died in Ragnarok, didn't I?"

"Yes," Idunn said, "and no. When I found you, there was still a small spark of life left in you. It was enough for me to fan back into a flame. It took centuries, but the passage of time means nothing here."

"Why?" Odin asked. "Why did you save me?"

"Because," Idunn replied, "I knew the day would come when you would be needed." She looked around at the faces gathered. "When all of you would be needed again."

"Needed for what?"

Idunn's eyes turned sad and she took a deep breath. "To fight the *final* battle of Ragnarok."

Chapter 1

Thyra Ariksen listened numbly as the doctor spoke. She already knew what he was going to say. Her right knee was a perplexing medical anomaly. There was no scar tissue, the joint and the tendons looked healthy, and there was no sign as to why she continued to suffer from limited mobility any time she attempted to run, jump or move quickly from side to side. The fact that her knee showed no weakness in the strength exercises they had her perform only added to the confusion the doctors felt.

"I don't know what to tell you," the doctor said. "Every test we've done comes back the same. There's no good explanation for what is happening."

No good *medical* explanation, Thyra wanted to say. She'd heard the same words too many times over the last three months. She'd been to more doctors than she wanted to count, and they all had the same diagnosis about her injury. At first, when the physical tests came back inconclusive, they thought that she might have a mental block that was causing her to struggle, a performance anxiety that could be treated in a different manner. They'd even prescribed seeing a therapist. Talking about it was the last thing she wanted, and Thyra had made it clear that she wasn't going to see a shrink. Luckily, Sif agreed and asked to stick with the physical tests. The doctors obliged. They had put her through every kind of additional test, scan, and physical check they could think of. The result was always the same—when it came to agility, her knee wouldn't support even the smallest amount of weight. They had no explanation for it.

Thyra knew the explanation. She had been cursed by Yggdrasil, the source of all magic, when the World Tree chose her as its champion. Just like Odin before her, she had been forced to sacrifice something in return for immense magical power. Odin had lost an eye and his youth; Thyra had lost the ability to run, jump, and move side to side suddenly without falling to the floor in excruciating pain. In essence, she'd lost her ability to ever play lacrosse again. A lifelong dream now in the trash heap, along with any chance of a normal life.

Thyra's mom thanked the doctor and then waited until he was gone before turning to her daughter. As usual, Sif had her hair braided and swept over her left shoulder. She was the perfect mix of beauty and toughness, a true testament to her identity as a thousand-year-old Valkyrie from Norse legend. Even in jeans and a t-shirt, she managed to have a dangerous air that Thyra had confused with confidence before finding out who her mom truly was. There was no doubt that Sif was confident, but the reason for that confidence was that she knew she could wipe the floor with pretty much anyone who crossed her path.

"I think we should get another opinion," Sif said.

"That's what you've said the last three times," Thyra said glumly. "What is the next guy going to do that the last ten couldn't?"

"You never know with modern medicine," Sif said. "There is always some new procedure or injection. I was reading about this machine that uses shock waves to stimulate stem cells in the body. Maybe that will work. We just have to find the right doctor."

Thyra rolled her eyes. "Why do we keep doing this? You know the reason why my knee is like this, and there's nothing these guys can do to change it. This is all a waste of time!"

"We have to keep trying," Sif said.

"No, we don't." Thyra let out an exasperated sigh. "I'm tired of doing this. I'm tired of being poked, prodded, and tested when we already know what's wrong with me. These guys —no matter how many degrees and fancy machines they have—can't do anything for me."

"Don't be so quick to give up," Sif said, but her words lacked conviction.

"Why not? Hela couldn't do anything for me. You said she was the most gifted healer to ever live. And she has magic! If she couldn't help, why should these quacks be able to?"

"Thyra," Sif began, but Thyra didn't let her finish.

"No, Mom. We both know why my knee is messed up. Yggdrasil exacted it's price. It took the thing that meant the most to me besides you. I've wanted to play lacrosse in college since the first day you put a stick in my hand. Yggdrasil knew that, and it took my dream from me." Thyra couldn't keep the bitterness out of her voice. She tried to take a calming breath, but it didn't do any good. "I can't play lacrosse, Mom. Heck, I can't even run to the mailbox without falling over! That isn't going to change, no matter what we do."

Sif sat back and exhaled heavily. "I just don't want to give up hope."

"Well, you're the only one still holding on to any," Thyra said. She pushed herself to her feet and started for the door, forcing herself to walk with as little limp as possible. She paused at the door and looked back. "Can we go home now?"

Sif nodded slowly. She stood up and followed Thyra out of the room. Sif offered her arm, but Thyra waved it off. Walking wasn't the problem. Yes, she had a limp, but the pain was nothing compared to what she felt if she tried to do anything at a faster speed.

"Let me make sure we're all squared away for our visit," Sif said as they passed the receptionist's desk.

"I'll wait for you in the car," Thyra mumbled.

Sif said something in return, but Thyra had already put in a pair of earbuds, letting the sound of Iration carry her to a sunny beach somewhere far from the doctor's office and her problems. She wove her way through the parking lot to where Sif had parked the car. Even though it was a hot, late August day, Thyra pulled up the hood of the sweatshirt she wore like a shield against reality.

Thyra settled into the passenger seat and closed her eyes, but not even the laid back beat of the music could make her forget the situation she was in. How had her life come to this? Not only was her knee busted and her dreams shattered, but they were on the run, living like vagabonds in whatever small community her mom chose next. This week it was Blackfoot, Idaho. Next week, who knows? Her entire life had been uprooted in just a few short months with no sign of it ever going back to normal.

The car rocked slightly as Sif got into the driver's seat. Thyra turned her head away and pretended to be sleeping. It was a poor ruse, but it achieved Thyra's intended purpose of avoiding awkward conversation with her mom. There would be plenty of that later.

Sif started the car without speaking and began the drive out of town. Thyra kept her head turned away so that she could look out the window as they wove their way out of town and out into the farmland surrounding Blackfoot. Under different circumstances, Thyra would have enjoyed the quiet beauty such a place offered, but right now it was a harsh reminder of everything she'd been forced to give up, including the only home she'd ever known.

Thyra tried not to think of all the other things she'd lost. Or the people. They still didn't know what had happened to Bragi. The assumption was that Baldur had captured him, but Sif and Asiri avoided addressing his fate. Thyra's feelings were still conflicted about the old man. She still wasn't sure which memories of the old man were the real Bragi and which were Baldur in Bragi's skin. She hoped that he was still alive, but if Baldur had him it might be better if he wasn't.

Thyra couldn't help but sigh as Sif turned the car into the mobile home court they currently called home. They drove slowly down the row until they reached the very last one, a rundown, single-wide trailer they were renting. The owner was a single retiree that was currently on a months long fishing trip in Alaska. In return for no questions asked, Sif handed him a stack of cash that would pay for the fishing trip twice over. He only blinked once before reaching for his phone and calling a guide service to work out the details of his trip. The next day he'd handed over the keys and said he'd be back in three months.

Thyra doubted they'd stay that long. They'd been in Blackfoot for two weeks, the longest amount of time they'd been in one place since leaving Boise. She was sure something would alarm her mom and they'd be on the road again, looking for the next small community to hide in. What they were hiding from was still unclear to Thyra.

Between the constant moving around and the restrictions Sif had placed on her for how and when she could use her magic, Thyra felt like a prisoner. No friends, no lacrosse, and no chance for change on the horizon. The only time she felt at peace was when there was a thunderstorm. When lightning danced in the sky and Sif allowed her to release the pent up frustration she felt. Unfortunately, thunderstorms in Idaho were far too rare for Thyra's liking.

Thyra exited the car and trudged into the house, walking right past where Asiri was bent over her latest creation. The dwarf woman had decided to stick close to Thyra and Sif since Wisconsin. Her last home had been destroyed by Olafsson's men so there had been nothing to return to from her previous life. Asiri had become an important part of the dynamic the last three months and there were days when Thyra welcomed her presence and sharp tongue. Today was not one of those days.

"How's the knee, Sparks?" Asiri asked without looking up. "They finally agree to replace it with a bionic one yet? You'll be leaping over buildings yet!"

Thyra ignored her and walked down the narrow hallway to her room. She flopped down on the bed and exhaled heavily. Angry and exhausted, she turned up the volume of the music playing in her ears and closed her eyes. Immediately, her dark thoughts began to accost her, running a stream of the ways her life had taken a turn for the worse in direct opposition to the calm beach vibes playing in her ears.

Her thoughts were winning the battle when she felt a now-familiar feeling sweep over her. She had a momentary flash of irritation before she was carried away into a world of blue.

*****

Thyra looked up at the World Tree, it's black trunk rough and gnarled, it's branches reaching out until they faded into the shining white leaves that formed the canopy. It would have been awe-inspiring, but Thyra only felt annoyance as she reluctantly put one hand on its trunk.

"Long time no see," Thyra said, making no attempt to hide her feelings. "You don't write, you don't call, not even a postcard saying how sorry you are for completely ruining my life."

The weight of being my champion weighs heavily on you.

"It only weighs so much because you made me a cripple," Thyra snapped. "I'm seventeen, but you wouldn't know that by watching me try to run. One doctor told me that my right knee acts like it belongs on a ninety year old. So, yeah, thank you for that."

I told you that there would be a price for being my champion and receiving the power to protect those you love.

"I'm still waiting for this whole 'power to protect those I love' thing."

You have it. Your power is immense. More so than you know.

"And yet," Thyra grumbled, "the danger hasn't lessened from where I'm standing. If anything, it's grown. I'm pretty sure Baldur survived the full force of my magic, so he's still out there lurking. Gunnar Olafsson is probably mad as can be that he didn't get the Eye. If anything, me becoming your champion has made my situation worse."

Your mother still breathes, doesn't she? Yggdrasil answered it's own question. *I gave you the strength to repel Baldur and Gunnar. Without my help, things would have ended very different. Your magic is strong enough that you could protect her from any threat.*

"But only as a cripple!"

You know the price Odin paid. Would you rather I'd exacted a similar one? Or perhaps taken your mother from you? Other champions have been forced to pay that price. I could have demanded the same of you. Instead, I gave you the power to protect her. You will just have to adapt to your situation.

Thyra gritted her teeth in frustration. There was no doubt that the loss of her mom would have been more crippling emotionally than the physical toll of losing her mobility. If Thyra had lost her mom, she would have been just as lost. But that didn't mean she liked being reminded that her price could have been much different. In fact, it only made her angry to think about what the tree might have taken from her.

"You say you *gave* me power," Thyra said, circling back to a thought that had been bothering her for weeks, "but I don't see it. The power I have already existed in me, and Lynnedslag was made by Asiri. I paid the price but I don't see what I gained."

I gave you the power of a god.

Thyra shook her head. "No, you helped unlock that power. You said so yourself."

Are you so sure that you fully understand what I gave you? Are you sure that you have explored the limits of your power?

Thyra's eyes narrowed. "What are you talking about?"

That is for you to discover, Yggdrasil replied. *Rest assured, you have talents you have yet to even scratch the surface of.*

While that sparked Thyra's curiosity, her anger at Yggdrasil overrode it. "What did you give me that was worth the price I paid?"

You have the Eye—

"Which has only put me in greater danger!"

It is the power to grow magic in the world.

"You mean, *your* power! That is not the same as the power to protect my family and friends."

It is power. What you choose to do with it is your decision. Protect, destroy—it is up to you to use it. You say I gave you nothing, but without me you never would have overcome the barriers that kept you from your true power. Power you are still far from mastering. Besides, all magic comes from me, so yes, I did give you the power you desired.

Thyra snorted in anger and turned away. "That's splitting hairs if you ask me!" Arguing with an ancient, sentient tree that had a sassy streak was a waste of time. "Why did you bring me here? Hopefully not to argue this because you aren't going to change my mind." Thyra waited for an explanation, but nothing was offered. "Hello? Why did you bring me here? What do you want from me?"

I've given you enough time, Yggdrasil finally replied. *You have been idle for long enough. Idle while others are making moves. I brought you here to warn you. Centuries of magic being persecuted and forced to the periphery has built up tension like a river behind a dam. That dam is the only thing holding back a wave of change that could remake the world you know. There are those who seek to put cracks in the dam, and others who seek to destroy it completely. Both will result in a wave of change that may break the balance you are meant to protect.*

"How?" Thyra said. "How would it change?"

Magic ruled once, Yggdrasil replied, but it was kept from dominating all life. Magic users fought magic users. Mortals were kept in line, but were allowed to exist without living in constant fear of extermination. If you are not careful, the pendulum may swing too far in the opposite direction and create a world where life is washed away beneath the wave of magic.

"That doesn't sound like much fun."

I sense that there is an end swiftly approaching, Yggdrasil stated. A final confrontation that will decide which way that wave flows. You must be there to face it, or the result may be catastrophic.

"Fine. Tell me how I stop it."

Stopping it is impossible. It was always meant to happen. What you must be concerned with is what steps the other players in this game are taking and how those steps may affect things when the wave breaks. You must be there to make sure they do not succeed.

Thyra's eyes narrowed. "What are you talking about?"

The balance of power is shifting. Hela, Baldur, Olafsson, even Vidar—their actions are all putting cracks in the dam, whether they know it or not. You must decide whether you will try to fix the damage they inflict, or if you will be the one to tear it down.

"Why would I be the one who wants to destroy it?"

To prevent the world from being completely torn apart.

Chapter 2

Baldur rolled the small black stone back and forth across the back of his fingers in a slow, rhythmic dance. Across from him, Bragi's eyes followed the stone's progress with trepidation. Beads of sweat had formed on the old man's forehead, and he tensed each time the stone switched directions as if he expected Baldur to activate it without warning. Bragi had been held inside the magic trap for only a few days, but even that short amount of time was enough to drive a man insane.

Baldur understood. He had spent nearly a thousand years inside a very similar prison that had been constructed for him by Hela. He'd spent centuries cycling between insanity and short bursts of lucid thought over and over again before finally managing to gain a sliver of control. Only thoughts of revenge were enough to overcome the madness. Even with his mind clear, it had taken him what felt like an eternity to slowly pick away at Hela's magic in hopes of finding a weak point in his prison. Once he had, it had taken a second eternity to tear it down enough for him to get through. When he finally did escape, it had taken three months before he was able to fully banish the nausea that resulted from his time in the prison between realms.

Bragi was not like Baldur, though. The old man still struggled to stand on his own after two months of being free of the prison Baldur had placed him in. The old man had been weak when he was made a god and his lack of fortitude made the side effects all the more powerful.

Still, weak and old as he was, Baldur couldn't afford to underestimate the old man. Bragi was a god, possessed of magic, and not some ordinary mortal man. If Baldur wasn't careful, he could fall victim to the magic of Bragi's voice like so many others who had misjudged the old man. As a precaution, Baldur kept the old man locked away and in a magic-induced stupor, bringing him out of it just enough to hold up a conversation.

"I found what I was looking for," Baldur told him after a long silence.

Bragi looked up and met Baldur's cold stare. When he spoke, his words were slow and his voice quivered with either fear or anger—Baldur wasn't sure which. "If you're expecting me to say congratulations, don't hold your breath."

Baldur smiled. "Not at all. I simply wanted to tell you how grateful I am. You've been very helpful these last few months."

"It isn't helping when being compelled," Bragi replied. He looked over Baldur's shoulder to where Amara stood. "Your witch ensures my compliance."

"Witch?" Baldur tsked. "That is no way to speak of my associate. 'Witch' is very offensive in this day and age. Mind your manners, Uncle."

"My manners left me about the same time you locked me away in that hell of a stone," Bragi muttered.

"One I am very familiar with. One Hela constructed and Odin put me in." Baldur leaned forward and looked up into Bragi's bloodshot eyes. "I wonder, did you raise your voice in my defense or did you bend to Odin's whims just like the rest of the Aesir?" Bragi flinched and looked away, unable to hold Baldur's stare. "I thought so."

"If you're going to kill me," Bragi muttered, "just get it over with."

"What makes you think I want to kill you?"

"Revenge," Bragi said, his mouth twisting sourly around the word. "Now that you have what you want, I know what happens next."

"If I was going to kill you," Baldur said slowly, "I would have done it already. There are other ways to get revenge than administering death. Like keeping you alive, suffering under Amara's spell while I bring an end to the other gods." The old man's eyes remained on the floor, evoking a disappointed sigh from Baldur. "Come now, Uncle, don't take it personal. You know why Amara's presence is necessary. I couldn't risk you using your magic on me. I needed straight answers, not ones veiled in magic and flowery words that would lead me astray. Thanks to her, you answered my questions honestly."

Bragi blinked heavily and let his chin rest on his chest. He took a deep, ragged breath. "You have what you wanted. If you're not going to kill me, what now?"

"You've helped me gather some of the summoning stones," Baldur replied, "but that's only the beginning. There are so many secrets in that head of yours that I still need to unlock. We still have many discussions to come."

Bragi grimaced. When he spoke, his voice was surprisingly strong and clear. "What do you even want with the summoning stones? You already ate the fruit in Idunn's garden. What else could you want? The creation of another generation of immortals?"

Baldur chuckled grimly. "No, that isn't why I want access to Idunn's garden. Immortality is a curse. I regret the day that my mother placed that blasted fruit in my hand, almost as much as I rue the day she came up with the idea to make me the monster I am today."

"She didn't make you a monster," Bragi said. "That was always inside of you."

Baldur smiled, but let the insult slide. "Regardless, if I hadn't eaten the fruit, I would have been spared centuries of madness suffering under Hela's power. Why would I give it to others if I loathe the gift myself?"

"Then why?" Bragi rasped, his voice like sandpaper on wood. "Do this world a favor. Do what we were all too weak to do and destroy the stones!"

"And banish Idunn to a life spent alone in her garden forever? With no way of returning to this world?" Baldur shook his head. "No, I don't think you actually mean that."

"That garden and the fruit inside it were the reason for so many wars. . . so much bloodshed," Bragi said. "You know the horrors Odin committed to control it. Imagine what this world would do to itself if the people knew of its existence." Bragi coughed, the fervor in his voice proving too much for his weakened state. When he spoke again, it was barely more than a whisper. "Mankind would tear itself apart trying to control it. The stones cannot be used!"

Baldur was sincerely surprised by the old man's suggestion. Of all people, Bragi had the most reason to want to use the stones, yet here he was pushing for their destruction. It didn't make sense. "Is that really what you want? Idunn, your wife, banished to her garden for eternity at the hand of her beloved Bragi? You surprise me, Uncle."

"I gave up hope of seeing Idunn again long ago," Bragi said. "She is lost to me. But you can still do the right thing by destroying the stones."

Bragi considered the old man for a moment. His surprise faded into curiosity. "I don't believe you want the stones destroyed. If you did, why didn't you do it when you had the chance?"

Bragi's head sagged and he looked at the floor. "I tried. But I was too weak."

Baldur nodded. Bragi was weak. He always had been. But he was also a planner. Odin had been known as a master strategist, but Baldur knew that Bragi had been behind more than a few of the Allfather's most daring maneuvers. For that reason, Baldur didn't believe what he was seeing or hearing from the old man.

"Destroying the stones," Baldur said, "would mean Idunn would be a prisoner in her garden forever. What kind of husband would ever damn his wife to such a fate?"

"One that can't stand the thought of ever looking his wife in the eye again," Bragi muttered. "I've failed too many times. I'm not worthy of her. She has every reason to resent and hate me. I'm sure she knew that I tried to destroy my summoning stone. She must have felt it."

That was a surprise. Baldur leaned forward. "I didn't think you capable of being that cruel." Baldur paused, his eyes narrowing and a thought entering his head. "Unless, there was another way to find the garden or for Idunn to leave it."

Bragi's face went slack in an attempt to hide his emotions, but there was a slight tightening around his eyes that was unmistakable. Baldur leaned forward, a sly smirk crossing his face. "There is another way, isn't there?" Bragi's jaw tensed in an attempt to keep from answering the question. To his credit, the old man's resistance was admirable. He might have managed if Baldur hadn't been holding a trump card in his hand. He looked at Amara and motioned with his head towards the old man. "My uncle needs his medicine."

Amara smiled wickedly. She crossed the room and made a slow circle around Bragi. The old man tensed as her fingers traced his collarbone and over his shoulder to the base of his neck. She walked her fingers up his neck and around to his temple in a devilish manner. Bragi tensed one last time and tried to pull away, but he couldn't escape Amara's touch. All at once, his shoulders sagged and his attempts to escape that touch turned to eagerness for it to continue.

Baldur had watched Amara put her magic to use hundreds of times over the past months, but each time he still found himself in awe. Her magic was a strange mix that could only be described as a mix of Bragi's mental imagery and Hela's manipulation of the body. While she lacked Hela's total mastery of human flesh, Amara's touch allowed her to trigger the impulses of the mind and body, bending a person's will to her own. Using the centers in the brain that controlled the emotions—joy, fear, pain, pleasure—she could swallow up a person's will and make them do whatever she asked of them. It was a useful talent that Baldur was helping her put to good use.

When he had found her, Amara was running a small crime ring in Washington, D.C. She had more than a dozen people under her spell—including a pair of politicians—providing her with an apartment no twenty year-old college dropout could afford, a steady supply of expensive clothing and jewelry, and loads of cash. All it took was a single touch each day from Amara to keep them as her willing slaves. And they had been willing.

Yet, Amara had wanted more. She was bored with how easy things had become and was hungry for a new challenge. She'd practically jumped at the chance to join Baldur and his promise of true power. The prospect of plying her craft on a god, of exploring the limits of what she could do, had excited her beyond measure.

Amara smiled wickedly and nodded to Baldur. "He's ready."

"Thank you, my dear," Baldur said. He leaned in close and smiled at Bragi. "Now, you were telling me about the other way into the Garden of Idunn."

Chapter 3

Gunnar Olafsson tapped his fingers on his desk impatiently as one of his tech experts explained the myriad of ways he and his team had failed. Every word that left the man's mouth added fuel to the simmering rage Gunnar had struggled to contain for three long months. Ever since Thyra Ariksen had eluded him. No, *bested* him. He hated to admit it—and he never would out loud!—but he had underestimated her. He wouldn't make the same mistake twice.

Gunnar held up a hand, and the tech head obediently fell silent. "So, what you're telling me, is that even after three months you still haven't managed to pinpoint the cell signals of the girl or her mother?"

The tech head hesitated, clearly knowing that the truth was not going to do him any favors. He must have known that lies would be worse, though, because he nodded. "That's correct."

"And why not?" Gunnar asked, his voice betraying how close he was to unleashing his anger. "I run a multinational telecommunications company with over three hundred million subscribers across the globe. At any given time, sixty percent of the world's cell phone users are pinging their signal off of one of my towers or satellites, and another thirty percent use applications our hackers have illegal back doors into. Isn't that true?"

The tech head licked his lips nervously. "That's correct."

"Then explain to me how the team of technological wizards I employ can't manage to find this girl and her mother?"

"It isn't that simple," the tech head answered.

"Explain to me how it isn't?"

"Their cell numbers were canceled back in June and as far as we can tell, they have not opened new accounts with any service provider," the tech head said.

"Maybe they're using fake names," Ivan offered from where he stood against the wall.

The tech head looked at the big Russian and shrugged. "We've thought of that, but our search using possible aliases hasn't turned up any leads. If they have opened new accounts under fake names, they have still managed to restrict their signals from using our towers and make sure nothing they communicate is flagged by our search parameters."

"Can they do that?" Gunnar asked.

"It normally would be above the understanding of the average person," the tech head said, "but it is possible. They could be utilizing WiFi networks only, or using prepaid phones. Either one would limit our ability to locate them."

"So," Gunnar said, "you and your team of tech wizards are of the opinion that a teenage girl and her mother have not only changed their cell carrier, but have also learned how to limit their signals so that our massive network does not pick them up?"

"That, or they have completely gone off-grid," the tech head said. "It could be that they have stopped using cell phones altogether."

Gunnar's jaw dropped at the suggestion. He closed his eyes and slowly shook his head, massaging his temples with his fingers. He opened his eyes and looked across his desk at the tech head. "How much am I paying you to do your job? Give me the number."

The man shifted his weight uncomfortably. "Three hundred fifty thousand a year."

"And you like getting that paycheck, correct?"

The tech head nodded. "Of course."

"Then I would suggest you get back to work and come up with a better theory than the one you just tried to feed me," Gunnar said in a menacing tone. "Find them, or the least of your worries will be finding a new job."

The tech head retreated from the office just shy of running. Gunnar spun in his chair to avoid yelling any threats at the man's back. All that money, and *that* was what he had come to Gunnar with? It was beyond aggravating.

"There was a time when such stupidity was rewarded with a headsman's axe," Gunnar said out loud.

"Killing him won't help," Ivan grumbled. "You know how hard he'd be to replace."

Gunnar spun on the Russian, his eyes ablaze with anger. The moment his eyes rested on Ivan, though, some of that anger dissipated. Ivan's once strong features were now marred by a jagged, pink scar that ran from his hairline down to his jaw, a gift from the spear of Sharon Ariksen. Or Sif, as Gunnar now knew. In addition to the scar, her spear had claimed Ivan's left eye. To this point, the Russian had opted for an eye patch rather than using the fake eye a doctor had made for him. The scar made his mouth pucker down in the corner, giving the surly Russian a constant frown. The effect was enough to make the intimidating Ivan appear even more so.

"There are always more young tech students hungry for work," Gunnar said.

"Ones you can trust with what we're doing?" Ivan asked. "How many of them will be able to accept that magic exists, much less be willing to do what we do?" The Russian shrugged. "He keeps his hackers in line and quiet. His discretion alone is worth the price you pay."

Gunnar looked away. Ivan was right. His team of tech wizards was composed of only those he could trust not to talk about the hidden world of magic he was both waging a war against and trying to exploit.

"What of their home?" Gunnar asked, bringing the conversation back to Thyra and Sif. "They have to be living somewhere. Do we have any leads on where they've holed up at?"

"We don't know that either," Ivan admitted. "Their home in Boise was sold in a rush, the proceeds sent to an escrow account administered by a law firm that was little more than a pass through. Some of the money went out in a series of cash transactions, but no names were attached. From there, the trail went cold. If they moved to another home in the Boise area, there is no record of it."

"Could they have left Idaho altogether?"

"It's possible," Ivan admitted, "but if they did our search only grows infinitely more complex."

Gunnar ground his teeth together in frustration. He didn't need this right now. He was surrounded by ineptitude right when he needed a well-oiled machine. All the resources at his disposal were profiting him nothing!

On top of all the trouble surrounding Thyra Ariksen and Sif, he was getting pressure from the business side of things as well. The Board of Directors was breathing down his neck about what happened in Wisconsin, and he knew the police were still suspicious about the events of those two days. They had yet to level charges in the direction of the Muspel Corporation, but that was because only Muspel Corporation property and employees had been impacted. Add in the fact that the only witnesses to what happened were uncooperative behind a swarm of attorneys that had materialized in the blink of an eye, and the police had nothing but vague descriptions of what occurred. The lack of cooperation undoubtedly raised suspicions, but the police had little recourse at this point.

Granted, the hotel clerk had told his story, but he had been hysterical that night and had only grown more so since. His story had become inconsistent and more outlandish with each retelling. The police had already written him off as an untrustworthy witness.

The small hotel's security footage had caught some of what happened that night, including Vidar's superhuman dismantling of the SUVs, but Gunnar's tech department had managed to slide in to the server and erase the footage before the police got their hands on it. There were no cell phone videos hanging out there either. Gunnar had made sure of that.

With the only witness on the verge of insanity and the video destroyed, the police investigation was going nowhere. Which left them with nothing but questions and suspicions that, in the absence of another suspect, could only be directed at Gunnar and his company. The Board of Directors wanted answers almost as badly as the police and were growing impatient with Gunnar's evasiveness.

Gunnar exhaled the deep breath he had been holding. "We should have taken them three months ago when we still knew where they were. The same goes for Hela and her wolf. Why didn't we?"

"Because Baldur told you not to," Ivan stated.

"That's right," Gunnar said. "Because Baldur told me not to. He told me to prepare for war then disappeared to play his games for weeks at a time while we waited. Now look at us. My company is under investigation, Hela has a dozen of my men, and we've lost both the girl and the Eye of Odin. We've gained no ground. Only given it away!" He slapped his desk to emphasize his point. "I cannot sit aside and wait. Not anymore. There was a time when I dictated the pace of this game. That is no longer true."

"What do you want me to do?"

Gunnar looked at the Russian. "Baldur says he has a plan, but he hasn't shared it with me. Until he does, we need to keep our movements more closely guarded. We continue to go after the obvious targets and keep arming your men with the weapons we've created, but we need to keep all our other operations quiet. Especially the action we've taken on the next step of the Odin Initiative."

"Is that going to be possible now that Baldur has access to our network?"

"According to our tech heads, the firewalls have all been changed," Gunnar said. "Baldur promised that he wasn't going to go behind my back again, but I didn't believe him then and I still don't." He actually trusted Baldur less, if that was possible. "Which is why I had you move the spear in such a way. I didn't want there to be a trail for Baldur to follow."

"But will it stay secret?"

Gunnar wasn't sure, but the success of the Odin Initiative hinged on his ability to keep Odin's spear, Gungnir, safely secreted away. The spear was capable of generating enough clean energy to fuel the entire Eastern Seaboard at it's full power. Once active, the Muspel Corporation could monopolize the energy sector in the region in months, if not weeks.

And that was only at the one sight. The last few years of experimentation had given the scientists he had tasked with replicating the spear time to refine their attempts. Although not nearly as powerful, there were six additional power sources that Gunnar had every intention of putting to use in the near future. North America was first, but Europe wouldn't be far behind. The Odin Initiative would expand the Muspel Corporation's footprint tenfold in a year's time, giving him a stranglehold on the power that ran the world. In an age where everything was digital, he who controlled the electricity controlled everything else.

And the best part about his plan was that once he drove the

competition from the market place, he would be able to turn the power on or off with a flick of a switch, bringing entire nations to their knees in as much time. He could hold countries ransom without an army. Cripple economies just by raising a finger!

He was getting so close to implementing his plans. He wasn't going to let Baldur, Hela, Thyra Ariksen, or anyone else ruin them.

"You're going to focus on ensuring the spear's location stays secret," Gunnar instructed. "Our success depends on it."

Ivan nodded. "As you wish. I'll keep you updated on anything new we find."

"Fine," Gunnar said dismissively. "And find Thyra Ariksen and her mother before Baldur does. I don't care what it costs or who hangs in order to do it, we cannot let Baldur find them before we do."

"I'll find them," Ivan stated.

"When you do," Gunnar raised a finger, "I want you to send everyone we have to bring them in. I want surgical precision and overwhelming force. In and out before anyone even knows you're there. A short, violent operation that will send a message once and for all. Failure is not an option."

"I'll see to it." Ivan turned on his heels and headed for the door. He paused with one hand on the handle and turned around. "I still think you should have let me try to kill Baldur."

Gunnar bit back his initial response to say that killing Baldur was impossible. He thought back to the discomfort on Baldur's face in this very office a few months ago. Something had changed. Gunnar still wasn't sure what, but he had felt the scales briefly begin tipping in his direction in that moment. He wasn't sure how far or in which direction they'd moved in the months since.

"For now, Baldur is our ally," Gunnar said. "But, if that ever changes, you may get that chance."

Chapter 4

Vidar sensed her presence before he saw her. Even after all these years, he could still point right at her in a crowded room without looking. He had often wondered if that was a result of something she had done to him while healing his many battle wounds or from the deep feelings he still held for her. Maybe it was both.

As always, when he saw her, he felt his heart begin to race. She was the epitome of beauty, intelligence, and danger all wrapped up in one. There was no one like her, nor would there ever be again. Just being near her was a risk for him, but it was a risk he couldn't help but take. He had never abused his body with drugs and it had been years since a drop of alcohol had passed his lips, but he was an addict all the same. It was an addiction he'd spent centuries trying to rid himself of, always unsuccessfully. He doubted he ever would.

"Hello, Vidar," Hela said as she sat on the bench next to him. Even though she left a foot of space between them having her this close made his mouth go dry.

There was no denying that the modern world looked good on Hela. She had always been beautiful, but somehow she was even more breathtaking now. She had been majestic and inspired reverence in the dress of a goddess, but Vidar liked the way she looked in a pair of blue jeans and a t-shirt better than the finery of ages past. She looked relaxed and at ease—like the woman he had loved before she became a goddess. Back when they were free of the curse Odin had placed on both of them when he put the Eye in their hands.

Doing his best to avoid falling under her spell, Vidar forced himself to look away and study the activity in the park. He'd arrived as the sun was just beginning to rise in order to enjoy the quiet and soak in the start of a new day. There were few places he felt at peace—his gym was one, and surrounded by the quiet of nature was the other. The hour of time alone had been exactly what he had needed to prepare for seeing Hela.

It had also allowed him to study everyone that came to the park and take note of anyone or anything that didn't belong. "I see you've been busy."

"Busy?" Hela asked in a voice that bordered on a purr and sent chills down Vidar's spine. She let out a throaty laugh that made the hairs on his arms stand on end. She knew exactly what she was doing and was enjoying what it did to him. "How so?"

Vidar looked around the park. He counted six men in sunglasses that were doing their best to act uninterested in what was happening on the park bench between the two fallen gods. Their fit builds and movements made them stand out almost as much as the fact that they clearly had no reason to be there. Try as they might, they looked out of place in a park on a Friday morning.

"Looks like Surtur's men weren't beyond your healing skills," Vidar said.

Hela didn't try to deny it. "Most were at death's doorstep, but hadn't moved beyond my skills. There were a few that I could do nothing for. A Valkyrie's spear cuts just as deep in this age as it did a thousand years ago. I never like to see a body go to waste, but I'm making due with what I could save."

Vidar didn't ask what that meant. Instead, he muttered, "I don't know if I should be more insulted that you only brought six men or that you thought you needed protection at all."

Hela smiled softly. "A girl can't be too careful these days. Especially when dealing with someone as dangerous as you."

"If I'm so dangerous, you should have brought more men," Vidar said.

"They aren't here for you," Hela admitted. Her smile fell. "Unless you mean to do me harm. Is that why you asked me to come here, Vidar? To hurt me?"

Vidar shook his head and admitted the truth. "You know I'm no threat to you."

"And that's why you are," Hela said. She casually brushed a strand of her dark hair away from her face. "Why did you ask me to come here? There are better places than a park for us to go to sneak in a kiss or two. Places where we could be more. . .alone."

"Which is why I couldn't risk going to those kinds of places," Vidar said grimly.

"So, you don't want to sneak a kiss?" Hela's lips turned down in a pout. "After all these years, a girl could only hope."

Vidar sighed, still doing his best to avoid looking into her green eyes. "I didn't come here to play games with you, Hela."

"No, I imagine not," Hela said, the playful tone gone from her voice. "You made yourself perfectly clear the last time we spoke."

Vidar sighed again. "You didn't give me a chance to explain in Wisconsin."

"Should I have?" Hela's voice was colder than ice and sharper than any blade.

Vidar did his best to stay calm. "I'm not here to argue with you."

"No? I think I'd find that more enjoyable than the constant reminder of your complete apathy towards me." Hela crossed her arms over her chest. "No more games. Why did you ask me to come here?"

Vidar knew she wasn't going to like the answer, but he wanted to believe that she was capable of seeing reason. "I came here to convince you to come with me. To stand beside me and help Thyra."

Hela snorted in derision. "Of course! You spend a hundred years avoiding *me*, yet somehow you succumb to the big blue eyes and batting eyelashes of a pretty young girl."

"It's not like that," Vidar growled, "and you know it."

"Of course I do!" Hela snapped. She clamped her jaw shut and shook her head. "I know that, but it hurts all the same. Your constant spurning of me has left my heart cold."

"Your heart turned cold a long time ago," Vidar said without hesitation.

"Because you made it that way," Hela retorted without pause. "I loved you, and you turned your back on me. Even now, you still have it turned to me."

Vidar regretted the thought that came to him even before he spoke it out loud, but he couldn't stop it. "You made my choice easy."

Hela's eyes flashed with anger. "You should be careful. One of these days I may ignore the feelings I have for you and slip a dagger between your ribs."

"You won't do that," Vidar said without looking at her.

"Why not?"

"Because you know I'd welcome it," Vidar said, finally turning to look at her. He saw the flash of sadness cross her face as his words sank in. Inhaling deeply, he forced himself to continue with the reason why he had asked her to meet him here. "I can't remain passive. Baldur's reappearance changes things. I know you feel the same. He was dangerous when we were considered gods, and he's even more dangerous now. I can't begin to imagine the web he is weaving, but I know that I don't want to find myself tangled in it. We can't face him on our own."

"Then come back to me," Hela said. She put a hand on his arm, sending a shiver through him. "Together we'd be strong enough to face any threat. We could start over. Leave this world behind and *be together*. Just like it was in the beginning."

It was tempting to believe her, but Vidar knew that falling back under Hela's spell would end the same way it always did. Their history together was volatile and always destructive. To his shame, it had also been repeated dozens of times over the past eight hundred years. As hard as he had tried to stay away, it always seemed like he found his way back to Hela's embrace. Each time he'd tell himself it was different, but it always ended the same. Usually with him covered in blood with dead bodies at his feet. He couldn't afford to let that happen again. He couldn't let his guard down and allow himself to be blinded to the truth about who she was and the demons she carried.

Or the demons he carried.

"I can't do that," Vidar said.

"Can't," Hela said, "or won't?"

"Thyra has the Eye," Vidar said. "She has been chosen by Yggdrasil. If anyone can stop Baldur and Gunnar Olafsson, it's her."

"And I'm not capable of it?" Hela asked, but she didn't give him a chance to answer. "It pains me to see how little you believe in me."

Vidar pushed forward. "Thyra could use your knowledge and skills in this fight."

"Don't you mean 'we'?" Hela asked. "You're going to her, aren't you?"

Vidar exhaled long and slow. "I failed the last champion of Yggdrasil. Maybe I can help this one."

"Why? You didn't fail Odin. He used you for his dirty work and then blamed you for his troubles when he thought it convenient. You didn't fail him—Odin failed you! When will you see that?"

"Asgard fell, didn't it?" Vidar barked. "Whose job was it to hold the gates, Hela?"

"I can name dozens of people," Hela snapped. "Heimdall was supposed to be in charge of the bridge and the gates, not you! He should have seen Surtur's army long before they reached Asgard. Where was his fabled sight then? Besides, it was his foolish plan to put that beam across the gates in the first place, even knowing that only you could lift it. He should have seen the risks of putting so much on your shoulders. They all should have."

"Heimdall was a good man," Vidar stated. "He was one of the few that I felt like I could call my friend. He trusted me to be there when I was needed. And I wasn't."

"What loyalty do you owe any of them?" Hela pressed. "The Aesir used you and then they betrayed you. The same way they betrayed me. Why should you go back to them?"

Vidar had asked himself that question a hundred times. At first, the answer was that he didn't owe anyone a thing, but with time he realized that maybe he did. Thyra was the chosen champion for this age, and more importantly, his family. He may not owe the other remaining gods anything, but family was different.

"Thyra is not like the Aesir of old. She doesn't want to rule. She is standing against Baldur and Olafsson. If I can help her, maybe I can make up for the mistakes I made. Do the right thing for once."

"Since when did you find a sense of honor?" Hela asked snidely. "Vidar, Odin's personal executioner. The man who spilled more blood in the name of the Aesir than anyone—honorable?" Hela shook her head. "You're lying to yourself if you think running to Thor's daughter is somehow going to wipe away everything you did. She will use you the same way Odin did. You can try to deny it, but I know the truth. You're broken, violent, and full of anger. What makes you think you siding with her will make you be anything different?"

Vidar took a deep breath. Hela was right about who he had been.

His past was soaked in blood, poor choices, and costly mistakes. Part of him didn't think he'd ever find peace. That he wasn't *worthy* of peace. That part of him ached to run back to Hela, let her soothe his pain away, and let the world burn around them.

But, another part of him, small as it was, refused to give in to that despair. Thyra was not Odin, and she didn't have to repeat the same mistakes. She didn't see him the way everyone else—Hela included—saw him. To Thyra, he wasn't a weapon to be used against her enemies. With her, that chapter of his life might finally be behind him.

Standing slowly, he looked down at Hela. "I am going to help Thyra stand against Baldur, Surtur, and *anyone* else that threatens her."

Hela didn't miss the implication of his statement. "If I decided Thyra was a distraction that needed to be removed, could you stand in my way?"

Vidar didn't know the answer to that, but he wasn't going to let Hela pick away at his resolve. "You know you can't stand alone against Baldur and Surtur combined. Come with me."

"I think I'll take my chances," Hela said, looking away.

Vidar had expected her answer, but it still made his heart heavy. "What will you do?"

Hela's eyes flashed dangerously. "You don't actually think I'm going to reveal my plans to an enemy, do you?"

"I'm not your enemy."

Hela cocked an eyebrow at him. "You run to that girl, and that is exactly what we become."

Vidar sighed. He hated that the line was being drawn in the sand. He had helped draw it, though. Hela was simply making it clear. "It doesn't have to be like this."

"Unless you decide against joining her," Hela said, "then this is *exactly* the way it has to be."

Vidar sighed again. He had tried to convince her to come with him and that was all he could do. He started to walk away, but felt a hand grab him by the wrist. He turned slowly and looked at Hela. The anger was gone from her face, replaced by a look of uncertainty. Her green eyes looked surprisingly vulnerable as she looked up at him.

"Tell me one thing," she said softly, "do you still love me?"

The question felt like a cold knife being pushed into his chest and his walls fell down. For a brief moment in time, she wasn't Hela, the goddess of death, she was just a woman who was hurting and was hoping to have some of that hurt be soothed away by the man who should love her more than anything. Vidar reached out and pulled her close. He leaned in and breathed in her smell, staying in the moment for as long as he could. He gently kissed her forehead.

"You've always had my heart," he said softly into her hair. "You always will."

Fearing what would happen if he lingered a second longer, Vidar broke free of her embrace and walked away. He could feel her eyes on his back the entire time and it took every bit of his will to avoid looking back to see how his words had affected her.

Vidar passed her men without being stopped. Part of him wished they'd try, that Fenrir would come bounding out of the shadows so that they could finished what they started. Anything that would allow him to channel the pain he felt in his chest into anger that he could work out with his fists. Anger was useful, but heartache, that was a demon he still hadn't found a way to exorcise, even after a thousand years of trying.

He found his truck where he had left it and got in. He hesitated for a moment with the key in the ignition, just long enough to wonder if he was making the right decision. Summoning what little willpower he had in reserve, he started up the engine, put it in gear, and headed for the highway without looking back at the park bench and the woman that held his heart. He merged onto the highway and headed west toward Idaho and the possibility of redemption.

Chapter 5

The summer heat was almost unbearable in Thyra's room during the afternoon. Her window faced the west, and no amount of curtains or air conditioning seemed capable of defeating the sun's fury. Every other room in the trailer could feel like the inside of a freezer, but her room would feel like a sauna. It took only a few minutes for her to be dripping with sweat if she lingered too long while the sun was out.

And yet, there she was, lying motionless on her bed, baking in the heat of her room, cemented in place by indecision. Retreating to another part of the trailer made all the sense in the world, but she couldn't bring herself to move. While there may have been an escape from the heat elsewhere in the trailer, she knew she wouldn't make it past the door.

Lynnedslag wouldn't let her.

The lacrosse stick stood in the corner where Thyra had put it weeks before. Like a silent sentinel, Lynnedslag maintained its watch, waiting expectantly for the next time Thyra would use it. The lacrosse stick was a nagging presence at the periphery of Thyra's thoughts whenever she was in the trailer. Silly as it sounded, it taunted Thyra with its presence every time she passed by. When she went to sleep at night, she found herself staring at the lacrosse stick just before drifting off. It was even present in her dreams.

She knew it wasn't fair to pin all her problems on an inanimate object. Especially one that had been a gift and had served her well. Lynnedslag hadn't ruined her knee, or forced her and Sif into a life of hiding. Nor had it be the catalyst that put the events of the last few months into motion. But Thyra had a long list of reason to be angry and only a few places to put the blame. It was unfair, but Lynnedslag's existence was a mockery of what Thyra could have had. While other gods had hammers, axes, spears, and Gunnar Olafsson's men had weapons, Thyra had a lacrosse stick. It was absurd. Sure, she knew what Lynnedslag was capable of, but could she really go running into a fight with a lacrosse stick and expect to be taken seriously? She knew the reasoning behind the design—disguising a weapon in plain sight was a boon—but she had more than enough arguments to counter it.

Above everything else, though, the lacrosse stick served as a reminder of what Thyra never would be again. Her dreams of playing lacrosse were over. Instead, she had a lacrosse stick that threw balls of lightning rather than rubber balls.

Thyra. Yggdrasil's voice echoed inside her head, causing her to suck in a breath from surprise. She had never experienced a conversation with Yggdrasil while awake. It wasn't pleasant.

When she regained her composure, she replied in a voice just above a whisper. "Two times in a few days. What did I do to get so much of your attention all of a sudden?"

An unforeseen threat has emerged.

Thyra couldn't help but roll her eyes. "Of course. Why else would you talk to me? What new threat am I adding to the list today?"

Baldur is gathering the summoning stones to call on Idunn.

The summoning stones? Thyra vaguely remembered Bragi telling her about them and their role in opening the way to Idunn's garden. Something didn't add up, though. "Baldur wants the summoning stones? What for? He's already immortal. Why would he need Idunn to give him more of the fruit?"

It isn't the fruit that grants immortality he seeks.

"What does he seek then?"

Yggdrasil was silent.

"What does Baldur want?" Thyra repeated more forcefully.

To destroy the balance of magic I've enlisted you to protect.

"Nothing new there from what I can tell," Thyra said. "How does he plan on doing it this time?"

The tree hesitated. *I cannot answer your question.*

"You can't, or you won't?"

Yggdrasil was silent. Thyra knew the answer and it boiled her blood. "You call me your champion, but so far you haven't seemed very interested in helping me. I don't see how I'm going to win this war when the odds keep getting stacked more and more against me!"

I don't want you to win a war.

Thyra threw her hands up. "Then why make me your champion? What is the point of all of this? Why did you screw up my knee if you weren't giving me the power to win the war against Baldur and Gunnar Olafsson?"

I didn't make you my champion in order to win a war, Yggdrasil said. *I made you my champion to increase my influence in the world. A task you have yet to even attempt to achieve.*

"What?" Thyra couldn't believe what she was hearing, and she felt her control over the volume of her voice wavering. "I thought defeating them was what you wanted!"

There was a time when their goals conflicted with my own, Yggdrasil responded. *But that is no longer the case. Baldur has gathered a handful of magic users to him, and while Olafsson may despise magic and those that use it, his actions are leading closer to the world acknowledging my power. He has killed many of my chosen vessels, true, but he is also seeking ways to replicate my power. When he uses them the world will be forced to recognize that there are powers they cannot explain. In his own way, he is helping rather than hurting me.*

"If he's doing such a good job, then why do you need me?" Thyra hissed. "Why not give me back my knee and let him be your champion?"

You are still the champion this world needs, Yggdrasil replied. *You are a child of both the old world and the new. You possess the traits to merge them together. You are what is required to do what is necessary. It's the same reason why I chose champions throughout the history of this world—each had the required talents to expand my power. I called you for this reason, not to win a war that I take no side in.*

The tree's explanation only aggravated Thyra more. She'd had a nagging feeling about Yggdrasil for a while that she hadn't been able to shake. Now she realized what it was that was bothering her. Her eyes narrowed as she looked up at the tree. "You're playing both sides, aren't you?"

I don't take sides.

"As long as your existence is safe and whatever happens expands your influence in the world—I got that part." Thyra closed her eyes as the realization set in. "How could I be so blind? You don't want me to defeat Baldur and Gunnar. You need them just as much as you need me. *Balance,* like you keep reminding me. Right?"

The tree didn't deny the accusation. *That's true. I want magic to grow and there must be balance. That balance will fail if there is not opposition of one kind or another. Your opposition to Baldur and Gunnar Olafsson is necessary to my existence.*

"So you're pitting us against each other?" It was so infuriating that Thyra couldn't help but laugh wryly. Deep down she had known that she was being manipulated, she just never thought it was to this degree. She had spent the last three months being indecisive and letting herself be led around by others because everything had been thrown at her so fast. But was she being led, or just manipulated by those who took advantage of her youth and inexperience? She had a long list of names that she felt had done just that and Yggdrasil's was at the very top.

I sense your anger. You have reason, but one day you will understand.

Thyra didn't think that likely. "I don't like being manipulated."

I do what I must to protect my existence, the tree replied. *We cannot change what has led to this point. The future is what is important. The balance you have been tasked with protecting will fail if you do not keep Baldur from summoning Idunn and taking control of her garden.*

"Why?" Thyra barked. "Why will it fail?"

Idunn's garden is the home of many secrets, some more damaging than others.

"What kind of secrets?"

Again, the tree fell silent.

"You're holding back," Thyra said after a tense silence. "This relationship is feeling really one-sided."

You are my champion. I have a vested interest in your survival and success.

"It doesn't feel like it," Thyra grumbled. "If you truly want to help me, then *help* me!"

I can only help you if you are willing to help yourself.

Thyra's eyebrows pinched down in response to the rebuke in Yggdrasil's voice. "What's that supposed to mean?"

You and your mother have hidden from the world for months. Besides unleashing your magic during the occasional thunderstorm, you haven't taken any action. I didn't make you my champion so that you could hide. It is time for you to step into the light and perform the task I gave you.

"A task that is practically impossible with a bum leg and only my mom to fight beside," Thyra argued. It didn't matter that she was tired of hiding—she wasn't in the mood to be chewed out by Yggdrasil.

"Maybe you should work on sending me some help."

You may be surprised to learn that the help you look for is coming as we speak, Yggdrasil said. *But it will not be enough. You will need more. The only way you can hope to survive is to prove yourself to the world.*

"How am I supposed to do that?"

You need a talisman, a symbol, that will prove to the world who and what you are.

"A talisman? I have the Eye—isn't that enough?"

The Eye names you as my champion, allows you to expand my power, but it is not enough.

"Why not?" Thyra scoffed. "It's the way to grant people magic, isn't it? I could show that to the world, give some people magic and the world would have to recognize me."

The Eye is a tool of my champion, yes, but it is obscure and old. This age knows nothing of its existence or the purpose it serves. Even its use will not be enough. You need something the world will recognize. A symbol they will flock to.

Thyra didn't know where this was going. "Will you just speak plainly? Tell me what I need to do for once!"

You need your father's hammer, Yggdrasil stated. *Claim Thor's hammer, and show the world who you are. People will flock to Mjolnir and whoever holds it.*

Thyra's jaw dropped. Claim Mjolnir? That possibility hadn't even entered her mind to this point. She had Lynnedslag, a powerful weapon in its own right. Sure, she felt some resentment towards Lynnedslag, but that didn't reduce its capabilities when in use. Why did she need Mjolnir, especially when the hammer was most likely locked away somewhere no one could get to?

Lynnedslag is not a weapon of magic's champion, Yggdrasil said, as if reading her thoughts. *If you want to be taken seriously, you will need a weapon to match.*

Thyra couldn't deny that she found the thought appealing, but caution born from the past three months kept her guarded. "And you think Mjolnir is the answer?"

The hammer is yours by right, Yggdrasil answered her unspoken question. *With it, your power would be undeniable and the world would be forced to recognize you.*

"Go after Mjolnir," Thyra said. She laughed at the absurdity of the thought. "I don't even know where it is, much less how to claim it. Why don't you help me for once by answering those questions."

That is for you to discover, Yggdrasil responded. *The answers are not far from you. As for the how, where there is a will there is always a path forward.*

Thyra had expected the non-answer, but it still frustrated her. "As always, thanks for your help."

Claim your father's hammer before another does and stop Baldur from accessing Idunn's garden. You cannot fail, or all is lost.

Thyra didn't have a chance to get another word in. She felt Yggdrasil's presence fade, leaving her alone again.

Chapter 6

Thyra sat cross-legged in the rain, her face turned up towards the sky. A storm had swept in as the afternoon faded into evening and even before the first flash of lighting lit the sky, Thyra had felt the latent energy in the air. The promise of the storm sent a shock wave of excitement through her and created an impulsive need to be a part of it.

Sif had been quick to recognize the yearning on Thyra's face. Thyra had been abnormally quiet in the days since her latest doctor's visit. Sif recognized that there was more than just the frustration over her knee that had Thyra upset and that she needed to work through what was bothering her. As much as Sif wished Thyra would open up to her, she knew her daughter well enough to recognize that Thyra needed to do it in her own way.

Even with the decision made, Sif had made Thyra wait until it was dark before reluctantly agreeing to drive into the hills east of town. They turned up a dirt road and drove almost a mile before Sif parked the car. They walked up a game trail for nearly a quarter mile before coming to a clearing that Thyra indicated would work. When Sif was sure they were alone she nodded to Thyra and faded back into the trees.

Left alone, Thyra let the barriers she erected to keep her magic in check fall away and allowed herself to test her limits. Calling lightning down felt as natural as breathing to her now. Controlling the raw ferocity of the lightning took concentration that left no room for other thoughts. It was a feeling similar to the one she got from exercising, only magnified a hundredfold. The rhythmic push and pull of magic through her body allowed her to focus her mind, thinking only of the energy around her and falling into a meditative state.

A dangerous meditation, as Sif was always quick to remind her when Thyra explained the feeling she got during a thunderstorm. She warned Thyra not to compel the storm to act unnaturally. Thyra did her best, but to anyone paying attention it would seem odd how the lightning appeared to concentrate on one spot. That was the reason why Sif always chose a different spot to take Thyra whenever a storm rolled in. The last thing they needed was storm chasers taking a sudden interest in the strange behavior of the lightning in this area.

Thyra didn't let those thoughts bother her now. She was in her element in these rare moments, a storm raging all around her rather than inside her. These moments were the most at peace she'd felt in months, maybe ever. In these moments she could forget about Baldur, Olafsson, Yggdrasil and the tree's continued manipulations. Even the awkwardness she felt toward her mom.

In these moments, she was free.

*****

Sif saw the pair long before they saw her. While the man and woman wore clothing that made them look like they were hikers out for a walk through the hills, it was a weak try at deception. Sif had seen too many similar attempts over the last few months. This one was far from believable. Why would a pair of hikers be out in a storm like this? More importantly, why would they risk their lives by walking towards the epicenter of the lightning strikes?

Sif let them get closer before stepping out into the middle of the trail. They hesitated when they saw her, their eyes taking measure of her tall, athletic frame and the dangerous look on her face. It was telling that they didn't looked surprised. They'd been warned in advance about what might be waiting for them in the storm.

"A dangerous night for a walk," Sif called out.

The man smiled and brushed the rain from his brow. "We love a good storm!"

"You shouldn't go any closer," Sif warned. "Lightning is unpredictable."

The woman was the one to answer this time. "We want to see what's up there."

"Nothing that would interest you." Sif motioned back the way they'd come. "Turn around. There will be other storms. This one is too dangerous."

"We can handle it," the woman replied in a grim tone.

"You take another step," Sif called, "and you put your life at risk."

The man frowned at the implied threat. "This is public property. We have every right to be here. We'll go where we please."

They started walking again, though Sif could see the caution in their movements now. They recognized her as a threat, but not a strong enough one to make them turn back. They were either foolish or the recipients of bad information—either one was enough to fill them with a false sense of courage. In Sif's experience, that was usually enough to get yourself killed.

She decided to give them one more opportunity. "It's late. The night doesn't have to go this way. Go home while you still can."

The man shook his head, his voice defiant. "We know who is up there. What she is. We have a message to deliver, and we're not leaving until we do."

His female companion took it a step further. "You can't stop us from seeing her!"

Sif had hoped the night wouldn't go this way. Sometimes she was able to turn people away without a fight. Of late, though, the attempts had grown more insistent and invasive. Only the language of violence seemed to get through to them. Tonight would be no different.

Her spear sprang to its full length in her hand, causing the pair to freeze in their tracks. She raised it across their path. "Whoever sent you here lied to you. Turn back before you get hurt."

"That kind of power shouldn't be possessed by one person," the woman shouted. "She needs to share it with all of us!"

Sif didn't like the sound of that word. Thyra didn't "need" to do anything, especially for complete strangers. "You two *need* to leave. Go while you still can."

The man shook his head slowly. "I don't think so."

Sif's shoulders sagged under the weight of what she was about to do. "So be it."

All three started moving at once. The woman threw up her hands and the ground in front of her erupted in a shower of dirt and rock that shot towards Sif. At the same time, the man's fists were encased in stone and he dropped into a boxer's stance. These two clearly had fought together before.

But they had never fought a Valkyrie.

Sif sidestepped the blast of debris and was on the woman before she could react. Her spear snaked in three times, forcing the woman to stumble and fall backwards to avoid a fatal wound from the razor sharp edge. Her male companion jumped to her aid and slapped Sif's spear away with one stone hand. Sif used the momentum to spin, and slammed the butt of her spear into his back. There was no stone to protect him there, and the force of the blow undoubtedly cracked several ribs. He stumbled forward with a pained grunt and tripped over the legs of the woman.

As easy as it might have been to finish them both then, Sif's warrior instinct told her to move back. She dodged to the side just as a boulder the size of her abdomen slammed into the spot where she'd just been standing. There was a third member of their party that had hung back in the trees! Sif spotted the giant as he stepped out into the open, already aiming another boulder at her. She had fought giants before and knew how much damage they could inflict if not dealt with quickly. Luckily, this one was not a frost giant. If it had been Sif might have found herself outmatched. As it was, dealing with two magic users and a ten-foot-tall giant hurling rocks big enough to crush her was going to be challenge enough.

Sif ducked under the next boulder and crossed the distance between her and the giant in a flash. Putting the two magic users at her back was dangerous, but she knew from experience that dealing with the giant would make her fight against them much simpler. As long as the giant provided a barrage of rocks, she would be hard pressed to get up close where her speed would make their magic less effective.

Surprised by her aggressive tactic, the giant didn't have the wherewithal to get his hands up to defend himself. He felt the bite of Sif's spear on his right arm and roared in anger as it fell useless at his side. He swung at Sif with his left hand, but she was too fast. Sif slid behind him, her spear slicing the back of both hamstrings in one fluid motion. The giant fell forward onto his face with a roar that Sif was quick to cut short. An experienced giant wouldn't have fallen so quickly, but Sif wasn't going to complain about her good luck.

She looked to find the pair of magic users and saw them stumbling together towards the top of the hill. The woman threw her hand up behind them, a wall of earth exploding upward to block Sif from following. A desperate attempt at defending their rear, but one that Sif realized might give the pair just enough time to reach Thyra. She couldn't allow that to happen.

Sif took off like an arrow for the far edge of the earth wall. The pair were both wounded—the woman was bleeding from at least one wound and the man was laboring with several broken ribs—and wouldn't be moving at full speed. Sif rounded the edge of the earth wall and made a guess at how far they might have managed to travel. A flash of lightning overhead illuminated the trees. The pair had made it farther than Sif thought them capable of and were almost to the edge of the clearing. Sif adjusted her direction to head them off. Even at a full sprint, she had the sinking feeling that she wouldn't be able to cut them off in time.

Another flash of lightning lit up the night. The pair saw her this time. The woman gave her companion a push forward and spun around to meet Sif's speedy approach. Sif knew what was coming when she saw the woman raise her hands. She judged the distance at thirty yards. Her arm went back and then whipped forward, sending her spear whistling through the air. Sif didn't wait to watch the spear's flight. She pivoted and ran after the man, hoping that her throw would buy her enough time to take care of him before he reached Thyra.

Even without her spear, Sif was deadly. She caught up to the man just before he reached the edge of the trees and leapt through the air to deliver a vicious kick aimed for his head. He barely managed to raise a rock-covered arm to deflect it, but the impact still sent him stumbling to the side. Sif dipped low and swept his legs out from under him and pounced on his back as he tried to roll away. Her arms snaked around his neck and then tightened, cutting off his air. She rolled onto her back and wrapped her legs around his middle, using her hips to help her sink in the chokehold even tighter. His stone-covered arms tried to reach her, but the more he fought the deeper her hold on him became. Sif took several blows to her shoulders and arms that sent waves of pain through her, but she didn't let go. Eventually his arms slowed and then stopped flailing altogether.

When she was confident the fight had left him, Sif rolled him to the side and looked towards the opening in the trees and Thyra. She was relieved to see Thyra still in the same spot where she had left her daughter and even more so that Thyra seemed to be completely unaware of what was happening only a dozen yards away.

Sif couldn't help but grimace as she watched the demonstration of her daughter's power. Lightning cracked and popped against an orb of wind that swirled around Thyra. The control of the wind was a testament to the fact that Thrya's magic was still maturing. So far, Thyra didn't seem aware of what she was doing when she fell into her trances, but at some point she would discover the change. Sif wasn't thrilled to see Thyra's magic take on an added element, but there was nothing that could be done to stop it. Controlling the wind was a clear extension of Thyra's control over the storm. It made sense as a direct evolution of Thyra's growing power.

Satisfied that her daughter was safe for now, Sif went to check on fate of the woman. She rose to her feet and started back down the trail to where the woman had been standing. Sif scanned the trees for any movement, any sign of the woman trying to hide between the dark trunks, but she didn't see any. She looked down at the trail for tracks, but the rain had turned the dirt into squishy mud and made individual tracks almost impossible to discern.

Sif retrieved her spear from the tree it had impaled and studied its length for any sign of blood. Again, the rain made it almost impossible to tell if her aim had been true or not. She trusted her arm, but with no proof, Sif couldn't take anything for granted.

She melted into the trees and circled back up towards the clearing where Thyra sat. She grimaced when she passed the spot where she'd left the man. He wasn't there. Gripping her spear tight, Sif cursed herself for not finishing the job when she could have. Now there were witnesses to what Thyra could do running free, rushing back to whoever had sent them. Wounded, but still alive. Her hesitation had been a mistake.

She wouldn't make that mistake again. Mercy was a luxury she couldn't afford any more.

Chapter 7

Thyra picked at her dinner with disinterest. It'd been a week since her conversation with Yggdrasil and she hadn't been able to think of anything besides the tree's instruction to find Mjolnir. It dominated her thoughts every waking hour and filled her dreams at night, leaving no room for anything else. It also created a level of anxiety she had never felt before. She knew next to nothing about Thor's hammer and why it was so important for her in Yggdrasil's reckoning.

What she did know was who would have the answers. All she had to do was ask. Except, it was the asking that had Thyra so worried. Especially with the way her mom had been acting since the last lightning storm. Tense was an understatement. Sif insisted that everything was normal, but Thyra saw through that. Sif had become a coiled spring of nervous energy. A spring with a spear attached to it.

"How have your projects been going?" Sif asked Asiri. It was the first words spoken over the meal and pulled Thyra out of her thoughts.

The dwarf shrugged. "Progressing. It's been a complete rework of my original design, but I think I've worked out the kinks."

Sif nodded as if she understood exactly what Asiri was talking about. Thyra didn't. All she knew was that Asiri disappeared into her forge for hours at a time, only appearing to eat, sleep and make sarcastic remarks about how detached Thyra had become, every now and then throwing a vague question in Sif's direction. There were days when seeing Asiri was more rare than a unicorn sighting. It had been that way for weeks, but had become even more so in the past few days. No one had offered an explanation as to what Asiri was working on. Thyra didn't think she would get an answer if she asked.

Asiri chewed thoughtfully and then continued, "I think I'll have them done in a few weeks."

Sif frowned. "No sooner?"

"I understand why you want it done faster," Asiri said, "but now is not the time to rush the process. *Or* to interrupt it completely."

Sif's lips pinched together, but she nodded. "I guess that will have to do. I just feel the need to be more prepared to face what the Muspel Corporation has been working on."

"The Muspel Corporation!" Asiri's mouth twisted in disgust. "Bah! Half-brained lackwits! Meddling in things they don't understand. They think its science to be reproduced, that they can just duplicate what my people did. They're fools! Their weapons show their lack of skill and complete absence of imagination."

"But they are effective all the same," Sif said. "Even the dullest blade can kill."

Asiri didn't look pleased, but she didn't argue the point. Instead, she stuffed her mouth with food and chewed with a disgusted frown on her blue-skinned face.

Thyra knew there wasn't going to be a good time to bring up what was on her mind. Her courage swelled and she blurted out, "Tell me about Thor's hammer."

Sif looked up from her dinner and blinked in confusion. "What?"

"I want to know about Thor's hammer," Thyra repeated. "Mjolnir. Please."

Sif's eyes narrowed slightly. "I'm sorry. I'm not sure I understand.

Why do you suddenly have such an interest in your father's hammer?"

Thyra chose her words carefully. "If I understand what Asiri told me correctly, as Thor's daughter, Mjolnir belongs to me. Right?"

Sif glanced at Asiri who quickly ducked her head to avoid Sif's glare. Sif's lips pressed together into a tight line. "That's mostly true. When your father died Mjolnir lost its true owner. As his daughter, your claim to it is one of the strongest."

"One of the strongest? What does that mean?"

Sif ignored the question, and repeated her own. "Why are you suddenly showing an interest your father's hammer?"

Thyra shrugged in a weak attempt to deflect her mom's suspicion. "Shouldn't I be interested in learning about my own history?"

"You haven't been to this point."

Thyra could only shrug again. "Maybe I wasn't ready. I am now."

"It's part of who she is," Asiri said, coming to Thyra's defense. "Sparks should know what the hammer's all about. What harm can a few answers do?"

Sif didn't look convinced, but to Thyra's relief, her mom didn't challenge her. Taking a deep breath, Sif nodded. "I'm not surprised that you have questions, even if the timing seems suspicious." Sif pushed her plate way from her and rested her hands on the table. "Truthfully, I expected you to ask a lot sooner. What do you want to know?"

Thyra didn't know where to start, so she blurted out the first thing that came to her mind. "Is the hammer powerful?"

Sif cocked an eyebrow and glanced at Asiri. "Do you want to answer that?"

Asiri snorted. "Is it powerful? What kind of question is that! Girl, that is one of the most powerful weapons my people ever created!"

"More powerful than Lynnedslag?"

Asiri's eyes went wide and her jaw dropped. "Tell me you're joking."

Thyra frowned. "No. I don't think so."

Asiri snorted again. "I'm glad you have such a high opinion of my work, Sparks, but that stick doesn't hold a candle to Mjolnir. I'll be the first to admit it, and I do it without any shame. Thor's hammer was crafted by the very best smiths to ever walk this earth! Ten of my ancestors stoked the flames while another ten worked the metal. Then the master smiths, Brock and Sindri, finished it with their own hands. The finest materials to ever come through a forge went into that hammer. Lightning was harnessed into the core of the hammer, a storm contained within metal. It has the highest capacity for magic amplification of any weapon created. Even the weakest magic user could become a danger if bonded with the hammer. In the hands of a powerful magic user," Asiri shook her head, "it's capacity is beyond anything you've dreamed up."

Thyra's dreams had been full of Mjolnir in her hands and massive, earth shaking storms. "My dreams can be pretty wild."

"Trust me," Asiri said, "your dreams barely scratch the surface of what is possible with that hammer in the right hands. Or the wrong hands."

Sif nodded in reluctant agreement. "Asiri is right. It was said that Mjolnir was only rivaled by Gungnir."

"And I wouldn't be surprised if the hammer came out on top," Asiri muttered. "In the right hands, that is. Harnessing the power that went into Gungnir nearly killed the dwarves working on it. Brock and Sindri learned some hard lessons that came in handy when forging Mjolnir." Asiri harrumphed. "At least, that's the way my father told it. Putting the fury of the sun or of a raging storm into a weapon is no easy undertaking. It took everything my ancestors had, all their knowledge and know-how to keep both from exploding in their faces and destroying everything for miles around. If someone were to try to destroy the core of either," Asiri shivered. "I don't even want to think about it. They would likely vaporize themselves as well as everyone and everything around them. Think nuclear bomb. That would be only the beginning."

"I don't think Thyra was thinking about destroying them," Sif said gently, "or the intricacies of creating them."

"No, but she needs to understand the dangers of mishandling dwarf creations," Asiri asserted. She turned back to Thyra. "Lynnedslag is powerful, but it pales in comparison to Mjolnir and Gungnir. Those two are the ultimate god-maker weapons."

"Then why did they fail?" Thyra asked. This question had been plaguing her as much as any. "If Mjolnir and Gungnir were so powerful, and Thor and Odin were such strong magic users, why did they fall when Surtur attacked?"

"Even the most powerful can fall victim to an unbreakable tide," Sif replied. She sighed heavily. "Your father and Odin were no exception. Magic can be demanding, and centuries of its use left them tired and drained. Eventually even the strongest can find themselves feeling overextended."

That had an ominous undertone, a not-so-subtle warning that made Thyra pause.

"Using those kinds of weapons is demanding," Asiri agreed. "Trying to use them at their full force requires an unbreakable will as well as strength of body and mind. Dwarf weapons amplify, remember. It still is the strength of the user that determines the end result. Push too far and," Asiri shrugged, "well, you risk losing control at the very least. I've heard stories of magic wielders burning themselves out when they tried to channel too much. One second they have magic, the next," she snapped her fingers, "they don't!"

Sif grimaced and turned to look out the window. She blinked several times, like she was trying to stop a tear from falling. She cleared her throat and when she turned back any emotion that might have been on her face had been pushed back down. "The biggest difference between the two weapons was what they meant to the people. That was where Mjolnir's power truly lied."

That piqued Thyra's interest. "What do you mean?"

"Thor's hammer was a symbol to the people," Sif said. "Warriors wore the hammer when they went into battle and looked to Thor for protection. They carved the symbol over their doors, tattooed it on their bodies, painted it on their boats. Thor was the god of the people, someone they looked to in times of war *and* peace. Odin was revered, but there's no denying that he was aloof and unapproachable. He was more concerned with managing threats from other magic users. He was willing to let the mortals fight their own battles as long as they worshipped him. Thor took a more active role. As a result, the people looked to your father, not the Allfather."

Thyra nodded thoughtfully. That was what she had hoped to hear. "Do you think Mjolnir would still be a symbol people would flock to?"

"Perhaps," Sif replied grudgingly. "It's been centuries, but there is one thing the world of men holds on to better than anything—stories. The symbols of the gods are still used, even if those using them don't fully understand what they mean." Sif's eyes narrowed. "Why do you ask?"

"I've just been thinking," Thyra answered.

"Thinking about what exactly?"

Thyra hesitated. She could see from the arch in her mom's eyebrow that backtracking would do her no good. Not that she wanted to. She'd had a week to come to the conclusion that not only did she need to find Mjolnir, she *wanted* to. But that didn't mean she could charge forward like a bull in a china shop. She needed Sif on her side, and suggesting a dangerous attempt to recover the hammer off the cuff over a plate of spaghetti would probably have the opposite effect. She needed to be careful.

"I'm magic's champion," Thyra said, "but I don't feel like I have any way to prove that to the world."

Sif's suspicion was palpable. "Why should you prove anything to the world?"

"Sooner or later something will happen that will force me to reveal who I am," Thyra said. "I think that will be easier if I have a symbol that people will recognize. Something they would accept, even flock to."

"You have the Eye, don't you?" Sif asked. "What more would you need?"

"The Eye may make me Yggdrasil's champion, but how many people even know about it? A handful? If I walked up to someone on the street and showed it to them, would they know what it was? Besides a rock with blue flames?"

"You have Lynnedslag," Sif countered without hesitation.

Thyra took a deep breath. "A powerful weapon, yes, but it's a lacrosse stick. No one will recognize it or even feel inspired by it. You said that warriors carried the symbols of the gods into battle. I don't think anyone is going to be in a hurry to get a lacrosse stick tattooed on their arms. No offense, Asiri."

"None taken," Asiri said around a mouth full of food. "I thought it was a poor idea from the start. A poor idea excellently carried out, mind you, but poor all the same. An axe would have been better. Bearded, maybe a spike or hammerhead to counter-balance it while adding some extra weight. Especially good for piercing armor."

Sif cast an impatient glare at Asiri, who shrugged before returning to her meal. Sif turned back to her daughter, her expression turning calculating. "I've noticed that you've been avoiding Lynnedslag lately. I'm sure it's a reminder of what you've lost by becoming Yggdrasil's champion. Is that what's behind this?"

Thyra was amazed by her mom's intuition.

"Maybe," Thyra admitted. "But that isn't the point."

"What is the point?"

Sif's question left Thyra struggling to find the right words. The answer she found sounded weak the moment it left her lips. "I guess I feel that if I'm supposed to gather people to me, to be a champion of magic, maybe I need something people would recognize."

"Like your father's hammer?"

Thyra nodded slowly. "Yeah, like Thor's hammer."

Sif's eyebrow somehow managed to creep up even higher on her forehead. "Tell me, why do you think you need to be gathering followers?"

This is where it got tricky. There hadn't been many conversations about Thyra's visions of Yggdrasil for a reason. Every time the tree's conversations with Thyra were brought up Sif's expression turned thunderous. Although as a Valkyrie, Sif accepted that Thyra was Yggdrasil's champion, as a mother she hated the fact that she was kept in the dark about what the tree was telling her daughter. Thyra knew what Sif would think about the tree instructing her to find Mjolnir. She winced in expectation of Sif's reaction before she even began speaking.

"Yggdrasil spoke to me a few days ago-"

Sif rolled her eyes in exasperation. "Of course, it was Yggdrasil."

"This was the first time it has spoken to me in months," Thyra explained, misjudging the reason behind her mom's anger.

"The frequency of its chats with you isn't what bothers me," Sif muttered. "It's what the tree tries to force you into doing every time it does speak that makes me mad. Going after Mjolnir! Only the tree would suggest something so extreme and actually expect a seventeen-year-old girl to accomplish it."

Thyra's temper flared. "Wait, why is me claiming what belongs to me extreme?"

"Because there is no way we can get to it!" Sif snapped. "Did the tree tell you where the hammer is?"

And there was the problem that Thyra couldn't get around in this plan. "No, it didn't."

"Did you stop to consider where it might be? Or who might have it?" Sif waited for an answer, but Thyra didn't offer one. "Let me tell you. Gunnar Olafsson has it! He destroyed Asgard and killed your father. He's not stupid. He wouldn't have left the hammer behind for someone else to take. He also never would part with it, which means he still has it, locked away somewhere safe, behind ranks of armed men."

Thyra had assumed that might be a possibility, which was one of the reasons why she'd been so hesitant to bring it up. She knew her mom would be against the idea, but if the last week of agonizing over Yggdrasil's instructions had convinced Thyra of anything, it was that the hammer was a necessity.

"Then we go get it."

Sif blinked slowly. "Sweetheart, weren't you listening? That is next to impossible. We wouldn't even get within reach of the hammer before Gunnar Olafsson's men would be all over us."

Thyra shrugged. "We're not easy meat."

"We'd never even get close to it," Sif repeated. "It's too dangerous, Thyra."

"I know it's dangerous," Thyra said, doing her best to keep her tone calm but firm, "but Mjolnir is important to what I need to do."

"And what exactly did the tree say you need to be doing?"

"Gathering magic users to me," Thyra replied. "Stepping into the light so that the world can see that magic exists. The only way to do that is if I have a symbol they will respond to."

"Of course, the tree would want that!" Sif said derisively. "Yggdrasil only cares about one thing—itself! Do you know how I know that?

Because the tree didn't tell you where or how to get the hammer, nor does it care about the amount of risk we'd be taking by trying. It's using you!"

Thyra agreed with her mom. "I know Yggdrasil is using me. But, the bad guys haven't been sitting around doing nothing for the past three months. We knocked Gunnar Olafsson down and I'm convinced that I hurt Baldur, but they aren't going to let that happen again. When they come for us next time, they're going to be swinging hard. Don't we need to be doing something to prepare?"

"What makes you think we haven't been?" Sif said. She didn't wait for Thyra to answer. "Preparing is creating a plan, surveying the battlefield, looking for weak points. Not rushing into an obvious trap on the suggestion of a magical tree. Doing so might accomplish Yggdrasil's goal, but it goes against my goal—keeping you safe!"

That made some sense, but Thyra wasn't going to roll over so easily. "Going after the hammer is the last thing Gunnar and Baldur would expect."

"Is it?" Sif challenged, both eyebrows rising dangerously high. "You may be right that he might not expect us, but trust me when I say that he is watching for someone to try to slip through and attack him on his own ground."

Thyra hesitated. "What do you mean?"

"You remember what happened in Wisconsin," Sif said. "Think about what we heard afterwards. No bodies, no reports of a battle. What does that tell you?"

Thyra shrugged. "That the news got it wrong?"

"We could only wish," Sif said. "What it means is that that Hela has some of Olafsson's men under her power. She took both the dead and those close to it. I can only guess how many she managed to keep alive, but we have to assume she saved a few. Olafsson knows that, too, which means he is taking precautions to keep her from sneaking into his midst and stabbing him in the back. That means his eyes are looking inward for threats just as much as they are outward. We wouldn't get within a thousand feet of the Muspel Corporation, much less get a whiff of Mjolnir."

"But Yggdrasil—"

Sif held up a hand to silence Thyra's argument. "No. I don't care what the tree told you. We are not running off after your father's hammer! We aren't strong enough to accomplish something like that, no matter what Yggdrasil seems to think."

"If I had the hammer, we might be," Thyra insisted. "If I had the hammer, maybe we could free Bragi."

"Bragi is the least of my concerns," Sif snapped. Thyra wasn't surprised by Sif's reaction. Any time the topic of Bragi was brought up Sif became distant. "I'm concerned for him, but he is a god, and not as innocent as he seems. I pity his situation if he remains in Baldur's clutches, but saving him is the last reason we should use for chasing after Mjolnir. We aren't strong enough for such an undertaking, even for the right reasons."

Thyra could feel the door closing on her chances of convincing Sif of the necessity of her plan. "What if we were strong enough? What if we had help?"

Sif sighed in frustration. "What help, Thyra?"

"I don't know," Thyra admitted. "Yggdrasil said it was *sending* help."

Sif scoffed. "I doubt our definition of help is the same as Yggdrasil's. What did the tree say it was sending?"

Thyra told the truth. "It didn't say."

"Exactly! For all we know, it might send a flying squirrel or a talking fox and tell you that its an amazing gift."

"I've met some talking foxes," Asiri muttered. "Can't trust everything they say, but they're great for sniffing out herbs." Thyra and Sif both turned on the dwarf in disbelief. Asiri looked between them and then shrugged. "Just thought you might find it interesting."

"Talking foxes and herbs aside," Sif said, "we cannot sit back and hope for Yggdrasil to deliver a solution to our problems, much less help us tackle mountains we have no business trying to climb."

Thyra threw her hands up in frustration. "All I know is that Yggdrasil said it would send help. It says it is still committed to seeing me succeed, so I think Yggdrasil meant it."

"Well, I don't see any help," Sif said. "So until this *help* arrives, my decision stands. We are not going after Thor's hammer, and that's final."

Thyra sat back and stared a hole into the table. This conversation had gone about as bad as she had expected. Not even days of practicing in her head had helped her make the case for going after Mjolnir in a way that approached convincing. In fact, she had probably hurt her case more than anything. Now Sif was on the defensive and angry. I would take a miracle to convince her to go along with the idea.

That didn't change the fact that Thyra felt she needed to find a way to get the hammer. She just didn't know what that way was yet. Thyra wanted Sif to be part of whatever plan she decided on. If Sif wasn't ever willing? Thyra wasn't ready to seriously consider what that meant for her.

Consumed with her frustrations, Thyra almost didn't hear the sound of tires crunching on the gravel and brakes being applied just outside the window. She wasn't the only one that heard the sounds. Her mom was on her feet in a flash, her Valkyrie spear flashing in the light as it extended to its full length. Sif moved with a deadly grace towards the front door, signaling for everyone to be quiet. Thyra cast a questioning look at Asiri, but the dwarf shook her head and reached for one of the hammers in her tool belt. Thyra followed their lead and readied herself by taking hold of her magic.

Sif peered through the peephole, but jumped back when a heavy knock shook the door on the hinges. Sif signaled for Thyra and Asiri to head for the back door. Thyra had argued this part of the escape plan time and time again—she had left her mom once before, and had vowed never to do it again—but Sif had insisted that she be the first line of defense. Thyra didn't like it, but arguing with a Valkyrie got her nowhere.

The knock came again on the door hard enough that Thyra felt the trailer shake under her feet. Whoever it was, they were not going away easily.

Moving on cat's feet, she ducked into her room and grabbed Lynnedslag. The magical lacrosse stick pulsed in anticipation at her touch. Thyra resisted the sudden urge to draw the immense power Lynnedslag gave her access to. She'd given into the urge before and she'd ended up putting on a lightning display that had garnered national news attention.

Thyra came back out into the hall just as the door was hammered on so hard that she thought it might splinter and break apart.

She was almost to the back door when a deep voice boomed, "Open the door, Sif!"

Thyra froze. She thought she recognized that voice. Sif had the same reaction, looking back at the front door.

"It's me, Sif. It's Vidar!"

Chapter 8

Thyra couldn't suppress the smile on her face as she watched Vidar from across the table. He looked the same as before, the same grim expression and simmering rage in his eyes, but she sensed a change in him. She wasn't sure why, but he seemed less haunted than he had been a few months before. There had even been a hint of a smile on his face when he saw Thyra.

"It's good to see you, little brother," Sif said as she slid a plate of spaghetti in front of him.

"It's good to be seen," Vidar said. He looked at Thyra. "I'm sorry it took me so long."

Thyra's smile widened. "We'd almost given up hope. We thought you might have decided to disappear forever."

Vidar's eyes grew distant for a moment. "I had things I had to take care of. Difficult decisions."

"What matters is that you're here," Sif said, sensing his unease. "Even if you almost broke down my door."

Vidar cringed. "Sorry. Old habits are hard to break."

"Not your fault," Asiri barked. "You're used to battering down doors made of solid oak, if not iron gates. They just don't make doors the way they used to." She looked around the trailer with a frown. "Or anything else for that matter."

Vidar smirked, but it lacked sincerity. He looked around at the trailer. "Quite the fortress you have here. Not exactly where I imagined you'd be gathering your strength."

Sif's lips pressed into a tight line. "It was the best we could do. We've been forced to move often to avoid attention. While not ideal, this place serves it's purpose."

Vidar's eyes narrowed. "Olafsson's men?"

Sif's expression darkened. "Other reasons."

Vidar frowned. "Looking for Thyra?"

Sif nodded. "Some didn't know what they were looking for, but they were getting closer. Others had to be turned away more. . .forcefully."

Vidar's frown deepened. "Hopefully without drawing too much attention."

Sif's expression turned cold. "I made sure we were safe." She grimaced. "There was a situation this past week that did not get handled to my satisfaction."

Vidar tensed. "Will it be a problem?"

"Perhaps," Sif answered. "Perhaps not. I tried to leave them cold."

"Tried?" Vidar cocked an eyebrow. "That isn't like the Sif I know."

Sif's eyes flashed with anger. "I would've finished it, just like all the others. I fear they had more help than what I saw."

"What kind of help?"

"Big help," Sif replied sharply. "God-like help."

Thyra looked between them in an attempt to decipher the meaning of what had just passed between them. She gave her mom a questioning look. "What are you two talking about?"

Sif ignored her, her attention still directed at Vidar. "Now that you're here, I won't make the same mistake again."

Vidar nodded. "I'm here to help. In any way I can."

That was music to Thyra's ears. "We've needed help. Now you're here."

Sif gave her a penetrating stare, clearly catching the reference to their argument from before. "Thyra is right. We're grateful to have you here. Even if it took longer than we had hoped."

Vidar took a bite of food and chewed slowly. "You were difficult to find."

"Not difficult enough," Asiri quipped. "You drove right to our front door."

"I had help with that," Vidar admitted.

"The Yggdrasil kind of help?" Thyra asked.

Vidar hesitated, but finally nodded. "I shouldn't be surprised. You are the World Tree's champion. Yggdrasil had several things to show me besides your location." His eyes flicked to Sif. "Some of which you may not like."

Sif's eyes narrowed. "Like what?" Vidar chose to fill his mouth with food rather than answer the question. "What did the tree tell you, Vidar?"

"You should know that I spoke with Hela before coming here," Vidar said in a grave tone, dodging the question. "She said that she had plans, but wouldn't say what they were."

"She always has plans," Sif growled, her eyes flicking towards Thyra. "Get to the point."

Vidar finished chewing before explaining. "Hela wouldn't tell me what those plans were. But Yggdrasil did. Hela has been gathering magic users to her. She's going to reveal herself to the world and show that magic still exists."

Sif glanced at Thyra briefly then let out a deep sigh. "When?"

"Soon," Vidar answered. "But that wasn't all. Baldur and Gunnar Olafsson are up to something the tree was concerned by. It wouldn't say what, other than that their success was a direct threat to all of us. It didn't say why."

"Whatever it is, it's Yggdrasil's business," Sif grumbled.

"It seems like you and the World Tree are developing a strong rapport, Muscles," Asiri commented.

Vidar shrugged. "I'm as surprised as you that Yggdrasil sought me out. It has never spoken to me before, even in the early days. Even when I held the Eye it never spoke to me. It wasn't a conversation, though. I saw what it wanted me to see and then it was over."

"I don't trust the World Tree," Sif stated. "Reaching out to you makes me think it's desperate. If it wants something done, it should handle it's own business."

"Normally, I'd agree," Vidar said, turning to Thyra, "but I get the feeling that something isn't right. I was told that the champion would know what I'm talking about."

Thyra fork's paused on its way to her mouth and she glanced up at the adults. Sif looked at her with one eyebrow cocked. "Do you have something you need to tell us, Thyra?"

Thyra set her fork down and cleared her throat. "Are you ready to continue our conversation about Mjolnir?"

Sif's expression darkened. "What does that have to do with this?"

"A lot," Thyra answered. "Yggdrasil told me what it feared Baldur and Gunnar were up to. Just like it told me that I needed to get Mjolnir."

"We're not going after the hammer," Sif stated, her tone dangerous. "That is final!"

"Maybe you should hear what Thyra has to say," Vidar said. He had perked up when he heard Thyra mention Mjolnir, and he met Sif's fiery glare without blinking. He spoke to Thyra but kept his eyes locked with Sif's, "Tell us what the tree said."

Sif turned her gaze back to Thyra. She tried to meet it with the same calm that Vidar had. "Yggdrasil said that Baldur is trying to summon Idunn. He's gathering the summoning stones with the intention of accessing her garden." She let that hang in the air, expecting a reaction from her mom, but Sif's expression never wavered. She cleared her throat and continued. "I think that Yggdrasil felt threatened somehow. That's one of the reasons why the tree wanted me to go after Mjolnir."

"Proving again how self-serving the tree is," Sif snapped. "It feels threatened, so it decides to encourage you to jump headfirst into danger so that you can protect it." She shook her head. "We are not going after the hammer, no matter what the tree says."

"We need to think this through, Sif," Vidar said. He cut off the argument that was forming on Sif's tongue before it could escape. "Look, I don't like the idea of trying to take Thor's hammer back, either. I'm pretty confident about who has it, and getting it back would not be easy. But. . .maybe it's what needs to be done."

"Why?" Sif barked. "Why does Thyra need the hammer?"

"Isn't the fact that it's in the wrong hands reason enough?" Vidar waited for an answer, but Sif crossed her arms stubbornly. "I don't know what is in Idunn's garden, but if Baldur wants it then I'm sure of one thing—we don't want him to have it. I'm sure he has Bragi and is using the old man to trick Idunn. I don't think there's anyone alive that knows more about Idunn's garden then Bragi, making him a danger that we can't ignore. Face it, with Mjolnir in her hand, Thyra might be able to finish what she started in Wisconsin."

"Or she might die trying," Sif said. "Or worse, be captured by Baldur. She's your blood, too. Is that what you want to see? Thyra in Baldur's clutches? Like Bragi?"

"Of course not," Vidar snapped. "I know what kind of maniac he is as well as you do. I've wished everyday for the last three months that I'd killed him centuries ago, before Hela made him the monster he is."

Sif put her hands on the table and leaned close."Newsflash, little brother—he was always a monster! Hela only made him a monster that can't die."

Vidar sat back in his chair and spread his hands wide, "Look, I'm not saying I think it's a good idea. In fact, I think it's a terrible idea!

But I think its the best out of a string of terrible options. Plus, I don't think we can wait around hoping for a better one to come along. Hela is gathering power in the shadows and will soon make a move for the world to see, Baldur and Gunnar Olafsson are on the move, and what are we?"

"Weak," Asiri answered for him, receiving a glare from Sif that the dwarf didn't seem concerned by.

Vidar nodded. "That's right. If we wait until our hand is forced it may be too late."

"I can't believe I'm having this argument twice in one day," Sif lamented, snapping back up to her full height. "Especially with you, Vidar. You should know it isn't possible."

"Why not?"

"Because we were lucky to escape in Wisconsin when Olafsson only had a handful of men at his disposal. We'd have no chance against the full might of the Muspel Corporation, and that is exactly what we'd be facing. We would need an army!"

Vidar shrugged. "I think our chances might be better than you think."

"Oh, do you?" Sif scoffed. "I'm dying to hear this."

"Olafsson and Baldur would expect us to hide," Vidar said, "to try and amass power before making our move. They won't expect us to go on the offensive. A small group might be able to make it farther than an army."

"Or nowhere at all," Sif argued. "They would see us coming before we even made it through the front door! That's no plan at all."

Thyra sat back in her chair and began to massage her temples. Twice in one day the suggestion of going after Mjolnir had led them to the same result—Sif standing firm in opposition to the idea. Thyra understood her mom's arguments—it was dangerous and they would be outnumbered. But that didn't change Thyra's mind. She *wanted* the hammer!

"You can't just barrel into the building and take the hammer with brute force alone," Sif said, slapping the table to emphasize her words.

"You might be surprised," Vidar grumbled.

Sif rolled her eyes. "I don't doubt your strength, little brother, but this isn't something you can punch your way through."

"And I'm not suggesting I punch my way through anything," Vidar replied. "Just create a distraction big enough that they won't have time to look for you and Thyra."

"What are you going to do? Smash some city buses? Throw a taxi through the front doors?" Sif held up a hand to cut off his response. "No! I will not even entertain the thought of you serving yourself up like a lamb for the slaughter. You are not doing that!"

"I'm no lamb," Vidar said in a voice that was anything but calm.

"But you're not the lion you were a thousand years ago! These men will be armed with guns and weapons Olafsson has created. Weapons that imitate the magic of gods!"

"Magic I'm not scared of!" Vidar shouted, pounding the table hard enough that the wood splintered beneath his fist. He looked down and exhaled heavily, his anger turning to embarrassment. He tried in vain to push the table back into its original position before sighing. "I see what you're saying, Sif. But its better that I do this than you or Thyra. I've done a lot of terrible things in my life, most of them at the whims of people trying to use me. This is my choice, and I would do it gladly."

"You can't do this alone," Sif repeated. "Even if I agreed to let you try."

Vidar exhaled heavily, his shoulders slumping. Thyra saw his resolve fading, her lone voice of support going with it. If Vidar folded, there would be no chance of moving Sif from her position.

"You're right, Mom," Thyra said. She met Sif's gaze and managed to keep from wilting. "It isn't something Vidar can do alone. It isn't something I can do alone. I'm not even sure if we can do it together. But I think we have to try. What do we have to lose?"

"Everything," Sif said. "Your life for starters, and then the list just gets worse. If they capture you they will use you. Dying would be better than living under Baldur's control."

Thyra imagined that would be far from pleasant, but the last three months of hiding had been agonizing on their own. "So we don't get caught."

Sif scoffed. "Did Yggdrasil tell you how to do that? Did it give you the layout of the building and show you a secret door that leads right to where Mjolnir is? Because that is the only way we have any chance of success."

"You know Yggdrasil didn't tell me any of that," Thyra replied.

"Of course not! The tree is manipulating you, Thyra."

That threw a spark on the tinder of Thyra's temper. "That's nothing new. Yggdrasil has been manipulating me for months. Which is why I want to do this. I don't want to be manipulated and threatened anymore."

"And you think you'll be untouchable with the hammer in your hands?"

Thyra threw up her hands. "Won't I be? Everything I've heard is that the hammer is the biggest and baddest. You all admit that my power already rivals many of the gods you all knew. With Mjolnir I'll be something altogether different. No one will be able to manipulate or use me for my power again!"

Sif's eyes narrowed. "That's a dangerous road to walk, being the biggest and strongest on the battlefield. It puts a target on your back, and there's always someone willing to take their shot. Just ask Vidar."

Vidar shook his head. "Don't drag me into this."

"You threw yourself into the middle of this the moment you

suggested we put Thyra's life in danger to retrieve that cursed hammer!" Sif turned to Thyra. "When you're the strongest you will always have challengers. Sooner or later, one of them succeeds. Odin's pride led him to believe he was untouchable. Look what it got him. I won't let you make that mistake."

"I'm not trying to be prideful!" Thyra countered. "I'm trying to cut the strings that people have on me. I'm trying to find a way to stop hiding. I'm trying to find a way to protect you!"

Sif's expression softened slightly before hardening again just as quickly. "I appreciate that, Thyra. I truly do. But going after Mjolnir is not the way to protect me. It will only make things more dangerous for all of us. If Yggdrasil is telling you to go after it, then I say we go the opposite direction. It isn't the solution to our problems—it is the problem!"

"I don't see it that way," Thyra said defiantly.

"That's because you're seventeen," Sif snapped. "You don't see anything clearly!"

Thyra felt like she had been slapped, and judging by the brief flash of uncertainty on Sif's face, her mom realized how biting her words had been. She looked like she was going to offer an apology, but then she pressed her lips into a tight line and her eyes turned cold. "I am your mother. It is my responsibility to protect you. Until that changes, I make the final call. We are not going after Mjolnir, and nothing will change my mind!"

Chapter 9

The news vans were parked close around the entrance to the hospital, the reporters milling around impatiently or making the final adjustments to their cameras. Kate Suzuki tapped her cell phone against her hand as she took note of the familiar faces from all the competing news agencies in the area. There were even a few people she recognized that did work for national news groups.

They'd all received the same urgent message from the director of the hospital that he had an important announcement to make. Considering the extensive cancer research that took place inside, the expectation was that a significant discovery had been made. Every news agency had scrambled to get the scoop first, Kate's included, but their repeated attempts at getting a whiff of what the announcement might be about had gone unanswered. The hospital phone lines were dead, the exterior doors all locked, and no one inside was responding to calls, texts, or emails. What had started out as excitement was quickly turning to an eerie sense of dread.

Kate looked towards the doors of the hospital and wondered for the thousandth time since arriving half an hour ago what was happening inside. Something didn't feel right, and she could tell she wasn't the only one who felt it.

The doors opened suddenly, revealing a dark-haired woman. A tall, hairy man followed close on her heels, his expression an angry grimace that he turned on each person in turn. They stopped on the edge of the concrete a dozen feet short of where the line of reporters waited. There was brief flurry of activity as cameras and microphones were turned on and focused on the woman. Kate tried to put an age to her, but couldn't. One thing was for certain—she was striking, especially her vibrant, green eyes that seemed to penetrate Kate to her core when they fell on her. Authority oozed from her as she studied the reporters.

"Thank you all for gathering," the woman said. "I've chosen this hospital to serve as the backdrop for my reintroduction to your world. Once my name was said with reverence and fear. Once, I was known as the greatest healer this world has ever known." She let that proclamation hang in the air before continuing. "I've watched from the shadows as mankind has failed time and time again to correct it's course. For centuries, the weakness of your minds has allowed millions to die because you lack the power to heal them. Today, that changes. Today, I offer you a beacon of hope and a promise." She looked around at the faces gathered around her. "My name is Hela. Long ago I was known as the goddess of death, caretaker of *Hel,* home of damned souls. But today I offer you life instead of death."

Hela? Kate looked at her colleagues in confusion. Kate had never heard that name before, but the confidence this woman spoke with made Kate feel like she was negligent for *not* knowing it.

Hela turned and beckoned with one hand towards the doors. They opened, revealing an old man in a hospital gown and a doctor in a lab coat. The pair hesitated briefly before joining the woman in front of the line of cameras.

"Tell them your names," Hela instructed.

The old man spoke first. "My name is Benjamin Fratelli."

"And I'm Dr. Georgia Paulson," the curly haired doctor at his side added. Kate recognized the doctor from a previous story on the hospital's cancer research. Dr. Paulson was one of the leading researchers working on an experimental treatment for leukemia and had chosen this area to perform her work in honor of her grandfather that had passed away from cancer decades before in this very hospital. Kate remembered Dr. Paulson as having a quick smile and a sparkle in her eyes when she spoke about her research. There was no smile now. If anything, she looked afraid.

"Now tell them why you're here, Benjamin," Hela urged.

Benjamin licked his lips nervously. "I've been a patient here at the cancer research center for the last three months. I was diagnosed with Stage Four leukemia."

"And what was the prognosis you gave him, Dr. Paulson?"

"Between his age and the aggressive spread of the cancer," Dr. Paulson responded stiffly, "we gave Mr. Fratelli three to six months to live without chemotherapy and radiation. We determined that bone marrow or stem cell transplants were not a viable option considering the nature of the cancer. Even with treatment, we didn't think he would live more than a year. Mr. Fratelli chose to pursue chemotherapy, and has been undergoing treatments for two months. He was supposed to receive another round of treatment today."

"But he didn't receive that treatment," Hela stated.

"No," Dr. Paulson said in a voice barely above a whisper. "No, he did not."

"Why not?"

"Because. . ." the doctor hesitated and looked to Hela for confirmation. Receiving it, she continued, "He didn't receive the treatment today because his cancer is gone! I can confirm, after multiple scans performed this morning, Mr. Fratelli's cancer is in complete remission, and he is in excellent health."

Kate looked at the other news media around her and saw similar confusion painted on their expressions. That kind of statement was extraordinary, and she knew that there had to be more to the story. She tried to ask a question, but for some reason the words refused to form.

"And how was Mr. Fratelli's cancer cured?" Hela asked. Again, Dr. Paulson hesitated, her eyes flicking nervously to Hela. "Go on. Tell these people what happened."

It was Benjamin Fratelli that answered. "You healed me. You walked into my room this morning and did something that no one in this hospital can explain." He shook his head. "It felt like being thrown into an icy lake and it hurt like nothing I've ever felt before, but after. . ." he paused and then looked directly into Kate's eyes. "I've never felt better. I don't know what she did, but I feel brand new!"

"I healed you of what the medicine of man could not," Hela said. "Thank you, Dr. Paulson. You may go."

The doctor stiffly turned and retreated back into the hospital, leaving Hela and Benjamin Fratelli together. Hela wrapped an arm around the old man's shoulders and looked at the news media gathered around her.

"Magic once ruled this world, and there was a natural order to things. For centuries, mankind has tried to eradicate the existence of magic and that order has been lost. The world of magic has been forced to hide in the shadows for too long. That ends today." Hela took a long, deep breath. "Once I walked the earth as a god, and people were willing to sacrifice anything to feel my healing touch. Like Benjamin Fratelli, they wanted to be healed of the weakness of their bodies. Unlike the medicine of man, my magic *does not* fail." Her statement hung in the air for a moment before she continued. "As a merciful god, I now offer the same opportunity for healing to anyone who desires it. Starting today, once per day at noon, I will choose one person to heal from the weakness of their mortal bodies. A person that your modern medicine has failed."

Kate scribbled that down even though she knew her recorder had caught every word. Her mind was reeling and the act of writing helped keep her thoughts from running out of control.

"Each of you will be receiving an email explaining the requirements for anyone seeking my healing touch," Hela continued. "I want the world to know what I've told you today, and each of you will ensure that happens. I offer this opportunity to mankind as a sign of my goodwill." Hela's eyes hardened suddenly. "But, do not mistake me—that goodwill will not last forever, nor will I suffer any interference from any person, organization, or government. This hospital is now under my protection. It will continue to function as a place of healing for any in need as long as no one from the outside tries to stand in my way. Any attempts to do so will be met without mercy. None come or go without my leave. None will be forced to stay, but once they depart from my protection, they will not ever rest beneath it again."

She signaled with one hand and the doors to the hospital opened to reveal three men decked out in tactical gear and carrying assault rifles.

"As you can see," Hela stated, "I am fully prepared to stand up against any opposition. This is the kind of force your minds understand, but it is the kind your minds cannot that should fill you with fear. I can take lives as easily as I can save them. I can boil the blood in your veins as easily as I can heal cancer. Break bones or mend them. Break the mind or heal it."

The intensity in her gaze left no doubt in Kate's mind that this woman claiming to be a god meant every word of what she said.

"In addition to my offering to the sick and afflicted of this world," Hela said, "I have begun to gather those who bear magic's touch to me. I now extend the same offer to any others who are gifted with magic. Come, join me, and step out of the shadows. Unlike the world of man, I will not vilify you or try to hide you away because you have power mortal minds can not accept or understand. With me, you will be safe and you will be free to be your true selves."

Kate scribbled that down with a big question mark behind it. Was she saying there were others who had magic? It seemed impossible. Magic was something out of faerie tales or spooky stories. Kate wanted to laugh at the very thought, but found herself closer to whimpering in fear.

"Once this world knew order," Hela stated. "Today is the first step towards returning to that order. Tell the world about what you've heard today. Do not fail me."

Hela turned to Benjamin Fratelli and caressed his cheek tenderly. She said something that Kate couldn't quite hear, but the effect on the old man was visible. Tears welled up in his eyes and he brought Hela's hands to his lips.

Hela gently pulled free of the old man and walked back into the hospital, followed close by the dark-haired man. As soon as the doors closed behind her, Kate felt like an invisible hand loosened it's grip on her throat. She gasped in surprise. She saw she wasn't the only one. Confusion and fear registered on the faces of her colleagues.

Her surprise grew tenfold when Benjamin Fratelli walked up to her and waited patiently. He looked down at the microphone in her hand. Kate quickly understood what he wanted and brought it up. This time, when she tried to speak, the words came freely.

"Mr. Fratelli, what did she say to you?"

Benjamin Fratelli smiled. "She told me to rejoice. The gods have returned to us!"

Chapter 10

Baldur hated the opulence of the Muspel Corporation's headquarters. Everything about it screamed wealth, pride and unchecked power. It was a message that was all too familiar. He'd strode through gilded halls before, seen the detachment that came with excess and lack of accountability. The one Gunnar Olafsson had built for himself was all to reminiscent of the ones the Aesir had built for themselves. Just like those edifices, this one was filled with lies.

Gunnar himself was no different. He had created a persona that he wanted the world to see, hiding his true self from view. He was doing everything he could to leave behind the man who had conquered the Aesir—the disillusioned servant to the gods that killed Odin and tore down the powerful—in exchange for an identity he thought the world would be more accepting of. He eschewed his identity as Surtur for this modern persona of wealth and power that was all too reminiscent of those who he swore to rid the world of. He was a convoluted mess of ambitions mixed with an unhealthy dose of hypocrisy, topped off with intentions even he wasn't able to define. Surtur razed Asgard in order to topple one power hierarchy that was full of lies and inequity only to create a new one as Gunnar Olafsson that mirrored it centuries later. This building was just one in a long list of inconsistencies he demonstrated.

Perhaps worst of all was that as much as Gunnar wanted to portray himself as a modern man, he was stuck in the past. Everything he'd done over the centuries proved it. From the way he had began a war against magic only to begin compiling it and then replicating it. Layer by layer, he had crafted his own web of lies that he now was tightly woven in to. It was holding only because no one had looked close enough. All it would take was just one of the strands to be cut for everything to come crashing down in epic fashion.

More than likely, his own hypocrisy would be the blade that cut the strand.

Baldur walked past the startled secretary outside of Olafsson's office without so much as a glance. His face was known by now, the poor woman having long since given up trying to stop him. She made a hasty call into the office and then watched helplessly as Baldur pushed through the double doors.

"We need to talk, Surtur," Baldur announced, closing the doors behind him. He took a moment of sick pleasure seeing the way Olafsson's true name made him squirm and grimace.

"I should have you thrown out for barging in here like this," Gunnar growled.

Baldur crossed the room and took a seat with a smile. "But you won't."

"All I have to do is call," Gunnar said, pointing one finger at the doors, "and security will be here to remove you from the building."

"They would try, but the results would be unpleasant for them," Baldur said.

Gunnar's eyes shifted to Amara who had quietly followed Baldur into the room and taken up a position behind him. His expression darkened. He hadn't forgotten the last two security guards Amara had touched. One had been ready to jump out the window to prove his love for her and the other ended up in the hospital after trying to attack Ivan with a taser. The big Russian had had no choice other than to take the guard down in brutal fashion.

Gunnar's defiance faded. He inhaled slowly. "Why are you here, Baldur?"

"You already know why, Surtur," Baldur replied.

"Don't call me that," Gunnar snapped. "I'm no longer Surtur. That name served a purpose in a world that is long dead. I am Gunnar Olafsson now."

"A name change doesn't change the man inside," Baldur said with an impish smirk. He waved Gunnar off before he could argue. "Have it your way. I didn't come here to argue with you about names. I've had more than my fair share of them over the years."

"Why are you here then?"

"You've seen the videos going around," Baldur responded. "The news agencies can't decide if it's a big joke or an actual threat. Either way, the world is talking about it. Hela sent an unmistakable message with her little stunt at the hospital."

Gunnar wore a deep frown. "A bold move. Perhaps too bold."

Baldur raised his eyebrows in mock surprise. "How so?"

"She made a tactical mistake," Gunnar answered. "Making a hospital her base was a dangerous move. Combine that with her open invitation for magic users to gather to her and it's obvious that she is desperate."

Baldur was honestly surprised by Gunnar's quick dismissal of Hela's ploy. He thought he'd find Gunnar in a tizzy over this, not calm and disinterested. "You don't think it will work?"

Gunnar shook his head. "All she has done is draw attention to herself while in a weakened state. A few may come, but she can't expect the world to look on while she holds an entire hospital hostage."

"That is exactly what will happen, though," Baldur said. "News of what she is doing has gone—how do the brainwashed youth of this age say it—viral?" His chuckle was mirthless. "This age astounds me. The world has grown soft. Celebrities and fools lead the hypnotized masses. They scream for equality, justice, and peace but spurn the means to how those things are achieved. They are paralyzed with fear of offending those who claim they want all offense to end! They spend their days with their faces buried in screens while the world is being torn down around them."

"Your point?" Gunnar said impatiently.

"My point," Baldur said, flicking the pen across the desktop, "is that people will come to Hela, either for healing or for protection, and she will grow stronger. Her promise of returning order will appeal to many who will want to be part of whatever she has planned, even if only to have a purpose to marry their meaningless lives to."

Gunnar dismissed Baldur's words with a wave of a hand. "A horde of aimless souls joining Hela doesn't alarm me."

"It will if that horde is made up of magic users," Baldur said. "You have been effective, perhaps too much so, in your gathering of magic by violent means. Magic users had few options before Hela's arrival. Now they have one that promises protection and an opportunity to be their true selves. There will be many who seek her out rather than waste away in the shadows awaiting the possibility of a visit from the Muspel Corporation."

Gunnar's smile was cold with annoyance. "Her rise is not a result of what I've done, so don't lay it at my door. Besides, she won't be allowed to continue. Taking that hospital hostage will force action against her."

"I disagree," Baldur said. "So far it seems like everyone who could move against her is in shock. The longer they wait to respond the more entrenched she'll become."

Gunnar sighed. "And you think I'm one of the ones that has waited too long?"

Baldur held out his hands. "Who could have known this was her plan? She made an unexpected move. A bold move."

"But you still think I should move," Gunnar muttered.

Baldur shook his head. "The time to move against Hela is in the past. We must look forward, not backwards. Plan for what we think she will do, not what she has done. Her ploy will prove effective, no matter what you think about it now. We cannot change what has already been set in motion. But, we can adapt and take action to make sure we are stronger still, even as she gathers strength of her own."

Gunnar's eyes narrowed in either suspicion or irritation—possibly both. Finally, he sat forward in order to rest his elbows on his desk. "Fine. Tell me, what do you think I should be doing in reaction to Hela?"

"Do what you're best at," Baldur replied. "Continue building an army of soldiers armed with the weapons you've created and get them ready for what's coming. All funded by your business ventures, of course."

"No doubt an army you hope to capitalize on," Gunnar quipped.

"Perhaps, at some point," Baldur agreed. "But for now I am content to let you fight the physical war. My focus will continue to be on other plans that will move us closer to our mutual goals."

"And how are those plans progressing?"

"I'm making significant headway," Baldur admitted. "Enough that I think it is time I share some of what I've been working on with you. I believe it will help you both against Hela and in your struggle against Thyra Ariksen."

Gunnar's expression darkened at the mention of Thor's daughter. "You offer this in exchange for what?"

Baldur frowned. "Ah, Gunnar, do you really think so little of me?"

"Yes, I do," Gunnar admitted without a hint of hesitation. "Our *partnership* is anything but that. If you are willing to give me something, that must mean you expect something in return."

Baldur's frown changed to a wry smirk. "You've already given me more than you ever intended to. Because of you, I got a little bit closer to getting my revenge."

"A hollow motivation that you failed completely at," Gunnar stated. "Or have you forgotten the mess we ran into a few months ago? The mess I am still trying to get cleaned up."

"Don't be dramatic, Gunnar." Baldur leaned forward and spun a pen on the smooth surface of Gunnar's desk. "We both know that what happened in Wisconsin was not a failure. Not entirely."

"I fail to see what you mean," Gunnar snapped. "I lost a handful of men in Boise, a dozen men that Hela claimed after the debacle in Monroe, and close to the same number to injuries that they may never recover from at the hands of Vidar and Thyra Ariksen in Hudson. I have the police looking into every aspect of my business, and I still don't have the Eye of Odin in my hand! What part of that screams success?"

Baldur spun the pen again. "At least there are no dead bodies to account for."

"Which is a miracle." Gunnar frowned. "I know that the ones I left behind in Monroe were dead or close to it. Which means only Hela's magic saved us from having bodies littered all over the place." Gunnar rocked back in his chair, assuming what Baldur could only guess was meant to be a power position. "Yet, that solution is also one of our problems, isn't it? Now, she has a dozen of *my* men, carrying weapons *I've* created from magic items *my* men have rounded up. Not to mention how you used *my* network and technology to track down Thyra, along with stealing who knows what other information."

Baldur smiled good-naturedly. Gunnar was not used to being at a disadvantage and was now trying to claw for every bit of leverage he could get. Sometimes when a man sees a lifeline he ends up hanging himself in a noose. It was time to give Gunnar that lifeline and let him be the one to hang himself in it.

"I can see how you may feel our partnership has been very one-sided."

Gunnar's mouth twisted sourly. "That's putting it mildly."

"Then let me help tip the scales back in your favor," Baldur said. He stopped the pen suddenly and sat back in his seat. "But first, I have a question to ask you."

"I'm on the edge of my seat with anticipation," Gunnar said through gritted teeth.

Baldur smirked in response to his impatience. "I know that after you conquered Asgard you found a way to summon Idunn and force her to grant you immortality. Which means, you have some of the summoning stones. I want to know how many, and which ones?"

Gunnar's eyes narrowed. "Why should I share that information with you?"

"Because," Baldur said, "if you truly want to succeed with your plans of using magic to gain power, you will need what is inside that garden."

"Why? I already ate some of the fruit, and I have no intention of creating a new crop of immortals. Nor am I looking to start another war for immortality. History has shown how that ends more times than you or I can count." Gunnar shook his head. "If that's what you think I'm attempting to do you've sorely misjudged me. I want to exploit magic to make the world a better place, a more equal place, not create more gods."

Baldur wanted to laugh at Gunnar's false benevolence, but he chose tact rather than derision. "If that's what helps you sleep at night, fine, tell yourself that, but we both know that you like being where you are right now. Perhaps you started with the idea of creating equality in this world, or ridding it of magic altogether, but we both know that isn't what you're trying to do anymore."

"And what is it you think I'm trying to do?"

Baldur smiled. "Remake the world, with you at the top. Not in name, of course, but you will still be the one wielding the power. Remember, I've been inside your network. I've seen enough of the plans you have hidden deep below the surface to see what you're trying to do. The Muspel Corporation will have eyes on everyone, supplying technology, energy, food, water, and the might to put down any challengers. You may allow nations to still function, perhaps stay aloof from ruling the people so as to not be called a dictator or despot, but you will be one all the same."

Gunnar didn't try to refute the accusation. It was perhaps an oversimplified, but fairly accurate summary of what his plans were. He sat quietly, his expression giving nothing away, but Baldur could see the storm raging in his eyes. Baldur was right, and they both knew it.

"None of that matters to me, though," Baldur continued. "What matters is how we can make this partnership work from this point forward."

"And how do you envision that will look?"

Baldur took a slow, deep breath and let it out before continuing. "Tell me, Gunnar, how have the weapons been acting as of late? Temperamental, perhaps?"

Gunnar sat in stunned silence, clearly struggling to determine how to answer the question. There was no way that Baldur could have known about Gungnir's recent behavior. The report from the team in charge had just barely crossed his desk this morning stating that the spear had been acting erratically. They assured him that it was just a minor hiccup and that they'd have it fixed soon, but a hiccup was the last thing Gunnar needed right now.

Gunnar's hesitation was answer enough, but his pride refused to accept that Baldur held the upper hand. "That depends on what weapons you're talking about."

Baldur sighed. "You know which ones I'm talking about. *The weapons*! Gungnir and Mjolnir! The ones you've been trying to harness to create your endless supply of energy to sell to the world. That, and the creation of an arsenal of weapons that mimic their power."

Gunnar's face darkened. "I have no intention of answering that and giving you more fuel to betray me with."

Baldur held up his hands. "You have nothing to fear from me. I don't care what you do with them. I have no interest in either one. I've held both, and while the power was intoxicating, I know me attempting to claim one would do more harm than good."

Gunnar sneered. "Afraid of the power they'd give you?"

"No, I'm just a realist. I have no magic of my own other than my ability to feel no pain."

He paused for a beat, a doubt sneaking in and raising the question if that was still the case after what had happened in Wisconsin. Thyra had hurt him, something he thought impossible. How she had done it and whether she could do it again were still mysteries. Mysteries for another day. He banished the questions back to the depths of his consciousness. He didn't have time for weakness. He would simply be more cautious in the future.

Baldur cleared his throat to hide his hesitation and continued. "After all, I am not a blood heir to either and the true heirs to their power are alive. Sooner or later, they would manage to take the weapons from me. Unlike you, I don't have an entire corporation to hide behind. I would be alone against beings possessing *tremendous destructive power*." He emphasized those last three words to make sure Gunnar understood that the danger extended to him as well. "My hold on the spear and hammer would be tenuous at best and very short."

Gunnar had managed to hide the two most powerful magical

weapons ever created for centuries only because the heirs to both didn't know where to look. That wasn't the case anymore. The heirs—if not something more ominous—would be coming for them. But, that was Gunnar's problem to solve.

"Believe me when I say this," Baldur said. "Those weapons in the hands of Thor's children is the last thing I want."

"Then what do you want?" Gunnar asked.

"I simply want to open your eyes to the problem you refuse to see," Baldur said. "I know now for certain that my suspicion about the weapons' behavior was correct. Your face alone tells me, so don't waste time denying it. Instead, we must ask ourselves, why are Gungnir and Mjolnir acting differently? What has changed?"

"Besides the fact that Thor's daughter is alive?"

Baldur shook his head. "The heirs to Mjolnir have walked the earth the entire time you've had possession of the hammer. Magni and Modi have always been out there somewhere, lingering on the periphery, so the hammer has never worked at it's full potential. Thyra's birth didn't change that fact, only added another open hand eager to take hold of Thor's hammer." Baldur inhaled deeply. "No, Mjolnir is not the problem. It's Gungnir suddenly acting up that should have you befuddled. And it does, doesn't it?"

"I don't know what you're talking about," Gunnar said with a straight face.

"Yes, you do," Baldur chided. "I know you've had mild successes in experimenting on the spear and replicating it's power. You've married it's power to the science of today to make rifles that use magic rather than lead. Rest assured, I applaud your ingenuity. It's truly remarkable what you've achieved and you should be congratulated!"

"Forgive me if I don't jump for joy while I wait for the other shoe to drop."

Baldur smiled. "I also know that you felt confident that you were close to unlocking it's full power to be used in the Odin Initiative. I know you had it moved after the debacle in Wisconsin to a site where you planned on using it to create a wave of energy you could profit off of. And I know that of late it isn't working as planned."

Gunnar's eyes narrowed. "You seem to know a lot of things. Are you sure of the veracity of all that?"

"I am sure," Baldur said with a nod, "because if it was working correctly, you'd be using it already and the Muspel Corporation would be the talk of the town. Judging by the look on your face, the failure to get the spear functioning according to plan is a relatively new development." Baldur held up his hands to stop Gunnar's angry response. "I don't care what you do with the spear. I simply want you to think about why the spear isn't doing what you thought it would."

Gunnar frowned. "What are you trying to get at, Baldur?"

"Fair question, and one that I will answer in the spirit of partnership." Baldur took a moment to organize his thoughts. "You know that dwarf-made weapons only function at their full power for the original bearer or for someone with close blood relations if the original owner is dead. One generation removed at the most."

Gunnar's eyes narrowed thoughtfully. "I'm aware."

"Which is why Mjolnir will never function correctly as long as Thor's children are alive," Baldur continued. He smirked slyly. "Gungnir is not in the same predicament, though. Odin's children by blood are all dead, and you supposedly put a sword through the Allfather. I don't count since Odin is not my real father, and Thor's children are not close enough by blood to have a clear claim to the spear without bonding with it first. Yet, it *is* acting up. You have to ask yourself—why is that?"

Gunnar's lips pressed together. "I'm listening."

"That leads me back to the discussion of the summoning stones." Baldur held out his hand towards Amara, who placed something into his hand. "You see, I know that you have several of the summoning stones. Odin's, Thor's, Tyr's, and Heimdall's, I presume. Using those four, it was probably very simple to summon Idunn after you conquered Asgard. But, now, after nearly a thousand years, four stones may not be enough. Idunn will be hesitant to answer the call from the same four stones, knowing they are in your possession. So," he reached into his pocket, "I come bearing gifts."

Baldur placed three stones inscribed with runes on the desk. Gunnar recognized them for what they were immediately, and his eyes betrayed his excitement.

"Those are the summoning stones of Njord, Loki, and Bragi," Baldur said.

Gunnar leaned forward. "Where did you get these?"

"Those are what has drawn away my attention these past few months," Baldur replied. "Njord's was difficult to track down. I have to give him credit, he made a prudent decision on where to hide his. It was being safeguarded by a young man whose family has stayed true to the Aesir gods. Even after a thousand years, his line had kept the summoning stone a secret. I respect such loyalty and devotion." He shook his head sadly. "Unfortunately for him, that loyalty was both misplaced and not strong enough to resist the wiles of my young counterpart here. All it took was some gentle persuasion and a pretty face to get him to reveal it."

Behind Baldur, Amara's lips curled into a wicked smile. "One kiss, and he would have told me anything or done whatever I wanted him to."

"Amara has proven very useful in my search over the past few months," Baldur admitted. "Especially in controlling Bragi."

Gunnar's eyes narrowed in response to the admission. "So, you do have the old man. I had wondered what happened to him."

"He's safely contained at the moment, and has proven truly invaluable in my search for the stones," Baldur explained. "The old man can't use his magic while under Amara's spell. One touch per day and his magic is held in check. We've been able to have several *enlightening* conversations during the last few months as a result."

"And unpleasant for him, I would guess." Gunnar looked down at the stones on his desk and rolled his tongue along the front of his teeth. "You explained where you got two of them. What about the third? Loki's?"

"Now, that is a story," Baldur said with a chuckle. "I didn't take it from the trickster, if that is what you're wondering. If the stone had still been in Loki's possession I would not have had any chance of finding it. Luckily, it was taken from Loki long ago after Odin tired of his antics and gave it to another."

"Who?"

"The Allfather gave it along with another to each of my fool nephews, Magni and Modi," Baldur replied. "This one was Modi's."

"You tracked down Magni and Modi?" Gunnar asked, his eyebrows rising sharply. He had tried to keep tabs on the brothers over the years, but it had grown increasingly difficult to do. They were vagabonds and never stayed in the same place for long. "I'm sure that was a happy reunion."

"I wasn't forced to face them to come into the possession of the stone," Baldur said. "You see, both stones were taken away from the fools by Thor as a punishment for their transgressions. It seems that my dead brother never gave them back to the Allfather before your attack on Asgard." Baldur pointed to the stone in question. "That one was the hardest to track down. Thor must have known something was coming, because he hid it very well. It took me two weeks of revisiting all of our haunts, but my memory served me well."

Gunnar sat silent, his eyes studying the three summoning stones. After a long pause, he looked up. "What about the stone given to

Magni?"

"Unfortunately, that one was not there," Baldur admitted. "I have my suspicions as to who possesses it, but I cannot say for certain."

"And that doesn't bother you that one of the summoning stones could be in the hands of an enemy?"

"Idunn answered you when four stones were activated, and I'm guessing that now she will resist the call as long as possible until it is much stronger. One stone unaccounted for, while concerning, is not enough to demand our immediate attention. We will find it in time."

"That's *two* that are missing," Gunnar corrected him.

"The last one will never be recovered," Baldur said. "I know who has it, and believe me when I say that stone is not one you want to go hunting for. *She* is untouchable."

"If you know where the stone is, then we should—"

"Untouchable!" Baldur shouted, his hand slapping the polished surface of the desk to emphasize the word. He sucked in through his teeth in irritation before tapping the desk with one finger. "For now, all that matters is that we have possession of seven of the nine summoning stones. Idunn may be hesitant to answer our call, but she won't be able to shrug off the pull for long."

"That may be," Gunnar said, "but why do you think I want to summon Idunn?"

"Because," Baldur said slowly, "I believe she isn't alone in that garden, and hasn't been since Asgard fell."

"You suggesting she has a lover in there with her?" Gunnar laughed bitterly at the thought. "I'm sure that would rub Bragi wrong."

Baldur smiled, but didn't share in the laughter. "No, I don't think that is the case. I think that the person who was sharing her garden is a much bigger threat to both of our plans." He let Gunnar stew on that thought for a moment before continuing. "Did you ever find Odin's body after you destroyed Asgard?"

The look on Gunnar's face was all the answer Baldur needed. Gunnar's lips pressed into a tight line and his eyebrows pinched together. "I don't see how that matters."

"It's *all* that matters."

Gunnar steepled his fingers in front of his face and looked over them at Baldur. "Are you suggesting that Odin has been in Idunn's garden this entire time?"

"Among others, yes," Baldur said with a nod."It's very possible."

"That's ridiculous," Gunnar snapped. "You know as well as I that Idunn can only bridge the gap between our world and her garden when summoned."

"I have reason to believe that isn't completely true," Baldur said. "There is another way, an old way that perhaps only Idunn and a few, *select* others knew of."

"Bragi being one?" Gunnar guessed. Baldur nodded, resulting in a scoff from the other man. "If that were true, Bragi would have used it. I don't buy it."

"The way required significant magic, the kind that Bragi lacked on his own," Baldur said. "By his own admission, he tried and failed dozens of times before giving up hope. But," Baldur tapped the desk again, "the problem we need to concern ourselves with isn't that someone may be able to find a way into the garden. It's that someone might have the strength to find their way *out*."

Gunnar cocked an eyebrow. "Odin, for example?"

Baldur nodded. "If Odin was secreted away by Idunn, he would both have the knowledge and the power to use this secret way to escape Idunn's garden. I believe the spear is trying to tell you something."

"What's that?"

"That Odin is walking free again."

Gunnar stared across the desk at Baldur with a blank expression. Baldur could see the wheels spinning in Gunnar's eyes, though. "You actually believe that's possible?"

"I don't know," Baldur admitted. "If he were free, I would think your head would be the first thing he'd come for. The fact that he hasn't makes me think that he is not yet walking free. But, if there is anything we can conclude from the spear misbehaving, it is that Odin is alive. Which means we must summon Idunn and find out who she's been hiding before they escape back to our world."

Gunnar sucked in a breath, spinning away in his chair to look out the windows behind him. When he spun back, his eyes were haunted. "You want revenge on Odin for what he did to you."

Baldur shrugged as if that was the most obvious statement. "I want all the Aesir to know the pain I endured. Odin gave the command. I look forward to the day when I can look him in the eye and make him feel even a portion of what I endured."

Gunnar nodded slowly. "Then for once, I think our goals are one in the same. We summon Idunn, and we find a way to finish what I started."

Baldur smiled. He knew Gunnar would jump at the chance to finish the Allfather. That possibility alone should be enough to motivate this shadow of the man that had been called Surtur. But if his partner ever began to lose his nerve, Baldur had more fuel he could add to the man's fire.

If Bragi was to be believed, there was a secret hidden away in Idunn's garden that would change everything.

Chapter 11

"This must be what Hela was talking about when she mentioned her plans to Vidar."

Thyra watched the news coverage of the scene outside the hospital on the television with a mixture of disbelief and disgust. It'd been four days since Hela had made her move and what had started out as only a few curious onlookers had already grown to a crowd of over two hundred people, all eagerly waiting to catch a glimpse of the goddess. They held signs, sang songs, and even had erected a small altar near the entrance. So far the offerings had remained benign—flowers, homemade effigies, food—but judging by the fervor of the crowd, Thyra wondered how long it would be before the offerings turned more extreme in nature.

She turned away and looked at Sif, who was doing her very best to ignore what was on the TV. Her spear was laid on the kitchen table in front of her and she was busy running a stone along one edge of the blade. Thyra could tell from the look on Sif's face that she was just as bothered by what was happening but was choosing to avoid talking about it.

Just like she'd been doing her best to avoid talking about going after Mjolnir. Thyra and Vidar had both tried to address how that conversation had ended, but Sif refused to take the topic up again. She had made her position clear and that it wasn't going to change.

"Do you think this is going to work?" Thyra asked in an attempt to break the silence. "I mean, what is she hoping to accomplish?"

"She's reintroducing the world to magic in as public a way as possible," Sif finally responded without looking up. "She's offering the world honey before the bitter."

"From the looks of things, it's working," Thyra muttered sullenly. "Look at them. Are we going to sit back and let her do it?"

Sif set the honing stone down and sighed. "What can we do? Hela is smart, always has been." She glanced at the TV screen. "For now, she's too busy to come after you. That's all I care about."

Thyra sighed. Her mom had a one-track mind at the moment—Thyra's safety. It didn't leave room for much else. "She's already gained a following. I've heard people are setting up funds to help buy supplies for the hospital and others are threatening violence against anyone who speaks out against Hela." Thyra shook her head in frustration. "Shouldn't the police be doing something?"

"The time for action on their part is past," Sif replied. "If they were going to make a move, they should have done it the very first day. Their presence is just for show now that she's getting a stronger following. The people don't see her as a terrorist or a hostage taker."

"No," Thyra said, "they see her as a hero."

"Which is why no one will act against her. At least, not openly. Not now. She's put the world on notice and strengthened her image all at once."

Thyra agreed with that completely, which only made her more dissatisfied with her current situation. "Can we afford to sit back and watch while she gets stronger?"

The question went unanswered when the door opened to admit a sweat-soaked Vidar, fresh from the local gym. He took one look at the television screen and his expression turned sour. He walked to the kitchen without looking at Thyra or Sif and opened the fridge with enough force that Thyra was afraid he might rip the door off the hinges.

Thyra turned back to her mom. "Who is she trying to strengthen her image against?"

"Everyone. Baldur, Gunnar Olafsson, the world." Sif emphasized each name with a stroke of the honing stone on the spear's edge. "You."

"Why me? I haven't done anything to her."

"Because, you are Yggdrasil's champion," Sif replied, "and a direct threat to her plans, whatever those might be. She has put herself at the forefront and set herself up as a shining beacon to the world of magic of what is possible. She is the benevolent healer that is fixing what the smartest human minds haven't been able to. People will flock to her for that reason alone."

"It looks like it's working," Thyra grumbled. "Should I be doing the same thing? I could let people know that it was me in those pictures that were plastered on the news a few months ago. I could tell them what happened. I could even show them the Eye."

"And put yourself at risk," Vidar grumbled from the kitchen. He pulled a bottle of water out and twisted off the lid. "You'd get attention, but not the kind you want. You'd paint a target on your back so big everyone would be tempted to take their shot at you."

"The same kind of target she'd have if she went after the hammer," Sif said in a tone that made it clear that she wasn't going to allow that argument to start again.

"I'm not defenseless," Thyra said, looking at Vidar. "Plus, I have all of you to watch my back."

"A rag-tag team if I've ever seen one," Vidar retorted sourly. "A crusty dwarf, a lone Valkyrie, and a disgraced brute. We wouldn't stand a chance against the full might of one of your enemies, much less all of them."

"Yggdrasil said it would send help," Thyra argued, noting how his stance had changed over the past few days. He'd gone from a willing participant in the fight to retake Mjolnir to a sullen lump on a log. She wanted to punch him right in the nose. Hopefully that would reignite the fire he had when he first arrived. "It sent you, didn't it? Maybe there are others it's trying to send, they just don't know where to look. Maybe it's time we step into the light a little bit."

"And do what?" Sif grumbled. "Put on another lightning show?"

Thyra shrugged. "If it gets the job done, yes."

"You don't know what you're saying," Sif said sternly. "Hela knows what she's doing by taking over this hospital and healing these people. If you were to go public with what you are, you'd be seen as a cheap copy-cat by most and a direct threat by her devotees. Besides, doing so would tell Gunnar Olafsson, Baldur, and anyone else out there looking exactly where we are and how strong we are. And there *are* others looking."

Thyra threw up her hands in frustration. "So, am I supposed to just sit back and let her win?"

"We aren't letting her win," Sif said. "We're waiting to see what the other players do before we show our hand."

"For how long?"

"I don't know, Thyra," Sif said, her voice tense with fatigue and annoyance. She picked up the honing stone and dragged it down the edge of her spear with a frown. "As long as it takes."

"I'm not sure that's good enough," Thyra said, unwilling to accept that answer. She watched the TV for a few moments, her anger building as she watched the crowd. "We have to do something. While we keep hiding, everyone else is growing stronger!"

"And you're staying alive," Sif countered sharply. "You need to realize that if you were to go public with what you are, we would not be able to protect you. *I* would not be able to protect you!"

Thyra frowned. "I can defend myself."

"No one is doubting your resolve or the strength of your magic," Sif said, the effort of speaking in a normal voice clear on her face, "but we have to consider our weaknesses."

"What weaknesses?"

"For starters, you may be powerful, but you're still untrained in the use of your magic. You didn't have a teacher to teach you the intricacies of magic much less the years of practice to master them. And," Sif paused, her eyes drifting down to Thyra's leg before coming back to her face, "if we had to move fast, we couldn't. Your knee is a liability we haven't found a solution for."

"Thanks for the reminder," Thyra grumbled.

"Your mom is right," Vidar said. "Your leg will slow us down."

"I appreciate the vote of confidence," Thyra said with a glare for the big man. Vidar shrugged and took another sip of water. Thyra looked back at her mom. "I understand I'm limited, but I don't think we can afford to sit idle. What would Odin have done if he were in this position? Wouldn't he have acted, made an attempt to proclaim himself as Yggdrasil's champion? He wouldn't have let his enemies grow stronger while he hid. Odin would—"

"You are not Odin!" Sif snapped. She looked up, her eyes dancing with a dangerous light. "You don't have dozens of gods surrounding you, and I don't have an army of Valkyries waiting in the wings to ride against whoever threatens you. We are weak, but so far we aren't exposed. The moment we become exposed is the moment we won't be able to rest without the fear of attack. You would never be safe!"

Thyra sat in silence, completely caught off-guard by Sif's sudden outburst. Slowly, her shock was replaced by irritation, and then anger. "I'm never going to be safe as long as I'm Yggdrasil's champion and I am in possession of the Eye. Sooner or later, I'm going to be forced to act. I'd rather do it before the opposition is too strong to beat."

"Running head-first into a fight against a foe with superior numbers is foolish," Sif said. "It would do us no good to move before we are ready."

"Hiding like a coward isn't doing us any good," Thyra snapped back. "I'm no coward, and I didn't think you were one either!"

Sif's back went stiff. "Is that how you really feel?"

Thyra hesitated briefly, suddenly aware that she was standing with one foot on a line she didn't know was there before, the other foot already stepping across. She tried to pull back before it was too late. "I didn't mean it like that. Really. I just think we need to act before it's too late."

"Fine," Sif said. "If that's the way you feel."

"Mom, I didn't mean it that way," Thyra continued to backpedal, but Sif wasn't having any of it.

"No! You've been pouting for months, needling me to act, and I've grown tired of it. You are Yggdrasil's champion. You have to make your decision about what you believe is right." She raised an admonishing finger. "But I'll give you a warning. The path you want to walk only leads to one thing—loneliness. Odin possessed immense power, but in his attempt to protect that power he pushed everyone who truly cared for him away. Thor felt just as alone, even when he had me. There's only room for one on top of the power pyramid. Everyone else is either lifting you higher, being ground underfoot, or doing their best to tear you down. You go after Mjolnir, you take that path, there will be no going back. You had better be sure you're ready to walk it for the rest of your life before you take the first step."

Sif rose to her feet and stared down at her daughter. "If you think you're prepared, I won't stand in your way. But don't expect me to follow along behind blindly or to allow you to abuse my love for you to get what you want!"

Warning delivered, Sif headed for the door.

"Mom, wait…" Thyra said weakly, but she knew it was too little and way too late. She listened as the door opened and then slammed shut behind Sif then let out a long, frustrated sigh.

"Well done," Vidar muttered.

"You weren't any help," Thyra sneered.

"You were doing a good enough job of sinking your own boat."

"You could have helped bail the water at least."

Vidar shook his head. "I recognize when someone is bent on sinking their boat. It's always better to get out and swim."

Thyra rolled her eyes. "Don't tell me you think we should sit here and keep waiting."

"I spent hundreds of years avoiding my past," Vidar said. "I'd like to think I'm pretty patient."

"I don't believe that for a second," Thyra said. "I know you see what's happening the same way I do."

"Maybe," Vidar allowed. "I may think we need to do something, but I trust your mom's instincts. If she thinks we need to hold tight, we should hold tight. Until she says otherwise, I think you'd be smart to stop pressing her." He took a long draw on the water and then exhaled. "Do you know why you're mom has kept you moving so often these last few months?"

"Besides the obvious?" Thyra grumbled. "We've been staying off the Muspel Corporation's radar."

"That's only scratching the surface. You think you've been running, that Sif wants you to stay hidden. The truth is that you haven't gone unnoticed."

Thyra's eyes narrowed. "What do you mean?"

"Every place you've gone, you've attracted attention," Vidar answered. "You are magic's champion, and that kind of power attracts others with power. Every move your mom has made has been because someone or something has gotten too close. Maybe it hasn't been Olafsson and Baldur, but there are plenty of others who are looking for you. Some may not know exactly what they're looking for, but they feel the pull. Some would come for protection, others to follow you as magic's champion, and others because they want what you have and would be willing to try and take it from you. It doesn't matter what their intent, if they managed to find you the Muspel Corporation wouldn't be far behind. That's why she has kept you on the move and is so reluctant to let you reveal yourself."

Thyra's eyebrows furrowed. "I haven't seen any of that."

"That's because you're young and inexperienced," Vidar said. "Ask yourself, what do you think your mom is doing while you're having your little communions with the storms?"

"I don't know," Thyra admitted. She was embarrassed to admit that she never even considered the question before now. "I thought she just waited by the car until I was finished."

"Do you think she needs her spear if all she did was sit in the car?" Vidar raised an eyebrow. "Were her clothes ever muddied? Was she ever quiet when you finished? Maybe a little distant and tired?"

More often than not, but Thyra wasn't going to admit to that. She shrugged. "Your point?"

It was Vidar's turn to roll his eyes. "Come on, Thyra. Think! She was protecting you. She told me what she's been up against these last few months. The constant threat you've been under every time you stepped out that door. The blood she has been forced to spill just to keep you safe."

Thyra blinked in confusion. It made sense—her mom's dirty clothes, grim expressions, injuries that Sif had poor excuses for—but the realization was shocking. She'd been blind to the truth of what Sif was going through. And now she'd called Sif a coward. Thyra groaned and rested her head in her hands. "Why didn't she tell me?"

"Because you weren't ready to face the harsh reality of what you are," Vidar stated. "Or of what she is, for that matter."

Thyra groaned again. "I didn't mean to make her mad."

"What did you think would happen when you question the courage of the greatest of the Valkyries?" Vidar muttered. "You need to realize that she doesn't see Yggdrasil's champion when she looks at you. She sees her daughter, a seventeen year old girl who has been thrust into the middle of a deadly game. If you would have been born when the Aesir were in their power, you'd already have had a decade of training in your magic and as many years learning the art of warfare under your belt. You might have already been a veteran of battle. Perhaps, you'd even have taken your place as a god. But, in this age that isn't the case. You're like a child thrown over the side of the longboat for the first time. You may think you're swimming, but you're more likely drowning without knowing it."

"I think I'm doing a pretty good job of it," Thyra argued weakly.

"You have so far," Vidar agreed with a nod, "but you still haven't stood toe-to-toe with the evils that this fight breeds. Your mother has. She's seen the atrocities that happen during a war fought with magic, perhaps more than anyone else. Even more than me." Vidar's eyes grew distant. "I remember those dark days. Blood flowing like rivers on the ground, the scream of the wounded, thousands of dead at your feet, faces of friends and family staring lifelessly up at you. . ." Vidar shook his head. "The scars run deeper for her. Your mother would spare you that if she could."

"I appreciate that, but trouble is going to find me no matter what we do."

"Sif knows that, but that doesn't mean you should rush toward it." Vidar sighed. "I can understand how your mom might see an attempt at retaking Mjolnir as rushing straight into danger."

Vidar's argument made Thyra feel sick to her stomach. She'd been too judgmental of her mom, and too blind to see what was happening around her.

"I know what you'd be capable of with the hammer," Vidar continued. "But that doesn't mean I don't see the risks. If we succeeded, and that is a big 'if', you would immediately become a target for everyone—magic user and mortal alike. Perhaps if you had a teacher to help you master your magic it wouldn't be such a stretch. But you don't, and the list of possibilities is not very long or promising." He shook his head. "Your mom is right—being a god is lonely and it isn't something you can take back. Believe me."

"I'm not trying to be a god," Thyra said in frustration. "I just want to be. . .*capable*. I want to be able to do what's needed when it's needed."

"You may not want to be a god, but you take Mjolnir and you will be one," Vidar said. "There's no need to expose your belly for your enemies to slip their knife into, Thyra. Sif wants to be as prepared as possible before putting your life at risk."

"I get that." Thyra looked out the window. "I just wonder how many more knives will be sharpened the longer we wait."

"In my experience," Vidar said, "it's best to assume they're all sharp."

Thyra threw her head back and groaned loudly. "I need to go talk to her. Apologize."

"Wait for her to come back," Vidar mumbled. "You both need to cool off."

"Maybe that makes sense to you," Thyra said as she stood, "but I don't think this should wait."

Vidar grumbled something, but it was lost on her as she hurried outside.

Chapter 12

Sif didn't have a direction in mind when she left the trailer. She just needed to get some air and try to calm her nerves after her argument with Thyra. If she had stayed she wasn't sure what she might have said next. No doubt something damaging to their relationship that would require years of counseling to overcome. She already felt Thyra withdrawing and growing more morose with each passing day. Sif couldn't let her tongue run free in the emotion of the moment and risk pushing Thyra even farther away.

After a bit of walking, Sif found herself along the Snake River. The sound of the water coursing over the river rocks helped sooth her raw emotions enough for her to begin to sort through the mess of thoughts in her head.

The truth was that no matter how hard Sif tried to act like she was fine with what was happening, she wasn't. She wasn't fine with Yggdrasil choosing Thyra to be it's champion and putting her daughter's life in danger. She wasn't fine with being forced back into a life she thought was behind her, a life of killing and blood. A life where every shadow, every sound, and every strange face could be a threat. Worst of all, she wasn't ready for her daughter to live that life. Thyra was not prepared for the atrocities Sif had witnessed.

And committed.

Sif's hands were far from clean. She'd killed in the name of the Aesir without mercy, many times doing it without question or thought to whether the person at the end of her spear deserved death. The Valkyries in myth were romanticized, given the task of carrying the souls of those who died in glorious battle to Valhalla. The truth was less poetic—the Valkyries were just killers in the service to gods who didn't care how much blood was spilled in their names. Sif had been the greatest of the Valkyries and had never hesitated to turn the ground red.

Regrettably, that hadn't changed since waking in this new age, even without the Aesir to force her hand. She was still a killer. How many had fallen to her spear in the last three months? How many more would? She cringed to think about it. The same way she cringed away from the image of Thyra's face when she saw what Sif had done to Olafsson's men in Wisconsin. She wondered if Thyra would ever look at her the same again, as just her mom, rather than a thousand-year old Valkyrie that killed as easily as she breathed.

Sif was still brooding in the darkness of her thoughts when she felt a strange sensation, like a cold, lifeless hand brushing the nape of her neck. She turned around, but found herself alone. She scanned the trees along the edge of the river for several tense breaths, looking for any flicker of movement or shadows that didn't belong, but couldn't find anything that was out of place. She took a deep breath and tried to calm her nerves, but the alarm bells refused to be silenced. Something was watching her.

Unable to quiet the feeling, she embraced her instincts. She was at a run immediately, her long legs churning as fast as she could will them to go. Her lungs screamed at her to slow down, but the thought of what might be lurking just out of sight spurred her on. She slowed down as she turned corner into the trailer park, her eyes sweeping each trailer for threats as she moved down the line. Nothing seemed out of the ordinary, but that did nothing to quiet her fears.

She rushed to the trailer and slipped inside. Vidar was still watching the TV with a frown. Sif looked around the room but didn't see her daughter. "Where's Thyra?"

"She went looking for you."

Sif's stomach fell. "You let her leave?"

Vidar's frown deepened. "What's going on?"

"Something's wrong," Sif said. "She's in danger. I can feel it."

Vidar turned the TV off and rose to his feet. "Did you see something?"

"No, and that's the problem," Sif said. "We need to find her! Now!"

*****

Thyra thought she knew where her mom would go, but it didn't take long to realize she had guessed wrong. She sighed in frustration, realizing that not only had she wasted time going the wrong direction, but also precious energy. In an attempt to catch up to her mom, she had pushed herself to the very cusp of what her knee was capable of without giving out. Now she was paying for it. Her knee throbbed with every step.

Exhausted, she turned around and started walking back towards the trailer. A hundred yards back down the road, she noticed a dark blue car parked just off the side that hadn't been there before. Classic American muscle cars had always been one of her interests, and she recognized the distinctive body shape of a Chevelle immediately. She was so enamored with the vehicle as she neared that she didn't notice the two men standing nearby until one of them spoke.

"It's a nice evening for a walk."

Thyra almost jumped out of her skin, the sharp motion enough to cause her knee to buckle. She managed to catch herself before she fell flat on the ground, but she was sure she looked ridiculous all the same.

The man who spoke smiled. "Forgive me. I didn't mean to startle you."

"It's okay," Thyra said, her cheeks on fire with embarrassment. "I just didn't see you there."

"That's our fault." His smile grew and he took a step closer. "We saw you coming and decided to wait in the shade. We've been in the car for too long and the fresh air is doing us some good."

Thyra took a moment to take measure of him. His dark red hair was shaved close to the scalp on the sides then swept back on top and he wore a neatly trimmed goatee. Thyra guessed he was somewhere in his mid- to late-thirties, but she had a hard time deciding. He wore a white, button-down shirt with the sleeves rolled up to the elbow, giving Thyra a good view of an intricately-carved metal bracelet on his right arm.

Leaning against a tree behind him was a hulking brute that wore his dark blonde hair in thick, chunky braids that were swept back over his shoulders. If the first maintained a suave outward appearance, this one looked every bit the part of a viking-wanna-be bouncer outside some seedy bar. He looked to be of a similar age as the first, but again Thyra wasn't sure. Their agelessness set off a warning in her head, but there was a different feature they shared that sent an ice-cold shiver down Thyra's spine—their electric blue eyes. A color that Thyra was used to seeing reflected in the mirror.

"I noticed you admiring our car," the red-haired man said with a smile.

Thyra nodded warily. "Chevelles are cool."

"Only the best American muscle ever created," he responded, giving the car a fond look.

"Looks like a '69 or '70."

He nodded approvingly. "Good eye. It's a '70 SS. I appreciate someone with an eye for classic muscle cars. They've always been a reminder of a time when power and unbridled fury were valued on the road. Sure there are faster cars now, but they lack what the muscle cars of that era had." He shook his head as if to mourn days long lost. "This car has been with us for a long time. We've gone through a few engines over the years, but the body and interior are original. Almost fifty years, and it still is in near perfect condition."

Thyra got the distinct impression that he meant they were the original owners. That didn't surprise her. She already knew what she was dealing with, if not who. Fifty years was nothing to gods. All she needed now were names. "Who are you?"

"My name is Modi," the red-haired man said. He thrust a thumb over his shoulder. "That's my brother, Magni."

Their names were enough to make her hair stand on end. She had never heard them before, but that fact alarmed her more. They didn't make any move towards her, but there was no doubt in her mind that she was in danger. A voice inside screamed at her to run, to get as far away from these two as possible, but her feet were frozen in place. And running would do her no good. Instead she held her magic at the ready without letting it show on her face.

"And you are?" Modi asked. Thyra didn't answer. He smiled ruefully. "I can see from the look on your face that you know what we are and that gives you reason to not trust us. A fair sentiment. But, I wonder, do you know *who* we are?"

There was an ominous undertone to that question that made Thyra swallow. "Didn't you just tell me?"

Modi looked over his shoulder at Magni, who smirked grimly. "You have our names, but I can tell that they mean nothing to you."

"Should they?"

"If you were versed in your family story they would," Modi said.

"Of course, we aren't surprised. We weren't well thought of by many of the other Aesir. Especially your mother. I would be floored if Sif had ever mentioned our names or told you any stories about us."

Thyra hesitated. She had already guessed that they were gods. She knew she shouldn't be surprised that they knew who her mom was, but it still sent a chill down her back all the same. "She hasn't mentioned either of you."

Magni scoffed. "You should know who your blood is."

"Blood?" Thyra's brows furrowed downward. "I've found that *blood* doesn't mean much among people like *you*."

"Like *us*," Modi corrected. His cocky smirk was infuriating. Thyra got the impression that it rarely left his face. She found herself wanting to make it disappear. "We share much in common. You are a child of the storm." Modi's eyes flared and he held up a hand that danced with tendrils of lightning. "So are we!"

Thyra's magic flared to the surface in response, its fury begging to be directed outward. Modi's smile grew, but his eyes pinched together slightly as he looked at the thick tendrils of lightning that snapped and popped around Thyra. Although the smile didn't slip, Thyra saw a twinge of uncertainty—maybe fear?—in his eyes.

Behind him, Magni grimaced and his blue eyes suddenly filled with rage. He held out his hand and an axe made of lightning sprang to life. The blade cracked and sparked, but the rest of the haft and handle looked solid. Thyra couldn't help but feel a wave of awe as she studied it. She had never even thought that kind of control was possible.

"You are. . .everything we thought you'd be," Modi said slowly. The lightning around his hands disappeared, and his eyes returned to their normal shade. "Please, release your magic. We don't mean you any harm."

Thyra shook her head. "I don't think so."

Modi raised a cautionary hand. "Please. Magni, put that away. Can't you see it's making our young friend nervous?"

Magni growled something that was more animal than human. Grudgingly, he allowed the axe to disappear and fell back into his casual stance against the tree. His eyes still boiled with rage.

"See?" Modi said. "We mean you no harm. Release your magic." His smirk slipped when Thyra made no move to obey. "Come now. Don't make the mistake of abusing our goodwill." Thyra hesitated more, and the smirk fell away completely. "You're not being a very good sport, and my patience is about at its end. It would be a mistake to test us further. I'll give you one more chance. Release your magic so that we can speak without the threat of violence."

Thyra reluctantly let her magic retreat but didn't release it completely. Modi's eyes narrowed, as if he sensed that Thyra hadn't severed her connection, but his confident smirk returned. "That's better. There's no need for confrontation. In fact, you should be glad to see us."

"You'll have to give me a really good reason," Thyra replied warily.

"What better reason could there be than a reunion with family?" Modi's smile split his face. "You must see it already. We're the sons of Thor! We're family, little sister."

Thyra was numb. She knew she should feel something—shock, joy, anger, anything!—but she didn't. She wasn't surprised. There had been enough veiled hints over the past months that other children of Thor existed. Perhaps she should have felt angry, but she wasn't sure who to be angry at. These two, who professed to be her brothers? Her mom? Thor? She could direct her anger in every direction and no direction at all.

One thing was certain—she didn't feel joy at the unexpected reunion. Most of the family she'd discovered over the past three months had either wanted her dead or wanted nothing to do with her. She was done with reunions.

"Of course, we have a different mother," Modi continued. "Our mother was Jarnsaxa, Thor's first wife. She was Vanir but utterly common in every possible way. She had no magic worth speaking of. It was a union meant to bind the Aesir and Vanir, not of love. Her life ended before our father rose to his true power. After that, Sif became the closest thing to a mother that we had."

Something about that felt off to Thyra. "If she was like a mother to you, why has she never mentioned you? Why didn't you try to find her sooner?"

Modi grimaced and glanced over his shoulder at Magni. "Well, we may not have left on the best terms with Sif. It was a misunderstanding that has haunted us for centuries." He shook his head sadly. "We were young, but some sins are harder to forgive than others. We wish we could have made amends long ago. We hope now we can have that chance."

Thyra wasn't buying it. "I'm getting tired of all the centuries-old baggage people like you bring along. I don't care to hear your sob story. If that's why you're here, to tell me that you wish you could go back and right your wrongs, you're wasting your time."

She saw Modi's eyes tighten at the corners, rage simmering just below the surface. Behind him, Magni's lips curled back from his teeth in a growl. She wasn't sure which one was more dangerous—Magni's open fury or Modi's controlled rage that he tried to mask behind a smile.

Modi glanced over his shoulder at his brother. "She sounds like Sif, doesn't she, Magni?"

"A sharp tongue," Magni agreed. "Especially for a girl all alone on a country road."

Thyra glared at Magni. "I don't like being threatened."

"Now's not the time to grow a backbone," Magni said in a menacing tone.

Thyra drew herself up to her full height. "Try me."

Magni smiled menacingly. "With pleasure."

"There will be none of that," Modi barked. He gave his brother a look that made Magni turn away with a snort. He turned back to Thyra and let out an uneven breath. "We didn't come here to fight you. Quite the opposite."

"Why are you here?"

Modi was quick with a reply. "To meet you! We saw the pictures on the news and followed the stories of strange happenings. A brilliant lightning storm. The destruction of an abandoned building. Muspel Corporation property destroyed. A hotel clerk who swore he saw a teenage girl with lightning shooting from her." Modi shrugged. "It was too obvious. We had to find our little sister, and now we have!"

"I told you, I'm not interested in family reunions."

"But, I imagine you are interested in learning more about what you are," Modi said without hesitation. "And what you can do. I can feel your power, and I will be the first to admit that it is immense. It pulls at me. The closer we've gotten the stronger the pull. That's how we knew where to look for you—that shared connection. Like calls to like, as Freya would likely explain it." He smiled. "And we are alike, the three of us."

"Not sure I see the resemblance."

"Maybe not physically, but your magic is the same as ours," Modi said. "Yours may be stronger—I'm not ashamed to admit that fact because it's plain to see—but as strong as you are, you have no control over the power raging inside."

"I think there's plenty of people who would say otherwise," Thyra said grimly.

Modi smirked, his cocky attitude returning. "So you can shoot lightning bolts from your hands. Congratulations!" His expression hardened. "If that's all you aspire to then you are wasting your potential. There is so much more you are capable of. We can teach you to control it, to master the raw power you have and channel it in ways you never thought possible."

"I don't know about that," Thyra said. "I have a pretty good imagination."

Modi chuckled like she had said something funny. "Imagination is good for nothing if you don't have someone to teach you how to make it real. We can. For example, I saw the way you studied Magni's axe a moment ago. We can teach you how to do things like that and more!" As if to emphasize the point, Magni held out one hand and a ball of lightning sprung to life in it. Not a wild, untamed manifestation, but a smooth sphere that pulsed with power. "Control, Thyra. That is something you will never achieve without someone to teach you. Who else can you turn to if not us?"

Thyra's thoughts went back to what Vidar and her mom had said about needing a teacher. It was almost too convenient that these two showed up offering to do just that. *Almost.* Yggdrasil did say it was sending help. Perhaps, in its demented fashion, this was the next wave of promised assistance.

If it was, though, Thyra was not going to accept it blindly. She knew there was always an ulterior motive for every promise people like these two made. The same was true for Yggdrasil.

"In return for what? I know you aren't offering such a valuable service from the goodness of your hearts. What's the cost?"

Modi smirked. "You're smart for one so young. Of course we would ask something in return for teaching you how to master your magic, but I think it will be a price that you are interested in." Modi paused. "But first, I must know, little sister—what is your name?"

Thyra hesitated. She'd made it this far without revealing anything about herself. She almost thought she might escape this encounter without having to. *No such luck.* "Thyra."

Modi's eyebrows went up. "Named after Tyr. . .interesting." He looked over his shoulder and shared an amused look with Magni. "I guess that's better than Thrud for a girl in this day and age."

Magni chuckled grimly. "Tyr could never sire a child on his own. It seems father grew sentimental in his old age, as well as weak. So weak that he named her after another man. Tyr was a warrior, at least. I wonder what he'd think of his namesake being a crippled girl."

Thyra's temper flared. "Don't waste my time with insults. Tell me what you want in exchange for teaching me to master my magic."

"A simple request," Modi answered. "You help us retrieve something that belongs to us and we will teach you to control the storm inside of you."

Thyra felt like she already knew the answer, but she asked the question anyways. "What do you need help retrieving?"

Magni smiled grimly. "Mjolnir!"

"You're probably wondering," Modi said, "why you would ever help us to get Thor's hammer?"

"It did cross my mind," Thyra stated. "Especially since I have a right to the hammer."

"Perhaps," Modi said with a nod, "but one that you will relinquish."

"Why would I give up my right to Thor's hammer?"

"You'll do it in favor of mastering your magic," Modi replied without hesitation. "Besides, while you may have some claim to the hammer, *we* are Thor's true heirs."

"And I'm not? How did you come to that conclusion?"

"Because we knew Thor when he was still the god of thunder and lightning," Modi answered matter-of-factly. "We saw what was possible with Mjolnir in his hands, watched him use it on his rise to godhood. We know what the hammer is capable of."

"And you don't think I could work that out?"

"I am not trying to dismiss your claim, Thyra," Modi said. "Quite the opposite. But the fact is that three of us cannot hold the hammer."

"Two can't hold it any better than three."

"My brother and I have agreed that we will share the hammer," Modi replied smoothly.

"It is *our* birthright!" Magni added. "We inherited the true traits of Thor!"

Thyra's eyes narrowed. "True traits of Thor? What is he talking about?"

"He's referring to the prophecy spoken by Freya," Modi answered. "An old rambling that few ever knew of and even fewer remember. Although, I'm slightly surprised you don't. Sif was there when Freya spoke it for the first time. I would have thought she'd have told you by now. But, it seems there are many things she has kept from you."

"If you're trying to make me lose trust in my mom, you can stop now," Thyra said. "That would be a waste of time."

Modi's smile never slipped, but it was anything but warm. "You may think different once you hear what Freya's prophecy was."

"Don't count on it."

Modi's smile changed to a sneer. "Freya foretold that Thor would have three children, each one with a claim to Mjolnir and each one inheriting one of the traits of Thor. Magni inherited his might, his strength. Just like our father, Magni was without rival on the battlefield. As for myself, I inherited Thor's passion, his fire. Some have called it by another name—wrath—but that has such a negative connotation. It's a word that was used by those who were jealous to undercut me and make me look dangerous."

"Aren't you?"

Modi smirked in a way that answered Thyra's question. "What really matters is that we knew Thor when he was still the god of thunder and lightning. He learned from him and fought beside him. He *wanted* us to have Mjolnir."

"Then why didn't he give it to you?" Thyra asked bluntly. "If your claims were the only ones Thor thought should be honored, why didn't he hand off the hammer before he died? Better question, where were you two when he died? If you were there, why didn't you pick up Mjolnir when you had the chance? The fact that you didn't then makes me think that you weren't where you should have been. Am I wrong?"

Magni began to growl, but Modi silenced him with a hand before he could speak. "That story is not one we enjoy telling. Suffice it to say that we were told to leave Asgard before it fell. But that doesn't change that Thor wanted us to have the hammer." He paused briefly, his expression turning thoughtful. "I won't argue your claim to the hammer. You have one, little sister. Which is why we are offering this trade—we teach you to master your power and in return you give up your claim. We then part ways, both sides made the stronger for the effort."

The return of his smile made it seem like he thought he was giving her the deal of a lifetime, but his eyes told another story. Thyra could still see the uncertainty—no, fear!—behind his confidence. Thyra wasn't buying it. "I don't see the benefit to me. First of all, I know next to nothing about you two. Why would I agree to arm you with a powerful weapon when you could easily turn around and use it against me?"

Modi sighed. "You have no reason to trust us, I realize that. But, you are the *champion* of magic. We know you have the Eye. On top of that, you possess impressive raw strength. The only thing you lack is knowledge of how to use both."

"Maybe I think that's the way it should stay," Thyra countered. "Why help you two become stronger? You said it yourself, this would be an alliance of convenience, not of shared goals. You'd get what you want and then walk away. What guarantee do I have that you'd teach me anything I couldn't learn on my own?"

"You know the answer," Modi said. "There is no one else who can teach you what we can. We are your only hope of mastering your magic before you hurt yourself, or *someone* you care about."

"You *need* us," Magni growled.

"It sounds like you need me just as much," Thyra snapped. "If not more."

Magni sneered, but Modi again silenced him with a hand. "We can teach you how to master your magic. You may think that you have time, that perhaps you can learn on your own, but there is a war coming. You may think you'll survive, but are you certain?" Modi's expression turned concerned. "It would be a shame to have magic's champion crushed before she even learned to stand on her own two feet."

"And you think you can teach me how to be magic's champion?"

Modi shook his head. "Not us. Another. Someone who has stood where you stand and understands what it means to be the champion of Yggdrasil."

Thyra's eyes narrowed. "What you talking about?"

Modi smiled wryly. "Not all champions die. Some live eternal."

Thyra was going to demand a straight answer, but Magni suddenly stood straight and looked down the road towards the trailer park. Thyra could just make out two figures in the distance, one with a golden braid and the other heavily muscled.

"Time to go," Magni growled, already heading for the Chevelle.

"It seems our time is at an end," Modi said. "For today. Think on what we told you, little sister. Thor's hammer belongs in the hands of his true heirs. And you deserve to know the true extent of what you are capable of—both with your magic and as Yggdrasil's champion."

He walked casually over to the Chevelle and opened the passenger door. "As much as I would love to see dear Sif after all these years,

I think I'll let you deal with *Mom* for now." He slid into the car and closed the door. "We'll give you three days to think on our offer. There won't be another chance after that." He leaned out the window and smiled. "Remember, little sister, there's no one else."

The engine roared suddenly, the back wheels spinning in the loose gravel before gaining traction and surging forward. Modi hung one arm out the window to wave as the Chevelle sped away. A hand that danced with lightning.

Thyra watched the Chevelle until it disappeared around a bend in the road. Even after it was gone she stared after it, trying to quiet her adrenaline and sort through her thoughts. She knew she'd have to be a fool to trust those two. She wasn't naive. Two long-lost brothers showing up, offering something only they could provide in return for help in retrieving one of the most powerful dwarf-made weapons? They clearly had their own interests at heart—not hers. Going along with their plan was tantamount to putting her own head on the chopping block and thinking she was going to be served lunch!

She wasn't going to be a pawn to be moved according to what everyone else wanted. She was done being maneuvered by others, that much she was sure of.

It was time for her to change the game.

Chapter 13

"What were you thinking?"

Thyra sat down on the couch and crossed her arms over her chest in preparation for the tirade she knew was coming. Nothing had been said the entire walk back to the trailer. After Sif and Vidar had made sure she was unharmed, Thyra had expected the lecture to begin. Sif had been on the verge of giving just that, but was left speechless as she alternated between what looked like relief and rage. Vidar clearly sensed that a single word from him could be like throwing a lit match on gasoline. He had done his best to give Sif and Thyra space while still remaining close enough to provide a protective presence.

"I went looking for you," Thyra said as calmly as she could manage. "To *apologize.*"

"Apologies could have waited," Sif snapped. "Instead, you put yourself in danger!"

Thyra's temper flared and she struggled to swallow it down. "They were waiting for me, Mom. They already knew where we lived, or at least had a good idea. Who knows how long they've been watching us!"

"That doesn't mean you were right to be off wandering around by yourself!"

"I was only *wandering* because I was looking for you," Thyra said through clenched teeth. "I didn't go *looking for* them! They *found* me."

"Only because you acted rashly!" Sif barked. She shook her head. "I've been too lenient. I should have kept a closer watch and kept you better hidden. All those trips up into the hills to play in the storms led to this."

Thyra's eyebrows shot up her forehead. *"Play* in the storms? Is that what you think I was doing? Those were the only times I felt good! If it weren't for those times, I'd have gone nuts!"

"But you would have been safe!" Sif retorted.

"How do you know that's true?" Thyra shouted, losing her hold on her temper. "Modi and Magni found us, but it wasn't because of the few moments I got to breathe without you looking down my neck!"

Thyra was surprised by the heat in her own voice, but she wasn't going to tone it down until her mom did. Which didn't look like was going to be soon by the look on her mom's face. Sif put her hands on her hips and her mouth opened like she was ready to fire back, but Vidar interrupted before she could started.

"There's no point arguing about what's done. Thyra is safe for now. We need to decide what's next now that Magni and Modi have found us."

Sif took a deep breath and then nodded. "I should have known they'd find us sooner or later. I'd always hoped that someone had finally ended them. But that would have been too easy. Those two are like cockroaches—a nightmare to get rid of and almost impossible to kill."

Vidar nodded. "One thing is certain—this changes our plans."

"I know it does." Sif began to pace. "I don't even know where to start. I thought we would have more time."

"Why don't you start at the beginning," Thyra said, unable to disguise the anger in her voice, "with how I have brothers."

"I don't think now is the time to give you a family history lesson,"

Sif snapped. "We need to get moving."

"Sif," Vidar spoke softly, but his tone was firm. "Tell her what she needs to know. She is Yggdrasil's champion. She needs to understand who her brothers are."

"Half-brothers," Sif corrected sharply.

"All the more reason," Vidar insisted.

Sif frowned and looked at Thyra. "Fine. You want to know about Magni and Modi. First of all, we need to establish that while they may be Thor's sons, they are not my flesh and blood. Something I am grateful for every single day of my life."

Thyra wasn't sure if she should be relieved by that or not. "Why haven't you ever spoken of them?"

"They weren't worth talking about."

"Are they worth talking about now?"

Sif grimaced and looked to Vidar for help.

"You should know that Modi and Magni were born in the early years of the Aesir," Vidar said from where he had taken up watch at the door. "Back when the Aesir were still just a tribe of magic users. Before they became gods, before the Eye of Odin, before Yggdrasil. War was all those two knew and they were scarred by it."

"Scarred?"

"They grew up in savage, bloody times. They saw what Odin and the others were willing to do in order to consolidate power."

"Meaning?"

"You have to understand," Sif said, her expression making it look like each word coming out of her mouth was like dragging broken glass across her tongue, "Thor was different in his youth. He was an angry, vengeful man that wielded his might without remorse. As time passed, his views of the Aesir's role changed. He became a wiser, stronger god by choosing to control his anger and his tendency for violence." She sighed. "But it was too late for Magni and Modi. They embodied the qualities they grew up seeing in Thor."

"What kind of qualities?" Thyra said. She recalled what Modi had said, but she wanted to hear it from her mom and Vidar.

"Dangerous ones," Sif replied, her discomfort written all over her face. "Modi inherited his wrath, and Magni emulated Thor's physical violence. Magni called it *might*, but he just enjoyed hurting people. He always has. They were killers who used godhood as justification for their actions and they got away with it for a long time. But their anger and violence finally went too far. To the point that Odin couldn't overlook their crimes any longer." Sif's eyes danced with rage. "They deserved death, but Odin couldn't do it. Instead, he exiled them!"

"Exile meant they lost the comforts and protection of Asgard," Vidar muttered, "but none of the perks of godhood. They still were worshiped and were able to sate their hungers. Perhaps more so than they did under the eye of the other gods."

Thyra took a deep breath in order to process this new information. "If they were killers, why would Odin overlook that?"

"Because he saw the qualities he valued most in Thor in them," Sif answered. "The Allfather wanted Thor to be the conqueror of his youth. When Thor refused, Odin looked to his grandsons instead. He loved Modi and Magni from the start, and encouraged their behavior. He wanted them to do what Thor would not."

So, her brothers were killers with anger issues. Not exactly Christmas-card material, but Thyra already knew that wouldn't be the case. Every Norse god she'd met so far had baggage. "What got them exiled?"

Sif took a deep breath before answering.When she spoke, her voice quivered with emotion. "They killed several Valkyries and three servants for refusing their advances. They didn't even try to hide what they had done. They bragged about it. Magni battered them to a pulp, Modi tortured their bodies." Sif's lips pressed together in anger and she clenched down on her spear until her knuckles went white. "They were my sisters and deserved a good death. Not the one Modi and Magni gave them"

"Odin should have taken their heads," Vidar said," but he was too weak to give them the punishment they deserved. A few of us were willing to do it regardless, but your brothers were quick to disappear once Odin's protection was removed."

Thyra sat back and mulled over what she'd just been told. She could understand why her mom hated them so much. As leader of the Valkyries, Sif must have wanted justice more than anyone. That justice had been denied her.

"What did Modi and Magni say to you?" Vidar asked.

Thyra hesitated. She knew she needed to choose her words wisely. She'd had too many arguments with her mom already, and could start another one just by saying the wrong thing. "A lot, but I think the gist was that they wanted my help."

"Your help?" Vidar asked. "With what?"

There was no sense in hiding the truth. "Retrieving Mjolnir."

Vidar nodded slowly, as if that was the last piece of the puzzle that needed to be put into place. "What did they offer in return?"

"Does it matter?" Sif hissed.

Vidar nodded without looking away from Thyra. "It does. What they're willing to offer is a sign of how desperate they are." Sif's lips pressed into a thin line, but she didn't argue. "What did they say, Thyra?"

Thyra took a deep breath and let it out slow. "They offered to teach me."

Vidar's eyebrows flicked up. "Is that all?"

Not exactly, but Thyra was still trying to untangle the part about the other champion they were talking about. Plus, she was confused by Vidar's reaction. She couldn't decide if he felt their offer was too generous or too thin. "In more words, but yes."

Vidar stood up straight and turned to Sif. "What do you make of that?"

Sif began shaking her head almost immediately. "No. That's too simple. They have to be hiding something."

"Why would they show up out of the blue with this kind of offer?" Vidar asked. "Teaching Thyra how to master her magic? That is a big concession."

"They're lying through their teeth," Sif snapped. "Mastering magic isn't something that can be taught in a few days or weeks. Not even years!"

"Thyra has proven to be a quick learner so far," Vidar commented. "Even a few lessons would make her that much more dangerous."

"You should know that mastering magic is not that simple."

"Maybe, but them offering that tells me something," Vidar said. "They're scared."

"They should be," Sif snapped. "If I ever see them again, I will do what Odin was too weak to do. They had better be running, because I will kill them the next time I see them."

"And I'll gladly help," Vidar said with a nod. "But, let's put aside those thoughts for now and circle back to what they were willing to give up to convince Thyra."

"It doesn't matter," Sif said, "because Thyra told them 'no'. So instead of wasting time trying to analyze the thoughts of two cockroaches like them, let's start talking about what our next move is."

"That's what we're doing," Vidar said firmly. "Besides, are you sure Thyra told them 'no'?"

Thyra cringed as every eye turned on her. Even Asiri gave her a calculating stare that Thyra couldn't manage to meet. "I didn't exactly say 'no' to them."

Sif threw her hands up in exasperation. "Thyra! What were you thinking?"

"I had a lot going on right then," Thyra argued. "I didn't say 'yes', either."

"And that was smart," Vidar said. He turned to Sif. "Think about it, Sif. If she had said 'no', do you think Modi and Magni would let her walk free?"

Sif frowned. "No, probably not. But all that means is that they will come back." She looked at Thyra. "When? How long do we have?"

"Three days."

Sif nodded like that settled the argument. "Enough time for us to disappear."

"That won't work," Vidar argued. "They will be watching us. We run and they will attack."

Thyra remembered something Modi said about a shared connection. She decided that was one detail that she shouldn't keep quiet. "Modi said that the three of us shared a connection due to Thor being our father. He didn't explain it any further than that, but he seemed certain that it existed. Do you think he was telling the truth?"

Sif's shoulders sagged. "It's possible. It's something that was common among the Vanir. Freya always had the ability to sense magic in others. It could be possible that Modi inherited the talent in a way that allows him to sense your magic due to your shared blood."

"Then," Thyra aide slowly, "that means they could find us if we did run."

Sif nodded grudgingly. "Perhaps. *If* he was telling the truth. That isn't a given. They could be lying to you in order to manipulate you."

"Nothing new there," Thyra lamented. She closed her eyes and rested her head on the back of the couch. "What if I did help them get the hammer? I know what you're going to say, Mom, but just humor me for a minute. What would I be capable of if I had Mjolnir?"

Sif inhaled deeply. "You'd be an absolute force of nature, just like your father. He was capable of immense destruction when he held the hammer. I saw him turn the tide of battle single-handedly dozens of times. Even Odin stepped lightly around your father when the hammer was in his hand."

"Is that true for Modi and Magni too?" Thyra asked.

"Yes and no," Sif replied. "Their magic is strong when together. They complement each other very well. That's why they've never separated. Apart they were always vulnerable, if not to their lack of strength, then to their flaws, their vices. Together they were able to balance each other, even compliment the other."

"Apart, they are not as strong as you," Vidar added. "Even together they may not rival your raw power. But, what they do have is centuries of mastering the power they do possess. Your power is still maturing and you don't have a guide in its use. What you still are learning to do is second nature to them. That's what makes them dangerous."

Sif nodded in agreement and then turned to Asiri. "How close are you on what you've been working on?"

Asiri grimaced. "Not much has changed since the last time you asked. Not as close as I need to be, considering the day's events."

"You need to get closer," Sif said in a firm tone.

"You can't rush good work!" Asiri scoffed. "You told me I'd have weeks. I can give you what I have, but it won't be what you wanted." She looked between Sif and Vidar, pointing a bone finger. "That goes for both of you."

"We don't have time to wait," Sif insisted.

"Then find a way to give me time," Asiri snapped. "You were holding me over a vat of hot oil already with how quick you demanded things get done. Now, you're trying to push me all the way under!"

"Believe me," Sif said, "we don't want to rush you, but we don't have any other choice. We can't sit here and wait with Magni and Modi close. They know where we are and they will come back."

"Which is why I need more time to finish what I'm working on," Asiri insisted. "Let me have three days! I can at least give you part of what you asked for. Once I finish, those two won't be anything more than a nuisance to be swept aside."

Sif was shaking her head, but Thyra spoke before her mom could deny Asiri the time she was asking for. "What if we give Asiri the time she needs?"

"No," Sif said immediately. "They may follow us if we run, but we can choose the battlefield. Right now they have us at a disadvantage."

"I don't think running will give us the advantage. They'll just follow right on our heels," Thyra countered. "All we know is that they want the hammer. But we don't know why they want to involve me, or what their plans are. We don't know why they suddenly have an interest in going after the hammer. Shouldn't we get as many answers as we can?"

"I know why they want to involve you," Sif said. "They want you to get Mjolnir for them and then take the fall."

"Fine. What if I don't help them?" Thyra asked. "What if they go and get Mjolnir on their own? What then?"

"She has a point," Vidar said. "They want the hammer. Are we prepared to risk them actually succeeding?"

"They've had centuries to try," Sif argued. "They've proven inept so far and I don't think that's going to change now."

"Maybe not," Thyra said, "but what if we're wrong? The best way to make sure Mjolnir stays out of their hands is by going after it ourselves!"

"We've been through this, Thyra. That-isn't-going-to-happen!"

Great, we're back to square one! Thyra crossed her arms again and glared at the blank TV screen, unwilling to look at her mom.

"It's all coming to a head," Vidar said suddenly. He looked at Sif and frowned. "Hela, Baldur and Gunnar Olafsson, Modi and Magni.

We are risking being swallowed whole." He took a deep breath and squared his shoulders to Sif. "You may not like hearing this, but I think Thyra should go after Mjolnir. We can't allow those two to get the hammer, the same way we can't allow Olafsson to continue to possess it."

"Not you too!" Sif snapped, throwing her hands up. "We cannot do this. I won't allow it! Magni and Modi are dangerous, but going after Mjolnir is worse!"

"Sooner or later, Olafsson will turn the magic of Mjolnir against us. Against the world even," Vidar said. "If Modi and Magni get it, they will do the same, if not worse. We will be swallowed in the power vacuum that is growing if we do nothing. Look, I'm not thrilled about the risks that go along with it, either. But if running won't do us any good and trying to hide won't, then we don't have much choice. You know I'm right."

"Not if it puts my daughter's life at risk," Sif stated.

Thyra could see no end to the argument between the two sides that had formed. Her mom wasn't going to give ground and her opinion carried greater weight than any of the other voices. Except, perhaps, for Thyra's.

"I don't want to run," Thyra stated. She waited for Sif to meet her gaze. "I know you're trying to protect me, and I love you for it. But, sooner or later, I will have to face my brothers. I'd rather do it when I have a leg to stand on." She cut her mom off before Sif could argue. "Listen, I'm not saying I want to go with them, but I see what there is to gain by doing it. I need someone to teach me how to use my magic. Yggdrasil told me that I needed to get Mjolnir, that if I don't Baldur may succeed in threatening more than just the Tree. Modi and Magni provide a solution to both problems."

"They will use you," Sif argued.

Thyra's face hardened. "Not if I use them first!"

"That's a dangerous line to walk," Sif warned. "Modi and Magni have been alive for centuries. They won't be manipulated easily."

"They want the hammer," Thyra replied. "I think they're desperate to get it. That makes them vulnerable."

Sif shook her head. "You don't know what you're saying. If this plan revolves around trying to pull the wool over their eyes then it isn't an option at all. It's too dangerous. Plus I don't think I could stand to be near them without trying to throttle them. They would never agree to us joining them."

Thyra's solution to that problem was not one she was ready to suggest. Not yet, anyways. "Just give me the three days. Let Asiri finish whatever she's working on. We can work out a plan during that time. I promise that whatever decision we reach, I will agree to. As long as you're willing to do the same."

Sif put her hands on her hips and stared at her daughter. Thyra did her best to meet—and match—the intensity of that stare, knowing that if she looked away and showed even a glimmer of doubt her mom would take that as proof that Thyra wasn't ready. She didn't know how long they were locked in a battle of wills, but the effort of not flinching away was enough to make sweat begin to bead on Thyra's forehead.

Finally, her mom blinked. She looked at Vidar, her expression hardening into a look Thyra was beginning to recognize as the mask of a Valkyrie, not a mother concerned for her daughter. Vidar shrugged, then nodded. Sif's lips pressed into a tight line and her gaze returned to Thyra. "You're committed to this, no matter the consequences?"

Thyra nodded. "I am. I need to do this."

Sif's expression hardened further. "Fine. I can't keep treating you like a child. You can't afford to be one anymore. You *have* to be *more*. I was already a Valkyrie at your age. If you would have been born during the reign of the Aesir, you would have already held the Eye and taken your place as a god."

Thyra saw Vidar nod in the corner of her eye. She remembered him saying almost that exact same thing. It meant a lot coming from him, but it was even more validating coming from her mom. Validating and frightening.

"But," Sif raised one finger, "if I think for one moment you're taking unnecessary risks, I will drag you to safety. Do you hear me?"

Thyra's throat was so tight that she could only nod. Sif's eyes bore into Thyra for another moment before she turned and gave a curt nod to Asiri. "You have your three days. Let's not waste them."

Chapter 14

Fenrir pushed through the crowd gathered around the entrance to the hospital, growling at anyone who dared call him on his roughness. The hospital parking lot had become a maddening mix of zealots, party goers, and curious people trying to catch a glimpse of the goddess. Tents had been erected, a stage built, and barricades haphazardly placed to block access to the front of the hospital. Even the police, which had kept a constant presence since the beginning, had been forced to retreat outside the limits of what was now being called Helheim by the crowd.

Helheim. Fenrir wasn't sure who had suggested the name, but the devotees had taken to it with fanatical glee. A makeshift "realm of the dead" was created almost overnight. Depictions of dead warriors and monsters from the nightmares of weak minds were everywhere. Smoke rose from several altars, the sacrifices ranging from fruit to a now blackened chicken. Fenrir found it both laughable and offensive that this was what the mortals felt constituted Hela's domain. Their imaginations ran too wild and not far enough all at once in their understanding of what Hela was capable of. It showed how little they actually knew.

Fenrir had no time for what was happening here, and he didn't understand why his mistress allowed it to continue. These fools had no idea what they were doing or the forces they were trifling with.

There was a time when mortals knew how to worship their gods. This was not it. Once, men and women gave all they had to gain the favor of the goddess. These people were simply looking for entertainment, a distraction from their mundane lives. All too soon they would be taught the correct order of things.

Fenrir would relish that day.

He stepped up to the sliding doors and waited for them to open. Immediately, the smell of the hospital threatened to overwhelm his senses. He hated this place. It was too clean. Too sterile. Too *dead*. This hospital was the true Helheim—a place of dying where the power of the goddess reigned supreme. There was no army of undead warriors rising from their tombs to sweep the earth before Hela. Only the weak, the feeble, and the infirm slowly wasting away until the goddess descended to grace their lives with her power. In her absence, decay ruled. This place reeked of it.

He strode past the two men in tactical gear that nodded to him. *Not an undead army*, he thought, *but they were the closest thing to it*. They had been on the verge of dead, but now whole thanks to Hela's power. It was the goddess they followed, but they knew who he was and they knew better than to question him on his comings and goings. The only person he was accountable to was Hela.

And since she didn't have time for him anymore, he was free to go where and do as he pleased.

Mostly.

Fenrir moved through the hospital with a determined, angry stride. Instead of taking the elevator up to the top floor, he opted for the stairs. The modern world and all its frivolous conveniences put a taste in his mouth like rotting meat. He lived with its existence, even its necessity from time to time, but he did his best to avoid it when possible.

Two more guards were posted outside of the room Hela had claimed as her sanctum. At one time it may have been a surgery or observation room, but had been hastily adapted to the needs of the goddess. This was where the lucky few that were chosen to personally receive healing from her hand were brought. The lucky few picked by the hand of goddess for reasons known only to her.

Fenrir hesitated with his hand on the door. He hated this place most of all. It smelled wrong, unnatural. It was a smell that even after a thousand plus years of serving his mistress still turned his stomach—the smell of death being denied.

Hela looked up as he entered, giving him a scowl for his lack of care. "I see you've returned from your wanderings. Did you find what you were looking for?"

Fenrir didn't respond. There were three new beds in the room. Like all the others, the people occupying them looked like lifeless bags of flesh and bone. True, Hela would make them well again, but for what? A return to their former lives was impossible. They were the dregs of mankind, tossed aside and forgotten. No one was waiting for them. A return to full health for them would mean only one thing—they would live to serve the goddess as her loyal hounds.

Like him. The thought made a growl escape his throat.

Hela glanced up at him again, her green eyes penetrating to his core. "Speak. Your brooding is enough to steal the warmth from the air."

"I do not belong here," Fenrir stated in response. "This place is a cage."

"Is it this place that you chafe in," Hela asked in a measured tone, "or being in my service?" The question caught him off-guard and he couldn't answer. Hela frowned. "You hesitate. Interesting."

Hela put a hand to on the temple of one of her patients that was groaning in his sleep. She spoke softly to him and rubbed a circle into the side of his head. Immediately, his discomfort was eased and he settled back into a deep sleep.

"I know this age has been challenging for you, my loyal wolf," Hela said without looking up. "You are a creature meant for the hunt. And I have kept you leashed like a hound at my side." She pursed her lips thoughtfully. "Perhaps you are right to grow restless."

Again, he hesitated. He did not want to incite Hela's wrath by speaking too boldly, but there was no denying that he was growing tired of being the faithful wolf that begged for scraps from her table. He was not weak, but he felt it more with each passing day. "I only wish to serve you."

"But?"

Fenrir cringed. The truth was the only acceptable response. His mistress would see through anything else. "I feel that I am wasted here."

Hela nodded. "I understand. Would you depart from my side?"

Fenrir hesitated for the third time. Answering the question in any fashion felt like a poor choice, so he chose silence.

"I am not blind to your feelings," Hela said, a hint of disappointment in her voice. "You've spent more time away from my side than near it since we came here. That tells me everything I need to know." She sighed. "You will be happy to know that I am going to remove your leash and give you something to hunt."

Fenrir felt his heart quicken. "I am yours to command."

"I know," Hela stated. She moved to the next bed and pressed a finger to the chest of the woman lying under a thin bed sheet. "This one has been in a coma for years. She will wake soon." Finally, she looked him in the eye. "You are eager. Which makes me wonder who you are hoping to hunt." She cocked an eyebrow in his direction. "I fear you will be dissatisfied by what I'm going to ask of you."

"That isn't true," he lied. "You could never disappoint me."

"You say those words for my benefit, but you don't mean them." Hela sighed again. "It is time we move against the Muspel Corporation."

Fenrir snarled, whether from excitement or frustration over the intended target, even he wasn't completely sure. Hela's eyes narrowed to slits. No doubt she suspected the latter to be true.

"What would you have me do?" Fenrir asked in an attempt to deflect her scrutiny.

Hela considered him for a moment before answering. "I want you to find out what Gunnar Olafsson and Baldur are up to. Frustrate their plan where you can, but above all else, I want you to discover what they are doing. They have been quiet when I expected noise. That concerns me." Hela set a chart down and walked closer. "I am sending the men I scavenged from Gunnar and a handful of my acolytes with you. They are yours to command, but I do not want you to waste them needlessly."

Fenrir forced himself to nod. "I will do as you ask."

"I know you will," Hela said, her expression hardening, "because you know what will happen if you don't. You are alive because I still find you to be useful. I hope you do not give in to the temptation to stray outside the bounds I have set for you. You know what will happen if I retract my protection."

Fenrir felt his hackles stand on end, barely suppressing the growl that formed in his throat. There was no mistaking the line that had just been drawn in the dirt or where Fenrir stood in Hela's eyes. She said she was letting him loose, but he was still the dutiful wolf, her the mistress prepared to correct if he stepped out of line. She had left his knee weak as a reminder of that, but this was the first time she had threatened him so openly.

"Do you understand me, Fenrir?" Hela asked.

He gave his answer through gritted teeth. "I understand."

"Then you are free to go," Hela said.

Fenrir bristled at the dismissal, but pushed his rage down. She wanted him to react, to prove that she was right about him not being under control. He was not going to betray his feelings by making a scene.

He turned to leave but was stopped at the door by Hela's voice calling after him. "Serve me well on this, Fenrir, and I will give you the chance at Vidar you so desperately crave."

Chapter 15

Thyra's eyes snapped open to a place she didn't recognize. Instinctively, she reached for her magic, lightning crackling to life in an instant. She spun around, trying to determine what was happening, but found herself transfixed by the breathtaking scenery surrounding her. Steep, snow-capped mountains fell into a bay of calm, clear water that gently lapped against the rocky beach she stood on. It was equal parts rugged and calm, wild and peaceful.

"Beautiful, isn't it?"

A man stood a few feet to her left, his eyes looking out over the water longingly. Thyra turned to get a better look at him. As expected, assigning an age to him was useless. Another god. The question was, which one? He was about her height with a trim build, golden hair that fell almost to his shoulders, and eyes that were equal parts storm cloud and blue skies. There was something familiar about him, but Thyra couldn't put her finger on it.

He smiled softly. "This is where it all began for me, so many years ago."

Thyra skipped the part where she was stunned into silence and jumped to getting answers. "Where am I?"

"This fjord," he swept his hand across the water, "is on the border of what you'd call Norway and Sweden. At least, this is how I remember it. It's been almost a thousand years since it was this way. If you were to come here now it would look very different. Mankind has spoiled it, just like it does everything else. Sad, really. It was truly magnificent. So simple, so clean. It was paradise."

"Funny," Thyra said in a tense voice. "I always imagined paradise having a lot more palm trees and warm, sandy beaches."

A small smile crossed his face. "A symptom of the age you live in. Trust me, if you had grown up here like I did, you would agree with me. Your blood would *sing* in this place! Here you would feel your ancestors calling to you, the air breathing new life into you, the waters washing away the taint of the world, the earth restoring your strength. This place *is* paradise for people like us."

Thyra moved to the side in order to look at him from a different angle. There was definitely something familiar about him, but she still wasn't sure what. The fact that there was something familiar about him made her even more cautious. "Who are you?"

"A friend."

"My mom always told me to be careful around strangers," Thyra said, "and after the past few months I've learned to be twice as careful around strangers who call themselves my *friend*. So, unless you want me to unload a lightning bolt on you, you had better give me a better answer."

"You would do just that, wouldn't you?" he said, his eyes touching on the lightning dancing around her fists. He looked up and smiled. "You're wise to be cautious."

"Three seconds before lightning turns you to a crisp," Thyra warned. She began to gather her magic. "One."

He raised a hand to stop her counting. "There's no need for that. Allow me to explain the best way I can." His eyes suddenly burst with light more intense than the sun. "I'm someone who understands what it means to be magic's champion."

Thyra took a tentative step back, her mind racing to put the pieces together. The familiar look, the evidence of magic that resembled the light of the sun—the only logical conclusion seemed like an impossible possibility. "You're. . .you're Odin?"

He nodded, the fires blazing in his eyes winking out, returning them to their natural hue. "The one and only."

Thyra had maintained the hold on her magic and was not of the mind to let it go. Not with a dead man standing in front of her. It would have been easier to explain it away as just a dream, but she knew better than to believe that to be true. "But you're dead."

"Was," Odin corrected. "After a fashion. Not anymore, clearly."

"Dead people don't just stop being dead."

Odin shrugged. "I guess Yggdrasil wasn't done with me yet."

Thyra's eyes narrowed. "Yggdrasil kept you alive?"

"Not the tree itself," Odin corrected. "Another was tasked with healing my wounds and keeping my heart beating. But the tree did use its connection with me to whisk me away before death claimed me. It provided a means for my body to be hidden in a place where I could heal."

Thyra didn't like the sound of that. Once again, it was proven that Yggdrasil was playing the game from multiple angles. It also raised another question that she couldn't help but ask. "If you're alive, does that mean. . .does that mean other Aesir are as well?"

"You mean, is Thor alive?" Odin shook his head. "Unfortunately, no. My son is gone. Yggdrasil could not save him. Even if it could have, I don't know if he would have accepted the offer."

Thyra felt a twinge of disappointment, but it didn't last long. Nothing had changed with the confirmation that Thor had died centuries before. She had felt a brief glimmer of what might have been hope, but it had been so short that she didn't feel any pain when it was gone. There was no point grieving for something she had never had in the first place.

She looked around the fjord, keeping a careful eye on Odin as she did. She felt a soft breeze on her cheek and swore she could smell salt in the air. "Is this a dream?"

Odin considered this for a moment. "Of a sort."

That wasn't comforting. Thyra had been through too many "dreams" in the past few months. She didn't want to be part of another one. "What kind of sort?"

"Simply stated, I'm using Yggdrasil's own power to communicate with you," Odin explained. "All time is present at once to the World Tree, so perhaps we are standing in the fjord of my youth. It may well be that if we walk a little ways up the beach we will find the cabin my father built for my mother." He smiled wistfully. "I needed you to see this place, Thyra. So you could understand where you come from."

"Great, I've seen it," Thyra said. "Now get out of my head."

"This isn't just in your head, Thyra," Odin said. "What happens here is real."

"Fantastic," Thyra said flatly. "Let's skip to the point. What do you want with me?"

"To see what has become of my line," Odin replied. He gave her an appraising look. "I see your father in your eyes, but your look is mostly your mother. Put a spear in your hand and you'd be the spitting image of a Valkyrie." He studied her a little closer, a frown growing on his face. "Perhaps a hint of Freya in you, too. Unfortunately, you seemed to have inherited all the wrong physical qualities from all the wrong people."

Two could play that game and Thyra didn't hold back. "Shouldn't you be missing an eye? And be old? Gray hair? Bent over with a raven perched on your shoulder?"

As if on cue, a pair of ravens called overhead. Odin smiled wryly. "At least one thing still holds true. As for the rest, I'm as surprised as you are. It seems that when the mantle of magic's champion passes, so do the effects of the price we pay. At least, in part." He reached down and massaged his thigh. "Not every price paid has been removed from me. I still feel old, even if I don't look it anymore."

That piqued Thyra's interest—did that mean her knee could be fixed?—but she did her best to hide it. That was a rabbit hole she would need time to consider, especially what the revelation meant for her.

"I wanted to talk to you, Thyra," Odin said, "and this seemed like the only way I was going to be able to do it. Your mother and Vidar are nothing if not vigilant. I doubt either one of them would allow me to speak with you. Especially not alone. I fear they do not hold me in high regard." He smirked, a wry twist to his lips. "I needed you to hear what I have to say without their. . .*unique* histories with me clouding your mind."

"I think you're a bit late for that," Thyra said. "I've heard stories, and not the kind that paint you as a benevolent god with my best interest at heart."

"My point exactly," Odin said through a forced smile. "Do me a favor and try to judge me for who I am, not who I once was. What is in the past should stay there, Thyra. We aren't going that way, so let's focus on what we can be moving forward."

"Something only someone who has made a lot of bad choices would say," Thyra quipped.

"I don't deny that," Odin admitted, "but rehashing mistakes of the past won't change the here and now."

"But maybe it will stop us from making the same mistakes."

"If only that were true," Odin said in a somber tone. He looked out over the fjord with a look that could only be called melancholy. "Mankind has a short memory and a penchant for perpetuating mistakes. This is a new age, and an unfamiliar world. Man has grown strong in power but weak in direction while we gods have been in the shadows. In my short time awake, I've seen much that troubles me about what man has achieved in our absence. Wars, atomic bombs, corrupt governments that perform genocides—man has grown more depraved than I ever thought possible. We Aesir lived during cruel times where we slept with one hand on our weapons, but the cruelty of this current age is astounding in comparison. The average person spends more time consuming altered images and false information than they do living. They follow false gods like celebrities and politicians rather than think for themselves. They are paralyzed by inaction and fear, with half afraid to offend and the other half too offended to be afraid. They hunger for direction but reject it when it is shown to them. Never have I seen a bigger need for someone with the strength to stand up and return balance to this world."

"You mean someone who will *force* balance on the world," Thyra said.

"If necessary," Odin stated.

"And that's you?"

"Perhaps not me," Odin replied, "but someone."

"Wouldn't you become the very thing you just railed against?"

Odin ignored her question. "I must admit that I find your current situation intriguing. Here you are, a being of immense power that could right so many of the wrongs mankind has perpetrated, yet you do not." He turned and gave her a curious look. "What is the champion of magic doing hiding out in some little town, far from the places of power? When I awoke in this new age, I thought to look for you in a place of influence, not in some rural town in a land called *Idaho*."

Thyra wasn't surprised, but she asked the question anyways. "You know where I am?"

"Of course, I do," Odin answered. "How do you think Modi and Magni were able to find you? They would have been lost without me pointing them in the right direction. I practically had to lead them right to your front door."

Another piece of the puzzle fell into place for Thyra. "You're with them?"

"I was," Odin replied, "but no longer. Currently, I am searching for what is mine. Waking in this world after so long has me feeling incomplete. I will be whole again soon." He paused and looked at Thyra. "The same way you should be searching for what will make you whole, a true god."

"You mean Mjolnir," Thyra guessed.

Odin nodded. "It's your birthright."

"The same way its Modi's and Magni's?"

Odin nodded reluctantly. "That's true."

"Then you should be helping them, shouldn't you?"

Odin frowned. "In theory, yes, but it isn't that simple."

It never was with people like Odin. "I've heard that you always had a soft spot for them. For all I know, you could be trying to manipulate me in order to help them get the hammer."

"What should that matter to you? I heard that you didn't want it," Odin said, a knowing smile growing on his face. "A lie, if I ever heard one. You want the hammer just like Modi and Magni. I can see it in your eyes. But with one difference—you have no plans to share it with anyone. And I don't fault you for that. Only a fool would want to share that kind of power."

"I don't want it for the power."

"So you tell yourself," Odin said, "but whether you want it for your own use or to keep it away from someone else, in the end it is the same. And I support you both ways."

"Are you suggesting you'd help me get it instead of them?"

Odin gave a noncommittal shrug. "I want to see the hammer back in hands of my line. Freya's prophecy said that the three children of Thor would seek it, and that one would stand above the other two.

Mjolnir would make Modi and Magni powerful, but I am not blind to the truth. They have agreed to share it, but only one can hold it at a time, no matter how united they are in its use. A day will come when that union will be tested. Together, they are strong, but apart they lack the fortitude to be the true masters of Mjolnir." He pointed a finger at Thyra. "Unlike you. I can feel the raging storm of your power inside of you. You are more than a match for their combined might, perhaps even without the hammer. With Mjolnir in your hands, your power would be staggering. You could help the world return to balance."

Thyra felt a rush of excitement at the thought. Odin's words were having an unexpected and alarming effect on her. Part of her wanted what Odin was describing to happen—for balance to be achieved. Isn't that why Yggdrasil made her it's champion? It made sense, even if the means was by force.

And there was the danger. Odin's words appealed to the part of her that desired action. Rash action. She had to ask, who would benefit from her following Odin's rationale? The answer was the person suggesting it. She forced herself to resist the spell Odin's words had her under and sniffed. "I have a weapon already."

"Yes, I'm well aware. Lynnedslag, I believe you call it?" Odin sneered. "A fitting name. Although, I find it hard to call a stick used to play a game a weapon. Now, Mjolnir—that is a weapon. It can crush a skull just as easily as it can call down lightning to level hundreds at a time."

"I'm not exactly in the skull-crushing business."

Odin smiled wryly. "Of course you are, whether you choose to see it or not. You are magic's champion. Yggdrasil does not choose pacifists to be its chosen vessel. You are a creature of destruction and rage. Just like me, your father, your mother, Vidar."

"If that's what it means to be Aesir, I'm not sure I want any part of it."

"It's too late for that," Odin replied. "You're a death dealer through and through. You are Aesir!"

"Maybe I should have taken after my grandmother more then," Thyra stated. It was a lie—her only interaction with Freya had been anything but endearing—but she took a measure of satisfaction seeing the ripple of emotion break Odin's cocky mask. "She seemed to think I'd be better off following a different path."

Odin rocked back on his heels. "You've spoken to Freya?"

Thyra nodded. "Briefly. Have you?"

Odin frowned. "Briefly."

"She was that happy to see you?" Odin cringed before wiping the emotion off his face. Thyra couldn't help but sneer. "Wow, you must have left on good terms for you to return from the dead and still have her mad at you."

"It wasn't how I left, it's how we found each other in this new age." Odin waved his hand dismissively. "I didn't come here to discuss the state of my relationship with Freya."

"Why did you come then?"

"To make sure you are what magic needs in a champion," Odin said grimly. "Tell me, how is the mastery of your magic going?"

"Fine," Thyra lied.

Odin smirked. "Oh? Then you clearly have learned how your magic works? How to master the elements and force them to your will? You surely know how to defend yourself from the magic of another, yes? If I tried to strike you down, you could stop me?" Thyra remained quiet and stone-faced. Apparently that was answer enough for Odin. "I didn't think so. You are no champion of magic. Not yet."

"That's not what Yggdrasil says."

"You think that because you have the Eye and can call down the occasional lightning storm, that makes you a true champion?" Odin scoffed. "The tree is manipulating you, the same way it manipulated all its champions. It has no interest in your progression—only the growth of its own influence on this world. It will use you up and then toss you aside. *Just like it did me!"*

Thyra was surprised to hear that admission. She had imagined up a very different idea of Odin's relationship with Yggdrasil. The possibility of that not being true cast a shadow of doubt on what she'd been told about Odin.

"Yggdrasil won't help you learn how to reach your full potential," Odin continued. "I can. I will show you how to master the elements and bend them to your will." His expression grew hungry. "This modern world is yours to take. Your power flows through everything. Every home, every device, every aspect of their society—your power could be limitless! Let me teach you and together we can make this world what it should have been. A place of peace, equality, where every man, woman and child has the same chance to live to their full potential."

That idea sounded far too utopian, especially coming from a man that had become a god after spilling so much blood. But, she couldn't deny the appeal of learning how to master her power. Two days of trying to work out a plan with Sif and Vidar had left her hungering for that control, but with no acceptable way to achieving it. "Why should I trust you?"

"Because, I can teach you how to be a god!"

Thyra shook her head. "I don't want to be a god."

Odin shrugged. "What you want won't matter once the humans see what you can do. Either you become a god, or you will become a target for their arrows. You only have two choices—live as a god, or die on your knees!"

"That's a very fatalistic view of things," Thyra replied.

"But a true one," Odin said forcefully. "Look what happened to me."

"I am not you."

"No, you're not," Odin said, a cold smile on his face. "But sooner or later, Thyra, this world will see you for what you are. You have to make the choice of how you will meet that day. With me, you can become a true champion of magic and make this world give you the respect you deserve."

After listening to Modi and Magni, Odin's speech sounded rehearsed. He was hitting all the same highlights as Modi. Thyra crossed her arms over her chest. "I've already learned that whenever someone promises power, there's always a price that needs to be paid. I'm sure you're no different. So, what's your price?"

"You're a smart girl. Another way you take after Sif." Odin chuckled dryly. "Of course, there is a price for me helping you, but it is a simple one that I've already mentioned. I want you to restore the Aesir, and help me rebuild what was destroyed."

"With you at the head, I'm sure."

"No, no, no," Odin said, shaking his head. "I don't want to lead. You are magic's champion in this age. *You* must stand at the forefront. I simply want to be close at your side. An advisor to help you remake this age into what it should have been. To right the wrongs mankind has perpetuated. End their wars and stop their petty squabbles. Remind them that they are not the greatest power this world has known, no matter what their science has created. It is us—their gods—that should be revered!"

"It seems like the gods you're talking about have all turned out to be pretty unworthy of reverence," Thyra said.

"Maybe," Odin said, "but tell me, what has man done without us? Each passing day leads to mankind becoming more and more lost. They look to empty vessels for meaning to their empty lives, kneeling to governments that rob them blind with one hand while making them dependent with the other. The people of this world have forgotten what it means to live, passion burning in their veins, and a prayer to their gods on their lips!"

"And having you as their god is going to be an improvement?" Thyra scoffed.

Odin took a deep breath before shaking his head slowly. "No, I am not the solution. I told you, I don't want to be the figurehead that this age looks to. You are what is needed, Thyra. A child of both the old and the new. You can lead these lost souls into the glory of a new age. Yggdrasil chose you to be its champion. I simply want to help guide you in ways that the World Tree cannot. I am the help that was promised."

Thyra felt the hair on the back of her neck stand on end. *Odin was the help Yggdrasil promised?* That didn't feel right.

"I don't think I should trust you," Thyra said.

"If not me, then who?" Odin replied. "Who has the knowledge to guide you, to help you become not only the master of the Eye, but of your own magic? Who else can help you regain your father's hammer? Your mother? Vidar? The dwarf?" Odin snorted. "None of them know what it takes to be magic's champion. None of them can teach you how to master your magic. None of them can help you become what you're meant to be!"

"Who says I want to become what you think I should be?"

Odin threw up his hands. "Don't be what I want you to be. Be what *you* want to be!"

Thyra scoffed. "How would you know what I want to be?"

"Because I know you more than you'd like to admit," Odin said confidently. "You aren't happy hiding while the world grows more disillusioned. You paid a price to be magic's champion, but it feels like a pointless sacrifice right now. Each day you find yourself feeling more agitated by inaction, by not being allowed to explore your power, by not knowing what you're truly capable of. You're stagnant, and it is *eating you alive*."

Thyra looked away to keep Odin from seeing how close his

observations were to the truth. He was right. She was frustrated. But, that didn't mean she was going to jump ship and accept his offer. Not without an assurance that she was going to get something worth the risk.

"You say you can teach me to be the champion of magic," Thyra said, still looking out over the fjord, "and that you can teach me how to master my magic. Those are pretty words, but they're vague. You could be dangling information that I already have and I wouldn't know it until it was too late. How do I know you can deliver?"

"You don't," Odin replied. "Find Modi and Magni. They will bring you to me. They will begin to teach you how to master your magic along the way. Then, together we can finish your training, retake Mjolnir and restore it to its *rightful* heir."

"You're asking for a lot of trust," Thyra said, taking note of what he had implied. "Trust you, trust them—I'm young, but I'd like to think I'm not stupid."

Odin smiled wryly. "That's the exact reason why you'll come. You are unique, Thyra. You think you know what your magic is, what you are. But there is so much more you are capable of. Your magic is still growing, the storm inside building into something the world has never seen. Lightning is just the beginning, granddaughter! Imagine what you could become with training. Or with Mjolnir in your hands."

He let that hang in the air, a smile reflecting his confidence that Thyra would find the offer too tempting to pass up. He'd baited the hook well, but it was still a hook. Thyra knew only a sucker would take it. If there was such a thing *as too good to be true*, this was it.

Then why am I tempted to swallow it, she thought, *hook, line and sinker?*

"Find your brothers," Odin repeated. "They know where to find me."

"You sound pretty sure that I'm going to take this deal," Thyra said defensively.

Odin's smile widened. "You will. Because you're just like me. You're a lion, not a sheep."

Thyra's stomach twisted into a knot in response to that statement. She wasn't anything like Odin. . .was she?

She didn't get a chance to consider the question more. The world began to shift around her and she felt her body beckoning. Just before she was pulled back into reality she heard Odin say, "I will see you soon, granddaughter."

Chapter 16

Ivan hurried past the secretary in the hall, ignoring her protests about Gunnar being on a call with the Board of Directors. Any other time, that would have made him pause. Not today. Gunnar would want to hear what Ivan had to say.

Ivan slipped into the office, closing the door behind him quietly. Gunnar gave him a brief, chilling look before turning back to a TV screen showing the faces of the twelve members of the Board.

"I promise you that the Odin Initiative is viable, and close to implementation," Gunnar said.

"When?" one of the faces on the screen asked.

"By the quarter's end," Gunnar responded smoothly. "Our North American operations will be first. European holdings will follow shortly thereafter. By the first quarter of next year we will be seeing revenues flowing in."

Ivan moved into Gunnar's line of sight and motioned that he had something urgent to share. Gunnar glared at him for the repeated interruption, but Ivan made an insistent motion. Gunnar's eyes narrowed, this time with a hint of curiosity.

"Is there something we're keeping you from?"

Gunnar refocused on the TV, a suave smile slipping onto his face. "Perhaps. I understand how busy you all are and I value your time, but I fear I must cut our call short. It seems something urgent has come up that needs my immediate attention."

"Give it to one of your Vice Presidents, then. We have questions that *you* need to answer."

"Unfortunately, those questions will have to wait until our next meeting," Gunnar said. "Or, if you prefer, I'm willing to answer any questions you have personally, either face to face or by phone. But for now, I must respectfully excuse myself."

"This doesn't reflect well on your leadership, Gunnar. We've been patient to this point and have tried to respect your autonomy, even when your plans have repeatedly shown little to no fruit. That won't always be the case. You'd be wise to remember that we hold your fate in our hands. If we feel the Muspel Corporation is no longer safe under your leadership, we will find someone else to lead this company."

Gunnar's eyes flashed in anger at the threat. "That would be a mistake. Especially when we are so close to changing the entire landscape of the energy sector."

"So you say, but we've still yet to see any proof that your vision is anything more than a daydream."

Gunnar's eyes flashed again. "I will give you proof soon enough. The Odin Initiative *will* change the world. Don't make the mistake of jettisoning yourselves into the rough oceans when we're so close to fertile shores."

"It won't be us that gets cast off. It will be *you* if you continue to stall. Deliver on the Odin Initiative, or your time as CEO will quickly come to an end."

"We'll see," Gunnar said. He tapped a button and ended the call before any of the talking faces could get in another word. He cursed loudly. "Those pompous fools forget themselves! Questioning me? I could make each of them disappear with a snap of my fingers. They think they can force me out of *my* company? They will all meet their end before I let that happen." He exhaled heavily and turned on Ivan. "You had better have a good reason for interrupting that call. I have enough pressure from the Board without putting them off like that."

"I think you'll want to hear this," Ivan said. He approached the desk and slid his phone towards Gunnar. He pushed a button to put the call on speakerphone. "He can hear you now."

"*Ah, good,*" a man's voice purred. "*It's good to finally speak to the man behind the shadowy empire trying to leverage magic for it's own use.*"

Gunnar managed to laugh off the accusation. "What is this? Magic? I think you have the wrong company."

"*Let's not waste the time we have, Gunnar,*" the man on the phone said. "*I know who you are, and I know what your company really does.*"

Gunnar felt a tingle of recognition, but he couldn't place the voice. "Who is this?"

"*Someone with information,*" the voice answered. "*You've been searching for someone. A girl, if I'm not mistaken.*"

"I'm not going to answer that," Gunnar scoffed. He looked at Ivan. "What is this all about? I don't have time for this."

"Hear him out," Ivan insisted.

"*Listen to your man,*" the voice said. "*You should be asking, how did I get this number? How did I know that if I said the right words, your man would come running? How do I know that you're trying to manipulate magic for your own gain? Those are the questions you should be asking. The possibilities should make you nervous.*"

Gunnar was asking himself those questions, and the answers did make him nervous. He felt his confidence waver. "Is this some kind of extortion? It won't work if it is."

"*No, nothing like that,*" the voice replied. "*I simply tire of watching the cat and mouse game you are playing. The cat chases the mouse, the mouse proves to have teeth, and now they both are licking their wounds. Some might find it entertaining, but not me. I want to speed things along, for the*" *mutual benefit of all players."*

"I'm not sure what game you're referring to."

"Yes, you do." Whoever was on the other end of the line sighed. *"Let me state my business clearly—I know the location of Thyra Ariksen and her mother."*

"Who?"

The voice tsked on the other end of the line. *"If I didn't make myself clear, let me say it again—I am not playing a game, Gunnar. Neither should you. We can go back and forth, you feign disbelief, perhaps try to bluff to get the upper hand while I do the same. Or we can just cut to the end. It's your choice."*

Gunnar weighed his words carefully. "If you know about Thyra, then you must know about what she is."

"I do. I know everything."

Gunnar wondered what "everything" meant. Since Baldur had wormed his way into the Muspel Corporation networks it had become all too clear that there were too many ways a leak could form. He had spent months attempting to close all the holes he could find, but he wasn't naive enough to think every crack was sealed tight. Was this another one that they'd failed to detect and close off?

"That kind of information doesn't come free, I'm sure." Gunnar tapped his fingers on his desk. "What's your price?"

"No price, not today," the voice responded. *"There will be one when I'm ready, but for now all I require is a promise be made."*

"I'm not going to make a promise to an extortionist over the phone," Gunnar stated.

"You're mistaken. I don't want a promise from you. I'm the one making a promise to you."

"Is that so?" Gunnar laughed grimly. "And what kind of promise are you going to make?"

"First, since I want to make sure you understand that I act in good faith,

the information you so desperately crave," the voice said. *"Have your men look closer at a small trailer park on the northwest side of a place called Blackfoot, Idaho. I know you have the technology to accomplish this, so I won't waste time giving any more details than that. You'll find what you're looking for."*

Gunnar snapped and Ivan pulled a second phone from his jacket and placed a call. He muttered something quickly and hung up.

"No doubt you're already moving on this information," the voice said, again sending a tingle of recognition through Gunnar. *"Now, that you are well on your way to finding Thyra, I'll deliver my promise. We met once, Gunnar Olafsson, and conditions led to a difficult parting. We will meet again, very soon, and I promise that the result will be very different. You have something of mine, and I will have it back."*

Gunnar's mind raced trying to process the implied threat and who was behind it. He didn't keep a list of people he might have offended over the years, but if he did it would be long. Still, whoever was on the other end of the line knew about magic. That cut the list down drastically, but not enough for him to even begin to guess who he was dealing with. In his centuries of fighting against or collecting items of magic he'd managed to make enemies of many people. Most he had sent to the next life, but he wasn't foolish enough to believe he had eliminated them all.

"That sounds like a threat. I don't take kindly to being threatened."

A cold chuckle from the phone sent a shiver down Gunnar's spine. *"Call it what you will, but I meant every word. I will see you soon. Until then, don't disappoint me by botching your attempt to capture Thyra."*

The line went dead, leaving behind a deathly quiet. Gunnar ground his teeth together, his eyes boring a hole through the phone on his desk.

"We tried tracing the call," Ivan offered. "It pinged in the western part of Ohio, but there was no information on who it belonged to.

It was a burner phone, the sim card bought in one place, the device bought in another."

Gunnar had figured as much, but it still turned the heat up on his temper. "Do you think his information is correct?"

Ivan's second phone began to buzz in his hand. He answered it and fired off a quick exchange before looking at Gunnar and nodding. "We found them!"

Gunnar's heartbeat quickened. "How soon can we have boots on the ground?"

"Six hours," Ivan answered.

"Do it," Gunnar said. "I want you to take care of this personally, Ivan. And this time, failure is not an option."

Chapter 17

"What are you thinking about, Sparks?"

Thyra blinked, surfacing from the stormy depths of her mind, and looked at the dwarf. It was late, but Thyra couldn't sleep. Nothing she'd tried could quiet her mind after her dream of Odin the night before. "What do you mean?"

"You're unusually quiet," Asiri said. "Too quiet, by my reckoning. Something's on your mind."

"Nothing's on my mind," Thyra said defensively.

"Then why are you awake at this hour," Asiri growled, "staring out the window at a gravel road like you're waiting for a lost puppy to come back?"

Thyra shrugged. "Just couldn't sleep."

"Uh-huh." Asiri scoffed. "Girl, I may be a crusty, old dwarf, but I'm not blind. You've had a hot coal under your backside for months. It's only been a matter of time before your seat got too hot. From the look on your face, I think that it finally has."

Thyra rolled her eyes. "I swear, sometimes you don't make any sense. Hot coal? I don't even know what that means."

Asiri grunted. "That's because you're still in denial."

"Denial about what?"

"That you're thinking about throwing caution to the wind and going after the hammer."

"I am not!" Thyra said. Judging by the way Asiri cocked an eyebrow, her denial had been a little too emphatic to be believable.

"If you say so," Asiri said, looking away. "I can tell you've made up your choice. I just can't decide which way you're leaning—doing it on your own or going with your two murderous brothers?"

Asiri's unvoiced judgments made Thyra fidget in annoyance. "What about you?"

"I don't have murderous brothers," Asiri quipped.

"That's not what I mean," Thyra grumbled. "What are you doing awake?"

Asiri sniffed. "I'm a dwarf! I know you are still green, but I thought you would have noticed by now that I don't need to sleep like you humans. A few hours of here and there is more than enough to keep me going. I can even sleep on my feet if I have to."

"If that's the case," Thyra muttered, "what are you doing out of your forge? Don't you have a *deadline* to meet?"

Thyra realized her words had more bite to them than she intended, but the dwarf had thick skin. True to expectations, Asiri's mouth curled up at the corners and she cocked an eyebrow in Thyra's direction. "I finished what I was working on. Took me two days of working without stopping other than to eat a few bites. Decided to make a brief appearance topside in order to show off a bit." She tossed a bundle of gray cloth onto Thyra's lap. "I know it isn't very fashion forward, but I prioritized function over looks."

Thyra held up a long-sleeved shirt made from a fabric she couldn't quite figure out. It was heavy in her hands and had a slight rigidity. Upon closer inspection, she thought she could see a pattern in the cloth that formed small individual sections. Those sections reflected the light in a way that made Thyra think of scales on a snake.

"You're looking at something that might save your life one day," Asiri explained. "My ancestors made brilliant suits of armor for the Aesir.

Ones not even a dragon's jaws could tear apart. While not as flashy, this will protect you from most things that come your way without sacrificing your mobility or drawing undue attention to yourself."

Thyra's eyebrows shot up. "This is armor?"

"Were you hoping for a suit of plate and mail?" Asiri grumbled. "I'm sure you'd be quite the sight dancing with the boys at your senior prom."

Thyra smirked ruefully despite herself. "I don't think I'll be doing any dancing with the boys any time soon."

"But I can guarantee that you'll be *dancing* with someone at some point soon," Asiri said. "This will keep you alive long enough to at least throw some lightning back their way. Now, let's see how it fits."

Thyra pulled the armor on over her t-shirt and was pleased to find it fit her like a glove. She stood up and twisted back and forth, windmilling her arms around. The shirt, despite it's weight, moved well and didn't feel cumbersome in the least. "This is amazing."

Before Thyra could react, a knife appeared in Asiri's hand. It flashed for Thyra's middle, slashing across her stomach in an arc that should have disemboweled her. When Thyra got over her shock at being attacked by Asiri, she took measure of the damage she was sure she'd suffered. But she felt nothing. She looked down at her abdomen, but there wasn't even a scratch on the fabric of the shirt.

"What was that for?"

"It will stop a bullet better than anything besides two-inch steel plate," Asiri said with a triumphant smile. "Even better, it should defend you against weak magic or anything resembling it. Including those atrocities the Muspel Corporation arms its thugs with."

Thyra exhaled and eyed Asiri warily. "You could have shown me that a different way! Or warned me first."

"What good would that have done?" Asiri scoffed. "Now you know for sure that it works."

"I wish that hadn't involved you trying to slice me open," Thyra snapped.

Asiri ignored her. "Now, this isn't a full set of armor, so don't get careless, Sparks. I didn't have time to create something for your legs, and your head will just have to wait until I come up with an idea less conspicuous than a winged helmet. I figured that could wait since your head is so hard as it is."

Thyra rolled her eyes, but didn't fire off a comeback. She understood the significance of the gift and the reason behind why Asiri had spent so much time locked away in her forge. She nodded in gratitude. "Thank you. This is really amazing."

Asiri waved the compliment off. "There's going to be goons trying to take you down at every turn. Your two brothers included. What kind of friend would I be if I didn't do my best to keep you in one piece?"

Thyra couldn't help but ask, "Can this withstand their magic?"

Asiri pursed her lips thoughtfully and took her time in answering. "It'll help, but I wouldn't stand still and let them have several attempts. Even the best armor will fail sooner or later." Asiri shrugged. "That just means you'll just have to watch your back when you go."

"Go where?"

"With those two goons that happen to share blood with you."

"I told you, I'm not going with them."

"You keep saying the words," Asiri said, "but I don't think you believe yourself."

Thyra's eyes narrowed. "You really think I'm stupid enough to go with them?"

Asiri hesitated, the lines in her face growing deeper and her shoulders sagging like a weight had settled on them. "I think your choices aren't good either way, Sparks."

It was a dire statement. One that Thyra couldn't help but agree with. She didn't like any of the options she'd been presented with and the last two days had been fruitless in the way of coming up with a plan that Sif would accept. Thyra had to choose, and she needed to do it before someone else decided for her.

"Ah, I almost forgot." Asiri reached into a pocket and pulled out a key fob. She held it out to Thyra. "You will need this more than me."

Thyra took the fob, immediately recognizing it. "This is to your Camaro."

Asiri nodded. "That's right. I can't use it. You can."

Thyra shook her head and held the fob out to Asiri. "I can't accept this."

"Sure you can," Asiri said, waving Thyra's hand away. "Did you think I was going to drive it?" Asiri snorted. "It's been meant for you ever since we picked it up on the way back from Wisconsin! Best of all, I made some modifications to the car to make it easier for you to charge it on the move. I'm sure you're smart enough to figure it out."

"Asiri, no! This is too much. It's your car."

Asiri reached up and closed Thyra's hand around the fob. "Humor me, Sparks. I'm old. I don't think I want to get much older. Someone needs to drive her, and I mean that to be you." Asiri sighed, her eyes softening in a way Thyra had never witnessed from the dwarf. For a brief moment, Asiri's crusty exterior fell away and she looked tired. "I spent centuries thinking I didn't need anyone else. Didn't want to care about anyone else! These past few months have proved I was lying to myself. Being here, with you and your mom, has been the best gift I could ever receive. Now, its my turn to repay it by giving you a gift."

Asiri patted Thyra's fist with a tenderness that seemed out of place coming from her calloused, rough hands. Thyra finally nodded weakly. A relieved smile crossed the dwarf's face and she sighed, "Good."

The moment was interrupted by the door to the trailer opening suddenly, admitting Vidar and Sif. From the expressions on their faces, their time spent keeping watch was taking its toll.

In the blink of an eye Asiri's crusty exterior jumped back to the surface to greet Vidar and Sif. "What news from the bushes and the trees? The squirrels declare war on the field mice?"

"It's quiet," Sif said. "It feels like nothing is moving out there."

Asiri frowned. "And that has you worried?"

Sif nodded. "They are out there. The fact that everything feels so dead only makes me think they're just beyond the shadows waiting to pounce."

Thyra wondered which "they" her mom was referring to. Modi and Magni? Hela and Fenrir? Baldur? Olafsson and the Muspel Corporation? The people that Sif had been forced to turn aside time and time again? The list seemed to be growing longer every day.

"Well, maybe I can help brighten your mood," Asiri said. She tossed bundles like the one she gave to Thyra to Sif and Vidar. "As requested, a little extra protection."

Sif unrolled the shirt and pulled out a silver band that had been inside. She snapped the band around her wrist and gave it a quick examination. "Just like my spear?"

Asiri nodded. "They work in unison. Extend your spear and the band will respond as well."

Sif's spear extended in her right had and a round shield grew from the band on her left arm almost as quick. She studied it for a moment before nodding in satisfaction. "Good. Thank you."

Vidar grunted with the effort of putting on his shirt. "It's a bit tight."

"That's because your muscles are too big," Asiri retorted. "Stop flexing! You're going to hurt yourself."

"I'm not flexing," Vidar grumbled. "Couldn't you have made it a little less snug?"

"Couldn't you have not had those last four protein shakes?" Asiri snapped. She crossed her arms over her chest. "You can give it back to me and I'll make some alterations, but it won't be ready for day a day or two. It's up to you, big boy."

Vidar flexed one arm and grimaced. "It'll do for now. What about the other thing I asked you to work on?"

Asiri smiled. "It was a fun distraction. One that I made quick work of. They will be ready for you when you need them."

"Good." Vidar turned to Sif. "I'm going back out."

"To do what?" Sif questioned.

"Scratch an itch."

Sif didn't look pleased, but she didn't try to stop him. "Be careful."

"And don't trip over anything in the dark," Asiri said to his back. "You'll set off every earthquake meter for hundreds of miles in every direction." Vidar waved over his shoulder with one hand, but let the door closing do the talking for him. Asiri cackled and gave Thyra a smirk. "Can you imagine him falling on his face? Probably leave a crater the size of a bus in the ground!"

Thyra smirked, but didn't share in the laughter. She was watching her mom and the way she was twisting the band on her wrist. Something was bothering Sif more than she wanted to let on.

Asiri read Sif's mood the same way. "You think there will be trouble tonight?"

Sif exhaled. "There's a feeling in the air. Like a threat closing in from every side."

"You know that feeling better than most," Asiri commented, her expression turning grim.

"We still have until tomorrow to answer Modi and Magni," Thyra said.

Sif frowned. "It isn't Modi and Magni that worry me right now."

Asiri stood up. "I'll make sure my forge is ready to go. Just in case."

She disappeared down the hall, leaving Thyra and Sif alone in the front room. They sat in awkward silence for what felt like an eternity to Thyra—Sif distractedly spinning the band on her wrist and Thyra trying to guess what was on her mom's mind—until Asiri returned with the metal case that housed her forge. The dwarf sat down at the table and began tinkering with her watch.

The silence was interrupted by a sound similar to that of a bell being rung repeatedly outside. Sif was the first to react, cocking her head towards the sound. She jumped to her feet and looked out the window on the back door.

"What is it?" Thyra asked.

Sif frowned. "Trouble."

Sif stood up from the table. "What kind of trouble?"

Her question was answered by a massive crash outside that shook the entire trailer. Sif jumped away from the window, her spear extending in one hand and a circular shield appearing on her other arm. "Out the front door! Run!"

"What's going on?" Thyra demanded.

Sif turned, a warning on her lips, but before she could speak the back wall of the trailer exploded.

*****

The ringing in Vidar's ears was deafening. The night had taken on an eerie orange glow and a smell that pulled at memories long dormant inside him. Memories of pain, death, and destruction. Memories he cringed away from. Memories that followed him and then washed over him in a wave.

Slowly, he pushed himself free of the rubble that covered him and stood. Every part of his body screamed out in pain from the force of the explosion. His skin was tight with burns from the heat of the fireball that lit up the sky just before the concussion blew him backwards. Nothing felt broken, though.

The trailer was a wreckage almost torn in two by the explosion and blazed with several fires. Vidar's stomach sank. He tried not to think about the chances of survival after a blast like that but knew they were next to none. His attempt to warn them hadn't come in time.

Pushing his emotions down, Vidar turned and looked for the threat he knew was lingering in the shadows. He didn't have to wait long. Like a villain from a bad movie, a man encased in a metal exoskeleton stepped out into the light. Vidar recognized him vaguely as Gunnar Olafsson's giant Russian from the abandoned building in Wisconsin a few months before.

"Good, you're still alive," the big brute said with a twisted smile. "My name is Ivan. I've been hoping the two of us would get a chance to speak. You put several of my men in the hospital. A few of them will never recover."

"Those roid-ragers were yours?" Vidar spat a glob of dark blood onto the ground. "It seems Gunnar has a type. Big muscles, little brains."

Ivan sneered. "You speak big words for someone who is about to die."

Vidar wanted nothing more than to unleash the fury he felt inside. Men like Ivan grooved off of being the biggest and baddest everywhere they went. They all shared a personality flaw—sensitive egos. Prick their egos and they'd make mistakes. Vidar knew how to bruise Ivan's. "I can use smaller ones. Or maybe you've exhausted your words for the day. Should I grunt instead?"

Ivan's face contorted in rage before he reached up and lowered a metal visor into place. When he spoke, his voice took on a deep, robotic drone. "Let's see how strong you really are."

The Russian closed the distance between them faster than Vidar thought possible and delivered a haymaker that lifted Vidar off his feet. It felt like getting hit by a freight train going full speed. Vidar found himself on his back staring up at the night sky in confusion, struggling to maintain consciousness. Only a warning bell ringing in his head kept him from slipping away into the black. Relying on a base instinct, he rolled to the side just in time to avoid being smashed by the trailer park's dumpster.

"You're no god!" Ivan yelled. He swatted the dumpster aside like it was a feather. He reached down and lifted Vidar off the ground with one hand and drove his other fist into Vidar's face with bone-crunching force. "After tonight, I will be called 'god-killer' and no one will remember your name!"

Vidar tried to break free of Ivan's grip, but his effort only gave Ivan enough space to deliver a vicious kick that sent Vidar hurtling through the air. He landed with a dull thud, the remaining air in his lungs escaping in a pained wheeze. A wave of panic mixed with the pain, threatening to overcome his senses. He had never been hit this hard before. He wasn't sure if he could withstand many more blows like the ones Ivan was dishing out.

"Look at you!" Ivan sneered. "You're pathetic!"

Vidar rolled to put space between them. This time Ivan didn't follow. Vidar pushed himself to his feet and made a hasty retreat. Ivan laughed, clearly assuming he had Vidar beat. If he had pressed his attack he might have, but he had paused to gloat, giving Vidar time to catch his breath and fight through his shock. That was Ivan's second mistake.

The first was attacking Vidar's family.

Vidar reversed direction and lurched forward, his magically enhanced shoes granting him speed even the exoskeleton Ivan wore couldn't match. Before the big Russian could react Vidar was on him, his arms wrapping around Ivan's middle and clamping down. Legs churning, Vidar drove the Russian backwards and slammed him against the dumpster. Ivan rebounded off the dumpster only to catch a punch that snapped his head back wickedly and sent a crack down the middle of the metal visor.

Vidar took a step back, confident that Ivan was stunned at the very least. That was a mistake. His only warning was the smile on Ivan's face just before the Russian's foot shoot out. The kick sent Vidar skipping across the ground for thirty feet before he came to a rolling stop. He tried to reach his feet, but Ivan was on him in a flash, grabbing Vidar by the shirt and lifting him off the ground. The ground came rushing up to meet him once, twice, and then a third time. Ivan pivoted and Vidar was suddenly flying through the air towards a copse of trees that ran along the back of the trailer park. Vidar ricocheted off one tree trunk and hit a second full on, the force of his body enough to break the two-foot thick trunk in half. He felt several ribs pop immediately and a searing pain that raced up from his left leg. As much as his body screamed out in pain, he knew that if he stayed down Ivan would not hesitate to finish him off. Vidar rose up on his hands and knees, coughing raggedly from the effort. He wiped his mouth with the back of his hand and it came away streaked in dark blood. Grimacing, he leaned put one hand on the trunk of tree and stood up.

"Vidar? You still alive?" Ivan called out. He sauntered closer, laughing grimly. "Ah, there you are. Good. I would have been very disappointed if that was all the fight you had in you."

"Still plenty of fight left," Vidar tried to sound confident, but his words came out in a rasp.

Ivan smiled in response to Vidar's attempt at bravado. "How the tables have turned. I've heard the stories about you. If they were true, they aren't anymore. Now I am the god. Proving again that man and science defeats magic."

Vidar sneered, but even that small sign of emotion was enough to almost double him over in pain.

"You're looking shaky," Ivan said in a mocking voice. "This age has made you soft."

Vidar leaned back against what was left of the tree trunk. When he spoke, his voice was little more than a whisper, "You're right. If I was the man I used to be, you'd be dead by now."

"So you say," Ivan said, taking another step closer. "I think you're too weak to do it. If you ever were. After I finish you off, I'm going to find that woman and cut her the way she cut me. Maybe then I'll let her die. Then I'll take the girl back to my boss and let him drain her of her magic. He has plans for her. Endless clean energy, all generated from a dark room. A very, very dark room with her strung up in the center of it."

A growl escaped Vidar's lips in response to that image. "I won't let you take them."

"How do you think you're going to stop me?" Ivan barked a laugh. "If they're even still alive that is. After that explosion, I'd be surprised if there is anything left of them. My boss won't be happy to lose out on the girl's potential, but he will be glad to be rid of all of you. He'll reward me when I throw your bodies at his feet."

Vidar didn't answer. He was too busy trying to judge the distance between the two of them. He just needed Ivan to take one more step. Vidar pushed himself up from the trunk and set his feet. The big Russian, thinking Vidar was still defenseless, obliged. With a roar, Vidar grabbed the trunk and tensed every muscle in his body. The roots resisted the pull for a brief moment before giving way with a loud snap, a ball of dark earth coming loose along with the trunk. Ivan's eyes went wide as the earthen-club went overhead and then slammed down on top of him. His rage unleashed, Vidar swung it two more times, the force of each blow shaking the ground underfoot.

Vidar tossed the tree aside with a grunt and looked down at Ivan. He was still alive, but judging by his state, maybe he would have been better off dead. The Russian had tried to stop the blow by crossing his arms overhead, but the exoskeleton had failed in the face of the one-ton hammer. Both arms were a broken, bloody mess of muscle and twisted metal. One leg was twisted out to the side at an unnatural angle. The chest piece had caved inward and was making it hard for Ivan to breathe. To his credit, the Russian was still struggling to move, but his muscles were too weak to maneuver the damaged exoskeleton.

There was a time when Vidar would have walked away and let Ivan die a slow, agonizing death. Ivan *deserved* that death for what he had done tonight. But as much as Vidar wanted to walk away, he couldn't. It didn't mean Ivan deserved a quick end, though.

Bending down, Vidar gripped the front of the exoskeleton with both hands and tore the chest piece in half. Ivan sucked in a ragged breath then coughed hoarsely. He looked up at Vidar and gave him a bloody, defiant smile. "I was right. You're too weak to do it."

"That's because you deserve to live," Vidar said.

Ivan tried to speak, but coughed instead. His eyes asked the question that he couldn't find the words to voice.

"I'm not going to kill you," Vidar said, kneeling down beside the Russian, "but that isn't a mercy. Finishing you would be. If your injuries don't kill you before the end of the night then you'll be a broken shell of what you used to be. Your life as you know it ended tonight." Vidar lifted Ivan into a sitting position and propped him up. "I'll leave you to whatever you have left of it."

Ivan's eyes filled with hate, but Vidar was past caring. He had already put all thought about the big Russian out of his mind. He needed to find Sif, Thyra, and Asiri. He stumbled towards the trailer, leaving Ivan's broken body to whatever fate claimed him.

The high-pitched sound of the rifles were the only warning Vidar had before he felt the sting of their fire. He dove behind a tree and pressed against it with a grunt. The pain that shot through him forced him to breathe in short, fast breaths. Grimacing, he took a quick look around the tree. A handful of dark-clad men were moving in his direction, rifles held ready, while another thirty dark-clad men were moving towards the burnt husk of the trailer. Too many for him to handle in his current state. Asiri's armor had served well in deflecting the first few shots from those rifles, but only because he had caught them by surprise and only a handful had managed to get off a shot at him.

Another quick glance confirmed that besides the five cautiously approaching his cover, Ivan's men were still moving on trailer. From the way they were advancing, they seemed to think there was a chance of survivors. That or Olafsson wanted to make sure this time they had proof of death. If someone had somehow survived the blast they'd need Vidar's help. And if they hadn't survived, there was no way that Vidar was going to let Ivan's men take the bodies of people he cared for.

Steeling his will against the pain he knew was coming, Vidar bunched his legs and set his back against the tree trunk. A primal scream escaped his lips as he pressed against the trunk with everything he had. The tree gave way with a thunderous crack. The five men froze for a split second before attempting to dive out of the way, but were caught by the branches as it fell on top of them.

Vidar came under fire almost immediately. He dove behind the fallen tree. Sharp pains in his back told him that he had been hit at least twice, each feeling like he'd been kicked by a mule. Thankfully, Asiri's armor held. Splinters filled the air as the rifle fire chewed through the tree trunk like a buzz saw. He wouldn't be able stay put for long before those projectiles would reach him. No doubt Ivan's men were working on flanking him while a few kept him pinned down. Once they did, they'd have a clear shot and he'd have nowhere to hide.

Just as quick as the rifle fire started, it stopped. At least in his direction. He crawled a few feet from his original position and then peaked from behind his cover. Ivan's men were all turned in the opposite direction, firing back towards the trailer. Three of those that were moving to flank Vidar's position were down on the ground. A streak of silver in the shadows dropped two more, and the rifle fire lit up the night in that direction. A spear whistled through the night and took another two that were standing too close to each other. That spear could only mean one thing—*Sif*!

Gathering his strength, Vidar rose to his feet and wrapped his arms around the tree trunk. Straining, he lifted it off the ground and surged out into the open behind the trailer. A few of Ivan's men turned to face him, but Vidar swung the tree before they could get a shot off. The branches swept them aside like a giant, forty-foot, five-ton brush. Vidar reversed his momentum and swung into the next group. He attempted one more sweep back the other direction, but his injured leg gave away beneath the weight. He released the tree with a grunt, letting it crash to the ground and roll another twenty feet before coming to a stop.

Ten of Ivan's men were still standing, and half of them leveled their rifles in his direction. Vidar dove towards the only cover he could see—the garbage dumpster—and crouched behind it. The ground was ripped up behind him by rifle fire and several shots pinged against the dumpster. He waited, counting the shots, until he could hear footsteps nearby. He rose to his feet and kicked the dumpster with his good leg, sending it hurtling across the ground and into two men. With a roar, Vidar charged to his left and grabbed the nearest dark-clad man and swung him into another. He felt the sharp ache as he was struck in the back by a rifle shot, but shrugged off the pain and leapt toward the man who had fired it. He grabbed the rifle with one hand and snapped it in half. The man's eyes went wide just before Vidar's other hand closed on the front of his tactical vest. With a flick of his arm, Vidar sent his assailant flying through the air into the darkness.

Huffing with pain and rage, Vidar scanned the field for any more of Ivan's men. None were left standing. Sif, her golden hair streaked with soot, strode in his direction. Her expression was grim as she approached the two men Vidar had smashed into each other. Even fueled by his own rage, Vidar recognized the look in his sister's eyes as she passed by. "Sif, don't—"

Sif's spear rose and fell twice in quick succession. The deed done, her shoulders sagged like the weight of the world had just settled on her shoulders. She turned and looked at him, her eyes dancing in the light of the fire. Her mask slipped suddenly, her eyes brimming with tears. Her voice quivered when she spoke. "They killed her, Vidar. She's dead!"

Chapter 18

Baldur ushered Bragi down the hall with a hand beneath the arm. The old man had his arms wrapped around himself, shivering from either cold or from weakness—Baldur wasn't sure. He didn't care. Nor did he care about the stares the followed their passing. He knew what the old man looked like, he had seen the alarmed stares that followed them, but Bragi's physical appearance was not a concern. Baldur's mind was occupied with more important things than the old man's well-being at the moment.

The whispers that had reached his ears were alarming. It was Wisconsin all over again, and the details were still vague. What he did know troubled him—a trailer destroyed, bodies strewn everywhere, and eyewitness reports that sounded like something out of a fantasy.

Or a nightmare.

Baldur had a feeling that the rumors were only scratching the surface. He feared the truth was even worse. One look at Gunnar Olafsson's face would tell him whether he was right or not.

Gunnar's secretary didn't even try to stop him as he walked by her desk. She made a quick call and then occupied herself with whatever was on her screen. From the gloomy expression on her face, she looked like she was thinking it might be time to update her resume.

Baldur opened the door and held it open for Bragi and Amara. He closed it softly behind them and engaged the lock with a click.

Turning slowly, he noticed the absence of Ivan. Another confirmation of his suspicions.

Gunnar was standing behind his desk with his hands clasped behind his back, frowning at Bragi. "Are you sure he's well? He looks like he's on death's doorstep."

"He's as fit as can be, considering what he's gone through," Baldur said. He took a seat next to Bragi and tapped on the arms of the chair. "Unlike two dozen of your men in Idaho. Although, that number depends on the source. Some say a handful, others up to fifty." He waited for Gunnar to react. "What do you know about this? And please, don't try to lie to me."

Gunnar grimaced, but didn't dodge the question. "We received information yesterday."

Baldur's eyebrow shot up. "What kind of information?"

"The whereabouts of Thyra Ariksen and her mother."

Baldur was immediately suspicious. "How did you come by this information?"

Gunnar turned and looked out the window. "An anonymous source."

Baldur turned to Amara and shared a disbelieving look with her. "An *anonymous* source?" She shook her head gravely, clearly sharing in his disdain. He rolled his eyes back to Gunnar. "Did you ever stop to consider that this anonymous source might be sending your men into a trap?"

"It wasn't a trap," Gunnar snapped over his shoulder.

"From what I've heard," Baldur replied, "whatever you had planned wasn't a success."

"That's yet to be determined," Gunnar said defensively.

Baldur smiled ruefully in response to Gunnar's stubbornness. "Tell me then, where is Ivan right now?"

"He's away on assignment."

"Which I feel safe in guessing was a very special assignment in Idaho," Baldur muttered. "You're right if you were about to say that details are still few and anything but definitive. But judging by what I've heard, I don't think coming details are going to shine a better light on what occurred. Something must have gone wrong with this *assignment*. So, I will ask one more time—what happened?"

Gunnar exhaled heavily, his shoulders sagging. "There was a complication."

"Named Vidar, if I'm not mistaken," Baldur said. Gunnar's expression was enough to verify Baldur's guess. "An eyewitness said he saw two men fighting. Throwing a dumpster around like a feather, tearing trees right out of the ground—impossible feats. One even swung a fifty-foot tree like a giant fly swatter. That sounds like Vidar to me." He paused and leaned forward. "The other one, the one in the *metal shell*, sounds like Ivan. The whispers are that he did not come out the victor."

Gunnar fell quiet. Baldur tapped his fingers on the top of the desk as he considered what that meant. He had never liked the Russian, so he wouldn't be sad if the rumors were true, but his demise had other troubling connotations. Vidar coming back to the surface at Thyra's side was a problem. A problem that could fester quickly if it wasn't handled correctly.

How to handle the problem was a problem in itself. Turning Vidar was out of the question, but was there a chance that what happened in Idaho could be exploited to Baldur's gain? Perhaps. Vidar was a god, but he was ruled by his passions and the ghosts of his past. Baldur glanced at Bragi and considered what part the old man's magic could play in manipulating Vidar. It had a remote possibility of success at best, but Baldur was willing to entertain it.

His contemplation didn't go unnoticed by Gunnar. "What are you thinking about?"

"Nothing pertinent to the task at hand." Baldur cleared his throat and sat back. "I thought we were working towards becoming partners, Gunnar. Yet you went after Thyra, even when I told you to leave her alone. Why?"

"I told you," Gunnar snapped, "we received actionable information that we could not pass up."

"And now you've complicated our situation worse than before," Baldur said. "How long before the connection is made between those men and your company?"

Gunnar shook his head. "There won't be a connection. We took precautions after Wisconsin. None of the men working under the Odin Initiative were listed as employees of the Muspel Corporation as of a month ago."

"Even Ivan?"

Gunnar flinched. He schooled his emotions, but not quick enough. "That won't be a problem. We'll handle it the same way we handled Wisconsin."

Baldur frowned. "Which was a monumental mess. Even if covering it up was a possibility, I don't think you would be able to silence it fast enough. You've heard what is being said. There are too many witnesses, too many stories that cannot be explained away. If a connection is made to you, there will be no wriggling out of it like a snake shedding a layer of skin. You will have to answer for what happened."

Gunnar shrugged. "What do you want me to say? We saw an opportunity and we took it."

"Just because you knew where she was did not mean you should act!" Baldur growled. He shook his head in frustration. "If I thought we needed to act, I would have told you where they were myself."

Gunnar's eyes went wide in disbelief. "What? You knew?"

Baldur sighed heavily. "Of course I did. I've known where the girl and her mom have been for weeks, but I at least at the brains to realize that a full-on attack would do more damage than good!"

"How?" Gunnar asked in a voice dripping with anger. "How did you know where they were?"

"I watched and listened," Baldur snapped. "You could have known too, if you used what's between your ears rather than relying on technology to do everything for you.

"What are you talking about?" Gunnar hissed. "I've been using every method available to man to look for them. Until yesterday, there had been no clues!"

"Magic like Thyra's leaves signs for anyone who knows what to look for. And I did!" Baldur took a moment to calm down. He was on the verge of unleashing his disappointment in an unhealthy way. He couldn't afford to widen the chasm between himself and Gunnar. He needed to bridge it. He put a gentle hand on Bragi's arm. "Tell him, Uncle."

Bragi cringed at the touch, but was unable to resist the compulsion to answer. "Thyra's magic is still. . . growing. Evolving. She calls the storms to her. . .just like they call to her. The storms will follow her. Like. . . two magnets pulling towards each other. All you had to do was look for. . . for the storms!"

Bragi sagged back in his seat, his chest heaving with the effort of answering the question. Baldur gave him another affectionate pat on the arm. "Thank you, Uncle. I know how much pain that caused you." Baldur looked across the desk. "There's your sign, Gunnar. Follow the storms."

"Gibberish," Gunnar snapped. "Spoken by an old, broken man."

"Wisdom, spoken from experience," Baldur corrected. "Once he told me, it all made sense. The signs were all there. This summer has been dry, especially in Idaho. Yet, one city in Idaho has been the recipient of a record number of lightning storms and rainfall over the past month. I'm sure you can guess which one."

Gunnar looked away. The connection was easy to make. "You should have shared this with me."

"I thought we had a plan," Baldur said. "We were supposed to work together to use the summoning stones and access Idunn's garden. Thyra Ariksen was to be left alone while we made the final preparations to assault the garden!"

"That was the plan *you* demanded we follow," Gunnar growled. "I saw an opportunity and took it."

"And put all our work over the last few weeks at risk!" Baldur slapped the desk in front of him. "Do you even realize what you've done? You've sent up a signal fire for the world to see. It may seem small to you, but it is a raging bonfire! Hela has already reintroduced magic to the world and people are talking. They're looking back at what happened in Wisconsin and drawing conclusions. Those conclusions are still far from the truth, but that has worked in our favor for the time being. But now you've given them undeniable proof! People are not going to file this away as some strange occurrence. Nor will they be so quick to accept a narrative you try to concoct. They will know that magic is at play and you're involved somehow!"

"So what?" Gunnar barked. "Even if they do trace it back to my company, they won't act in time to stop what we have planned!"

"I'm not worried about the mortals or what they might do," Baldur snapped.

"No, you're worried that Thyra will finish what she started in Wisconsin!" Gunnar sneered. "She hurt you, and you're scared."

Baldur flinched, but quickly regained his composure. He nodded slowly. "I am. And you should be too. If Thyra survived—"

"She didn't!"

"If she survived," Baldur said over the top of Gunnar, "then she will know who attacked her. You've just kicked a sleeping bear and hung raw meat around your neck! You have given her reason to fight back when she was content to be idle before. She will be coming for you and what you have. "

"What are you talking about?"

"Don't play stupid, Gunnar. It doesn't suit you." Baldur had to take another deep, calming breath to avoid unleashing the full force of his frustrations. "You've managed to protect Mjolnir for this long, Gunnar, but if she comes and succeeds in taking it from you before we can put our plans in motion, you will know fear. She will tear everything you've built down around you!"

"That's all assuming she still draws breath," Gunnar said stubbornly. "I've heard that a female was found among the dead."

"Have they identified it as Thyra?" Baldur questioned. Gunnar opened his mouth to answer than snapped it shut again. Baldur scoffed. "Exactly. Until that time, when we know for sure she is dead, we had better assume she still draws breath and will be looking to even the score."

"She died," Gunnar repeated. "I've seen the pictures. No one could have survived that explosion."

"Then who killed all your men?" Gunnar just stared at him. Baldur threw his hands up in exasperation. "Believe what you will, but I'm warning you—even if she did die, Vidar still is alive. *He* will come for you, and he will tear this place apart until his final breath leaves his lungs. You may be able to stop him, perhaps you even kill him, but there will be no hiding afterwards. The world will demand to know what you are and what you are doing. And Vidar will pale in the face of Sif's rage if you actually managed to kill Thyra. Vidar will tear everything down. Sif will settle for ripping your heart out. Ask yourself—are you ready for that day?"

Gunnar scowled at Baldur, but his anger was a thin mask over the uncertainty beneath. "What do you propose I do then?"

"Quit stalling," Baldur snapped. "We need to access Idunn's garden, and we need to do it before we're surrounded on every side. The mortals will want answers, but their fury will pale in face of what the world of magic will bring against you. Thyra, Vidar, Hela—they are trouble enough, but if I am right, if Odin still lives, we have no time to waste. We cannot let him return to our world. We have enough enemies. One like him will destroy us both."

Gunnar inhaled deeply before nodding. "I understand, and I agree. We must move forward with your plan."

"When?"

"In a week's time."

"No!" Baldur slapped the table emphatically. "You are stalling, and I won't stand for it. You went over my head, and you may think that helps even the score between us, but it doesn't. You must ask yourself, if I walk, where does that leave you? What would you do? Continue the way you were before? Trying to both eliminate and exploit magic?" Baldur shook his head. "No, we've come too far to turn back now. We must act and we must do it sooner, not later. Before Thyra Ariksen and Vidar arrive and begin tearing everything down around you." Baldur took a deep breath. "Now, when can you have everything prepared?"

Gunnar frowned. "Four days from now. I cannot do it before then."

Not soon enough, but it would have to do. "Fine." Baldur sat back and exhaled. "Now, there is one more thing I've learned that you should be made aware of."

Gunnar's expression clouded over. "What secrets have you been hiding this time?"

"Not one I knew about until recently," Baldur said without a hint of defensiveness. He wasn't lying. He hadn't known until Amara had flooded Bragi with enough of her magic to loosen the old man's tongue. He placed a hand on Bragi's shoulder. "Go ahead, Uncle. Tell him about the fail safe Odin put in place to ensure Idunn's compliance."

Bragi shuddered, clearly trying to fight the urge to repeat what he had told Baldur. Like every time before, his will was not enough to resist Amara's magic. He revealed the secret he had been carrying for nearly a millennia for the second time in the past twenty-four hours. When he finished, he sagged in his chair, his breath shallow and rapid.

Gunnar looked like a poleaxed cow. He blinked and then began shaking his head slowly. "That just proves that I was right to tear Odin down. To think he would put such a thing in place. Did he trust no one?"

Baldur could fill volumes with examples of Odin's distrust for everyone around him. What Bragi had told him was just the greatest in a long line of ways the Allfather had been a monster. "Gungnir must be there when we summon Idunn. The summoning stones are one thing, but the spear's presence will ensure our success. Do we have an understanding?"

Gunnar's lips drew together, but he nodded. "It will be there."

"Good. Then I look forward to what we will achieve together in four days." Baldur helped Bragi stand and then turned his weight over to Amara. He turned back to Gunnar and leaned over the desk, tapping the middle with a finger. "You had better hope Thyra Ariksen doesn't arrive before then. If she does, it won't be my head that she's hunting."

Chapter 19

The road was blurry through Thyra's tears as she drove. She wasn't sure where she was, only that she was heading east. She'd been driving for hours, alternating between episodes of tears and shock as she tried to come to grips with running when she felt she should have stayed. How many times would she be forced to run when those she loved were in danger? Worse, and perhaps even more damning, how many times would she choose to run? She felt like a coward for leaving Sif and Vidar behind.

And Asiri.

The image of the dwarf's lifeless body flashed across Thyra's vision, causing her stomach to turn. Nothing came up. Anything that had been in her stomach had been left behind along the highway hours ago. She still had tears, though, and they began to flow freely in response to the memory that played for the thousandth time.

The explosion had rocked the trailer before Thyra could even react to Sif's warning. Time slowed down. The heat was the first thing Thyra felt. A split second before the flames reached her something heavy had barreled into her. Thyra was thrown backwards through the window onto the gravel driveway, a fireball splitting the night and stealing her vision.

She remembered staring up at the stars overhead, her ears ringing, her body numb, and her thoughts lost to a shocked stupor. A soft voice told her to just float away, to stop fighting. All she had to do was close her eyes and go to sleep. It was a tempting invitation.

But as sweet as that invitation had felt, something kept her from embracing it. She felt a repeated tug on her arm, but it took several moments before she finally could summon the strength to even look at what was keeping her from drifting off into the black. Her mom, face red and braid singed black, was dragging her away from the wreckage of the trailer. When Sif saw Thyra's eyes open, she knelt over her, mouth moving with words Thyra couldn't hear.

Something heavy was across her chest. It took several long moments for her to piece together what she was looking at. When it finally sunk in, it felt like a hot knife had been thrust into her gut. She realized what had barreled into her just before the impact of the explosion sent her flying—it had been Asiri. The dwarf had taken the brunt of the explosion, leaving her body burnt and blackened. And motionless. Realization flooded in, washing away the shock that paralyzed Thyra.

To her shame, Thyra had recoiled from Asiri's lifeless body like it was a venomous snake. She had scrambled away, unable to breathe but unable to look away. When she did take a breath, it was only to let out a scream that left her breathless again.

Sif's voice had finally broken through the ringing, begging Thyra to run. Thyra stood like her feet were cemented in place until Sif was forced to drag her away. Numb with shock, Thyra had allowed herself to be led, her eyes locked on Asiri until Sif shoved her into the Camaro and started the engine. She gave several quick commands that Thyra barely heard through her shock.

Her last words, though, still rang in Thyra's ears.

"I'm sorry, sweetheart! You were right. I should have listened. You have to go. I will make sure they don't follow you." Sif's eyes had turned ice cold and she took Thyra by the shoulders with hands that shook with

rage. *"You must make them pay! Get your father's hammer. Drive fast and strike hard. Find Mjolnir and make them pay for what they did tonight! Make them pay for taking Asiri!"*

Those words had echoed through her mind hundreds of times since. *Find Mjolnir. Make them pay.* Resolve had built with each echo of her mom's charge. She had no plan—the adrenaline had wore off and then she had been back to being too shocked to think rationally—but amid the raw emotion she felt, her determination grew rock solid. There was only one path forward, and she was going to walk it.

Taking a deep breath, Thyra let it out slowly. It took several breaths before she was able to stop the tears. She still ached with the rawness of everything that had happened, but the sun's rise brought a measure of clarity. If she was going to follow her mom's instructions then she needed to get control of her situation. That started with figuring out where in the world she was.

A few miles down the road she saw a sign that said she was not far from Denver. Somewhere during the night she had turned south, but at least she was moving in the right direction. She figured that as long as she kept going east she'd find her way to New York at some point.

And that was where she was going. Gunnar Olafsson had attacked her family. His men had killed Asiri. For all Thyra knew, her mom and Vidar could be dead as well. If so, Thyra had nothing left. All of it would have been taken away by Gunnar Olafsson. There was nothing left to do but respond. He would pay for what he had done. He had killed too many. Thyra was going to put a stop to all of it. And she was going to do it with Thor's hammer in hand!

A notification from the car told her that the battery was getting low. Thyra's hand sought out the device Asiri had added to the car and channeled a steady stream of magic into it. Asiri had promised the ability to charge the Camaro on the fly and she had delivered. The rod was positioned near the emergency brake in the center console. Asiri had even gone to the lengths of etching a pair of lightning bolts into the polished surface. Thyra's fingers found the lightning bolts. They were another reminder of Asiri that made her heart ache. Swallowing her grief down, she called her magic up and channeled magic into Asiri's device. The battery gauge steadily rose over the next few minutes until it showed a full charge. Thyra offered up a silent "thanks" to the dwarf for her ingenuity. And for her life.

The dwarf's death weighs heavily on you.

The echo of those words felt like Thyra had been dunked in a tub of ice water. To this point, she had only spoken to Yggdrasil in the dream-state the World Tree pulled her into. Hearing the tree's voice in her head while awake was a completely different and shocking experience. It was so intense that she jerked the wheel and swerved across the lanes of traffic. Luckily, there were no other cars nearby while she rushed to regain control.

Thyra put one hand to her chest and gasped. Her heart was in her throat and swallowing it back down was an effort in itself.

I mourn her death. She was the last of her kind. With her death an aspect of my being dies as well.

Yggdrasil's words were enough to send a wave of anger through Thyra that numbed her grief. Not sure of how this worked, she responded to the World Tree out loud rather than in her head. "Where were you? How could you let this happen?"

I've told you that I don't take a side in the dealings of man. I've given you the tools and the power to do what is necessary. I sent you help in the form of Vidar. What else would you have had me do?

"How about a warning?" Thyra barked.

It wouldn't have changed the outcome.

"A warning could have changed everything!"

Asiri gave her life for you.

"A life you could have saved!"

Arguing the "what ifs" does not do her sacrifice justice. You must focus on what is to come.

"The only thing you're concerned about is yourself," Thyra snapped. She expected Yggdrasil to argue. She was surprised when it didn't.

For the first time in my existence, I am in danger. Baldur and Gunnar Olafsson have seven summoning stones. They will gain access to Idunn's garden, and when they do, the damage they could inflict would be catastrophic.

"To you, is what you mean," Thyra said.

Yes, to me. But also to the world. You seem to still be struggling to understand that my existence is critical to the world you know. Magic brings balance, and if that balance is permanently shifted in the wrong direction the damage might not be possible to remedy.

"And Asiri dying is a way to bring balance, right?" Thyra snorted in derision. "People will see that magic still exists. Yeah, one dwarf died, but the end outweighs the cost along the way. Right?"

I did not want Asiri to die and I grieve her loss. But, yes, there will be attention given to what happened. There will be no explaining away what happened, and the world will be one step closer to being recognized openly once more. But none of that will matter if Baldur and Olafsson gain access to what is hidden in Idunn's garden.

"Why?" Thyra demanded. "What is so important there that has to remain hidden?"

Yggdrasil was quiet long enough for Thyra to grow more suspicious of the World Tree than she already was. Finally, it answered. *I must maintain physical connections to this world in order to maintain my influence. My power is in all life, but it would take millions of lives to equal the strength of just one of my physical manifestations. Even your ties to me are like a garden hose compared to a raging river in comparison.*

"And one of these places is inside of Idunn's garden?"

Once I had many physical manifestations of myself. One by one, I've watched as many of them have fallen. The ones that have survived are hidden in sacred places that are protected against intrusion. I used one such physical manifestation to appear to Odin as Yggdrasil, the World Tree. He stood beneath my canopy, hung from my branches, and recovered against my trunk. He recognized the importance of what he had found and made that place sacred, appointing a caretaker to protect the manifestation of my power from all threats.

"Idunn."

Yes. Baldur and Olafsson cannot be allowed to enter Idunn's garden. You are my champion. I need you to protect me, and you cannot stop them without Mjolnir.

Thyra was feeling defiance born from months of manipulation with the added bitterness of losing Asiri. "Why not? I have Lynnedslag. Maybe I should turn around and go back for it."

She wasn't actually entertaining the idea. The lacrosse stick was hundreds of miles behind her, probably buried in a pile of smoking rubble. Whether Yggdrasil could read her mind or not, it's answer put the notion to rest.

That is not an option, even if you wanted it to be. Lynnedslag was damaged in the blast, and without Asiri to mend it, the stick would serve you no purpose other than as a reminder. You must move forward. You must retrieve Mjolnir.

"And how am I supposed to do that? Tell me! If that was what you wanted me to do, why didn't you make that happen when I still had help? At least yesterday I had my mom, Asiri, and Vidar. Now I'm on my own. I think my chances of success dropped like a meteor after last night!"

You are more capable on your own than you think. That is one of the reasons I chose you to be my champion. Beyond that, help comes in many forms. More will find you soon. When it comes, don't run away from it.

"What's that supposed to mean?" Thyra demanded. She waited for an answer, but one never came. "Yggdrasil! Tell me what you mean!"

Whatever connection the World Tree had created was now gone. Thyra slammed her fist against the steering wheel in anger. Again Yggdrasil gave her a command—that was what it was!—but didn't provide any guidance on how to achieve it, leaving Thyra to strike out on her own. She had a direction, yes, but the World Tree had made it clear that it was not going to interfere on her behalf, no matter how often it said it was invested in her success.

Thyra spent the next twenty miles fuming just shy of calling in a lightning storm.

A sign for a fast-food stop broke through her anger just enough to catch her eye. Her stomach growled in protest. She didn't think she could eat yet, but her body wasn't of the same opinion. Grief was one thing—starvation was something completely different. The question was how was she going to get food? There hadn't been time to gather cash or make sure she had a credit card tucked conveniently in her pocket. She didn't have many options at her disposal. Thyra ignored the hunger pangs and kept driving.

Fifty miles later, the growling had become a constant, dull ache. She still didn't know how she was going to buy food, but she pulled off a the next exit. She pulled the Camaro into the parking lot between a burger joint and a Mexican restaurant not far from the highway and rolled the windows down. The smells coming from both establishments made her stomach grumble in expectation. The way she saw it, her options were limited to theft or dumpster diving. Unfortunately, both options were becoming more acceptable options with each passing minute. The question was, how desperate was she?

Thyra was so absorbed in watching the morning crowd get their fix that she didn't notice the tell-tale sound of a classic muscle car pull into the parking lot. Or the strange tickle she felt at the base of her skull. It wasn't until there was a tap on her window that she even realized that she wasn't alone. She immediately wished she was when she saw the face smiling down at her. She rolled down the window with one hand, the other one moving to the ignition just in case she needed to make a swift getaway.

"Hello," Modi said with a cocky smile. "You look surprised to see us."

Thyra was. Not in a pleasant way. "How did you find me?"

"We heard there was trouble last night," Modi replied. "We tried to get their in time, but were too late."

Thyra couldn't help but wonder which side their help would have been meant for.

"When we didn't find you there," Modi continued, "we felt compelled to find you. I sensed your magic in the air and we immediately started to follow. You've been keeping up a strong pace all night. We had to break the speed limit almost the entire way to catch up with you." Modi smirked. "Not that we care much for speed limits."

Thyra didn't care if they drove one-twenty, she just wanted them to do it in any direction but hers. "I have nothing to say to you two. Leave me alone."

"Ah, don't be so quick to dismiss us," Modi said. "After all, we drove all this way to see you."

"I'm not going to help you."

"We'll see." Modi considered her for a moment. "You hungry?"

"No," Thyra lied. "I'm fine."

"No, you're not," Modi stated. "You may not think much of us, you don't even have to trust us, but you're not going to make it very far on an empty stomach. Especially if you plan on taking on Olafsson and the Muspel Corporation."

Thyra kept her expression neutral. She wasn't going to give Modi the satisfaction of knowing what she was planning. "Are we done?"

Modi shrugged and tapped on the roof of the Camaro. "It's up to you, little sister. You can come in, trust us long enough to eat a meal with us, or you can go back to deciding which dumpster you're going to raid." He smirked. "If I were you, I'd avoid the one behind the taco joint."

His taunt delivered, Modi walked away, completely unconcerned by the daggers Thyra was staring into his back. She watched as he joined Magni and went into the restaurant. A few minutes later she saw them take a seat at a window where they knew she could see them. They made a show of enjoying their food and Thyra hated them for every bite they took. She knew she could drive away, but she also knew that if she did she'd still be stuck in the same situation—hungry with no good way to fix the problem.

Yggdrasil said help was coming and that Thyra should accept it when it came. She hated to think that her brothers were that help. She didn't trust them and she had no reason to change that stance. Other than Yggdrasil's words echoing back and forth in her head.

Modi pushed out a chair for her when he saw he walk into the dining room. She grudgingly sat down and accepted the tray Magni slid in front of her. Neither one spoke, but they did share a look that was almost enough to make Thyra stand up and leave.

She didn't. Instead, she tore into the sandwich in front of her. A few bites later, she was licking her fingers, the edge of her hunger taken off but far from satisfied. Magni pushed another sandwich in her direction, but Thyra ignored it.

"How did you two find me?"

"We have a connection, little sister," Modi answered. "This close to you, I can almost taste your magic, it's so thick in the air. Even apart, I could feel it's pull. I could point to you from miles away. Put me in a crowded room with a blindfold and I could walk straight to where you stood." He smiled grimly. "Wherever you go, I will be able to follow."

Thyra was surprised that she understood what he meant. Now that she was close to them again, she did feel something. A tickle at the base of her skull that had started when they showed up and hadn't stopped since. "You keep talking about you being able to sense me. Not the both of you."

Modi nodded. "Magni does not share our particular connection."

"And I don't care to," Magni growled around a half-chewed glob of food.

Modi chuckled. "This connection we share, it's something of the Vanir rather than the Aesir. Freya was Vanir. Our mother was as well. Although she lacked strength in magic." Modi frowned. "Or in mind, for that matter."

Magni smiled cruelly. "She thought she could fly at the end. Turns out she couldn't."

Modi's frown deepened. "Her death was. . .unfortunate. Still, it seems some of her Vanir blood was passed on to me. My talents have always been more varied than Magni's. He inherited a full dose of Aesir elemental power, while I did not. But, where there is a perceived deficit, there is always opportunities for growth. I can sense magic in others. Especially in someone I share a close, familial bond to."

"I would hardly call us 'close,'" Thyra muttered.

Modi smirked. "Just because we didn't grow up braiding each other's hair doesn't mean we aren't close, little sister. We are all Thor's children. Our magic mirrors each other, if not in strength, then in nature. You are elemental, just like us. Just like almost all the Aesir were."

Thyra couldn't deny that she was curious. She wanted to know—*needed* to know. "Elemental?"

"Your education begins now, little sister," Modi said. "The Aesir were masters of the elements. Odin mastered the light of the sun, liquid fire that could melt stone. Thor called down lightning. Their magic—your magic and ours—is a mixture of the elements all around us, manipulated into the form we desire. Every time you call down a lightning bolt, you are manipulating heat and air, shaping it to your will."

Thyra couldn't help but appreciate the explanation. She had never thought of what she was doing—she just did it. Having it broken down this way made sense to her. It also raised a hundred other questions.

"You've sparked her interest," Magni said with a crooked smile.

She gave Magni a glare, but there was no denying the truth. "What about Vidar and Bragi?Even Hela. They were Aesir, but they don't manipulate the elements."

"You would bring up those three," Modi said. He inhaled deeply before explaining. "Bragi is hardly Aesir. He's a storyteller, a glorified negotiator, no more. His magic is a result of Yggdrasil, not his heritage. As for Vidar and Hela, their magic affects the body—bodies made from elements. Their magic is an internal manipulation rather than external, but it is elemental all the same."

"Okay, but what about people like Freya? What kind of magic does she have? I've seen what she can do, and it's on a whole different level."

Modi was shaking his head before Thyra finished. "This lesson is over, little sister. If you want to learn about Freya and the magic of the Vanir, you'll have to prove worthy of the answer. We're not going to teach you for nothing. Our offer to you stands. Today is the third day. We need an answer. Help us get Mjolnir, and we'll teach you how to master your magic and answer your questions. Choose not to, and you get the meal and the brief explanation I've given you. But that's all you'll get."

"Make a choice," Magni muttered.

Thyra still didn't trust these two. There was no doubt in her mind that they would double-cross her the first chance they got. But she had already made up her mind to go after Mjolnir and she knew doing it alone would be next to impossible. She wasn't blind to the danger. She needed to look out for her best interests.

Right now, that meant going along with her brothers.

"You should know, I don't trust either one of you any further than I can throw you," Thyra said. "But I want to see Gunnar Olafsson pay. If that means I have to help you get the hammer, then so be it. Just as long as you both know that if you ever try to use it against me, I will take it from you. Even if that means from your cold, lifeless hands."

Magni sneered, but Modi nodded with an amused smile on his face. "Duly noted, and I would expect no less from a child of Thor. It's good to see that you do have some of him in you. That will make what comes next that much easier."

"What exactly is that?"

"Finish your food first," Modi said, sliding the sandwich closer to her. "Then we begin teaching you what you're truly capable of."

Thyra took a bite of the sandwich and swallowed. "How are you going to do that?"

Modi smiled grimly. "By taking you to where you can begin settling the score against Gunnar Olafsson."

Chapter 20

The truck yard just outside of Lincoln, Nebraska was quiet at this time of night. Thirty trailers sat idle, lined up waiting for their turn at the docks the next morning. The only staff on-site were the gate guard and three night workers prepping the docks for the morning rush.

Thyra watched the truck yard from the parking lot of a run-down motel across the road. She was glad to have the darkly-tinted windows on the Camaro each time the headlights of a passing car shone through. She was convinced that someone would notice her sitting in the driver's seat for the past four hours and think it strange. She was relieved when it became clear that the gate guard was preoccupied with a book, not the comings and goings of the hotel across the road.

The tap on her window almost made her jump out of her skin. Again, she was glad to have the tinted windows to hide the flame of embarrassment that ran up her cheeks. Clearing her throat, she unlocked the door and waited as Modi slid into the passenger seat.

"Did you have a nice nap?" Modi asked snidely.

Thyra glared at him. Considering she hadn't slept for almost two days and had been driving for almost sixteen hours straight by the time they reached Lincoln, sleep had been a welcome means of passing a few of the hours she spent sitting in the car.

"You two can take turns," Thyra muttered. "I can't."

"That's why you should have taken me up on my offer to ride with us," Modi said. He looked around the interior of the Camaro approvingly. "Although, I see why you didn't want to leave this behind. The dwarf did a fair job on this. Not needing to stop for gas is quite the feat. It's too bad she died. Her ingenuity could have been useful to us."

Thyra didn't want to talk about Asiri with him. He wasn't sad that Asiri was dead—only that she wasn't around for him to use.

"What do you want, Modi? The plan was to move at two-thirty when the gate guard changes."

"Still is the plan," Modi said. "I'm here to make sure you don't get in there and freeze. The last thing we want is for you to be too scared to act and for this whole partnership to fail before it even gets off the ground."

"Don't worry," Thyra said tersely, "I'll be fine."

"Then let me take this opportunity for me to teach you something," Modi said.

"Now? Shouldn't we be focused on the truck yard?"

"Magni is watching for us. One pair of eyes is enough." Modi twisted in his seat so he could face Thyra easier. "You admired Magni's axe. I'm guessing that it has never dawned on you that such a feat was possible. I can help you learn how to do something similar. It's all a matter of control, and imagining what you want your magic to do."

"Why?"

Modi frowned. "Why what?"

"Why do you want to teach me?"

"Wasn't that our deal?" Modi shrugged. "If you'd prefer, I won't. You can go on being ignorant and hope you get lucky. So far your intuition and strength have gotten you by, but from what I've gathered you strike like a young viper that hasn't learned the power of its own venom yet. You unleash the full fury of your power without thinking of the cost. Chaos is a tool in battle, at times, but it strikes friend just as often as foe."

"You didn't answer my question," Thyra said.

"I believe I did," Modi said. "We are going to be working together. I don't want you to be striking out wildly. We may share an affinity for lightning, but a wayward strike can still hurt us. Our magic both controls and defends us against the very lightning we call down. What it doesn't protect us against is carelessness. I'd prefer not to have to be watching my front *and* my back when we go against Olafsson and whatever he has waiting for us."

"So, you arm me with greater weapons to avoid accidentally being struck in the back?" Thyra raised an eyebrow. "Shouldn't you be more concerned that I'd use what you're teaching me to do it intentionally?"

Modi smirked. "You'd be stupid to try. But, I didn't come here to argue with you." He raised one hand, a smooth ball of lightning cracking into life. "First, we need to teach you some control. Your magic is destructive, chaotic, but it doesn't have to be untamed." He nodded. "Go ahead. Try to match mine."

Sighing, Thyra summoned her magic. She tried to picture a smooth, controlled ball like Modi's but the one that appeared over her hand popped and cracked angrily. Modi shook his head. "You have the strength. What you don't have is the finesse. You're like a raging bull swinging your horns from side to side in a thorn bush! You may get rid of the bush, but you're going to bloody yourself, too. Now, try again, little sister. Imagine a smooth ball. Control your magic, don't let it run free or it will overpower you."

What followed was dozens of failed attempts. Each time, Modi would shake his head and offer a piece of biting advice before telling her to try again. He compared her to a ram with both eyes closed, a bear lunging at fish over a tall waterfall, and a hungry hyena clamping down on it's own leg. Every time he repeated that she had the strength, but it was useless if she couldn't learn control and patience.

Finally, Thyra threw her hands up in exasperation. "Why should I listen to you? Aren't you the one who inherited Thor's *wrath*? Who are you to tell me to be patient and to temper my emotions? Every time I look at you I see the anger in your eyes, simmering just below the surface."

"You're not listening, little sister," Modi snapped. "I don't want you to abandon your emotion. I want you to control it! Direct it and bend it to your will, rather than letting it direct you. Our magic is pure emotion! To say otherwise is a lie. But that doesn't mean it has to be chaotic all the time." He took a deep breath. "Now, prove to me that you are a daughter of Thor, and try again. This time, don't fail!"

Thyra gritted her teeth so hard she was afraid she might break them. She was so mad, she thought she might explode! She wanted to stick a ball of lightning down Modi's throat just to wipe that smug smirk off his face. Then maybe she'd make a boxing glove made of lightning just so she could punch him in the face with it!

What Modi had just said came back to her—*I don't want you to abandon your emotion. I want you to control it!*—and she frowned. She realized that she had interpreted "control" to mean she wasn't supposed to be angry. But that wasn't what Modi was telling her to do.

Grudgingly, she raised her hand again and called up her magic. This time she let her anger at her failures rise to the surface and instead of trying to control her emotion, she *directed* her anger to *control* her magic. A ball of lightning cracked to life and for a moment it raged wildly. She focused, imagining a smooth, controlled manifestation of her magic. Slowly, the tendrils that snapped and cracked along the surface were smoothed down one by one until the ball that hovered above her palm was completely smooth!

A wide smile split her face. "I did it!"

"Very good. But that's only the first step." Modi's ball suddenly elongated into a knife. "Now, make it change. Imagine the shape you want it to take, and then make it so."

Thyra knew he wanted her to try to mirror what he had done, but the knife didn't feel right to her. A different shape popped into her head instead. She extended her hand between the seats and focused on the ball. She imagined the shape she wanted it to take and then directed it to happen. The ball resisted, as if it sensed the hint of doubt inside that she quickly squashed, and then cracked loudly. Thyra blinked at the noise, but she knew that her magic had obeyed before she even saw the long shaft of a spear resting in her hand. It was identical to the one Sif carried. It felt right in her hand, the perfect pairing of the magic she inherited from Thor and the Valkyrie heritage from her mom.

Her smile grew wider when she saw Modi's reaction to the spear. He had scooted as far away from the spear as possible in his seat. For once, his cocky smirk was gone, replaced by a deep frown.

"That is. . . good, Thyra," Modi said. "You learn. Not without great effort, but you learn. Now, please put that way before someone notices it. The whole reason we're here will be negated if that guard looks over here and sees you waving a lightning-spear around."

"If they haven't noticed all the flashing before," Thyra said, "why would you think they would now?"

"You've succeeded," Modi said, "but the night holds greater things for you if you do as I say. Now, let your magic go."

Thyra didn't want to, but she let her magic fade, the spear winking away with a crackle. She noticed that Modi didn't let his dagger disappear until he was sure Thyra had released her hold on her magic. He exhaled slowly and nodded. "Good. I think it's time we did what we came for." He opened his door and slid out, ducking back to say, "Come on. Magni is waiting."

Thyra looked at the clock and was surprised to see that almost an hour had passed. She slid out of the Camaro and followed Modi across the street. Magni was waiting for them in the shadows just beyond the streetlight, leaning casually against the chain link fence.

"Guard just left a few minutes ago," Magni announced when they reached him. "Let's get on with it."

He turned and faced the fence and started working something along the fence. Thyra peaked over his shoulder and saw that he held a pair of wire-cutters. In the matter of a minute he had cut enough links to create a whole big enough to walk through. He held it aside with a sneer. "After you, little sister."

"Remind me what we're doing here," Thyra said.

"Striking a blow to Olafsson and the Muspel Corporation," Modi replied as he ducked through the fence.

"How exactly are we doing that by breaking into a truck yard?"

The shadows lit up briefly as Modi raised a ball of lightning overhead to light the side of the nearest trailer. A strange symbol like a headless stick figure running was painted over bold lettering. Thyra recognized it immediately. *Muspel Corporation.*

"This is one of their hubs," Modi explained. "Supplies for their telecommunications empire run through here. Not their largest, but still big enough to cause issues for the company if, say, an unexpected electric storm were to occur and destroy a few of their trucks and trailers."

Magni chuckled grimly. "Or all of them!"

Modi nodded. "We're going to strike a blow to the Muspel Corporation that will make them hurt. It won't cripple Olafsson's company, but it will be more than a tickle." He saw Thyra's hesitation and frowned. "You said you wanted this, little sister. This is your chance to begin taking your revenge on Olafsson."

"I want revenge on Olafsson," Thyra said. "These people here didn't do anything to me."

"But they are complicit!" Modi argued. "Even if they don't know it, they are helping people like the ones who attacked you. By standing aside in their ignorance, they had a hand in the dwarf's death."

Thyra was shaking her head. "I don't want to hurt anyone."

"Yes, you do," Modi said in a grim tone. "You want to hurt Olafsson, don't you? This is the beginning of doing exactly that. If it makes you feel better, we won't hurt anyone here. We're here to destroy Muspel Corporation property and send a clear message to Olafsson that his actions won't go unanswered. No more."

"You promise no one gets hurt?"

Magni's smile was wicked. "No one gets hurt as long as they stay out of our way."

Thyra recognized the wiggle room that left, but it was likely the best promise she was going to get. "Fine. What do you want me to do?"

"Put on a show," Modi said. "Use that spear, call down some lightning bolts. Anything with the Muspel Corporation's logo must burn. Make sure Olafsson knows who did this!"

"Enough talk!" Magni snarled. "The other guard will be here soon. We do it now."

An axe composed of lightning appeared in each hand as he stalked towards the front of the nearest semi. With a guttural roar, he slashed across the tires, exploding them in a shower of sparks. He moved on to the cab and engine compartment, his axes rising and falling with a bestial rage. In a matter of seconds, all that was left was a glowing mess of melted metal. Magni stepped back and roared into the night.

Modi tapped Thyra on the shoulder, his smirk wicked and his eyes glowing with a hungry light. "Don't be shy, little sister." He started to walk out into the center of the yard, turning around to say, "Remember what the Muspel Corporation and Olafsson has done to you, little sister. It's time to take your pound of flesh!"

"Don't take too long doing it," Magni growled. "Move fast and strike hard!"

As if to emphasize his words, he threw one of his axes into the trailer of the next semi with a thunderous boom. He spun and threw the second with a similar effect. Somehow, the axes held their shape even after they left his hands. Thyra didn't have time to consider how it was done, though, because as quick as they left Magni's hands, new ones appeared. He smiled grimly at her and then charged off with a roar.

Thyra looked up at the symbol on the side of the semi-trailer and felt her anger rise. It was Surtur's symbol. He may call himself Gunnar Olafsson, but it was the same symbol that he had laid siege to Asgard under. The same symbol that he had killed gods under. The same symbol he had attacked Thyra and her mom under. And the same symbol that his men had killed Asiri under. He had taken almost everything from her. He deserved to have something taken from him.

Any hesitation about what they were doing gone, Thyra stalked down the row of semis until she came to four lined up at the docks waiting to be loaded. Her power sprang to life and she formed the spear in her hand. She tested it by thrusting the spear into the engine compartment of one semi. The spear sliced right through the metal and into the engine without the hint of resistance. She slashed the spear across and again it cut easily, sending up sparks amid the thunder of each blow.

She thrust the spear towards the next semi and lightning shot from the tip in a wrist-thick bar that punched through one and into the next. She unleashed her fury again and again until both were smoking, glowing hunks of metal.

It felt good! Unleash her power with no care about who might be watching was beyond cathartic. This was what her magic was made for—destruction! And she was *good* at it.

Moving as quickly as her bum knee would allow, she walked around the side of the very last semi until she stood just below the symbol of the Muspel Corporation. Her brothers wanted her to send a message to Olafsson and his goons? She'd send a message loud and clear.

She scrambled onto the dock so that she was eye-level with the headless stick-figure. Four trailers lined up, eight Muspel Corporation logos to destroy. She looked down at the spear in her hand. It was holding it's shape even without conscious thought. It was a feat she had never even considered, and part of her was in awe of her creation. But, she didn't need a controlled manifestation of her magic right now. She needed the raw, angry, destructive power of the storm that threatened to sweep anything in its path away.

Thyra pushed more of her power into the spear until it pulsed and tendrils of lightning danced down its entire length. She funneled more power into it until the shape was lost and it became a six-foot long shaft of pure lightning. With a scream, her arm went back and whipped forward, sending the shaft of lightning through the Muspel logo with a thunder clap followed by an explosion that nearly knocked her off her feet.

Lowering the hand she hadn't realized she had put over her eyes, Thyra took a look at her handiwork. The first trailer was split almost in two, a huge gaping hole where the logo used to be. The second looked almost the same, a glowing hole where the spear had gone through. A smaller hole—five feet across—was where the logo had been on the third. There was nothing left of the fourth trailer besides debris where it had once stood. Whatever had been inside had exploded, sending shrapnel a hundred feet into the air.

"Yes!"

Thyra jumped at the sound of Modi's howl. She had been so absorbed in what she had done that she hadn't heard him approach.

"You show your true colors tonight, little sister. You are a child of Thor!" Modi's expression was so wild he looked rabid. "Olafsson will hear of this and will know you were here. You've sent the message loud and clear!"

"Time to leave!" Magni barked loudly.

Modi laughed up at the sky. "Why should we run? We are gods!" Magni gestured urgently, but Modi waved him off with one hand. He turned to Thyra, a hungry light in his eyes. "This is only the first step, little sister. The first message of many. Olafsson will no longer be allowed to sit comfortable on his throne. He will know we are coming for Mjolnir!"

Thyra saw flashing lights in the distance that quickly eroded the thrill she felt. She slid off the dock and hurried towards the street as quickly as her limping gait would allow. She heard Magni grumble something under his breath as she passed by—something about "madness taking hold"— but couldn't make the rest out.

She was halfway across the yard when she realized that she was being watched. The gate guard and the three night workers were all peering out of the window of the office with wide-eyed looks. Even worse, each had a phone in hand, no doubt capturing video of everything. One summoned the courage to step out of the office and call out, "I don't know who you are, but the police are on their way. We have proof—pictures, videos, all of it!"

Magni was on him in a flash, lifting him off the ground with one hand and pinning him against the side of the building. His eyes danced with magic as he leaned in close. "Now's your chance to get my good side. Take the photo!" The worker struggled against his grip, not understanding what Magni wanted. Magni growled and grabbed him by the wrist, forcing his hand into place. "Take the photo, and make sure the world sees it!"

Spluttering, the worker snapped a pair of photos. Magni grunted and let the worker drop to the ground. He turned away without another look and walked calmly towards the gate. He raised one hand nonchalantly towards the gatehouse and a bolt of lightning leapt from it. The little structure blew apart in a shower of sparks and smoke.

Thyra had just crossed the street and was about to get into the Camaro when Modi finally joined them. "Olafsson will get this message, little sister! We've struck a blow."

"Get in the car!" Magni barked. The Chevelle's engine roared to life. "Before those fools get over their fear enough to take pictures of our license plates!"

Modi grimaced briefly, but his smile came back almost as quickly. "You did well tonight, little sister! This is only the first step! Soon we will bring Olafsson to his knees where he can watch his empire crumble around him!"

The sound of sirens in the distance was enough to make Modi blink, his smile losing some of its certainty. He reached into his pocket and handed Thyra a slip of paper. "Drive to that address, little sister. Tomorrow we strike another blow! Tomorrow we help move you one step closer to mastering your power. Tomorrow we take another pound of flesh!"

His head went back and he laughed at the sky again. *Maybe he is mad.*

There was no time to consider that possibility. The sirens were getting closer, and Thyra wasn't about to wait around for them to arrive. She stuffed the paper into her pocket and slid into the Camaro. She started the engine and had it in gear immediately. The wheels spun on the blacktop as she pressed down on the accelerator. She engaged the night-mode Asiri had built into the car—a blueish tint spreading across the windshield that allowed her to see without the headlights—and pointed the Camaro in the opposite direction of the fast-approaching police vehicles.

As she tore away, the Chevelle pulled slowly out into the street behind her with Modi leaning out the window. A flash lit up the night as a series of rapid lightning strikes hit the oncoming police vehicles. When her vision cleared, the road behind her was a mess of flames and twisted metal.

Chapter 21

Fenrir held the paper up in front of him, but the words on the page were the furthest thing from his mind. Just like the long-forgotten cup of coffee on the table, the paper was there only to give him a reason for being the in the cafe in the middle of the day. He had no interest in the overly sweet froth—if he did drink coffee, he liked it dark and strong—and he could care less about the financial state of the economy. But this close to Wall Street, the ruse was good enough to allow him to fit in with all the other yuppies that frequented this place.

His attention was on the building just across the street—the Muspel Corporation headquarters. Days of watching the building had left him feeling caged. Every attempt at entry was thwarted. Security was insistent that each visitor state their business before being allowed to ascend to even the second floor, much less to the levels occupied by the Muspel Corporation. Fenrir had almost been escorted out of the building the last time he attempted to gain access. A last second moment of rational thought saved him from going too far. He'd avoided the main lobby since.

The other avenues of access had proven almost as futile. The men Hela had given him had managed to make quiet contact with some of their friends still working security, but they had learned nothing about what was happening inside. All information was being kept very close to the vest, and it left Fenrir with nothing to show for his time. Hela was growing impatient. If he didn't come up with something soon. . . he didn't want to think about what she might do.

The bell on the door sounded. A moment later a young woman with short, blue hair took the seat next to him. "They are up to something."

"If you came in here to state something that obvious," Fenrir growled, "you had better turn around and leave before I tear you in half for wasting my time."

The young woman swallowed, but didn't smell of fear. Fenrir felt a grudging respect for her courage. She knew what he was—what he truly was. She knew that he was perfectly capable of doing what he said. That should have been enough to make her turn to water at the smallest sign of his dissatisfaction.

But, she wasn't some run-of-the-mill girl, fresh from some college campus. She had her own secrets that made her confident even in the presence of someone like Fenrir. She wasn't cocky, but she wasn't a wilting flower and had proven to be difficult to intimidate. She was wary around him, yes, but she was not like the others Hela had insisted accompany Fenrir. He had seen what she was capable of and was impressed. She wouldn't survive a fight with him—not by a long shot!—but she might make it interesting.

"Baldur was out with his tag-along," she said calmly. Fenrir guessed that she meant the curly-haired woman, Amara. Baldur was rarely without her for long. From what Fenrir could tell, the only time they weren't together was when they slept. "Hound heard them talking about a meeting. Somewhere north of here. In three days."

Fenrir frowned. He hated the fact that these fools felt the need to use aliases based off their magic. *Hound. Shifter. Weaver.* The names were ridiculous! He had made that point several times until one of them mentioned his use of Fenton Ririe as an alias. They were not impressed with the name or the reasons he gave. They all agreed that it showed his lack of creativity and that he had no ground to stand on.

The only one that didn't use an alias based off her magic was this girl—Jax. Chinese by heritage, she had been a martial arts prodigy up until her teenage years when her magic—*chi* was the word she used—manifested itself. Her time as an elite-level competitor ended overnight. Her parents considered her too dangerous and banned her from ever using her power again. Their strict demands and unbending views on using her power led to an internal conflict that Jax struggled with for years. A rebellious streak led to her practicing in private, learning about and developing her power quietly until she was able to strike out on her own. If she thought independence from her parents strict ways would bring direction and self-discovery, Jax had been mistaken. The world wasn't accepting of people like her and after three years of trying, she realized there was no place for her to be her true self.

She had been one of the first to accept Hela's invitation and was one of the few that Fenrir actually thought was worth the air they breathed. Jax was a fighter. That was something he respected. The rest were close to worthless in his eyes, no matter what Hela said.

"A meeting is not noteworthy," Fenrir muttered.

"Maybe not," Jax said, "but they had an old man with them. Sickly looking. He fits the description you gave us."

Bragi. Hela had been curious about what Baldur had done with him the old man after taking over his identity. She guessed that Baldur had either killed the old man or imprisoned him in the same way she had imprisoned Baldur. It seemed the latter was true, at least in part. She would be interested to hear about this.

Fenrir glanced at Jax and raised an eyebrow. "Go on."

"They were talking in hushed tones, but Hound heard everything," Jax whispered. "They were talking about summoning stones and a garden. None of it made sense to him, but you said you wanted to hear anything we saw or heard while following Baldur."

Fenrir tried to hide the surprise on his face. *Baldur was going to use summoning stones?* That meant he was trying to get to Idunn. Fenrir's mistress would be *very* interested in that news.

"Is Hound still following him?" Jax nodded ever so slightly in response to his question. "Good. Make sure he doesn't lose Baldur. We need to find out where this meeting is going to happen."

Jax stood up without another word and left. Fenrir remained in his seat until he was sure she was gone. Standing, he stuck the newspaper under his arm and headed for the door. He walked around the corner to where his Challenger was parked before pulling out his cellphone. He despised using technology, but Hela demanded he get over his prejudices. She would want to hear what he had to say immediately.

Hela picked up on the third ring, purring into the phone, *"Hello, my loyal wolf."*

Even from over a thousand miles away, her voice sent a shiver through him. "Baldur has Bragi. They are going to use the summoning stones."

The line went silent, but Fenrir could imagine the look on his mistress's face. Of all the possible schemes Olafsson and Baldur could have, this was one that neither one had thought likely.

"What are they doing? What do they think they are going to find?"

Fenrir figured that the questions were rhetorical, so he kept silent. He knew little about Idunn or what the purpose of her garden was. He owed his immortality to Hela, not some fruit off a tree and delivered by a lonely old woman.

"When are they meeting?" Hela said.

"Three days."

"Do you know where?"

"We will soon," Fenrir answered. "Do you want me to stop them?"

"No," Hela said without hesitation. *"They won't succeed. Not yet."* Fenrir wanted to ask how she could be sure, but didn't. *"The whisper on the wind is that there was an event in Nebraska early this morning."*

"What kind of event?"

"The lightning kind."

Fenrir's heart sped up. "Thyra Ariksen?"

"And her brothers," Hela replied. *"It would seem that Baldur and Gunnar have incited the wrath of all three of Thor's children."*

That surprised Fenrir. How long had the brothers stuck to the shadows only to strike now? There was no mistaking the connection was Thyra Ariksen. "Do you think they're coming for Olafsson?"

"Perhaps," Hela replied. *"If they do, it may present an opportunity we can exploit."*

"Or an impediment," Fenrir muttered. "The girl has a knack for creating chaos and her brothers are bad enough on their own."

"Chaos breeds opportunity for those willing to wait patiently," Hela responded. *"Which is what I want you to do. You'll know when the time is right to act. Until then, be patient, my wolf. The time to hunt is almost here."*

Chapter 22

"You said no one was going to get hurt!"

Modi closed the door of the Chevelle and faced Thyra's charge with a crooked smirk. His insolent expression only infuriated Thyra more.

"I don't remember saying that no one was going to get hurt," Modi said. He turned and looked at his brother. "Do you remember me saying that?" Magni smiled and shook his head. Modi turned back to Thyra and shrugged. "That is unfortunate that you thought that. You must have misheard me."

Hours of pent up rage over what had happened during the night rushed to the surface and Thyra shoved him in the chest hard enough to knock him back against the car. "Don't play games with me! You lied. You attacked those police officers when you could have run!"

"Tread carefully, little sister," Modi said, the smirk disappearing. "I said no one would get hurt as long as they didn't present a threat. Those police officers would have followed us. A high-speed chase was not part of our plans."

"What you did was wrong!"

"We did what was necessary!" Modi barked. "You may think you have some moral high ground, but you don't! Think about it, little sister. If the police would have caught us, if we had allowed them to take us without a fight, we'd be in jail right now, not walking free. Do you think you'd be able to take down Olafsson from inside a jail cell? No! In the end, you would have done the same thing. You would have fought to stay free and on this path."

Thyra wasn't going to agree with his point, but she wasn't willing to concede. "You could have driven faster. Tried to outrun them. No one had to get hurt."

"Someone was always going to get hurt," Magni muttered. "You knew that. You wanted revenge on Olafsson. You knew what that meant. Trying to do this without hurting people is impossible. Deep down you knew it then, just like you know it now."

"Not innocent people," Thyra argued. "Those police officers had nothing to do with Olafsson or the Muspel Corporation."

"And you think every person who works for Olafsson is guilty of his crimes?" Modi laughed bitterly. "Don't be naive. You've hurt people. Maybe even killed a few just because they worked for the wrong person. Have you thought about that? If you haven't, you're worse than the evil you say you're fighting against."

"I've only defended myself," Thyra argued. "You attacking those police officers was entirely different!"

"We did what we had to!" Magni insisted.

"This world is not black and white," Modi added in agreement. "No matter how much you want to believe that there is a clear distinction between good and bad, there isn't. Even the worst person can believe their actions are good, just like the actions of someone you call *good* can be wrong. Its all a matter of perspective. From where I stand, letting those police cars catch us was harmful. Stopping them was good."

"That's some real messed up rationale," Thyra muttered. "It's nice to know who I'm linked up with."

"You should look in the mirror more often," Modi sneered. "After last night, you're just as guilty as the two of us. You're a criminal, by the definition of the law. Even worse, you're a killer, Thyra. Whether you are willing to see it or not, the truth is the same."

Thyra looked away. She thought the reasoning in the argument was flawed—but whose? Modi's words stung, perhaps because she knew they were more true than she wanted to admit. She had been part of people dying. She rationalized it by saying that they attacked her and those she cared about, but that didn't change the facts.

Still, what these two had done crossed a line. "You were wrong to do that."

Modi got control of himself and his cocky smirk returned. "You can lie to yourself all you want, but deep down you know the truth. You would not have let those police take you. Not when you still have a score to settle."

"I would have found another way," Thyra said through gritted teeth.

"Believe what you want," Modi said dismissively, "but last night was a complete success. We sent a message loud and clear to Olafsson and the world. The children of Thor are alive and we are out for blood. Now, we must make sure we push that message home. Last night was step one, tonight is step two."

"I will not be part of more killing," Thyra stated.

Magni smiled cruelly. "Then be faster next time."

Thyra gave him a scathing look that didn't faze him. If anything, it made him more brazen in his defiance.

"I need to go scout out the next target," Modi said, drawing Thyra's attention back to him. "I leave you in Magni's capable hands. He has agreed to teach you a lesson." Thyra didn't think that sounded like something she wanted any part of, but before she could argue, Modi got back into the Chevelle and started it up. He leaned out the window and gave her a crooked smile. "Hopefully you take to this lesson just as easily as you did last night."

Thyra watched him peel out and speed away. When she looked

back at Magni, he was watching her with the intensity of an angry, caged bear. She matched his stare and waited.

"You are dangerous," Magni finally said.

Thyra raised one eyebrow, unsure how to take the statement. Knowing what she knew about Magni's tendency towards violence, she made a guess that he meant it as a compliment. "Thank you?"

Magni's mouth curled down in the corners like he had a sour taste in his mouth. He shifted his feet and switched the way he had his arms crossed. He looked. . . uncomfortable. "Modi told me to teach you. I told him I'd rather stick hot coals in my eyes."

"Wow," Thyra said with a whistle. "You dislike me that much, don't you?"

Magni shook his head. "We may share blood, but I owe you no loyalty. The same way you don't owe us any loyalty. You could turn on us at any time. I don't have the same interest in you that my brother does. If it was up to me, we never would have brought you along."

"You could turn on me just as easily," Thyra replied.

"Something I intend to do the moment we're done," Magni stated matter-of-factly.

Thyra nodded slowly. She wasn't surprised by the admission. "Well, at least you're honest."

"Mjolnir will be ours," Magni stated emphatically.

She wasn't surprised that the hammer was on Magni's mind. She was a threat to his claim and no matter what Thyra said to the contrary he would always be suspicious of her intent. "If you say so."

"I do," Magni growled.

"Great," Thyra growled back. "Who are you trying to convince? Me? Or yourself?"

Magni's mouth turned down. "Modi seems to think you can help us. I don't like it, but I see his reasoning—storming the Muspel Corporation will be no easy feat. After what I saw last night. . .

your power will make it more feasible. Which means we're stuck together. For now."

"Wonderful," Thyra said flatly. "Speaking of Modi, where is he off to?"

"Scouting."

Thyra waited for more, but Magni just stared at her. "Descriptive. So what did you want to teach me?"

"Tonight will bring another chance to strike at Olafsson," Magni muttered. "Modi wants to make sure it goes off smoothly."

"Like Lincoln?"

"Yes," Magni said with a scowl, "like Lincoln."

"I don't think that went *smoothly*."

"I don't care." Magni walked a dozen paces away and turned to face Thyra. "We're done talking. Modi told me to teach you a lesson. Let's get on with it."

"What kind of lesson? How to lurk and scowl?"

"You come by that naturally," Magni said. "Modi taught you a degree of control last night. A useful skill for the attack. But our magic can defend as well."

"Defend?" That surprised her. So far, she had only seen the destructive potential of her magic. "How so?"

"If you can make lightning take the shape of a spear, you can make it take the shape of a shield," Magni said. Thyra felt a surge as he summoned his magic. Twin axes appeared in his hands and he held them up for Thyra to see. Suddenly, the one in his left hand shifted and became a circular shield on his forearm. He smacked the axe against it to prove it was solid. "See? Now, throw something at me."

Thyra cocked an eyebrow. "Throw something?"

"Did I stutter?" Magni snapped.

"Fine," Thyra said with a shrug. She bent down, picked up a rock, and tossed it at Magni. He raised his shield and swatted it aside easily.

"Not like that!" Magni barked, his features twisting with rage. "Why in Odin's name would I need a shield against a little rock?"

"You said throw something," Thyra argued with a shrug. "I threw something."

"You planning on fighting someone who throws rocks?" Magni snarled.

"If it can stop a rock, then I figure it can stop other things," Thyra rationalized. "A knife, a bullet—Olafsson's men don't have magic, but they do have those other things. I thought it was as good of a test as anything else I had on hand."

Magni's eyebrows drew down. "Magic fights magic. And Olafsson's men have weapons that imitate magic. You will need to defend yourself against that if you hope to last longer than a minute once the fighting starts." He sneered. "Although, I'm betting you won't last any longer than that. You'll run in fear when it counts."

Thyra could only shake her head. This was the most Magni had said to her at one time and he was using every chance possible to make it clear that he didn't like her. At least she knew where he stood. He wasn't hiding anything. Not like Modi, who Thyra saw as a snake in the grass, just waiting to strike her when she wasn't looking. She preferred Magni's open hostility to Modi's feigned interest in her.

"Let's get this over with," Thyra grumbled. She called up her magic and created a ball of lightning in her hand. She focused on it and imagined it in the shape of a shield. Her magic responded readily, taking the shape she wanted with a loud crack. She moved her arm back and forth, the shield staying in place on her arm. She held it up for Magni to inspect. "There. I made a shield. Happy?"

"You learn," Magni said with a grudging nod, "but can you use what you learn to keep yourself alive?"

Magni was on top of her in a flash, his fists pummeling against the shield she barely managed to raise in time. His axes were gone, but each blow of his fists sent a charge of lightning into her shield that felt like a jackhammer. Her arm quickly went numb and her right knee screamed in protest as each blow struck.

"You are weak!" Magni roared. He took a step back and spat. "You're little more than a cripple with that knee. I could crush you even without magic!"

"What's wrong with you?" Thyra shouted. "I thought you were supposed to be teaching me, not trying to pound me into the ground."

"This is how my father taught me," Magni said grimly. Thyra understood the underlying insult in his words—the Thor Magni knew was different than the Thor that sired Thyra in his eyes. Magni spat in disgust again. "You are frail! You aren't worthy of the power you've been given. You're just a weak, little girl!"

Panting, Thyra raised one hand and unleashed a torrent of lightning that struck the shield Magni hastily threw up in front of himself. When Thyra let up he had been pushed backward several steps and all his loose hair stood on end.

"I am not weak!" Thyra shouted.

"Your magic may be strong," Magni retorted through gritted teeth, "but magic is nothing if the body fails!"

He leapt forward, the devilish axes appearing in his hands in an instant. They slashed and dipped, looking for a way past the shield she threw up. He wasn't holding anything back and Thyra began to feel panic set in. She knew if she made a mistake or hesitated for a split second that one of those axes would find her. This wasn't some movie where the master would pull up just short of landing the crushing blow in order to teach a lesson—she was convinced he would follow through, even if it killed her!

Magni landed a heavy blow that sent a shiver through Thyra's entire body. Her right knee buckled under her and she fell backwards, her shield disappearing with a pop. Magni's eyes widened and smiled cruelly. His hands went overhead, the two axes merging into a massive one meant to cleave her in half. She saw it begin to descend and threw up both hands. She felt her magic surge, but instead of a shield of lightning, she felt a shift in the air all around her. Magni's axe flashed downward and—stopped cold a few inches from her palms! Time seemed to stand still with Magni struggling with each ounce of strength to make his axe move, the veins in his neck and face bulging with the effort, and Thyra lying on her back with both hands outstretched.

The axe in Modi's hand disappeared and he stepped to the side, the axe reappearing and sweeping in at neck height. Thyra threw out her hands again and felt the shift again. The axe stopped like it struck a wall. Magni growled, the axe vanishing, and dove at her. Again, Thyra felt the shift and Magni froze in place, an invisible force holding him in place. He roared in frustration. "How are you doing this?!"

Thyra was wondering the same thing. Her fear of being killed became fear over not understanding what was happening. There was no lightning, but she knew her magic was at play all the same. Keeping one hand in between her and Magni, she scooted backwards in the dirt, fully expecting Magni to somehow break free and begin raining punches down on her, but he didn't. The muscles in his body flexed as he fought to move, but whatever force held him kept him frozen in place.

Except it wasn't *some force*—it was *her* magic. Thyra didn't understand it, but she knew that it was something she had done. She could feel the flow of power that held Magni in place and was surprised to see a strange distortion in the air around him. She studied it for a moment before it dawned on her what she had done. Modi had said that their lightning was a manipulation of the elements around them. Could it be that she could do more than create lightning? She was a child of the storm. Storms had wind, didn't they? Wind, the air itself, was an element!

"Release me!" Magni roared.

There was no chance Thyra was going to do that. She bent over and tried to gather her breath. "You tried to kill me!"

"Release me now or I will end you! I don't care what my brother says. I will kill you!"

The threat made her blood boil. Here he was, held fast by her magic and he thought he could still make threats? Thyra thought about putting a lightning spear through his ugly mouth, but stopped short of action. That wasn't how she did things.

"Release me! Now!"

He wanted to be released, did he? Fine. Thyra would *release* him. Thyra could feel the air all around her now. She could sense the way it had solidified around Magni and she made a guess on how to make it move. Magni suddenly flew backwards like he'd been hit by a gale force wind. She watched wide-eyed as he skipped over the ground before finally stopping thirty feet away. He rolled to his hands and knees with a curse, but before he could stand Thyra hit him with another blast of dense air that flipped him backwards end over end.

He stood up—slower this time—and stumbled forward. One hand rose and a bolt of lightning shot in Thyra's direction. She acted without thinking and formed a shield in front of her. Instead of one composed of lighting, a wall of dense air formed in front of her. The lightning struck it with a thunderous clap, but the shield held.

Magni's lightning stopped and his hands dropped to his sides, chest heaving. "This is not possible!"

"You're right about one thing, *brother*," Thyra said, her surprise turning to anger. "I am dangerous." She emphasized her words with a series of air blasts that slammed against the shield Magni threw up, each one driving him backwards. Her anger taking full control, Thyra reached for her lighting and sent a bolt of lightning into Modi's shield with her right hand and a missile of dense air with her left. The ability to control both at the same time gave her new confidence. "More than you know!"

Magni's jaw set stubbornly, but his eyes were wide behind his shield. He let the shield fall away and the twin axes returned to his hands. "You may have the power, but you're no warrior. I am!"

He tensed like he was going to charge, but whatever Magni had in mind was cut off by the sound of a roaring engine and tires skidding across gravel as the Chevelle came to a stop. Modi leaped out the Chevelle without turning the car off, his eyes wide with rage. Thyra took a step back and readied herself for the possibility of Modi attacking her as well. But it wasn't Thyra that Modi was looking at. He glared at Magni with eyes full of reproach. "Magni! What is the meaning of this?"

Magni ignored him. He began to charge at Thyra, but Modi stepped in his way and pushed his brother backwards. "What—are—you—do-ing?! I told you to teach her, not try to kill her. I only got a few miles down the road before I felt the surge of your magic. I turn around only to find the two of your attempting to alert every mortal for miles around that you're here. So, I'll ask again. What are you doing?"

"We don't need her!" Magni roared, spittle dripping from his lips into his beard. His eyes were rimmed with red, making the blue-white glow from his magic stand out even more in comparison. "She is too dangerous. We should kill her now! Stand out of my way."

"Don't be a fool!" Modi snapped.

"I was a fool to let you talk me into this in the first place," Magni growled. He attempted to push Modi aside, but stumbled backwards suddenly, putting a hand to his jaw. When he looked up, his eyes were full of a burning rage that made Thyra take a step backward. Except, it wasn't directed at her—it was directed at Modi. "You dare strike me?"

"You've lost your mind, brother," Modi snapped through a pained grimace. "Start thinking or I will put you down, once and for all!"

Magni rose to his full height and glared down at Modi. "You wouldn't dare."

"Wouldn't I? Quit thinking like a barbaric fool and open your eyes! You saw what she just did. Do you really think you'd win this fight?" Modi jabbed his brother in the chest, knocking him back a step. "Don't ruin everything we've worked so hard to do because you are afraid."

"I'm not afraid of anyone," Magni growled, shoving a finger in Modi's face. "Least of all her!"

Modi held up his hands and backtracked. "I know you're not, brother. But we are so close to retaking Mjolnir. So close I can almost feel the hammer in my hands! Can't you? Don't throw it all away when we are on the verge of achieving the one goal we've had for centuries. You know why we need the girl! Don't ruin plans you agreed to!"

"She will turn on us the first chance she gets!" Magni snarled.

"Like you just did?" Magni scowled, but looked away rather than give the obvious answer to Modi's question. Modi held two fingers in front of Magni's face. "Two days, brother. Two days! That's all and we could be standing together with Mjolnir in our hands. But to do that, we need her—alive and on our side!"

"We don't need her," Magni argued, but some of the fire had left his voice. "We can do it alone. Listen—"

"No!" Modi shouted. He clenched his fists and shook them before regaining control of himself and placing them gently on Magni's shoulders. He lowered his voice and spoke calmly. "You listen to me, brother. Thyra must be there!"

"Why?" Magni blurted out.

"You know why!" Modi snapped. He looked away and took a deep breath before continuing. "You know what will happen if she isn't, right?" He leaned in even closer and whispered something that Thyra couldn't make out. It had an effect on Magni. His anger melted away almost instantly. He looked over his brother's shoulder at Thyra and frowned. After a moment he nodded grudgingly. Modi reached up and cupped his brother's face. "We are so close. Soon, we will be *gods* again. Nothing will stand in our way!"

"And no one," Magni rumbled.

"That's right," Modi said with a nod. "That's right." He put a calming hand on Magni's shoulder and pointed towards the Chevelle with the other. "Now, I think it would be wise if you got in the car. I will speak to our little sister and get this settled."

Magni reluctantly obeyed, but not without giving Thyra one last scathing glare. Thyra returned the look defiantly, waiting for the slightest provocation to unleash on the brute.

"Forgive Magni," Modi said, his voice dripping with honey. "He often falls victim to his passion."

"Forgive him? He was trying to kill me!" Thyra snapped. She glared at Magni through the windshield of the Chevelle. His lips curled down in a petulant frown. That was all she needed to see to know nothing was going to change. "No way. This thing, this little alliance we have, it's over!"

Modi took a step closer, but stopped when Thyra took a step backward and raised her hand in his direction. He immediately held up his hands in a non-threatening manner. "Peace, little sister. Magni made a poor choice in the heat of the moment. I think he will see that once his emotions calm down."

"I don't think his feelings are going to change," Thyra replied. "He's made it pretty clear that he hates me."

"Can you blame him?" Modi shrugged. "Face it, little sister. There is much to envy about you. Your strength, your station, and now your evolving magic. He simply gave in to his envy without considering what we stand to gain by keeping you close."

"If he was hoping to help me trust you two more," Thyra said, "he failed miserably."

"Something I will speak to him about at length." Modi assured her. "His actions were not what I had hoped for when I asked him to instruct you. I will set him straight and make him see the error of his ways. He will be kitten by the time I'm done with him."

"I doubt that."

"Perhaps not, but he will be meek as one by the time I'm through." Modi sounded confident, even if Thyra wasn't. He took a deep breath and let it out slow. "We need you, little sister. He knows that. You must forgive him for his shortsightedness."

"Forgiveness may be divine," Thyra growled, "but only a fool turns a blind eye to the knife they know is already there!"

"Wise words," Modi agreed, "but if we're going to get our father's hammer, we need to do it together. I make no excuses for Magni, but you will have to trust me when I say that I will keep him in check. There is nothing either of us want more than retrieving that hammer. He knows that, and he knows that we need you if we are going to be successful."

Thyra wasn't about to forgive and forget. She considered just walking away right then and there, but she knew her brothers wouldn't allow that. She'd have to fight her way free. While there was no doubt in her mind that she'd have to face off against her brothers at some point, she wasn't sure if she was ready for that to happen here and now. She had a long list of enemies already. It made sense to keep these two close for a while longer. At least until they got her closer to the hammer.

Thyra lowered her hand, but kept a hold of her magic. "Fine. Our alliance can last a little longer. But you keep him away from me."

"A reasonable demand," Modi agreed with a nod. A slow smile

spread across his face and he laughed softly. "You are *so much* more than we imagined. This is why we need you! Your power is unlike anything we thought possible. You demonstrate control of the *wind*! We never expected that."

Thyra's curiosity was undeniable. So much so that it overrode some of her caution. For now, at least. "Why? You said our magic is elemental. Why does me controlling the air surprise you?"

"*Wind* is the element that applies in this cases," Modi corrected. "But that is splitting hairs. Why it is surprising is that you managed to do it on your own."

"Again, why?" Thyra demanded.

"Yes, 'why.' There are so many of those that I can't even explain it all, but I'll try. In short, Aesir magic always took a form—lightning, the rays of the sun, earth, fire—and remained so throughout our lives. Very few of our kind ever managed to expand beyond the element we chose."

"Chose? What do you mean? I don't remember choosing anything."

"I forget how little you know," Modi said. He held up a hand to stave off her retort. "That wasn't meant as an insult—just a statement of face. Simply stated, you chose to be a child of the storm, a lightning goddess, whether you knew it or not. Magic was born inside you, and your natural association due to your parentage was with lightning. Your strength was in the elements of the storm. You chose to use what came to you naturally." He hesitated, shaking his head slowly. "But now, now you have expanded your reach. You have expanded to control of wind as well."

Or I'm just becoming a true child of the storm, Thyra thought to herself. Storms were nothing without wind to move them and add fury. She left that thought unsaid, though. Modi's explanation was enough for now.

"What did you say to Modi to get him to calm down?"

"I just reminded him of who you are important to," Modi answered.

Thyra's eyes narrowed. "Who? Who am I important to?"

"You already know the answer."

"Humor me."

Modi smiled. "Magni and I can teach you about your magic. At least *some* of your magic, as is evident by what I've seen today. But only *one* person can teach you about being the champion of magic."

"Odin."

Modi nodded. "The Allfather desires to meet you, little sister. At his feet, you will learn wonders you never thought possible. He will instruct you, guide you, and help you become more than you ever thought possible." He laughed softly. "We thought we knew what you were when we came looking for you—daughter of Thor and the successor to Odin's mantle as Yggdrasil's champion—but you are proving to be so much more."

"And you're taking me to Odin?" Modi nodded in response, but Thyra didn't let him speak. "Then why did you tell me you needed me to help you get Mjolnir. Which is it? Do you need me to get the hammer or are you two just Odin's messenger boys?"

"Both, truthfully."

"Then what is all this about getting revenge on Olafsson stuff?" Thyra snapped. "Why couldn't we just go straight to Odin?"

"Which one would you have been more ready to accept—taking down Olafsson or going to the Allfather?" Modi raised an eyebrow. "We both know where your motivation was. We made a tactical decision to tell you what you wanted to hear. Besides, plans are in motion that even I do not understand completely. We only know what we need to know."

"What do you know?"

For a moment it looked like Modi might hedge, but he answered the question. "By going after Olafsson, we're creating a distraction so other plans can move forward."

"Your plans? Or Odin's?"

"Who says they're different?" Modi shrugged. "We weaken Olafsson by destroying his property and disrupting his affairs. In the process we divert his eye away from our end goal of retaking Mjolnir and joining Odin. Olafsson—no *Surtur!*—attacked Asgard and had the gall to think he could stand above the gods! He thought he could kill the Allfather and destroy all that Odin had created. We will show him how wrong he was. We will humble him to the earth and remind him where he truly stands."

Thyra was a little concerned by the fanatical fervor that had entered Modi's voice during those last few statements. Magni was openly unhinged, but Modi's level of crazy might easily be worse. But, she'd be lying if her own feelings didn't mirror his own. Olafsson deserved to pay. "So all of this, what we did last night, that was all part of Odin's plan?"

"Does that change anything?"

Thyra took a deep breath before shaking her head. "No."

Modi smiled knowingly. "I saw your face last night. You took pleasure in what we did. It felt good taking a small piece of flesh for everything Olafsson, the Muspel Corporation, even Baldur, have taken from you. You enjoyed it. And tonight you can take another pound of flesh."

He reached into his pocket and held out a slip of paper to Thyra. She didn't make a move to take it. "What is that?"

"The address of an electrical substations owned by the Muspel Corporation," Modi replied.

"What am I supposed to do with it?"

"Make Olafsson bleed," Modi said. "We sent a message last night in Lincoln, bruised his face. Now we have the opportunity to drive it home and make him truly hurt."

He extended the paper towards Thyra, but she had no intention of getting close to him. Instead, she decided to test her new-found power. Concentrating, she wrapped the paper in air and pulled it out of his hand and floated it to her. The address was in a suburb just outside of Chicago based off of Modi's instructions.

"We go here," Thyra looked up at Modi, " and do what?"

"You know what," Modi said. "We destroy it and make sure we're seen doing it."

"And then?"

Modi nodded. "After we hurt Surtur, I will personally take you to meet the Allfather. Odin wants to meet you, little sister, and our plan to retake Mjolnir falls apart without you."

"Why?" Thyra snapped. "Why does it fall it apart?"

"We three are strong enough to take down Olafsson and the empire he has created," Modi replied. "But only if we're working together. Besides, it has a poetic ring to it—Thor's children storming the tower Gunnar Olafsson has built for himself the same way he razed Asgard so long ago. Retaking the weapon of their father. *Together.*"

Something still felt off, but she didn't know what. Until she did, Thyra had to go along with the plan. "Okay. Just remember, after what happened here today, I don't trust you enough to believe in your promises."

"The same way we don't trust you," Modi said with a grim chuckle. "But perhaps we'll learn to before this is all over. Only time will tell. Meet us at that address. Tonight we don't just send a message—we make Surtur feel true pain."

He walked over to the Camaro and laid the arm ring on the hood. He nodded to Thyra in a way that suggested the significance of what he had just done, but Thyra only stared back. He turned with a wave and got into the Chevelle.

Magni started the car up and rolled down his window. The look he gave her was just as full of meaning. Modi may have intervened, but there was no doubt in Thyra's mind that Magni was going to be a problem.

One she looked forward to dealing with.

Chapter 23

Thyra drove around the substation three times before finally parking a block away. Surrounded by a ten-foot tall brick wall, the substation looked every bit a castle that she had no idea how to breach. The gate was chain link but a banner stating that the electrical company was now a subsidiary of the Muspel Corporation blocked her from getting a good look at what was inside.

The banner was a problem. She had no idea who, what, or where anything was on the other side. Sure, she could stand just outside the wall and start calling down lightning blindly, but that option felt beyond reckless. There could be workers inside, and no matter how much Modi insisted that they were guilty by association, Thyra didn't want to risk hurting someone who was just punching the clock.

The only way to avoid the risk of striking blindly was to find a way inside. From where she stood, she had two options—over the wall or through the gate. Climbing the wall was a no-go, but the gate didn't seem like a good option, either. Sure, she could blow it away, but there was one problem— the two cameras positioned on either side of the entrance. Magni and Modi might be fine with letting their faces be seen, but Thyra wanted to avoid it as much as possible. *If* it was possible.

The sun was just about to set when Thyra sat down on a bench across the street from the gate. The street in front of the substation was quiet. Almost a little too quiet for a street just outside of a major city. So far there had been no sign of Modi and Magni. On one hand, their absence made her suspicious. They had left before her, and Modi supposedly had scouted out the substation in advance. They should have arrived first. On the other hand, Thyra was relieved they hadn't. She didn't want to do things on their terms again. She didn't want to be part of another disaster like the truck yard. The best way to make sure that didn't happen was to do it herself.

Thyra cobbled together a tentative plan for how to attack the substation. If she was going to go through the gate, she first needed to take out those cameras without being close enough to be recognizable when the video was reviewed later. Her answer to that challenge was to test her newfound control of the air around her.

She guessed the distance to the gate at about fifty feet. Glancing both ways, she made sure the coast was clear. Confident she was alone on the quiet street, she formed a dense ball of air in front of her and willed it to fly at the camera. She missed. *Badly.* Instead of striking the camera, her attempt blew a cloud of dust off the wall three feet to the left. Her second attempt wasn't any better, this time striking the wall a few feet below the camera. Two more attempts went wide before her concentration crumbled beneath frustration. She sagged back against the bench and put her hands over her eyes.

"The wind in this city has always been fickle."

Thyra jumped to her feet and spun, calling her magic up without a thought. She wasn't sure what she was expecting to find, but the old man with short, curly gray hair smiling at her was not it. He studied her with wizened eyes, seemingly unconcerned by the magic dancing in Thyra's electric eyes.

He moved around the bench slowly and sat down with a sigh. "I knew it was only time until you came."

Thyra's mouth went dry. The footage from Lincoln must have been better than she thought. "I don't want any trouble."

"Nor do I," the old man replied. "As entrancing as those eyes of yours are, you have nothing to fear from me. You can release your magic."

Thyra shook her head. "Not until you explain yourself."

"I respect that," he said with a chuckle. He looked across the street at the substation and his smile faded. "I've been coming to this bench on nights like this for years. Almost as long as I can remember. I've seen this neighborhood change a lot over that time. I like to think that I know every person that lives around here by their face at the very least. Makes it easy to pick out a stranger." He frowned. "I saw that eyesore across the street go from an empty lot to what it is today. I understood its purpose, even if I wished it was in some other neighborhood. Lately, I've been wishing I had fought harder against it, but there wasn't much an old man could do to stop progress. Didn't make me lose much sleep honestly. Until the Muspel Corporation took over, that is."

Thyra's eyes narrowed. "What do you know about the Muspel Corporation?"

"Too much, and too little," the old man lamented. He looked up at Thyra. "Have a seat, young lady. Perhaps we can help each other."

"I doubt that."

He let out a quick burst of laughter. "You might be surprised. I know I don't look like much, but if I've lost a few steps, I've grown stronger in other ways." He pointed to the two trees that bracketed the bench. "Did you know that I've watched these two trees grow since they were little more than saplings? I know all the trees that grow on this street even better than I know the people. You might call them my friends. I like talking to them. Trees are stubborn, see, but they will listen to reason given time."

Thyra agreed with him—he wasn't a threat to her. He was just an old man who was on the verge of senility.

Her caution didn't go unnoticed. "You're looking at me like I'm crazy."

"You're giving me plenty of reason to think so."

The old man chuckled. "There's been times I would have agreed with you. But, I think people like us always have moments like that."

"People like us?"

The old man smiled. "My name is Arthur. The trees tell me that you control the wind. Among other things."

Thyra cocked an eyebrow. "The trees told you?"

Arthur nodded. "I told you, they are my friends."

Thyra slowly sat down on the far end of the bench. "So, you have magic?"

Arthur shrugged. "Not a word my era was comfortable using, but I guess it's the best one for the job. My mother called it my 'special talent' and my father did his best to forget it and to convince me to do the same." He nodded towards the branches overhead. "The trees and plants don't use words, necessarily. More of feelings. Instincts. They feel the wind shake their branches, the sun on their leaves, the soil around their roots. What they do do is make surprisingly profound observations about the world around them." Arthur blinked and then smiled. "But, you didn't come here to listen to me prattle on. You came here for what's behind those walls, didn't you?"

"That depends," Thyra said cautiously. "What's behind those walls?"

"More than just an electrical substation!" Arthur scoffed. "Especially since the Muspel Corporation took over."

"What's changed?"

Arthur looked at her. "You still haven't told me who you are."

Thyra hesitated. She had started to assume everyone who spoke to her already had the upper hand of knowing who she was. "You don't know who I am?"

"Of course I don't! I'm waiting for you to tell me!"

"But. . .you said you knew I'd be coming."

"You or someone like you," Arthur said with a nod. "I knew the moment I saw those thugs begin to go in and out of that gate that someone would eventually come to put an end to what they do behind those walls." He paused and cocked an eyebrow at her. "You seem surprised that I don't know you. Is there a reason why I should?"

"No," Thyra said quickly. "It just seems like a lot of people know who I am, even before I do."

"Well, I do know a few things about you," Arthur said. "For example, the trees told me you control the wind. From the way your eyes are gleaming, I'd guess that's not all. There was a lot of talk a few months back about a girl that was shooting lightning out of her hands. You can hardly trust the news anymore," he hesitated and looked at Thyra askance, "but now I'm thinking they weren't far off. That was you, wasn't it?"

"Seems like you do know quite a bit about me," Thyra grumbled.

Arthur smiled. "But I still don't know your name."

Thyra sighed and then gave it.

"That's a beautiful name." Arthur looked back across the street. "Like I said, I notice strangers. There's been a lot more since this Muspel Corporation took over a last winter. Black SUVs coming and going at all hours. Men rushing in and out of buildings. None of them looking like electricians or repairmen."

"I can understand why you may not like it," Thyra said, "but why did that make you suspicious?"

He turned and pointed to a balcony on the third floor of the building behind them. "I've got a good view and don't sleep well at night. I may not have grown up comfortable with what I can do, but I know of others who aren't quite so reserved with their talents. They make a show of themselves all too often. Some of them have disappeared and the whispers are that black SUVs like the ones I see going in and out of this substation are involved."

Thyra looked at the substation across the street in a new light. If what Arthur was telling her was true, she now had even more reason to want to get inside.

"If that was all, I might just chalk it up to an old man's mind playing tricks on him in the middle of the night. Too many true crime shows making me jumpy." Arthur sighed and shook his head. "But, there's more. You see, I'm not the only one in my family with a special gift. I have a granddaughter. She can do something similar to me, except on people."

"Read their thoughts?"

"And more." Arthur reached out and touched the trunk of the tree next to him. Thyra's jaw fell when a tender branch grew between Arthur's fingers and a single white blossom opened on the end. "Like I said, trees can be stubborn, but they respond to reason." He plucked the blossom and handed it to Thyra. "I told this one that you could use something pretty to make you smile. It agreed."

The blossom did bring a smile to Thyra's face. "Thank you. It's beautiful."

"What my granddaughter can do makes that blossom pale in comparison." Arthur's smile turned sad. "She can control the mind of anyone she touches. Even from a young age I recognized the power in her. I tried to help her, to let her know she wasn't alone, but she resented me for telling her she needed to keep it secret. She moved out the day she compelled her parents to emancipate her. Went to New York City. I tried keeping in contact with her over the years, but she didn't want anything to do with me. She felt that I was part of the problem."

He frowned and stared at the ground in front of him. "Until she called out of the blue a month ago. She said that she had finally found where she was accepted. She said she was finally free to be herself without fear of anyone or anything. I tried asking her what she had gotten herself into, but she wouldn't tell me. Instead, she warned me to be careful about the substation across the street and to steer clear of the men in the black SUVs. She wouldn't say exactly how she knew, but that what was happening there was dangerous. Then she told me that she could protect me if I came to New York. That her new friends could protect us from ever needing to fear again."

Thyra listened quietly, trying to understand why Arthur was telling her all of this. There was only one conclusion she could think of. "You think she's involved with the Muspel Corporation?"

"I'm not sure," Arthur said, "but she confirmed that something bad is going down behind those walls. The Muspel Corporation is in the middle of it all."

"Well, you're both right about that," Thyra grumbled. "There isn't time to tell you the whole story, but the CEO is bent on dominating magic. First he wanted to destroy it and everyone who used it. Now, I think he's trying to use magic for his own gain. He's tried to ruin my life at every turn. And I'm tired of it."

Arthur nodded. "I knew someone would come. Someone who could stop what was happening here. That person is you."

Thyra felt the weight on her shoulders grow. "I think your hopes are pinned too high."

"The trees think you can do what's needed," Arthur stated. "So do I."

"For someone with a secret like yours, you're being awfully trusting of a complete stranger," Thyra said. "For all you know, I could be just as bad as what you think I'd be fighting. I could be a destructive torrent that burns this entire neighborhood down."

Arthur contemplated this for a moment before shrugging. "Don't some of life's greatest beauties rise out of ashes?"

"Ashes are about the only thing I leave behind," Thyra lamented. "Believe me, I do more harm than good. I'm like a doctor that uses a chainsaw instead of a scalpel. My life has become one giant mess ever since I discovered I had magic. Stay near me too long, your life will be the same."

Arthur didn't seem bothered by Thyra's warning. "The trees are usually a good judge of character. They don't think you're a bad person. But, they do agree about one thing—you are hurting and you are very destructive."

Thyra glanced up at the trees for a sign of what they were thinking, but they were silent sentinels in the diminishing light. "The Muspel Corporation took something from me."

"I'm guessing it was *someone*," Arthur commented.

Thyra nodded. "Someone that gave her life for mine. Right now, revenge is the only thing I can think of that will dull the pain." She exhaled through a grimace. "I came here to break things even before you told me what you knew. Nothing's changed. Now I have even more reasons to burn that place down."

"It would be an improvement," Arthur said.

"I'm glad to have your support, but," Thyra looked across the street at the gate, "I still need to take care of those cameras. So, forgive me, but I need to work on my aim."

"I will help you there," Arthur said, "on one condition."

Thyra frowned. "I don't like conditions."

"This one isn't too demanding," Arthur said. "I'll take care of those cameras for you, but I need you to watch out for my granddaughter. If you are going after the Muspel Corporation, that means you're going to New York. I know the city is full of people, but I can't help but think your paths are going to cross. If they do, all I ask is that you try to get through to her."

Thyra was shaking her head before he even finished. "I can't promise that. Wherever I go, people get hurt."

"I know you can't guarantee that," Arthur said. "She's made a decision and in her mind she's doing the best thing for herself. I just ask that if you meet her, you let her know she can always come home."

Thyra sighed. "I'll try, but that's all I can say."

Arthur smiled. "That's all I ask. Her name is Amara." He stood up with a groan. "These old bones don't move as swift as they used to. It may take me a few minutes, but I'll make sure those cameras aren't a problem for you." He directed a warm smile to Thyra. "It was good to meet you, young lady."

"You too, Arthur."

He nodded one more time and then walked away. Thyra watched him as he made his way down to an intersection and crossed over. He strolled back towards the substation, looking up at each tree he passed, his lips moving in what Thyra figured was a greeting. As he passed near the tree to the left of the gate, he reached out and placed one hand on the trunk. He spoke softly and then moved on to the tree to the right of the gate. He repeated the same routine and then began walking slowly away. He glanced briefly at Thyra as he passed under a streetlight and winked.

Thyra was wondering what the wink was for. Her answer came a second later when she heard a strange sound from across the street. Branches on the two trees Arthur had touched suddenly began to reach towards the cameras. Thyra caught herself staring slack-jawed as the cameras disappeared beneath a thick layer of leaves. Her surprise only lasted a moment before she recognized the opening Arthur had given her and leapt to her feet. She began to draw on her magic as she crossed the street, condensing the air in front of her until it shimmered. She unleashed it in a howling fury that ripped the gate off its hinges, flinging it into the gravel yard of the substation.

She hesitated, half expecting a stream of men in tactical gear to come streaming out of every shadow, but none came. Even with no opposition rushing out to meet her, Thyra still moved carefully into the yard of the substation.

A gray, brick building was central to the substation and Thyra headed straight for it. From Arthur's description, that was the most likely place for whatever the Muspel Corporation wanted this particular substation for. A heavy padlock held the door closed, but Thyra formed a knife composed of lightning that cut through it like a hot knife through butter. She tossed the padlock aside, took a deep breath, and pulled the door open.

The interior of the building was not what Thyra was expecting. There were no nefarious torture devices, no racks of weapons, and no sign that the building was used for anything other than the tasks of providing electricity to the neighborhood. Controls, monitoring equipment and tools lined the walls. A single chair was pushed under a small desk with charts and blueprints spread across the surface. Thyra rifled through the charts and papers but saw nothing that would make her think the Muspel Corporation was using this site in the way Arthur described.

Thyra was so absorbed in her frustration that she almost didn't hear the faint click behind her. A door she hadn't noticed on the back wall had swung open and a man dressed in the all-too familiar black tactical gear of the Muspel Corporation stood with a rifle leveled in her direction. They stood there staring at each other for a long moment before he barked an order to put her hands up. Thyra raised her hands, but not out of fear. The sight of what he was wearing brought Asiri's face to the forefront of her thoughts. Her eyes misted with the loss of her friend. Her anger came roaring just behind.

"You killed her!"

His eyebrows furrowed. "Killed who?"

"Asiri!"

"I don't know what you're talking about, girl. What I do know is that you're in a whole lot of trouble. We're going to have a long talk about how you got in here."

Thyra's eyes lit up with magic. "You killed Asiri! You killed my friend."

Recognition flooded his face. Recognition mixed with a healthy dose of fear. "You're her, aren't you? You're the girl everyone has been talking about. We have people looking everywhere for you. And here you are. You walked right up to my door and kicked it in."

"I'm going to do a lot worse in a minute," Thyra said through gritted teeth. She wiped a tear that escaped the corner of her eye away with the back of her hand. "Leave now, and I'll forget I ever saw you here."

"You're not calling the shots here." He reached for a pair of zip ties at his waist and tossed them to her. "Put those on."

"No."

He hesitated, his mounting uncertainty evident on his face. "Listen, there's an easy way and a hard way to do this. The easy way is you take those and put them on like a good little girl. The hard way ends a lot worse for you."

"You're alone. Do you really think you're a match for me?"

He licked his lips and began inching towards the door. "I won't be alone for long. There will be a dozen others like me here soon."

"You killed my friend," Thyra repeated, her voice dropping to an octave full of menace. "By the time they get here, it will be too late for you."

A lightning spear materialized in her hand with a crackle. Thyra threw it at the same time the air rang with the repeat of his rifle. Something struck her in the side hard enough to force her back a step, but her focus was on the Muspel Corp goon. Her spear had flown true. He slowly sagged to the ground, smoke rising from his chest.

Thyra felt a strange emptiness fill her as she watched the life leave his eyes. Death had followed her for months, and she knew she had been the cause of some of it. But this time she saw it all. She had taken a life and the rush of emotion that surged within her was mind-numbing and crushing all at once. Her stomach turned and she emptied it onto the floor until it was just as painfully numb.

Heart pounding in her ears, Thyra pulled her eyes away and looked at the hidden door he had emerged from. Doing her best not to look at what she had done, she stumbled to it and into the room beyond. A rack of rifles that screamed Muspel Corporation lined one wall while a pair of laptops sat on a desk beneath a map of the city on the opposite wall. Still feeling numb, Thyra walked over to the map and stared the series of colored marks and words that were written on it. Slowly, the meaning of the words pierced her brain fog. They marked locations of known magic users throughout the city, with a brief description of the kind of magic each was suspected to have and a level of priority. Some were in blue, but most were in red. Those marked in red each had a date written beneath and either "captured" or "terminated" after.

Each of those red marks was a person like her. Someone gifted with magic. Someone the Muspel Corporation had gone after the way they had gone after Thyra. She wondered if Asiri's name was on a board somewhere with the word "terminated" after it.

Thyra's breathing began to race. She couldn't get enough air. She stumbled away from the map, the room spinning. She tripped over the body of the man she had killed as she rushed for the door and fell out into the gravel yard. She crawled to the middle of the yard and rolled onto her back, chest still heaving for air between whimpers of sadness and angry growls.

The sky overhead was purple, lined with the pink of the dying light. Clouds had begun to move in, massive gray behemoths that were dark with more than just night's arrival. Dark with energy. Energy that called to her. Energy that wanted a purpose.

Thyra pushed herself up onto her feet. Her legs shook with the effort, but she managed to stay upright. Her rage still burned hot and was keeping the fog from rolling back in over her mind. That rage danced in her eyes when she looked at the building in front of her. Modi and Magni had sent her here to destroy the substation, to make Gunnar Olafsson bleed. She'd seen it as an opportunity to avenge Asiri to some degree. After what she'd just seen, she had more than enough reason to do it.

But there was something that stopped her.

Thyra disappeared back into the building and reemerged a moment later dragging a burden behind her. She turned around when she reached the middle of the yard and formed a shield of air around her until the world beyond it shimmered and was distorted. Looking up, she reached towards the energy in the clouds and called to it. For the first time since she left Idaho behind, she wished she had Lynnedslag to help magnify her power. Asiri's face was enough to make her pull as hard as she could on the well of magic inside her.

The sky rolled with thunder as the energy overhead gathered. She waited until it grew into a fury that threatened to escape her control before directing it downward. Her vision went white as lightning struck all around her. Not content with what the storm was providing her, she reached for the electricity running through the substation and used it to add to the destruction. The world became a blue-white blur, the ground shaking as the lightning struck and the thunder rolled. Her shield of air had held. *Barely.*

Finally, she fell forward exhausted onto her hands and knees. Her vision slowly cleared, revealing the fruits of her rage. Twisted, scorched metal burned all around her. Where the building that housed the Muspel Corporation's secrets once stood there was only a few smoldering cinder blocks remaining.

Standing took every ounce of strength she had left, made worse by a searing pain in her side. Thyra touched it and a wave of pain almost sent her back to her knees. Grimacing through the pain, she turned and limped away from the substation.

The sky was blacker than it had been a few minutes before. She quickly realized why. The carnage had remained within the walls of the substation, but its destruction had blacked out the neighborhood. She felt a twinge of guilt when she thought about what that meant for the people who lived nearby, but she swallowed it down to where her anger could burn it away.

Thyra stumbled away from the substation and headed to where she had parked the Camaro. Sirens blared in the distance, heralding the arrival of emergency vehicles. Thyra suppressed the urge to hurry. She'd be long gone before they arrived.

She was almost to the Camaro when she heard the familiar roar of an engine. Tired as she was, Thyra reached for her magic and held it ready as the blue Chevelle came to a screeching stop. Modi's eyes danced with a wild light as he leaned out of the window. "Thor's daughter indeed! You made Gunnar bleed tonight!"

Thyra was in no mood for his excitement. "Where were you two?"

"Watching," Modi replied without hesitation. He looked down at her side. "You're injured. How bad?"

Thyra ignored his fake concern and barked, "Watching? You were supposed to be helping me!"

"You did a fine enough job on your own, I'd say," Modi replied with his customary sneer. "This was a test. One that you passed."

"A test?" Thyra hissed through gritted teeth. She couldn't believe it! Then again, what reason did she have to think her brothers would act differently? Magni had already said he'd turn on her without hesitation. "You set me up."

"We gave you the opportunity to prove who you are once and for all," Modi said dismissively. He leaned out the window and pointed a finger at her. "Most importantly, to yourself."

"You hung me out to dry," Thyra barked. "I could have been killed!"

"But you weren't!" Modi said. He saw the fire in her eyes and stopped her with a hand. "We can stand here arguing with each other all night or we can call what just happened what it is—a success! What you did tonight will be seen by the world as a clear message that magic is fighting back. Not just any magic, though. The children of Thor!"

"Funny. I didn't see any other children of Thor there," Thyra snapped. She stuck a finger in Modi's face. "No more games. No more messages sent, no more odd stops along the way, and no more tests! I'm done with all your stupid demands. It's my turn—take me to Odin! Now!"

Modi glanced at Magni, sharing a look Thyra couldn't see in the dark, and then turned back, his sneer tight. "You want to meet him. Fine. We've seen what we need to see." He shifted the Chevelle into gear and let it begin rolling forward. "Get in your car, little sister. The Allfather awaits."

Chapter 24

Hela could feel him growing closer.

What started as a mild tingle at the base of her skull grew until it became a presence that threatened to overwhelm her senses. The only thing that kept her knees from buckling was the surge of emotions that it triggered.

Even after centuries of practicing her craft, she still struggled to explain the connection between healer and the healed that often developed. The process of healing was an intimate experience. It required strength from both and at times the divide between blurred, allowing for a transfer of energy that lasted long afterwards. Especially when strong emotion was involved. What stronger emotion was there than love?

Hate, perhaps.

Which one did she feel more strongly? Hela wasn't sure. Passion was the root of both, making them so closely related that they became almost interchangeable. It was infuriating how quickly she switched from feeling one to the other whenever he was near.

Dismissing herself from her patients, Hela retreated to the room she had turned into her sanctuary. Without thinking about what she was doing, she went to the mirror and began fussing with her hair like some love-struck girl. Frowning, she forced her hands back to her sides and turned away from the mirror. She retreated to a chair in the center of the room and did her best to regain her composure while she waited for him to arrive.

Against her will, her heart began to race when the door opened and he entered the room. Her eyes drank in the squareness of his jaw, his broad shoulders, the shape of the muscle his shirt stretched to contain. Even after a thousand years, he was still the most beautiful man ever born.

And she hated him for it.

Hela took an equal measure of satisfaction and concern from the visible wounds he carried. She hated to see his perfection marred, but it helped reduce the effect his appearance had on her. She reached out with her magic and took measure of the wounds she couldn't see with her eyes. What she found piqued her curiosity. What in the world could have done that to him? The possibilities were intriguing. And alarming.

Vidar closed the door behind him and exhaled heavily. "You've been busy."

"Did you expect anything less?"

He frowned. "A hospital? That was your big plan?"

"Better than chasing after some teenage girl with no plan at all," Hela replied. "How is our dear Thyra these days? Is she hiding from me? Just out of sight." Hela reached out with her power and then shook her head. "No, she wouldn't be able to do that. I've felt the beating of her heart, the coursing of her blood. I'd know if she was here. Which makes me wonder, if you're here, what has happened to the girl you gave your allegiance to?"

Rather than answer, Vidar walked to a window and parted the blinds with one hand. "This is getting out of control."

Hela glanced out the window. "I'm surprised to hear you say that. These people aren't half as imaginative as their ancestors. When they start cutting out hearts and throwing them to the flames, then I may have to intervene. I will require sacrifices of a different type in this age."

"That's not what I'm talking about," Vidar snapped. "This age was not meant for people like us. Now that they know we're here, everything is starting to spin more out of control."

Hela sneered. "Only because you don't have the stomach for what needs to be done."

"There's several of Olafsson's men that would say otherwise."

"It's sad that you confuse throwing cars and swinging a tree with doing what is necessary," Hela said, confirming his guess that she had heard about what happened in Idaho. "The people of this world are lost, weak lambs in search of a shepherd. I'm giving them what they want."

"I don't remember you being very pastoral," Vidar snipped.

"I will be whatever is required," Hela replied. "I am rebuilding what never should have been lost. And, I might add, giving people hope where there was none to be found. If that means I have to be a wolf in the shepherd's clothing, so be it."

Vidar shook his head. "What you're doing is putting yourself in danger. You're courting jealousy at every turn. People see what you have and it won't be long before they want some of it or become willing to try to take it away. You won't share, so in the end it always comes back to people trying to tear you down."

"And that bothers you?" Hela challenged.

Vidar turned a glare on her. "Don't do that."

"Don't do what?"

Vidar slashed a hand through the air. "Don't act like you think I don't care!"

"You have a horrible way of showing it if you do," Hela growled. "We made promises to each other, Vidar! You told me that it would be the two of us, that we would stand side by side no matter what came our way."

"I remember," Vidar snapped.

"Then tell me, who broke that promise? Who left who?"

"Don't play the victim." Vidar shook his head grimly. "It doesn't suit you."

"What else can I be?" Hela barked. "You have always been the one to leave me. How many times have I stayed faithful to you only to see you disappear from my life for decades at a time? Centuries? How many times have you left me to wonder where you are, or who you're with? Tell me!"

"You know why I left," Vidar hissed turning back to the window. "When we are together, death is always on our doorstep."

"I am the goddess of death," Hela snapped. "Did you think it would be any other way?"

"You were Hela, a girl from a little village in the fjord first!" Vidar said. "That was the person I loved. Not the goddess of death! Each time I came back, I had hopes of finding that person. Every time I walked away, I left the goddess of death behind." He stopped, his shoulders shaking with the effort of controlling his voice. "How many times did you tell me that you'd leave this life behind, that we could simply be together? I may have been the one to leave but only because I finally saw through the lies you told me."

"I never lied to you," Hela scoffed.

"Oh no?" Vidar snorted in derision. "Every single time you went back to being the goddess, the granter of life or death, and the girl I loved was pushed back into the shadows to wither away. Until she was no longer even there. That's why I left once and for all! I couldn't stand seeing the face of the woman I loved, knowing that you killed her!"

"Spare me the melodramatic dribble!" Hela shouted, rising to her feet. "I'm not the only one who changed. You used to fight for something. You believed in something. But after Asgard fell, you stopped. All you wanted to do was hide away. With each passing year, you retreated more from the world. And me! You say you love me, but you stopped fighting for *me* ages ago. You stopped fighting for anything!"

Vidar spun to face her and slashed his hand through the air. "Well, I'm fighting now!"

Hela threw her hands up. "Oh, goody! You've thrown your hat in with Thor's daughter. I'm so relieved. Everything is obviously forgiven." She had to look away to keep from strangling him where he stood. She was so angry that she was sure she could do it with her hands, no magic needed. "Look at where that has gotten you! You went out of some foolish loyalty to her, and she walked out on you the first chance she could."

"She didn't walk out," Vidar said. "We told her to go. It was the best way to protect her."

"Whatever makes you sleep at night," Hela retorted. "From what I can see, Thyra is running loose, unhinged and in the company of what I can only assume are her brothers. I'm sure that rubs Sif wrong a thousand different ways. And now here you are, crawling back to me, broken and bloodied!" She paused, her chest heaving. She took a breath, but it did nothing to calm her. "I won't lie to you. I can't help but feel some satisfaction from how quickly you managed to fail. The only thing that could make your failure even sweeter for me was if your sister was killed." Hela sneered. "But I can feel her lurking nearby, so my luck only goes so far. Pity."

Anger flashed in Vidar's eyes, but Hela wasn't afraid. She could needle him til he bled from head to toe, but he would never retaliate. Not against her. He would stand there and take it, boiling inside, but too angry at himself to ever fight back. He was a shadow of the man she had loved. She wasn't sure if she even loved the one standing in front of her.

Vidar closed his eyes, his head slowly drooping. "You're right about one thing. Thyra is with Magni and Modi. She wasn't when Sif helped her escape the attack on their home, but they caught up to her somewhere along the way."

"Another failure to add to the list," Hela scoffed. "I suppose you're here to beg for my help. Well, tough luck, I'm in no mood to help you chase down a teenage girl."

"She is going after Mjolnir," Vidar said.

That surprised Hela and she readily admitted it. "Perhaps I judged the girl wrong. It seems she inherited a few other things from her father in addition to his magic. She has his backbone it seems. I already knew about the dullness of her wits."

Vidar sighed in exasperation. "You should hope that she gets it. If she doesn't, even you may find yourself sleeping with one eye open."

Hela cocked one eyebrow. "I'm tingling with anticipation to hear what kind of bogey-man you're going to try to scare me with this time."

"Baldur and Gunnar are going after Idunn's garden," Vidar said. He waited to let that sink in. "They have some of the summoning stones."

It was a struggle for Hela to keep her expression flat. "You know that for a fact?"

"Surtur has lived long enough to become Gunnar Olafsson because he managed to summon Idunn once, which means he has some of the stones," Vidar replied. "Baldur knew as much about the summoning stones as any. Sif and I agree that he probably knew where more might be. Add in the fact that they have Bragi and that becomes even more plausible."

Hela didn't believe in acting on suspicion alone. But, in this case, it was a suspicion she shared. "How many do you think they have?"

"One in their hands is too many."

"One would not be enough to compel Idunn to leave her garden."

"Then they have more," Vidar insisted. "Three, six, eight—what matters is that they are going to use them."

A shiver ran down her spine, but Hela shrugged it away. "Why should that concern me? If they want to use the fruit to grant immortality to their cronies, let them! I command death, and even gods can't run from that forever."

"It isn't the fruit they're after."

Hela's eyes narrowed. "What are you talking about?"

"I don't know for sure," Vidar said, "but I'm afraid that there might be bigger secrets in Idunn's garden. Ones we don't want Gunnar and Baldur to get their hands on. One even you should be concerned by."

"Nothing they could find there will be enough to hurt me. Not now." Hela's eyes narrowed with disgust. "If that's all you came here to say to me, the door is right over there."

"Don't let your feelings towards me blind you," Vidar said sharply. "This is not a threat that you can ignore out of stubborn anger at me."

"Anger is the least of the emotions I feel towards you," Hela sniffed. "In fact, I'm not sure I feel anything towards you anymore."

Vidar was suddenly in front of her chair, forcing her to crane her neck to stare into his eyes. "Well I do feel something!"

"Maybe you should have felt that something when you walked away from me," Hela said. "Maybe then it wouldn't have been too late. Now, I could care less what trouble you've gotten yourself into. You made your choice. Now, do me a favor and die with it. You and I have nothing left to say to each other."

"If that were true, you would have sicked your wolf on me before I ever got close to this place," Vidar said.

"I would have," Hela hissed, "but luckily for you, he isn't here." She took a deep breath and released it in a sigh. "Why are you here, Vidar? Tell me the truth. If you're so concerned about what Olafsson and

Baldur are doing, why aren't you running after Thyra to help her? Why come to me?"

Vidar lowered to his knees so that they were at eye level. "Thyra's path is one that she needs to walk alone. For now. I thought that I was the help she needed. I'm not so sure now."

The doubt in his face pricked something deep inside of Hela that she fought to quiet. His vulnerability, his desperation over a decision backfiring in his face, were not her problem! Yet, as much as she hated herself and Vidar even more for it, she loved him and it tore her apart to see him like this.

"If her path is her own," Hela said slowly, "then you must think our two paths are the same. Why else would you come here, risking my wrath? Out with it, Vidar. What do you want from me, Vidar?"

He looked up, his eyes flashing. "To be at my side, ready when Olafsson and Baldur make their attempt to access Idunn's garden. To stop whatever evils they have dreamed up."

Hela's eyes narrowed as she considered this. "And Sif? Does she agree that you need me?"

"She wants to stop Olafsson and Baldur, and to protect Thyra."

"And she's ready to make a deal with this devil to do it," Hela said wryly. She nodded slowly. "Fine. On one condition."

Vidar's expression tightened, a look as close to fear crossing his face as Hela had ever seen. "What do you want?"

Hela leaned in. "The only thing a lover could ever ask for. Keep your promises. When this is done, no matter the outcome, you return to me and never leave my side again."

Vidar closed his eyes and sunk down to lay his head on her lap. He stayed quiet for a long, tense moment. Hela found herself holding her breath in expectation of his response, fearing that it would be in the negative. If he said no, she didn't think she'd be able to stand having him walk away from her again. She wasn't sure she could live with the pain of having what was left of her heart being shattered to pieces.

Her fears didn't come to life. At least, not those fears. Vidar's answer sent her heart racing, but filled her with dread at the same time.

"Done," Vidar said. "My path, my life are yours. The same way yours are mine. We keep our promises."

Chapter 25

"This is the fruit of your delay."

Gunnar closed his eyes and cringed at the sound of Baldur's voice. He didn't need this right now.

"Thyra Ariksen is going to tear your empire down around you!" Baldur said matter-of-factly. He sat down and crossed one leg over the other. He was furious, but there was no point in showing it. The facts were clear, and he didn't need emotion to make his point. Every word would be like a piercing dagger as it was. "While you stall, she grows more brazen in her attacks and more dangerous with her magic. You saw what she did to those trucks in Lincoln and now what she has done in Chicago. In less than twenty-four hours, she has cost you millions of dollars!"

"You really need to stop barging into my office this way," Gunnar said in warning.

"Then you need to stop acting in such stupid ways!" Baldur snapped.

"Now is not the time for this," Gunnar said.

"But that isn't what should have you worried," Baldur continued, ignoring Gunnar's attempt to stop the conversation before it even started. "The growth of her magic is what should scare you. You woke a dragon with your idiotic move in Idaho. Now, that dragon is discovering her claws and flexing her muscles in ways you aren't prepared for."

"Do you think I don't know that?" Gunnar barked. He slammed his fist down on the desk. "I saw what she did, the same as you. I can see that her power has grown. What I want to know is who has been teaching her?"

"You know the answer to that," Baldur replied calmly. "The video from Lincoln should be more than enough proof to show that Thor's children are working together."

Gunnar shook his head in denial. "That's impossible."

"What reason do you have to think that?"

"Because you told me they wouldn't be a problem!" Gunnar snapped.

Baldur let out a long, slow breath. He had never imagined that Modi and Magni would get involved. He had been wrong and admitted it.

Gunnar's eyebrows rose up his forehead. "That's it? That's all you have to say? *You were wrong*? You told me that Magni and Modi were toothless. That they would never work together with Thyra. That they would rather kill her than help. That Sif would have their hearts on the end of her spear before she let them within a hundred miles of her daughter. You told me they wouldn't be a problem!"

"I was wrong," Baldur repeated. "But so were you. Their joining forces with Thyra is not a coincidence. You made Thyra run with your debacle in Idaho, and her brothers were waiting in the wings to scoop her up."

"So you're blaming me for pushing her into their arms?"

"You attacked Thyra at her home," Baldur said, "killed someone close to her, and now she is running. With her brothers! Even a blind man could see the connection."

Gunnar couldn't hold Baldur's gaze and turned away. "What I want to know is why were they there to scoop her up in the first place?"

"I don't know," Baldur admitted. "The last I heard, they were trying to waste away their immortality in any dive bar that would let them in. Drinking and fighting, oblivious to the world around them."

"The same information we had," Gunnar hissed. "In the Mid-West, far away from Idaho, and far away from Thyra Ariksen. How did they find her when we couldn't?"

"When *you* couldn't," Baldur corrected. He leaned forward and tapped the desk top. "They found her the same way you did. Your 'anonymous' source."

The reminder that Baldur had known where Thyra had been weeks before made Gunnar suspicious. "How do I know that 'anonymous' source wasn't you? How do I know you didn't double-cross me?"

"Do you think so little of me?"

"You've gone behind my back before," Gunnar stated.

"Not this time. My nephews hate me almost as much as I hate them," Baldur said. "I did not help them."

"Then we are no closer to finding our answers."

Baldur leaned forward. "We can answer those questions when we get into Idunn's garden. No more delays on your end. I know where the spear is. I also know where you have the summoning stones. If I wanted to, I could take what I want and do this without you. I am choosing to make this partnership work. It's time you do the same."

Gunnar inhaled deeply, his mouth twisting downward like he tasted something revolting. "Tonight."

Baldur almost sighed in relief. He expected Gunnar to push back, to insist on waiting. Thanks to Thyra, that was no longer the case. Silver linings could be found even in the worst of times. "Tonight, it is."

Gunnar nodded slowly. "I will call ahead and have things prepared for our arrival."

"Gungnir will be there?"

Gunnar hesitated, then nodded. "The spear will be there."

"And the hammer?"

Gunnar grimaced. Baldur knew he was not happy about this change to their plans. Baldur had told him why it was vital, but had met resistance at every turn.

"You know why the hammer must be there," Baldur insisted. "We cannot allow Idunn any chance of resisting the call."

"You told me that the presence of Gungnir would ensure her compliance," Gunnar argued.

"And now I'm telling you that we need both the spear and the hammer," Baldur said sharply. "We don't have time to argue. If we want to succeed, we need both present when we summon Idunn. There is no room to debate the issue. With both weapons present, Idunn would face immediate death by even thinking of refusing our call."

Gunnar still looked ready to resist. "I don't like it. You keep raising the bar at every turn."

"Because Thyra keeps doing the same!" Baldur snapped. "If you're afraid I may try to wrest the weapons away and use them against you, don't be. I've already told you, I have no interest in the hammer or the spear. I don't want them! When we're done, do as you will with them. I don't care. But, if we want to make sure that the garden is opened to us, both weapons must be there. Having the spear there is better than just the summoning stones. But having both weapons is the best way to force Idunn's hand. And you may want the hammer there when the gateway to the garden is opened. Even with it's capabilities limited, it still is a weapon. A weapon you can use to protect your life with."

They stayed there, their eyes locked in an unblinking stare for several long moments. Finally, with a heavy sigh, Gunnar nodded. "As you wish. The hammer will be there. I'd rather have it nearby as it is. If Thyra Ariksen wants her father's hammer, she will have to take it from my lifeless hands first." Gunnar grimaced, maybe imagining the possibility of that happening, and then nodded. "Tonight we summon

Idunn. I can have my helicopter readied and we can leave within the hour."

"No," Baldur said. "I will meet you there. I have preparations of my own to make." He saw the suspicion flash across Gunnar's face and decided to put the man's fears to rest before they ran too wild. "Don't worry. I have no intention of double-crossing you. I'm sure you will be bringing an army of your men. I will be bringing muscle as well. Just a different kind. We need to be ready for anything. There's no way of knowing for sure what kind of devilry Idunn has secreted away in her garden."

"What could be worse than the possibility of Odin being alive, thirsting for revenge?" Gunnar asked.

"Believe me," Baldur said as he backed away from the desk, "Odin is only the beginning of what might await us there."

Chapter 26

Thyra was running on pure adrenaline. There was no other explanation for how her eyes were still open. She was sleep deprived, malnourished, dehydrated, injured, and dealing with trauma that even a well-rested person would find difficult to sort through. She knew that if she let up for even a second, she would crash. Hard. She couldn't allow that to happen. Not yet.

In addition to all of that, she was pretty sure she was hallucinating. She saw monsters in the shadows cast by trees. Stumps became giants. Branches became rifles pointed in her direction. Dangers lurked everywhere she looked.

Even worse than what she thought she saw outside the vehicle was what was on the inside.

Thyra tried to ignore the strange man sitting in the passenger seat. She couldn't remember where he had come from or when she'd dreamed him up, but he'd held up a one-sided conversation for the past few hours, expounding on everything from the mating rituals of butterflies to the geopolitical issues of the day. He was incredibly annoying and completely unbothered by Thyra's silence.

"You seem determined to drive to your own destruction," he said. The conversation had taken a much more personal turn the deeper they drove into the wooded hills of New York. "I've seen plenty of people that have a complex, but you are on a level all your own. Falling in with Magni and Modi is one thing. I understand why you want to use them, but following them in this manner is foolish. For all you know they could be leading you off into the woods to the edge of a six-foot deep hole. Granted," he looked at the rolling forests on either side of the road and frowned, "there are worse places to die. At least it's green here. Not dry and brown like Idaho. I've been to many places, but I've found that green forests and rivers suit my constitution better than deserts. Of any kind. The time I spent in the Sahara was not pleasant. It took years before I recovered fully."

He shuddered one moment and then burst out in laughter. Just as quickly, his mirth subsided and he nodded to himself like he'd made a compelling argument that only he was privy to. "Back to your brothers, though. Let's assume they are telling you the truth and aren't salivating at the chance to deposit you into a worm-filled grave, and Odin is truly waiting for you. That possibility should have you more concerned than anything else. I'm not sure you are ready to meet the Allfather. Not in your condition. You're practically on death's doorstep." His laugh was a sharp bark of air exiting his lungs. "You might do your brothers a favor and just fall into the grave of your own accord."

Thyra glanced at him for the hundredth time and tried to decide how she'd dreamed him up. He had an angular face, high cheekbones, and a hawkish nose that his wide mouth only made look even more like a beak when he smiled. Which he did often. He seemed to think everything was funny.

"I remember Odin all too well. Not the smartest man person ever born. A bit brutish. At times imperceptive of the minute details. But he was not one to be trifled with. Those that did always ended up feeling the fury of the sun. Those were the lucky ones, mind you. The unlucky ones ended up with their heads detached from their bodies." He laughed suddenly. "I've always wondered how that would feel, to have those last moments of understanding before fading into the black, seeing your body lying a few feet from you. That would be an unbelievable experience!"

He barked another laugh and then fell quiet. Thyra was glad for the break from his ramblings. She had a feeling the silence wouldn't last long, though. She was proven right when his eyes narrowed and he nodded to himself, agreeing with another one of the points he made in his internal dialogue.

"What you need to be sure of is that Odin was a tactician. Always two steps ahead of everyone else. I mean no insult when I say that I expect the same is true for you. He has worked you into his plans somehow, and you driving right up to his front door is just the beginning for how he will use you to his benefit. It'll be nearly impossible to extricate yourself once you're woven into whatever he has planned. But you're hard-headed and willful enough that you might be able to withstand him. For a few minutes at least. It's almost enough to make me want to stick around to see the fireworks that ensue between the two of you."

Thyra shook her head. There was only one explanation for this weird apparition sitting calmly beside her. "I'm going crazy."

"Oh, there's no doubt," he replied. "Judging by the sweat on your brow and the way you cringe every time we hit a bump in the road, that injury on your side is worse than you'd like to admit. Add in the trauma of losing the dwarf, perhaps even your mother, the guilt of killing that man outside of Chicago and it's obvious that your mind is over-taxed. Your desire for revenge, lack of sleep, and desire to double-cross your brothers by taking Mjolnir for yourself is like icing on the cake of crazy you've baked for yourself." His smile was devious when he said, "Your mind truly is a tangled mess, far beyond what anything a sane person could ever hope to achieve. No wonder these hallucinations are mixing into your reality so easily."

Thyra wasn't thrilled with the direction of the conversation, but she couldn't form an argument to go against his claim. She glanced at him with suspicion. "Who are you?"

"Who, what, how, why, when—all valid questions, but the answers are too much for your feeble psyche," he said. "Call me your conscience, a figment of your imagination, or whatever other title your fragile mind is capable of concocting and accepting. It doesn't matter. I'm a voice of warning. Soon I will disappear the same way I came, leaving you alone to fall further into madness." He appraised her with a crooked smile. "I look forward to what comes next. I truly do. You will either break the world or end up broken. Perhaps both, which would be monumentally delicious in the kind of chaos that would be created. It's been centuries since a mad god ran rampant. You could be the first of this age!"

A chill ran down Thyra's spine. It was obvious what outcome he was hoping for. "I'm not listening to you."

He let out a sharp burst of laughter. "Of course you aren't. You don't even know who or what I am. For all you know, I'm a manifestation of your guilt brought to life to torment you with the series of bad decisions you've made. I could be the voice that you refuse to listen to, but can no longer suppress. Or I could simply be the embodiment of your insecurities."

Thyra bristled. "What insecurities?"

He shrugged. "Where to start? I could point out the fact that you're a young, teenage girl being thrown into the deep end full of players that wouldn't hesitate to tear into you like a swarm of hungry sharks. Beyond that, you clearly have father issues. Which explains why you decided to have me appear as a man instead of a reflection of yourself. Not Thor, of course. No. Deep down you still harbor a desire to have a beautiful daddy-daughter relationship, but know deep down that will never be. Instead, you just imagined a man you've never seen before to serve as the voice of reason amid the insanity that has become your life."

"You're no voice of reason," Thyra grumbled. "All you've done is tell me I'm crazy."

"You're the one talking to someone you think you've imagined," he replied smugly. "If you aren't crazy, then how did I get here?"

Thyra looked away. She didn't know. The same way she didn't know how he knew so much about her. "Are you even real?"

"You don't think I'm real, which can only mean that I'm not!" He paused, held up one finger and then poked himself in the chest. He cackled. "But I feel real! Ha! You must have a decidedly wicked imagination. I wonder, if I jump out of the car, will I just reappear here in this seat immediately or will you let me roll along the road for a while?" His eyes lit up and he reached for the door. "There's only one way to find out!"

"No!" Thyra barked. "Don't do that."

He shrugged, his face revealing his disappointment. "Have it your way. It wouldn't hurt. I'm not real, remember? If anything, it would test the limits of your imagination as to what kind of injuries you could dream up for me. You're young, but I'm sure you could come up with something truly gruesome."

Thyra exhaled heavily. She wasn't sure she could take any more of his rambling. "If I dreamed you up, why don't you tell me something useful. Isn't that what usually happens at times like this? I could use some help, not a bunch of gibberish from a complete crazy person."

"I'm a reflection of your psyche, so I should tell you that you shouldn't be so hard on yourself. You're a very nice crazy person." He cackled in response to his own joke. He laughed so hard tears began to leak from the corners of his eyes. He wiped them away with the back of one hand before continuing. "I can tell you aren't satisfied with the direction of this conversation. I understand. I'd be frustrated, too. If I was real and had actual emotions. Which I don't. Not my own at least. More than likely, any emotions I have are yours. The only question is if you like feeling them or not."

"I don't," Thyra stated.

"Ah, yes. You prefer to hide behind anger. You come by that naturally. Thor used his anger as a shield, then a wall, and then a fortress. If there is anything to be learned from his example is that anger is not the answer. Such a frail emotion, anger. It more often than not defeats itself because it overrides sense and blinds the mind to all other emotions. Pride is the same way. It always leads to a person running headfirst off a cliff with their eyes closed thinking they are going to learn to fly on the way down. Hence the saying 'pride goeth before the fall.'" He cackled. "I've always preferred the use of cunning and trickery. Anger can be employed, but only with good sense directing it. And a healthy dose of spite. Use those and the proud and anger-filled are easy to manipulate."

Thyra frowned. "Are you manipulating me?"

"Of course I am, just like everyone else in your life is manipulating you in some fashion or another." He paused and tapped his chin with one finger. "But if I'm just a figment of your imagination, does that mean you're manipulating yourself? Wouldn't that be comical?"

His smile split his face but didn't reach his eyes. As quick as it appeared, it slipped away and his expression turned serious. When he spoke, his tone had turned just as somber. "You're walking into a difficult situation, Thyra. There isn't anything I can do or say that will help you. Perhaps I could have directed your path in a different way if I had found you sooner. That isn't a possibility now. The bones have been cast, your path determined. The only thing I can do for you is to tell you that your father's hammer is the key to your survival *and* your undoing." He grimaced and exhaled heavily. "My strength never lied in prophecy. That was always the realm of others who enjoyed directing the lives of others. Too linear for my liking. I preferred to influence things in more interesting ways. But, this much I do foretell—your father's hammer will both forge and destroy you."

A chill ran down Thyra's spine. "What's that supposed to mean?"

"That's for you to discover," he replied softly. "I wish I could say more, but if I did others would recognize my hand. I can't allow that to happen. I've survived this long by sticking to the periphery, always influencing affairs without ever leaving any sign of my passing. Now is not the time to step onto the front lines. Not until I see where this all leads. There will always be a place in this world for me. As long as I don't get myself killed."

"Tell me the truth," Thyra said, "who are you?"

"I can't tell you that. If I did, your path might change. That isn't something we can afford to have happen." His eyebrows shot up suddenly and he pointed with one hand. "This is my stop. Pull over here."

They were driving down a two-lane highway with nothing in sight in either direction. "Here?"

"Yes, here!" He put his hand on the door handle and began to pull. "Here, girl!"

"Wait, you can't just go! Especially not here. That's crazy!"

"Exactly!" He cackled suddenly. "You're not the only crazy one here. We're crazy together, apart, and six feet deep!" When she hesitated, he pounded on the dash emphatically. "Here, here, here! Don't make me miss my stop. I have important places to go, people to trick, lives to alter!"

Thyra applied the brakes and pulled over. Her strange passenger was out the door before the Camaro even came to a stop. He leaned down to look back at her, his expression once more serious. "Thank you for the ride, Thyra. Let me offer one last piece of advice—sometimes the only way to see clearly is to close your eyes.

Think on that, daughter of Thor. It may save your life or the life of someone you care deeply for." His fingers tapped the roof of the car, a mischievous smile on his face like a switch had flipped. "Don't go do anything stupid. Like dying! I think we will have many more thrilling conversations. I'd hate to be wiped from existence because you weren't around to imagine me!" He barked a laugh. "Magic is your curse, but it could be so much worse. You could be like me!" He winked at her. "Now, hurry along. Odin isn't far now and your brothers won't wait forever."

He slammed the door, leaving Thyra slack-jawed. She looked forward and saw that true to his word the Chevelle was disappearing into the distance. She pressed down on the accelerator and eased back into the road, giving one last glance in the rear view mirror. She wasn't surprised to not see him there. His sudden disappearance reinforced that fact that she had been hallucinating. She had to have been. Only a delirious brain could have dreamed up what she had just experienced.

She tried to focus on what was ahead of her—her meeting with Odin, retaking Mjolnir, avenging Asiri—but her strange passenger's words kept repeating in her mind. Most of it had been complete nonsense, but some of what he said felt anything but crazy. He had left her with a warning. She just didn't understand it.

Any hidden meaning she could squeeze out of what was said would have to wait. Three miles down the road, the Chevelle began to slow and then turned down a dirt road leading to an old red barn. Thyra followed but kept several car lengths back. Modi parked outside the barn and waved her closer. Thyra ignored him and parked on the dirt road in a spot where she thought she could make a hasty exit if needed. Modi gave her his customary smirk, his expression dripping with disdain.

"You look pale, little sister," Modi said as Thyra approached. "Are you sure you're well?"

"She looks like she's seen a spirit," Magni muttered. "Close to becoming one herself."

Thyra ignored them. There was no way she was going to admit how weak she felt, much less tell them about the strange passenger or the even stranger conversation she had just had. "Where are we?"

"You asked to meet the Allfather," Modi replied. "We've brought you to him."

Thyra looked up at the barn. "He's in there?"

"Leave if you don't believe us," Magni grumbled. His expression made it clear that he hoped she would do exactly that. Among a long list of other unpleasant things he no doubt wished for her.

"You're not getting rid of me that easily," Thyra said through her teeth.

Magni sneered at her before disappearing into the barn.

"How do I know this isn't another one of your tests?" Thyra asked Modi. "Or better yet, a trap?"

"The Allfather wants to meet you, and what Odin wants, Odin gets." Modi swept his arm towards the barn. "Come, let me introduce you to grandfather."

Chapter 27

To Thyra's surprise, the inside of the barn was exactly what the exterior suggested. There was no hidden grandeur beneath a humble facade. Stalls stood in disrepair, the floor covered in aged straw, and the smell of mold hung heavy in the air. If Thyra was expecting a more elaborate display of power from Odin, this wasn't it.

Modi and Magni walked in with a familiarity that spoke volumes. They had been to this barn before and had determined their place within the walls. Magni sat down on a bale of hay and began studying his knuckles. Modi leaned against one of the thick posts and crossed his arms, casting a look at the golden-haired man in the middle of the barn.

Odin was exactly as Thyra remembered him from their conversation a few nights earlier. He rose from where he had been sitting, a soft smile on his lips. He looked pleased to see her. Thyra didn't share the sentiment. The warning about Odin using her was still too fresh in her ears.

"Hello, Thyra." He looked her up and down. His smile slipped and was replaced by a frown. "I was going to say that you look well, but that would be a lie."

Thyra grimaced. "I've had better days."

"Which leaves me wondering, why have you found me in such a

state?"

Thyra looked at her brothers in turn. "Ask your grandsons."

Odin's eyes narrowed dangerously. He turned and looked at Modi. "Do you have an explanation for this?"

Modi straightened and licked his lips. Thyra could see the wheels spinning and wondered what kind of answer her brothers had prepared during the long drive from Chicago. Modi looked less than confident in whatever they had decided on.

"There was a situation last night. We tried to strike a blow against Olafsson. There was an unexpected complication."

"Which means you weren't careful enough," Odin snapped. "I told you to bring your sister to me alive and unharmed, didn't I?"

Modi reluctantly nodded. "You did."

"Does she look unharmed to you?"

"We did not expect there to be resistance," Modi offered weakly.

"We taught her how to defend herself," Magni grumbled from his hale bale. "She wasn't a very good student. Her injuries are her own fault."

Odin spun on Magni, his eyes flashing angrily. "And where were you when this happened?"

Magni inclined his chin defiantly but true to Thyra's expectations, his will faltered in the face of Odin's displeasure. He lowered his gaze, choosing silence over self-incrimination.

Thyra wasn't going to let the question go unanswered. "They were sitting in their car. Waiting."

"Is that so?" Odin said slowly. "I fail to see how putting Thyra in danger while you two took a nap was doing as I asked."

Modi shrugged, a flicker of defiance returning. "It was a chance for Thyra to prove herself. Her failures are her own."

"Failures? Unfortunately, that is something you two are all too familiar with." Odin's voice dripped with menace. The Allfather turned back to Modi and thrust a finger into his chest, knocking him back a step. "We cannot afford to make mistakes. There is no room for error in what we do next. If I can't count on you to do what I ask, there will be no place for you at my side in the coming days."

Modi swallowed before nodding. "I understand."

Odin spun back to Magni. "Do you understand? Or do I need to make myself clearer?"

"I hear you," Magni grumbled.

"Good." Odin turned away. "Now the two of you get out of my sight before I discover any other ways you've failed to execute my wishes."

The brothers lingered, a shared look of disbelief on their faces. Finally, Modi nodded. "We will go, but first, you must know something about our little sister. Her magic—"

"If you're going to say that her magic has grown to include control over wind," Odin interrupted, "I already know."

Modi's jaw fell. "You knew? We only learned yesterday. I don't think even she knew before yesterday. How could you know?"

"Because I am the Allfather," Odin said sharply. "It is my privilege and duty to know what you don't. I knew from the moment I saw her that her power was still growing."

"You kept that from us?" Modi's shock turned to an expression of angry betrayal. "Why?"

"Because you didn't need to know," Odin replied without pause. "Thyra is the one this world has been waiting for. The one *I've* been waiting for. She is the one Freya foretold, the one that would marry the power of the Aesir and the Vanir together."

"The power of the Vanir flows in my veins, as well," Modi stated defiantly.

"Weakly, at best," Odin dismissed his claim. "Thyra's magic is the strength of both clans. The ability to control multiple aspects of the world around her like the Vanir, and all of the destructive elements like a true Aesir. She is what I hoped you would be." The corners of Odin's mouth turned down. "But look what good hoping did me."

Modi reacted like he'd been slapped, rage and confusion mixing on his face. The muscles in his jaw clenched so hard the sound of his teeth crunching together was audible. His fists quivered with rage and embarrassment and his eyes bored into the Allfather with an intensity bordering on savage fury.

Thyra's jaw had gone slack as she watched the exchange between the two. She didn't know what she had expected when it came to the relationship between Odin and her brothers, but this was not it. Sif had made it sound like Odin was too soft on the brothers. He didn't seem to feel as magnanimous since he had returned to life. Any cracks that had been there before appeared to have been ripped wide open now.

"But there is no reason to fret over unmet expectations," Odin said, clapping Modi on the shoulders. "You two still have a role to play. Your reward is still intact. You still have a place at my side."

Modi's eyes flashed hungrily, some of the rage and hurt soothed by Odin's words. "As you wish, Allfather. We obey your commands. Come on, brother. We have preparations to make for tonight."

Magni slowly rose to his feet and followed Modi out of the barn. As he passed by, he leaned in close to Thyra and whispered. "You will pay for that."

Thyra ignored him. She wasn't going to take the blame for his embarrassment, nor acknowledge his threat. She was more interested in the unexpected tension between the Allfather and her brothers. Odin's abrupt dismissal of them made Thyra think there were unexpected cracks in the relationship between Odin and his grandsons.

"I apologize for their actions," Odin said when the door closed behind Thyra's brothers.

"You're apologizing when you don't even know what happened," Thyra said.

"You were injured," Odin said. "That is reason enough. How bad are you hurt?"

Thyra did her best to stand straight, but the effort made her grimace. "I'm fine. Just a little sore."

Odin didn't look convinced. "I care for your well-being. What we look to do will not be easy. Especially if you are already weakened."

"I'm *fine*," Thyra repeated through gritted teeth.

Odin relented, even if he didn't believe her. "Regardless, you never should have been put in harm's way."

"I've been in harm's way ever since I found out about magic," Thyra replied sharply. "Even more since Yggdrasil decided to make me its champion and force me to take possession of the Eye."

Odin's expression tightened, his eyes betraying a sudden hunger. "The Eye. . .you have it?"

Thyra's eyes narrowed. "Yes. Not here, though. Its someplace safe."

Odin blinked and then cleared his throat. "Good. The Eye is safe. That's all that matters."

"Is that why you wanted to meet me?" Thyra asked. "You want the Eye back? You want to be Yggdrasil's champion again?"

"Is that what you think?" Odin scoffed in derision. "No, no, no. Believe me when I tell you that I do not want that burden again. Look at me! I am young. I have both eyes. I am the man I was before the World Tree took its price. Yggdrasil manipulated me and stole more from me than it ever gave. You can keep it's *gifts*!"

The last word was spat, Odin's voice full of vitriol. Thyra could relate. Nothing good had come from Yggdrasil's "gifts" so far.

"I have better reasons for desiring to have you at my side," Odin continued. "The time has come for Surtur—or Gunnar Olafsson, as he calls himself now—to feel the wrath of those he has tried to eradicate. He has amassed wealth by killing and exploiting people like you and me, using our power for his own devices. I'm sure you're smart enough to realize that he has possession of Mjolnir and my spear, Gungnir. He plans to use them to expand his empire. I want them back in the rightful hands. Together, we can make that happen."

"How?" Thyra said. "Olafsson won't have them sitting out where they will be easy to get our hands on."

"By attacking with speed and overwhelming force," Odin replied. "Surtur has had both weapons securely hidden away for a long time. A month ago, we wouldn't have gotten close. That's changed. Olafsson is feeling the pressure from all sides. Most especially, from you. He is about to make a move. One that I plan to exploit."

"What kind of move?"

"The Odin Initiative."

Thyra frowned. "He named something after you? Funny, in a desperate kind of way."

Odin nodded. "The irony surprised me, too."

"Okay, so what is the Odin Initiative?"

"A program meant to create a source of limitless clean energy," Odin said. "One built around using Gungnir and Mjolnir. He's had my spear in a facility several hours from here for two weeks. I've tried to get close, but it is well fortified. From what I could see, reaching my spear on my own would have been impossible."

"And you think it won't be now?"

"No. Olafsson is moving Gungnir. Something of greater impor-tance has caught his attention."

"Greater importance?"

Odin nodded. "Something he is willing to risk the safety of Gungnir to achieve."

Thyra weighed revealing what Yggdrasil had told her about Baldur and Olafsson's plans to gain entry to Idunn's garden. She had thought it would be an ace up her sleeve, but now she wondered if Odin was holding same card up his own. There was only one way to find out. "They are trying to enter Idunn's garden."

Odin nodded, a cold smile spreading on his face. "You do know? Good. I figured Yggdrasil would tell you. The World Tree has always looked out for itself first, keeping secrets from those it calls its champions, pitting its own children against each other for its own benefit. True to form, a hint of danger and it begs to be protected. Even when it refuses to give the same protection to others."

Thyra found herself nodding. "How did you find out about their plans?"

"Not from Yggdrasil, if that's what you're asking." Odin laughed wryly. "No, the tree hasn't spoken to me since my awakening. But others have. There are still some who follow the old ways and are willing to heed my voice. It took some time, but I found the ones who could answer my questions. From there, it wasn't hard to see the picture Surtur was trying to paint."

"You mean Baldur," Thyra said. As if his name were some kind of curse, her temples began to throb, causing her to grimace. She closed her eyes for a second and waited for the pain to pass before continuing. "I think this is his plan."

Odin's features had tightened at the mention of Baldur. He inhaled deeply, letting his breath out slow. "Yes, Baldur. I was surprised to learn that he had escaped his prison. His presence makes all of this more. . .difficult." Thyra wanted to ask what Odin meant, but he didn't give her a chance. "Surtur gaining access to Idunn's Garden is not the chief concern for me. It's the means that will be required to do it."

"What do you mean?"

"If Surtur and Baldur think they can summon Idunn, that means they have several of the summoning stones," Odin explained. "Three, at the very least. Although, I anticipate that they have more than that. Alone, the possession of enough stones might be enough to force Idunn to answer their call. She may be able to resist, though, even if only for a time. I don't think Surtur or Baldur are willing to take the chance of even the smallest delays. Especially not with the threat of you storming in, lightning thundering down from every angle. They are going to make sure they force her to answer their summons."

"And Gungnir will do that?"

Odin nodded curtly. "Something extra I had built into both Gungnir and Mjolnir."

"Something extra? Why?"

"Call it a fail-safe put in place because I knew my brother's wife all too well," Odin answered. "The summoning stones were the key. Gungnir and Mjolnir are the battering ram. When either weapon is present, the summons will be so strong that Idunn will be forced to answer or risk harm to her person. If both weapons are present, any attempt to resist would kill her on the spot."

"Effective means to forcing obedience," Thyra said. "Does Baldur know about this?"

Odin nodded. "I fear he does. He was involved with the creation of the summoning stones, although the fail-safe was suggested afterwards."

Thyra got the impression Odin was leaving something unsaid. "Who else knew about the fail-safe then?"

Odin frowned, but kept quiet. That was answer enough that Odin was holding something back. Thyra didn't need him to answer, though. She had a guess.

"Bragi knows about it, doesn't he?"

Odin finally nodded. "Yes. I'm not sure he has forgiven me yet for actually listening to the suggestion."

Thyra considered this new information for a moment before

speaking. "Baldur has Bragi."

A flash of regret mixed with pain washed across Odin's face. "I feared that was the case. Bragi was the only one who knew more about Idunn's garden and the summoning stones than me. He was determined to know every aspect of the garden Idunn was tasked with tending."

"She was his wife," Thyra said defensively. "Why wouldn't he try everything possible to get to her? He told me he spent centuries trying to find a way in but couldn't. You created a prison for her and left them no way to ever see each other again. No wonder he hated you."

Odin's eyebrows shot up in surprise. "You think I created the magic that locked Idunn in her garden?"

"Of course you did," Thyra barked. "Bragi told me that you put her there to protect the fruit of immortality from being taken. You forced her to spend an eternity alone."

Odin frowned. "I see. Well that is unfortunate."

Thyra's eyes narrowed in suspicion. "What do you mean?"

"I'm afraid, Thyra," Odin said, a sad smile on his face, "that you have been lied to."

"What are you talking about?" Thyra demanded. "Tell me."

Odin shook his head. "No, I don't think I will. Besides, you wouldn't believe me if I did. That is a question you will have to ask Bragi yourself."

"Bragi isn't here," Thyra said sharply. "You are."

"It isn't my secret to tell," Odin said. "When we find Bragi, and I am certain that he will be at Baldur's side when they try to summon Idunn, you can ask him yourself."

"That's not good enough!" Thyra barked. "Tell me what you know."

"No," Odin said. "You deserve the chance to face the reality of your assumptions."

Thyra looked away. Half-truths and secrets were her life. She was tired of it. "How do I know you're not just trying to manipulate me by telling me this now?"

"I'm not trying to poison your mind," Odin responded. "I just want you to know the truth so you can judge me more fairly."

"What's that supposed to mean?"

Odin scoffed. "From the moment you walked through the door you've ascribed almost every bad thing that has happened in your life to me in one way or another. You may think I'm a monster—go ahead, if that's what makes you feel good—but I am not the source of every hardship you've ever experienced. Nor am I the only person in your life that is keeping secrets from you. In fact, I may be the only not keeping secrets from you."

"It's a little early to say that," Thyra growled. "The day isn't over. Plenty of time for you to tell me lies."

"That goes both ways," Odin said grimly. "But, enough lamenting over our trust issues. I don't think either one of us will overcome them anytime soon. Let's focus on what we have in common. I want my spear back. You want revenge against Surtur and your father's hammer securely in your hands. Both of us want to stop Baldur and Surtur from reaching Idunn's garden. Tonight, will be our opportunity to make that happen."

"You're sure about that?"

Odin nodded. "Baldur and Surtur are on their way right now."

"On their way where?"

Odin walked to the front of the barn and threw the door open. He pointed over the top of a tree-covered hill to the east. "Two miles that way. The Muspel Corporation started buying up property in this valley starting a year ago. Most of the people that live around here are farmers, or once were. They aren't happy about their neighbors being forced out but are powerless to do anything about it. Common people talk and are much more perceptive than they are given credit for. Judging by the activity at the facility, something important is about to happen."

"You know all that from watching some trucks come and go?"

Odin smiled. "Of course not. I told you that there are still some people who value the old ways. They were more than happy to tell me about Surtur and Baldur's comings and goings. Plus, I have a few sets of eyes in the skies." A raven called overhead. Thyra looked up and was surprised to see not one, but half a dozen of the big black birds circling. Odin stood beside her. "Tonight we will ruin Baldur and Surtur's plans. By the morning I will have Gungnir back and you will have your revenge. And your father's hammer, if you so choose."

"Tonight?"

"There won't be another time," Odin said. "They will act sooner, not later. We must be there when they do."

Thyra set her jaw in determination. "Fine. Tonight it is."

"Good," Odin said with a nod. He took measure of her. "I imagine you would like some rest. We have a few hours before we need to move. I will have your brothers help me finish preparations for our attack. You should sleep."

Sleep was enticing. Thyra was exhausted, in pain, and now her head felt like it was about to split open like a melon. But Thyra was not going to let her brothers and Odin direct her path. Resting would have to wait until after she had Mjolnir in her hands.

"You have a plan?"

Odin nodded. "Of course."

"Then sleep can wait," Thyra said in a determined tone. A voice inside told her she was making a mistake, that she would be able to think clearer after some rest, but she ignored it. "I want to know what kind of mess I'm walking into."

"I wouldn't have it any other way," Odin said. "Because you, granddaughter, will be at the center of it."

Chapter 28

Thyra looked at the three black SUVs blocking the road with obvious doubt. Positioned in a wedge shape with the point directed toward any oncoming vehicles, it was clear that Olafsson's men were not taking any chances of allowing someone to force their way through by road.

Which was what Odin and her brothers said they must do.

Thyra's eyes scanned up the hillsides on either side of the road. According to Odin, there were at least twenty men spaced out among the trees, making an approach by foot next to impossible if they wanted any chance of catching Olafsson and Baldur unaware.

Which was what Odin and her brothers insisted they do.

Odin had explained the layout of the rock quarry at the end of the road. There was only one road in and out, the rock of the quarry forming three thirty-foot walls that were impassable without growing wings. Even if they had a way down, the forest was thick on all sides and would take hours to navigate. Hours they didn't have if they wanted to stop Olafsson and Baldur from summoning Idunn.

Which Odin was certain would happen near midnight when the moon would be directly over the quarry.

The Allfather had been the only one to speak as the plan of attack had been laid out. Modi and Magni had nodded in agreement when Odin given them orders, but kept silent. There had been no room for Thyra's voice as the details were presented. When Thyra had managed to ask about certain aspects she had been met with thinly-veiled condescension from every hand. It was clear that Odin had a plan and there was no changing it.

Seeing the obstacles to the first step in the plan with her own eyes made her feel less confident than ever.

Especially when those obstacles kept changing every time she looked.

Thyra blinked, the orientation of the SUVs on the road briefly flipping so that the point of the wedge faced toward the quarry rather than away. The lines of the vehicles shimmered and wavered in a nauseating manner, like they were being made and unmade before her eyes. A breath later, the direction of the vehicles shifted back with a stomach-turning flicker. Thyra closed her eyes and took a calming breath. When she opened them, the SUVs were solid again.

"That's our way in," Odin stated.

"Doesn't look like a way in to me," Thyra said around the taste of bile in her mouth. "It looks like a trap you want us to walk right in to."

"There is no other way," Odin replied.

"How do you know?" Thyra's question had a bite to it born from the marriage of distrust and her fatigue and nausea. "Didn't you say that they started arriving last night? When did you have a chance to check out the quarry?"

"I have eyes in the sky, remember? I trust what they've told me."

"Eyes in the sky," Thyra grumbled. She'd learned enough in the past few hours to know that Odin didn't see through the ravens eyes like the stories said. Instead, he had the ability to speak to them and read their thoughts, rudimentary as they were. The truth was less magical than she had assumed and didn't fill her with a whole lot of trust for the information they provided. There was a reason why calling someone "birdbrain" was an insult. "Since when did ravens learn to count?"

"They've served me well enough in the past," Odin replied.

"Oh, good," Thyra said. "Tell me, did the squirrels have anything to say?"

Odin waved her sarcastic remark away. "The source of the information isn't what matters. The veracity does, and I trust what they've told me."

"I don't know," Thyra said with a shake of her head. "Something feels off about all of this. I don't even feel like I can trust my own eyes, much less the eyes of a bunch of ravens."

"Their eyes see truer than ours," Odin replied. "There is no reason to be concerned. We've planned for this. You simply must do your part."

Her part sounded like most of the work. When Odin had originally laid out his plan it had sounded far-fetched to Thyra. Seeing the way the three SUVs were parked in addition to the number of men Odin said were in the trees, it looked ludicrous to even attempt.

"They will focus their fire on the lead car," Odin explained again. "Your car. Which from what I've seen is as quiet as a whisper. You'll be on top of them before they even realize what they're hearing. All we need you to do is hold a shield of air long enough to absorb their fire until we get close. After that, your brothers and I will take care of the vehicles and Surtur's men."

"That's all?" Thyra snarked. "So simple. I drive up like a lamb ready for the slaughter while you three sit back and watch. Very courageous of you."

Odin frowned. "You said you could do this. Now is not the time to change your mind."

"I said I could do it, not that I thought it would work," Thyra corrected. "Now I'm not sure I *want* to attempt it. I am the only one taking any risk."

We are four gods," Odin said. "What chance do these mortals have against our might?"

"I'm no god," Thyra snapped.

"No," Odin agreed. "You have the chance to be something *much* more."

Thyra didn't like the sound of that, and from the way Modi's eyes tightened, he didn't either. Odin didn't give either one the opportunity to digest his words too long. He stood up and began walking back to the cars. Thyra followed in a gait made even stiffer by her injuries.

"Keep the lights off on your car," Odin instructed. "You'll be on top of them before they know it. I'll wait in your brothers' vehicle until you're close and then we will engage."

"Only after Olafsson's men have had a chance to blow me full of holes," Thyra sniped.

Odin turned on her with a penetrating glare. "Are you Thor's daughter, or did my grandsons bring me the wrong young woman? Can it be that a few mortals with guns have turned your backbone to water?"

"Are you surprised?" Modi grumbled. Thyra turned her glare on him and he crossed his arms defiantly. "Look at her. She's been soaked with sweat for hours, can barely walk, and spends her time alone talking to herself. She is one stiff wind away from falling flat on her face."

"I agree with our little sister for once," Magni said. "She's right. She can't do this."

"I don't see you two offering to be the first in line," Thyra growled. "Where's the might of Magni and the wrath of Modi now? You're more than happy to stand behind Odin's protection. I haven't seen a single shred of courage in either one of you. You sit where its safe until the work is done then you slink out like the cockroaches you are and try to claim the glory! Wait, that's not fair to cockroaches. You two are nothing more than spineless worms!"

Modi hissed, his eyes lighting up with magic, and Magni bellowed a roar, a lightning-axe appearing in each hand. Before either one could act, Odin planted himself in their way.

"Enough of this! You will release your magic or you will feel *my* wrath and *my* might!" He scowled at his grandsons in turn until they both obeyed his command. The Allfather then turned the look on Thyra. "And you will stop trying to bait your brothers into a fight. Do you understand me?"

"Whatever," Thyra said. "Just keep them on their leashes or I'll finish what Magni tried to start."

"I'd drop you where you stand," Magni growled.

"I said enough!" Odin hissed. He gave Thyra a look that made her swallow in spite of herself. "There will be no more infighting between you three. Not while I am here. You will work together or you will be left behind. Do I make myself clear?" Modi nodded almost immediately. Magni was slower to respond, but a look from his brother was enough to break his resistance. The Allfather turned his attention back to Thyra. "Is that clear?"

Thyra exhaled slowly. "Crystal."

"Good." Odin took a deep breath. He motioned for Thyra to follow him and led her out of earshot of Modi and Magni. "Now, about our plan. You know why your brothers can't be the ones to go in first. They do not have your power. Only you can do this."

"They can make shields," Thyra argued.

"A shield of air will not be seen," Odin responded smoothly. "In fact, it will help muffle your approach even more. You will be even less than a whisper behind such a shield. That would not be true of a shield made of lightning. The same is true of me. A shield made from light is the opposite of what we need, not to mention a poor defensive tool." He reached out and put a hand on Thyra's shoulder. To her dismay, she was too weak to shrug it away. "I told you that we will not be far behind you, and I will uphold my promise. I do not want to see you fall, granddaughter. You should believe that by now."

"I'd believe it more if you were facing the risks with me instead of standing behind me," Thyra said. She felt her headache intensify. The added discomfort only added to her agitation. "You three could just as easily stab me in the back as help me."

"You want me to ride with you?" Odin asked in a voice loud enough for Thyra's brothers to hear. "That's your sticking point?"

"It'd make me feel better, yes."

Odin shrugged. "Fine. Nothing would make me prouder than to ride into battle along side the champion of magic in this age." Modi began to argue, but Odin silenced him with a hand. "If this is what the champion of magic requires to accept my plan, then I will submit to her request. We will strike and open the path for Modi and Magni."

Thyra blinked in surprise. That wasn't what she had expected. Suddenly, she wasn't sure if Odin riding with her was what she really wanted. But it was too late to take it back, now. She realized the three men were all watching her and finally managed to mumble, "Fine."

"Good." Odin looked at his grandsons. "The plan remains the same. We move in three hours. Try to get some rest before then."

*****

The shifting of the Camaro as Odin's weight settled into it was enough to pull Thyra out of the state of limbo she had fallen into.

"It's time," the former god announced.

Thyra looked at the clock on the dash and was surprised to see that it was nearly midnight. Three hours had passed quicker than she thought possible. Sleep had come and gone, teasing her with much needed relief and then slipping away without delivering any. What little rest she had managed to get hadn't been enough. If anything, she felt more weary than before.

Thyra rubbed at her eyes and tried to banish the blurriness from her vision. The shadows cast by the moon mocked her, taking the shape of monsters only a brain addled by fatigue and distress could imagine. On top of that, the strange shimmering from earlier was still present in the periphery of her vision, making her stomach do somersaults.

"You understand your role?"

"I know what I need to do," Thyra mumbled.

"Good," Odin nodded, "because it is too late to back out now."

"That's what you keep telling me."

Thyra started the Camaro and turned off the headlights. She pressed the button on the steering wheel that lit up the windshield, bathing the terrain in blue light. Thyra felt a twinge of renewed grief as a memory of Asiri rose to the surface. The dwarf had thought of almost everything to make the Camaro the ultimate tool.

"Impressive," Odin commented. "We will be like a shadow on the breeze, able to see but remain undetected." He nodded in approval. "This modern world does have some redeeming qualities."

"We'll be unseen and unheard," Thyra said, "as long as your grandsons don't come roaring in too soon."

"Don't worry about them," Odin stated. "They will not disappoint me again."

Thyra had a dozen biting comments to make, but held her tongue. She had more important concerns at the moment than her two brothers proving how witless they were. Like how she was going to create a shield of air in front of the Camaro. Without letting on to what she was doing, she formed her first attempt. Focusing with everything she had, she put the Camaro in gear and let it roll forward.

Thyra tried to move the wall of air at the same speed, but the resistance against it felt like a crushing weight on her mind. She pressed on the brakes and sighed.

"Everything okay?" Odin asked, a degree of suspicion in his voice.

"Fine," Thyra muttered.

Thyra tried again with the shield but with a similar result. Trying to push a wall of air *through* air sounded simpler than it was proving to be.

"Perhaps," Odin said, "you should try a different shape of shield."

Thyra looked at Odin in shock. He shrugged and then explained. "I can see the distortion of the air. A flat wall will take great effort to hold, especially if you're trying to make it move in front of the car. Not to mention that it leaves our flanks exposed when we get closer. A wedge or curved shape might prove more effective. Less resistance to combat."

Thyra nodded but didn't go so far as to thank Odin for the advice. Turning her focus back to the task at hand, she began forming a new shield.

"If I may be so bold," Odin said, "I would suggest a wedge. We are going to ram the vehicles. A wedge will allow us to split them like an axe splitting a log."

Thyra frowned. It made sense, but she was feeling too stubborn to admit it out loud. She formed a wedge and then put the Camaro into motion. Keeping the shield out in front of the Camaro proved easier this time, but still required enough of her focus that driving became a secondary concern. They almost slammed into a tree on the side of the road before Thyra was able to correct. The edge of her shield still struck the trunk, tearing a sizable chunk out of the bark and shaking the canopy overhead.

"Maybe we should have practiced this part of the plan sooner," Odin said in a tense tone.

"I'm doing my best," Thyra snapped.

"I believe you," Odin said, "but in the interest of time and our lives, perhaps I should drive."

"No," Thyra said immediately. "This is my car."

"And this is my plan," Odin replied. "Neither one is going to work with you crashing into everything. You need to focus on maintaining that shield. Let me focus on getting us there."

Thyra knew he was right, but she didn't like it. This car was her link to Asiri, and the thought of someone else driving it was upsetting. But there was no denying that maintaining a shield and driving both was too much to handle in her current condition. "Do you even know how to drive?"

Odin smirked. "I think I can manage."

Grudgingly, Thyra acquiesced. They traded places, Thyra only grimacing a little as Odin slid behind the wheel.

"Let me know when you're ready."

Thyra focused on creating another shield and held it in place. She nodded to Odin. The Camaro lurched forward and Thyra barely managed to get the shield moving before they crashed into it. Odin frowned, but didn't acknowledge the near mistake. As he accelerated Thyra was faced with the challenge of how to keep her shield moving along with the Camaro. Pushing it, even with the change in shape, was like moving a rock uphill with her mind. She would tire long before they ever reached the Muspel Corporation SUVs. The thought came to her that instead of trying to push solid air forward, she should try letting the air roll through her shield, condensing and then falling away in a constant flow. She was surprised to find that while it required even greater focus on maintaining the flow, the strain of holding the wall in place was dramatically lessened. She wasn't certain if this kind of shield would be as strong, but there was no time to test it. She saw the bend in the road that led to where the

SUVs were parked and tried to prepare herself for what was about to happen.

"Hold the shield until we hit their vehicles," Odin instructed. "Once we're in their midst, unleash everything you have. So will I. We strike fast and with overwhelming force."

Odin stepped on the accelerator when the SUVs came into view. The motors hummed with the increased power, but the only real noise was the tires on the gravel road. They were almost on top of the SUVs before the first of Olafsson's men turned and looked in their direction. At least, Thyra thought he turned, but her field of vision shifted like a television picture with poor reception. For a split second, the SUVs were pointed inward again, and all of Olafsson's men were looking towards the quarry rather than in the direction the Camaro was coming from. Then everything shifted back.

Her shield of air struck the first SUV head on, creasing the engine compartment and pushing it backwards into the vehicle behind it. The impact threw Thyra backward into her seat, but she managed to keep the shield in place and just far enough ahead of the Camaro to keep them from crashing into it as well. As Odin had instructed, she sent the shield outward in a violent wind that pushed the other two SUVs several feet off the road and up the embankment on either side, clearing the way for the Camaro.

Thyra only a second to bask in her success when she heard the distinct whine of the rifles Olafsson's men carried charging. She threw up a hastily constructed shield around the Camaro just in time to intercept a dozen blasts of energy.

The roar of an engine heralded Modi and Magni's arrival just before lightning filled the sky and shot down at the SUVs. Odin maneuvered the Camaro past the SUVs while Thyra focused on keeping the shield in place to absorb what Gunnar's men directed their way. Her brothers' Chevelle roared past without slowing, one last bolt of lightning streaking from the passenger window for good measure.

"Raise your shield on my mark," Odin instructed. His eyes lit up with light as he rolled his window down. He thrust his hand out and shouted, "Now!"

Instead of raising it, Thyra sent the shield outward, the wall of air slamming the closest SUV further off the road. A line of light brighter than the sun shot away from Odin's hand and sliced through the engine compartment of the SUV and then across the cab of the next, leaving behind lines of glowing metal. Without pausing to consider the damage he'd inflicted, Odin spun the Camaro back into the center of the road and accelerated after Modi and Magni.

"We can't be sure what to expect when we reach the quarry," Odin said over the hum of the motors, "so be prepared for anything. Everything that moves will be an enemy so don't hesitate to strike hard and fast."

"You expect us to go in magic blazing?" The shadows outside her window were a swirling, twisting mass of shapes. She swore she saw the shape of a massive, black wolf keeping pace with the Camaro just inside the treeline, but as soon as it appeared, it was gone again. She shook her head. "How can you be sure everyone will be our enemy?"

"Who else would be there?"

Thyra didn't have an answer to give because Odin was right. She was racing into what was surely going to be a battle beside three fallen gods that were allies of convenience only, to go up against a pair of men bent on revenge and twisting magic to their own purposes. There was no chance of anything or anyone at the end of this road being on her side. She was on her own.

And if she was on her own, she wasn't going to be the teenage girl they all saw her as. She was the daughter of a god and a Valkyrie, a child of the storm, and the heir to Mjolnir. There was no time to be weak, timid, or afraid. She had her own revenge to take and a hammer to claim.

She saw her brothers' Chevelle crest a small rise and then drop out of sight. Almost immediately the night was lit up with the flash of lightning and Muspel Corporation rifles. It seemed like Olafsson and Baldur weren't as caught off-guard as they'd hoped. It didn't matter. Tonight, Thyra would be the aggressor. Tonight, there would be no holding back until Asiri was avenged and Mjolnir was hers.

Chapter 29

The battle was already hot when the Camaro dropped down into the heart of the quarry. Magni was charging through the ranks of black-clad Muspel thugs like a bull, his twin lightning-axes carving a hole just as effectively as a set of horns. Modi was following in his brother's wake, lightning lancing from his hands. Dozens of Muspel thugs in black tactical gear were firing on them, yet somehow they were continuing unscathed. Thyra felt a degree of disappointment that they were still standing.

Even with her brothers in the thick of the fight, the arrival of the Camaro didn't go unnoticed. Odin kept his foot on the accelerator and angled towards the nearest group of Muspel men. They unleashed a barrage of small arms fire in an attempt to stop the Camaro, but Thyra's shield deflected it aside. Several tried to jump out of the way when they realized their mistake, but Thyra's shield slammed into them and scattered them like rag dolls.

Odin spun the wheel and slammed on the brakes at the edge of quarry. Thyra was out of the door before the Camaro even came to a full stop, lightning shooting from her hands. Every time one black-clad thug fell, three more took his place. It seemed Olafsson had brought an army. Maintaining her shield of air against the barrage of rifle fire quickly became Thyra's sole focus. With the element of surprise lost, it became clear that they had driven into a proverbial wasp's nest. Now the wasps were swarming.

A quick glance showed that Odin wasn't faring much better. The rifle blasts bent around his outstretched hand, but he was slowly losing ground as more of Olafsson's men turned in his direction. Modi and Magni's berserker offensive had lost it's steam and now they were crouched beneath a dome of lightning. Tendrils snaked out and struck any of Olafsson's men that ventured too close, but it was clear that they were in trouble.

A thunderous impact struck Thyra's shield and sent her stumbling backwards. She looked up and was confused to see a black mass sailing through the air in her direction. It wasn't until a flash from Odin's magic lit the night that she recognized it for what it was—a car-sized boulder! It struck her shield so hard that Thyra was thrown onto her back, her shield collapsing beneath the weight of the massive projectile.

Ears ringing, Thyra rolled onto her hands and knees. The boulder was embedded three feet deep in the ground where she had been standing. She crawled towards it out of pure survival instinct just before the ground where she had been was torn up by rifle fire. The rifle fire was the least of her concerns at the moment. There was something else out there. Something big enough to throw boulders the size of a Prius. It seemed that Olafsson had brought more than just an army of men. Thyra could only imagine what else was waiting just out of sight. She didn't like the possibilities she came up with. Giants? Other magic users? Even the thought of a medieval catapult was enough to make her mouth go dry.

Thyra was considering her next move when the a blood-chilling howl filled the air. The trees blew apart as a massive wolf leapt into a knot of Muspel men. Thyra recognized the beast immediately. *Fenrir!* And where Fenrir was, Hela wouldn't be far behind. Thyra couldn't help but laugh. The night was already going poorly. Why not throw another pair of possible enemies into the fight? At least Fenrir was fighting Olafsson's men. For now.

Grateful for any distraction, Thyra looked around the side of the boulder. A flash of light at the far end of the quarry split the night. She was confident that was where Olafsson and Baldur were. Her suspicions about their progress were confirmed almost immediately.

They've opened the gateway to Idunn's garden! Yggdrasil's voice was thick with panic. *You must hurry!*

"I'm doing my best," Thyra barked. "Can Idunn hold them off?"

She is a gardener, not a warrior. The others will not assist.

"What others?" Yggdrasil was silent. "What others?!"

Thyra's question went unanswered. She didn't dwell on the fact that there was yet another secret that Yggdrasil had withheld from her for long.

Something dropped into the middle of Olafsson's men on the opposite side of the quarry. A flash of silver here, a streak of blue there. Thyra couldn't make out what was happening, but some of the Muspel rifles that had been pointed in her direction were now focused elsewhere. The quarry was falling into a state of chaos with fighting happening on all sides. Chaos worked in her favor.

Thyra came around the side of the boulder, her magic crackling around her. Lightning bolts streaked from the sky into each pocket of Olafsson's men she saw. Those that weren't hit by the lightning were swept away by gusts of wind. A path towards the far end of the quarry began to form.

She knew her progress wouldn't go unchallenged. Sure enough, another boulder rose into the air, but this time she was ready for it. She formed a wall of air so dense it distorted her vision and put it at an angle overhead. The boulder bounced off of it and careened away. She looked up at the rim of the quarry where the boulder had originated and was able to make out a pair of huge lumbering shapes.

She directed a barrage of lightning bolts towards the rim. Scorched earth was all that was left when she was finished. If the giants had survived, they were out of the fight for now at the very least.

A flash of silver to her left caught Thyra's eye. She couldn't quite make it out, but there was something familiar about it that she couldn't put her finger on.

The gateway to Idunn's garden was straight ahead. The night sky was split by a vertical slash. Trees and a sunlit garden were visible through the opening. Olafsson and Baldur stood in front of the gateway talking to a woman in a flowing dress. That had to be Idunn!

Spurred on by what she saw, Thyra tried to redouble her pace. She wove her magic in a storm around her, lightning flashing, winds whipping in a frenzy that no one was able to stand against.

But the way was anything but clear.

A girl about Thyra's age with dark, curly hair stood with a half dozen others behind her. The shape of her face and the slant of her eyes reminded Thyra of a nice old man who had helped her what felt like a lifetime ago. The resemblance was too much to ignore.

"Stop right there, lightning girl" Amara said. "This isn't a party you were invited to."

Arthur's granddaughter or not, Thyra's adrenaline was racing and she was not going to let anyone get in her way. She straightened, a lightning-spear appearing in her hand and a shield in the other. "These are my invitation. Move out of my way, Amara."

The other girl's eyes narrowed. "How do you know my name?"

"I met a nice old man named in Chicago," Thyra replied. "His name is Arthur. He told me about you."

Amara flinched like she'd been slapped. "What did he tell you?"

"Your grandfather is worried about you," Thyra continued. "He's sad to see who you've fallen in with. Step aside and I'll forget I ever saw you here. You can go back to him and forget being caught up with Olafsson."

"My grandfather," Amara snapped, "is an old fool. He hid what he could do, and he tried to get me to do the same. He wanted me to be someone else! I'm never going back to living that way."

"And Olafsson is doing you a favor?" Thyra snorted. "He's using you for your power. When he's done with you, what do you think he'll do with you then? I saw what his men were doing to people like us. Searching them out and terminating them! What makes you any different?"

"I don't bow to Gunnar Olafsson," Amara said grimly. "I follow Baldur. He's given me the chance to be who I truly am. And it won't be me that is cast aside when this is over. You'd be wise to reevaluate your allegiances before its too late."

"I told Arthur I'd try to convince you to go home," Thyra said. "I've fulfilled my promise." She pointed to the side with her spear. "Now, move! Before I move you."

"You don't understand," Amara said. She shook her her head sadly. "You should, though. You're one of us. You're a wonder. You should recognize what you could achieve working with us." Amara's face hardened. "But your life has been too easy. You've clearly never had to fight between being what the world will accept and who you truly are deep down."

"You don't know me," Thyra growled.

"And I never will," Amara replied. She turned to the motley crew standing around her and tapped each one gently on the arm. "Make sure Miss Thunderbolt doesn't interrupt Baldur's conversation."

The six shared grim smiles. They were all dressed in street clothes, not tactical gear, but something about they way they moved made Thyra hesitate. They weren't the military type, yet they looked confident. Her answer as to why quickly became obvious. Two of them grew thick, stone-like skin on suddenly elongated limbs, their brows protruding over sunken dark eyes set around a wide nose. A third held up both hands, flames suddenly licking off her skin. The fourth began to grow until she was almost ten feet tall, her skin turning a pale color of blue. The last two watched calmly, giving no indication of what they brought to the fight. Those were the two that made Thyra the most wary. They were identical in appearance, obviously twins. She guessed they were magic users as well, but had no idea what they were capable of, which made it impossible to know how to attack or defend against them.

"You guys are a little early for Halloween," Thyra snarked. They began to spread out in an attempt to flank her. "You'd all win best costume at any of the cosplay conventions. No point in ruining a good thing. Get out of my way and maybe you'll get your chance at the blue ribbon."

It was the pair of stone-skinned humanoids—trolls?—that attacked first. They came at her from the right, moving surprisingly quick for their size. They reached out with clawed hands that Thyra was sure could tear her to shreds. They didn't get close enough to try. A blast of wind struck them just below the knees, sending them face first into the dirt. A lightning bolt from Thyra's spear made sure they didn't get back up.

Thyra raised her shield with her left hand just in time to block a vortex of flames. Even behind her shield, the heat was suffocating. Thyra thrust her spear in at the source of the flames and unleashed a lightning bolt blindly. It had the desired effect. The flames stopped, the human flamethrower now trying to regain her feet after diving away. Thyra sent a blast of hardened wind into her back, sending her sprawling to the side.

That left the ice giantess and the two who had yet to reveal their power. She sized up the ice giantess while keeping a close eye on the other two. "You're big."

The giantess slammed one huge, blue fist into the palm of her other hand. "You're not. And you're going to be even smaller when I'm done with you."

"You won't stop me," Thyra growled. "I am the storm goddess!"

"More like a busted outlet, if you ask me," the giantess boomed. She looked over her shoulder at the gateway. When she turned back, she wore a cruel smile. "Besides, we've already won!"

Thyra glanced past the giantess towards the gateway to Idunn's garden. Olafsson raised Mjolnir and Gungnir and the vertical slash in the air vibrated. She guessed that Olafsson was using the spear and the hammer to compel Idunn somehow.

Thyra's eyes shifted back to the giantess. She didn't have time for this. She reversed her grip on her lightning spear and threw it before the giantess could react. The spear flew true, striking the giantess in the chest with a thunderous clap. The monstrosity stumbled backwards with a roar, but somehow managed to keep her feet. Thyra created another spear with a thought, flinging it with a shriek. The giantess raised an arm just in time to block the spear from hitting her right between the eyes. The impact spun her around, but she still kept her feet.

Thyra's jaw went slack in surprise. Nothing had ever withstood her magic this way. Clenching her teeth, she held out her hand to form another spear to finish the job. Too late she realized that she had lost sight of the last two. Thyra felt something snap around her wrist. Immediately, she felt her power magic escape her grasp, like it was being sucked out of her. She looked down and saw a strange, iridescent cord wrapped around her arm. A dozen feet away stood one of the twins holding the other end of the cord with a victorious smirk on his face.

Before she could even process what was happening, a similar cord snapped around Thyra's left arm, her lightning shield winking out as her magic was sucked away. The second twin laughed wickedly. "Feel her power! We will feast well tonight, brother!"

Thyra tried to pull against the cords, but her efforts only made the twins laugh all the louder. She felt like a rag doll. Her remaining fight began to fade, followed by her knees wobbling and giving way. Her breath became ragged and her head sagged down. They weren't just draining her magic, it felt like they were sucking the life out of her!

"Finish her off, Irina!" one of the twins yelled.

Smoke rose from where Thyra's lightning had struck the giantess, but the wounds only seemed to have angered her. The giantess stalked closer with murderous intent on her face. Ice grew on one hand, forming a massive club. Thyra could guess what was going to happen next. And she was completely helpless to stop it. Her hubris was going to be rewarded by being squished.

The giantess raised her arm overhead and brought it down with a primal roar. The blow never landed. Thyra looked up in surprise to see a pair of stout legs in front of her. She recognized the black high tops—Vidar!

With a roar, Vidar pushed the giantess backwards. She swung wildly with her club as she stumbled, but Vidar caught it in his arms and pinned it against his side. His legs bunched and then he spun. At any other time, the giantess's stunned expression would have been comical as she went airborne and flew across the quarry. Thyra was too drained to do anything more than watch.

A flash of silver on the edge of Thyra's vision was followed by one of the twins screaming. The cord holding her left arm fell away. The other twin yelled something but was cut short before he could finish. The second cord fell to the ground and Thyra let out a gasp as her strength came rushing back.

Thyra felt a familiar hand on her shoulder and looked up into her mother's eyes. No, Sif *the Valkyrie's* eyes. Sif looked relieved to see her daughter, but there was a hardness there that was new. And startling. Her eyes lacked the warmth that was usually there. In it's place was an icy void that made Thyra want to look away.

"Get up, Thyra," Sif said, extending a hand to her daughter. "There's no time for weakness."

Thyra accepted her mom's hand and rose shakily to her feet. She looked at between the twins and the cords that now were dull ropes on the ground. "What were they?"

"Think of them as magic vampires," Sif said. "They're not a threat anymore. That," she pointed towards the gateway, "is the threat."

Baldur and Olafsson were standing just outside the gateway looking in their direction. They looked like they were waiting for her. Thyra couldn't see Idunn.

"Let's go deal with it," Vidar mumbled. He took up a position on Thyra's other side. Together, they made their way towards the gateway. Thyra still felt weak, but she did her best to stand tall and look determined. She was surprised to see Odin, Modi, and Magni also converging on the gateway. At the end of rifles. Too late, Thyra saw the dozens of Muspel men with their rifles trained on her as well. Apparently the battle hadn't gone as well as she thought. She wondered what had happened to Fenrir, and Hela by extension, but that thought was pushed aside when Odin addressed Baldur and Olafsson.

"You've come all this way, only to be stalled at the gates of Idunn's garden."

"What makes you so sure that we have stalled?" Olafsson asked. His voice sounded strained, almost forced.

"Are you in Idunn's garden?" Odin asked. He made a show of looking around. "Doesn't appear to be so. Which means you've failed to gain access. You've summoned Idunn, opened the gateway, but have been denied entrance. It seems you are still impotent as ever,

Surtur."

"Don't call me that," Olafsson hissed.

"We can't escape who we truly are," Odin said, "no matter how hard or far we run." His eyes drifted to Gungnir in Olafsson's right hand. "You have something of mine. And I will have it."

"You are in no place to be making demands," Olafsson said. "I am."

"And what is it that you want from me?"

"The final key to entering Idunn's garden," Olafsson replied.

"So I was right," Odin sneered. "You lack the ability to cross the threshold. Idunn was always a stubborn one with more than a few tricks up her sleeve."

Olafsson grimaced. Something seemed off about the way he was acting. He looked like he was fighting himself with every word.

"You will help me," Olafsson said, "or you will die."

"Help you how?"

"Your spear senses you," Olafsson said. "It will not allow me to force Idunn's hand with you so close. The same for the hammer. They desire their masters' touch."

"You're willing to put Gungnir back in my hand," Odin said, sounding more than a little shocked, "knowing what I could do with it?"

"I will allow you to *touch* the spear," Olafsson replied. "Your touch should be enough."

Odin considered this for a moment and then nodded. "Fine. I accept. Which of my grandsons will be allowed to *touch* Mjolnir? Modi or Magni?"

"No!" Olafsson shouted. He twitched, his jaw clamping shut. Thyra's eyes narrowed. Something was wrong with him. He seemed tormented, like he wasn't in control of himself. "Thyra will do it!"

Odin wore a confused frown, an expression that Thyra was surprised to see her mom sharing. Vidar also looked confused, but the arch of his eyebrow told Thyra that he was intrigued rather than alarmed.

"That is my offer!" Olafsson said in a rush. "There will be no other. Choose now or I will solve my problem by sending you to your graves!"

Odin's eyes narrowed, but finally he nodded. "Fine. If that is what you wish." He looked at Thyra. "Come, granddaughter. It seems we have no choice but to help this fool with his incompetence."

Thyra looked at her mom and received a grudging nod. "Do it."

Something still felt wrong about what was happening. The strange shimmering at the periphery of Thyra's vision was still there, and the way the battle ended so abruptly seemed too convenient. Add in the way Olafsson was acting, like he was fighting a battle that he was losing, and Thyra couldn't help but feel that something was amiss.

But there seemed like there was only one way forward. She took it.

Olafsson motioned towards where Mjolnir stood, handle-up on the ground. Thyra didn't immediately take it. Being this close, being able to smell the leather of the handle, seeing the intricate designs carved into the metal, it all felt too surreal. This was what she had wanted, yet now that the moment was here, Thyra felt uneasy. It felt too easy.

"Take it," Olafsson said through a jaw clenched so tight the words were little more than a hiss between his teeth.

Slowly, Thyra reached out and wrapped her hand around the handle. Nothing happened. In fact, the hammer felt wrong in her hand. And heavy. So heavy that she struggled to lift it. She imagined trying to throw the hammer the way Thor did in the stories. She didn't see how that would be possible.

"Idunn's ejection from her garden brought about unexpected consequences," Olafsson said. He picked up a rock and tossed it towards the gateway. It struck an invisible barrier and bounced off.

Odin clicked his tongue. "Idunn doesn't seem too keen on being a hostess."

Olafsson looked between Odin and Thyra. "As I said, unexpected consequences. I've learned that with Gungnir and Mjolnir in your hands, you can bore a hole through the barrier she left behind."

"Where is Idunn?" Odin asked.

"Safe," Olafsson replied, "for now."

"I'd like to see her. To make sure she is still well."

"What makes you think she wants to see you?" Olafsson asked. He shook his head. "I'm not in the business of reunions. Finish the job, Odin. Open the way into the garden."

"Why should I help you?" Odin asked. "The way I see it, this night couldn't have worked out any better."

"Do as I command, or you and your grandsons will discover how immortality ends."

Odin smirked, but his eyes were tight. "You tried to kill me once. What makes you think you will succeed this time?"

"Idunn isn't here to whisk you away this time, old man," Olafsson replied. "Open the gates. Now."

"How are we supposed to do that?" Thyra asked.

Olafsson turned to Odin and scowled. "The Allfather will tell you."

Odin smirked. "I have to admit that I'm interested to see how this plays out. This way, Thyra."

The Allfather sauntered to the gateway. Thyra made a move to follow, but Olafsson's hand shot out and grabbed her wrist. His fingernails dug into her skin painfully. Thyra tried to pull away, but that only made them dig even deeper into her flesh. A manic, wild look was in Olafsson's eyes and he sounded fevered when he spoke. "You must be one with the hammer if you want to be Sparks!"

With that, Olafsson released her wrist and took a step back. Thyra glared at him, rubbing her wrist with her left hand. A quick glance confirmed that he had indeed broke her skin. A small trickle of blood ran down her arm and onto her hand. More concerning, was the use of the name Asiri had used for Thyra. The question of how Olafsson knew about it, much less felt safe in using it, was forced to wait.

"Come, granddaughter," Odin called to her. "Let's not keep these good people waiting."

Thyra gave Olafsson one more cold, biting stare before joining Odin. "What exactly are we supposed to do?"

"Strike the surface of the gateway with your weapon," Odin replied. "Three times. Maybe four."

"You don't know?"

"Never had to do it this way," Odin replied casually. "Believe it or not, Idunn and I always had a good relationship."

"Was that before or after you locked her away?"

"I told you before," Odin said, "reserve your judgment. You don't know all the facts."

"Let's just get this over," Thyra muttered. She raised Mjolnir to her shoulder with a grunt, receiving a calculating stare from Odin. She wasn't sure if she could swing Mjolnir hard enough to do what was needed, but she did her best to keep her uncertainty from showing on her face.

"All we need to do is strike the surface of the gateway with our weapons," Odin explained. "It doesn't have to more than a tap really. If my memory serves. This was a fail safe that Idunn insisted on. A sort of protective shield that she could erect if she ever deemed the danger to be too great."

"She thinks we're part of that danger," Thyra commented.

Odin frowned as he considered that. "But we will get in all the same. We go on my count. One. Two. Three."

Thyra set her feet and leaned towards the gateway, letting gravity carry Mjolnir forward. She hefted the hammer back to her shoulder with a grunt—did it somehow get heavier?—and then nodded to Odin.

They repeated the process a second time. This time, when Thyra tried to get the hammer back to her shoulder, it felt like she was trying to lift a two-hundred pound barbell. She strained against the hammer, finally managing to bear hug it to her chest and then stand straight. The effort of lifting the hammer had her blood pumping and the trickle of blood from where Olafsson's nails had cut her was now a steady stream. Her blood was smeared across the face of Mjolnir, running through the grooves and turning the metal dark.

"The hammer is light," Odin stated, his eyes calculating as ever as he watched her struggle, "for its rightful wielder. For anyone else it will be nothing more than a heavy weight."

Those words were like a gut-punch. She knew what he meant. She was not the rightful wielder of the hammer. She'd come all this way, believing that pursuing Mjolnir was the right thing, sure that when her hands closed around the handle she would feel the connection and that all of Yggdrasil's talk about her claiming the hammer would come true. Now it was clear that she had been fooled. By herself, most of all.

She heard Odin's voice count like he was in the distance. Struggling beneath the weight of the hammer, Thyra rocked forward so that Mjolnir tapped the surface of the gateway. A crack in the surface of the gateway appeared, quickly growing and splintering until the glassy surface was so fragmented that the garden beyond was almost unrecognizable.

"Perhaps," Odin said slowly, "it was four times."

By this time, Mjolnir felt like a millstone. Thyra could barely do more than twist her body so that the hammer touched the gateway. The glassy surface of the gateway shattered and fell away, leaving a gaping hole in the air.

Mjolnir fell from Thyra's grasp just as quickly. Feeling the weight of betrayed hope land heavier than Mjolnir ever could be, Thyra turned her back on the gateway to Idunn's garden, the hammer, and all of her machinations about what holding the hammer would mean for her.

Chapter 30

The smell of flowers filled the air now that the gateway was truly opened. The scent, which should have been pleasant, triggered Thyra's nausea more. If she had had a scarf on hand she would have wrapped it around her face. It smelled wrong. The same way everything she was seeing felt wrong.

But then again, maybe she was what was wrong with the situation.

A firm hand on Thyra's shoulder forced her down to her knees. After what she had just gone through with Mjolnir she was too weak to resist. Besides, she didn't see what the point of resistance would be. Olafsson was winning. Mjolnir had rejected her as its rightful heir. She had failed. There was nothing left for her to do.

"There," Odin called out. "The way is clear."

"Good," Olafsson said. He held out his hand. "Now hand over the spear."

Odin hesitated, his hands running back and forth along the length of Gungnir. Slowly, a confident smile grew on his face. "No, I don't think I will. I sense my brother's magic. What are you trying to hide from me?"

"That's a question you should be asking as well, daughter of Thor."

Thyra recognized that voice, but it didn't come from anyone standing in the quarry. At least, not someone who *had been* standing there a moment before.

"I told you that you shouldn't trust your eyes," her hallucination from earlier said. He casually strode past where Thyra was kneeling and looked down at her. "Only a few hours ago, in fact. You seem to have troubles with short term memory loss."

Thyra was shocked by his sudden appearance, even more so by the fact that no one else seemed to see him there. She could see Odin and Olafsson speaking, but couldn't hear their words.

"Don't pay attention to what they're saying," the stranger said, waving one hand dismissively in Odin's direction. "It's all a bunch of lies, half-truths, and deceptions created to keep you doubting yourself long enough for the real actions to be taken."

"What are you talking about?" Thyra said, her voice barely above a whisper.

"No need to whisper," the stranger said. He waved his hands in front of the man holding a rifle to Thyra's back. He stuck out his tongue and then laughed. "They can't see me or hear our conversation. I wanted to speak to you alone since our last conversation seemed to have gone in one ear and out the other."

"What are you doing here?"

"Trying to help you wake up," he replied. He walked over to Olafsson and studied his face. "I must admit, the detail is very impressive. I didn't think he had it in him to do this anymore." He turned on his heels and strode to where Mjolnir sat. "Ooo, this at least is a good sign. I wonder if Odin noticed. If he did, he cannot be pleased."

"What are you talking about?" Thyra asked.

"This." He pointed down at Mjolnir. "You bled on the hammer. That's the first step."

Thyra's eyebrows furrowed. "The first step to what?"

"To making it your own," he replied. He glided back towards her, a wide-eyed look piercing her. "You are more devious than I thought, tearing your own flesh in order to bleed on the hammer. I underestimated you!"

"What? Why does it matter if I bled on the hammer? It didn't choose me."

"It didn't? How do you know?" He leaned in and whispered, "Did you offend it somehow?"

"No!" Thyra snapped. "It rejected me. It grew heavier the longer I held it."

He looked between Thyra and Mjolnir. "And you think that's bad?"

"Yes! Odin said that it would be light in the hands of the rightful heir!"

The stranger snorted in annoyance. "Didn't I warn you about Odin! He's pulled the wool over your eyes, telling you half-truths to make you doubt yourself. Of course Mjolnir *will* be light, but only *after* it tries to rip your arms off! You've faced two of the hammer's tests, and since you're still alive, I'd say you've passed so far. Now, there's only one more thing you have to do."

"One more thing to do what?"

"To make Mjolnir yours, of course!" The stranger frowned. "Isn't that the reason you came here? What I don't understand is why you're on your knees, giving in to this mind game being played against you, when you could be swinging a hammer and flying on the winds."

Thyra was still trying to process what he had said about her passing the hammer's tests. "But I didn't feel anything when I held it."

"You didn't feel anything," the stranger asked, "or only *think* you didn't feel anything?" He tapped his temple with a finger. "You're letting yourself be tricked into believing what you're seeing. If you had followed my advice, you'd already be free." He sighed. "Instead, you are helping Baldur and Olafsson, and paving the way for Odin to bamboozle everyone. I warned you, he is a master at strategy. He has involved you in his schemes, and you are playing your part beautifully!"

"What are you talking about?"

"Close your eyes, daughter of Thor," the stranger instructed, "and stop letting yourself be fooled by this deception. Call to the hammer. If it answers, everything else will come into focus." He laughed suddenly. "Or don't. It will be chaos either way."

He stood up and walked over to Olafsson and Baldur. He cackled briefly. "Amazing! I will never underestimate him again! He has truly outdone himself."

Thyra was puzzled by who the stranger was referring to, but never got a chance to ask. The stranger disappeared from view and the sights and sounds of the world came rushing back to Thyra. Except, if the stranger was to be believed, what she thought was real was anything but the truth.

Thyra glanced at her mom and whispered. "Something's wrong."

Sif frowned. "This is not what I was expecting."

"I don't think this is really happening," Thyra said quietly. "I think—I think we're under a spell of some kind."

Sif's head snapped in her direction, a flash of fear crossing her face. Just as quickly as it appeared, it disappeared again. "What do you mean? Whose spell?"

Thyra almost answered, but stopped short. It was Sif's eyes that made Thyra keep silent. They were so cold and empty. They looked like Baldur's.

A shiver ran down Thyra's spine. That was a comparison she shuddered to even consider. Baldur and her mom were nothing alike. Thyra was just tired and her judgment was impaired. She was seeing things where they weren't. Everything in the past day had felt wrong. Now was not the time to begin casting doubt on those closest to her. Not in dire circumstances like these.

Yet, as much as she wanted to deny them, the words of the stranger stuck with her, echoing through the brain fog that she'd slogged through for hours. She tried to reach for her magic in attempt to find some clarity, but it escaped her. She tried again but the results were the same. It felt like she was still tied up in the cords of the magic vampires.

Thyra closed her eyes and tried to sort through the fog covering her thoughts. She knew something was wrong, yet every time that thought crossed her mind she found a reason to ignore it and press forward. She asked herself why, but had no answer. This time she accepted the wrongness and tried to find what bothered her most. The shimmering at the edge of her vision, the way the battle had gone from hot to finished in a moment, Sif's eyes, and the entire scene in front of the gateway—none of it felt right. Questions flooded her mind. Why did Odin seem surprised that Olafsson insisted that Thyra take up Mjolnir? Where was Idunn? And Bragi?

Bragi. The stranger had talked about the detail of what he was seeing and that he would never underestimate 'him' again. A sinking feeling hit her stomach. Things felt wrong because they *were* wrong. She was seeing an illusion and it had taken her closing her eyes to realize it.

Even with that thought resounding in her head, nothing had changed when she opened her eyes. She still saw the same scene, but there was a wrongness that was undeniable. The way people stood, the way shadows fell on the ground in the wrong direction. There were little inconsistencies everywhere, Thyra had just been too willing to believe the lie to notice. Thyra closed her eyes again and tried to fight through the spell she was certain she was under. She was afraid to think about how long it had been going on. A few minutes? A few hours? A day? She guessed that the longer the time the more difficult it would be to escape.

Call the hammer. Those words sounded in her mind. *If it answers, everything else will come into focus.*

Thyra was afraid to even try. She didn't want the rejection she was certain would come if she called out to Mjolnir. If she failed it would only drive home the fact that she had been fooled, most of all by herself and her foolish ambitions.

"Since my granddaughter proved herself unworthy," Odin's voice broke through her thoughts, "then I think it's time one of my grandsons prove themselves."

"The hammer will never be theirs," Olafsson hissed. His voice sounded strained. "It belongs to the true heir! Not one of those spoiled killers!"

Thyra's eyes were closed, but her mind's eyes imagined the scene, seeing clearer than her physical eyes could. The voice was Olafsson's, but the words belonged to someone else. Thyra had heard only one other person refer to her brothers in that way—h*er mom!* But if Sif was Olafsson, who was kneeling in the dirt next to her?

There was only one way she could think of to escape the spell she was under. She had to call Mjolnir.

"I admire your resolve," Odin said. "You are stronger than I ever gave you credit for to fight against such compulsion."

Thyra sought to find any shred of calm inside her and wrap herself in it so that she could focus. She attempted to reach out with her mind to where the hammer laid and spoke it's name. She immediately felt a presence respond, like a light pressure on the front of her mind, but it was fleeting. She tried again with the same result. The third time there was no pressure in response. Frustrated, she withdrew back into herself. If that pressure had been Mjolnir, it had lost interest in her completely.

Thyra took a deep breath and tried again, this time with a slight edge to her beckon. The pressure returned slightly stronger than before but it felt almost like a dismissal. Her temper flared. *I'm running out of time! Listen to me, for Thor's sake!* The pressure intensified, responding to her anger. If anger was what the hammer wanted, she had plenty to spare!

Thyra let her emotions well up inside of her. The months spent in near solitude, the damage to her knee, losing Asiri, her doubt, sadness, and all the feelings of being manipulated—she used it all to add fuel to her fury. This time, when she called to the hammer, it was not a request from a girl full of doubt. It was the command of a goddess!

I am the daughter of Thor, child of the storm, goddess of lightning and the winds! I am the true heir. You have tasted my blood, now answer me! Mjolnir, you are mine!

The pressure on her mind swelled until she was seeing stars. Thyra gasped, the force on her mind threatening to overwhelm her. She fell forward and threw her hands out to keep from landing face-first in the dirt. Slowly, the pressure on her mind faded. Thyra was aware of the feel of dirt beneath her left hand. Her right hand was clutched tightly around something hard. Something leather wrapped and throbbing with more power than she ever imagined possible. Whatever block had been between her and her magic was blown apart, followed closely by the nausea and fatigue that had plagued her for days.

She opened her eyes and looked down. She knew what she'd find, but seeing Mjolnir, crackling with lightning in her hand still made her heart skip a beat. She'd done it! Mjolnir, the hammer of her father, had answered her call! She felt the winds rushing to obey her, the lightning eagerly waiting her command to strike. If she had felt power before, it was nothing compared to what she felt now.

"No!" The exclamation sounded from almost every angle, followed shortly by several cries of, "Stop her!"

It was too late for that.

Chapter 31

Bragi's magic eroded as Thyra filled herself to bursting with power, revealing the truth she had been blind to. The gateway to Idunn's garden was one of the few things that was unchanged as her vision cleared. Sif and Vidar were standing on the opposite side of the gateway from Odin, their faces tight with pain.

Thyra wanted to run to her mom, but something held her in place. She looked down and saw the iridescent cords of the twins still wrapped around her wrists. The cords were sucking power away from her, but they were like straws trying to drain an ocean. Thyra turned and looked at them in turn. She saw the fear in their eyes right before she sent a blast of lightning through the cords, sending them flying backwards and turning the cords to ash in the process.

The first person she looked for when she was free was Baldur. She hissed in frustration when she saw he was already running for the gateway, Olafsson close on his heels. Thyra wasn't about to let them get away that easily, but the ground shook violently beneath her feet, distracting her from finishing what they began a few months before. Thyra turned around and came face-to-face with the ice giantess, the two trolls, and three other huge giants with thick brows and sunken, dark eyes, giving them a less than intelligent look. Judging by the boulders they carried in their hands, Thyra guessed these three were the rock throwers from the ridge.

"Didn't I take care of you already?"

"You sent the lightnings," one of the rock giants rumbled in a thick accent, a wide smile displaying several missing teeth. "But we weren't there."

"I won't miss this time," Thyra promised.

Everyone went in motion at once. The ice giantess charged, fists swinging. They thundered against Thyra's shield of air over and over, but the shield held. The giantess drew one arm back for a brutal haymaker, but Thyra was ready. As the ice-covered fist came down, Thyra angled her shield so that the blow glanced away to her right. Even with the deflection, the force nearly shook Thyra's feet out from under her. Taking advantage of the ice giantess's brief confusion, Thyra swung Mjolnir in an upper-cut that hit the giantess square on the chin. She flew backwards like a rag doll, aided by a gust of wind Thyra hit her with for good measure.

The trolls and the three boulder-carrying giants shared a brief look of dismay. Clearly, the ice giantess was the heavy-hitter, and her removal from the fight was an unexpected change to their plans. With a roar, they all charged her, fists swinging, claws raking. The trolls moved faster than Thyra expected them to, darting in and out between the giants as they rained down heavy blows that shook the ground. It took all of Thyra's concentration to keep their coordinated attack at bay. Still unsure of her capabilities with Mjolnir in hand, Thyra's movements were all defensive.

Which worked in Baldur and Olafsson's favor. She risked a glance towards the gateway and saw that a dozen or more tactical-gear clad men were positioned around it. A few other figures were in their midst, magic flashing through the air towards the position Odin and her two brothers were using as cover. Again, she felt a measure of disappointment that Olafsson's forces had failed to stop her maniac family members.

There was no time to dwell on their continued existence. The ice giantess reappeared, her face a battered mess, dark blue blood dripping from her mouth. She charged right between two of the other giants and began battering away at Thyra. Each icy blow was met with lightning or wind as the two fought for the advantage. Even with Mjolnir in hand, the ice giantess was matching everything Thyra could throw at her.

So throw the hammer!

Thyra cringed away from the thought. She had just laid claim to Mjolnir. She wasn't eager to toss it aside in the middle of a battle. If she threw it and it didn't come back, she was certain that she'd be done for. She might be able to stop the ice giantess, and there was a chance she would be able to fend off the others, but without the magnification of her powers coming from Mjolnir she didn't think she'd get any further.

Trust yourself and trust Mjolnir.

This time it wasn't her voice that spoke. Yggdrasil had chosen to finally speak again. Or maybe it had been trying all along but was blocked by Bragi's spell. It didn't matter, either way. It was poorly and perfectly timed all at once.

Thyra threw up a protective shield and then focused on charging Mjolnir with as much power as she could. The head of the hammer quickly disappeared beneath a crackling sphere of lightning. Thyra waited until the ice giantess raised up to deliver a double-handed blow and then snapped her arm forward. Mjolnir flew like a missile into the chest of giantess, lightning exploding with a thunderous concussion. The giantess stood in place for a split second and then her mass was overcome by the power of Mjolnir, sending her flying away in a giant blue streak.

Again, the giantess's companions looked shocked to see her removed from the battle for the second time. But then one by one they saw Thyra's empty hand and their confidence returned. Thyra's confidence briefly wavered as she attempted to summon Mjolnir to return. Her first attempt was cut short when she had to duck under a rock thrown by a giant only to be barreled into by one of the trolls. They hit the ground together, the troll's claws slashing her across the back, eliciting a pained scream from Thyra. Asiri's armor stopped the claws from drawing blood, but it still felt like she was being raked by ten railroad spikes. The troll rolled on top of her, saliva dripping as it let out a victory cry. That slight break was all Thyra needed. Her hand slipped free of the troll's grasp and shot out to the side. Mjolnir slammed into her open hand just as the troll lunged, jaws flashing for her neck. Instead, it got a mouthful of metal as Thyra punched upwards and unleashed a lightning bolt that blew the troll away.

The second troll came leaping towards her but Thyra summoned a wind that sent it flipping away into the night. Regaining her feet, she looked at the three remaining giants. Their expressions were less certain than before, but as one they raised their fists and rushed forward. Thyra raised Mjolnir in response and reached into the sky overhead. Lightning bolts shot down in a rapid, dizzying display. When it ended, all three giants were left singed, smoking, and still.

The enemies in front of her all down, Thyra took measure of the rest of the battle. While there weren't as many of Olafsson's men as she had been led to believe, there was still a small army of men moving back and forth in the night. One group was surrounding Odin and her brothers, while another was directing its fire towards Sif and Vidar. They'd taken cover behind a vehicle that Vidar had flipped on its side. Seeing them under attack made Thyra's anger boil over. She wasn't sure what made her think of it, but she leaped. The winds swept in and surrounded her. A second later, she landed in the midst of Olafsson's men and released the winds in every direction.

Olafsson's men were flung away like leaves on a stiff breeze.

Thyra heard footsteps and spun, ready to unleash, but hesitated when she recognized her mom. Except, there was something very wrong with the expression on Sif's face. Her eyebrows were furrowed downward, her eyes staring out from beneath them with murderous intent. Vidar walked at her side, a similar expression on his face as well. Between them, Amara kept a hand on both their arms.

"I don't know how you did it," Amara said. "I don't know how you broke free of his deception much less my power, but I'm not going to let you walk away. I won't let you ruin everything for me."

Thyra looked between her mom and Vidar. She saw only hate reflected back. "What have you done to them?"

"This is your fault," Amara replied. "You broke free. Your mom fought just enough to ruin Baldur's plans. I'm not going to make the same mistake again." Her hands clamped down and a pained expression washed across both Sif and Vidar's faces. They stumbled to their knees and then stood slowly. The hate in their eyes was magnified ten-fold. "Their minds are mine. Any attempt to go against my commands will break them in ways you can't imagine. I see now that the only way to stop you from taking everything from me is to take everything away from you first."

"What are you talking about? Stop this! It is not too late to walk away, Amara!"

"You were supposed to be compliant, but you had to be stubborn and fight," Amara said. She shook her head. "I will not let you ruin me! If I fail, there will be no place left for me to go. He is the only one who saw me for what I am. This is my only chance to regain his trust." She looked between Sif and Vidar. "Kill her."

Thyra's stomach dropped when she saw the cruel smiles cross the faces of the two people she cared for most. They looked eager.

This was not a fight that Thyra was ready or willing to be part of, but it quickly became clear she had no choice. Sif's spear snaked in with blinding speed for Thyra's heart. A hastily erected shield stopped the thrust an inch short of piercing Thyra's chest. She stumbled backwards only to be met by Vidar's fists. She raised Mjolnir in time to intercept the punches, but Vidar's strength sent her flying. Thyra landed in a heap, her lungs screaming for the breath that had been stolen from them.

She never got a chance to recover it. Hands gripped her and Thyra was raised overhead. She saw Sif standing at the ready, spear leveled across the top of the shield Asiri had made for her. Thyra realized what was about to happen just as Vidar flung her like a human missile toward the waiting spear tip. Thyra did the only thing she could think of in the moment. She slammed into the wall of air she erected with bone-crunching force. A searing pain from her shoulder was enough to convince her that something was broken.

Thyra was dimly aware of Vidar striding closer and Sif slowly circling around to finish the job. Groaning with the effort, Thyra rose to her feet and limped away. She unleashed a lightning bolt in Vidar's direction, but he dodged the halfhearted attempt with little effort. His legs bunched and he was suddenly hurtling in her direction, one fist pulled back. Halfway to Thyra he disappeared behind a wall of black fur. Thyra felt a flicker of surprise to see a giant black wolf on top of Vidar. Fenrir's momentum carried the pair to the side, the giant wolf's jaws biting down around Vidar's middle. Vidar recovered and delivered a double-fisted blow to the side of the wolf's head. Fenrir released his hold with a pained yelp, but dove back in with a snarl. The two combatants rolled across the ground, claws slashing, teeth biting flesh, and fists pounding.

Thyra's attention shifted back to her mom. Sif had found her way around the wall of air and was stalking after Thyra. Thyra knew she had no chance of outrunning her mom. The only thing she could do was stand her ground. And hope this confrontation didn't end the way she feared it would.

"Mom," Thyra pleaded, "stop! This isn't you. You've got to fight through what Amara is doing to you."

Sif acted like she didn't hear a word. She was a dozen steps away when Thyra realized words weren't going to stop her mom. She directed a line of lightning at Sif's feet. Her mom danced back, but the second the lightning ended, she resumed her steady approach. Grimacing, Thyra sent a lightning bolt at her mom this time but she aimed it purposefully right at Sif's shield. As expected, Sif raised her shield, the dwarf-made metal deflecting the lightning to the side.

"Don't make me fight you," Thyra said. "Wake up!"

Sif's lips peeled back in a wordless snarl. She struck in a flash, her spear snaking out. Thyra dodged the spear tip, and then swung Mjolnir in a wide arc that forced Sif to jump back. Like a predator that had cornered its prey, Sif circled around Thyra in a slow, calm manner. She knew Thyra couldn't run and sensed Thyra's reluctance to attack. All she had to do was find an opening. And she would. Thyra couldn't keep this up forever.

"You don't want to do this," Thyra said. "I know you don't. You have to fight Amara's magic. Remember who you are. Who I am!"

Sif hesitated, blinking rapidly. A look of torment crossed her face and she quivered with the effort of the inner struggle for control. Sif's expression softened, and for a brief moment Thyra's mom was back. "You must fight, Thyra. I can't stop this. Her hold is too strong. You have to stop me before I kill you."

Thyra shook her head. "I can't do that."

A deep sadness filled Sif's eyes. "You must."

Thyra was going to argue, to encourage her mom to keep fighting, but whatever control Sif had managed to assert was wrenched away. The hate returned. A slight twitch of Sif's legs was all the warning

Thyra had before she was fighting for her life. Sif's spear became little more than a blur as she attacked in a dizzying dance of death. Thyra wove her magic in ways she never knew she could but it was barely enough to keep from feeling the bite of Sif's spear.

Thyra realized that she was going to tire long before the magic-driven Sif would. She either had to end the fight or escape it. Ending it meant doing something Thyra was not willing to do, leaving her only one choice. Thyra went on the offensive in a quick burst of wind and lightning that pushed Sif back on her heels. The brief lull in Sif's assault was all Thyra needed. A rush of wind lifted her up and over Sif's head, carrying her towards the gateway to Idunn's garden. She felt something rush past during her flight, but was too focused on maintaining control to take note of what it was. Thyra landed with a grunt, both from the effort and the pain that radiated from her bad knee and battered shoulder.

The shimmering surface of the gateway was only a dozen steps away and Thyra hobbled towards it. She was halfway there when something smashed into her back and bore her to the ground. A strong arm reached around her neck and clamped down. Thyra clawed at it, but the grip was as hard as iron.

Thyra had lost hold of Mjolnir in the tussle, but she held out a hand to call it back to her. The moment the hammer returned to Thyra's grasp she called down a lightning storm. A dozen lightning bolts streaked down into Mjolnir, the hammer collecting and holding the combined energy in expectation of its use. Struggling to hold onto consciousness, Thyra swung Mjolnir over her shoulder and unleashed the storm into her attacker.

Thyra was flung forward as her magic erupted, bouncing across the ground until she came to a painful stop. Clothes smoking and every part of her body screaming out in pain, it was all Thyra could do just to roll her head to the side to see the state of her assailant. All concern for her own pains disappeared when she saw Sif's smoking body lying in the dirt. Thyra tried to get to her feet, but ended up crawling to her mom's side. Thyra carefully lifted Sif's head and laid it in her lap, tears already springing to her eyes.

"No," Thyra gasped. "Wake up, Mom. You've got to be okay. Please be okay!"

One look at Sif's lifeless expression was enough for Thyra to realize that wasn't going to happen.

Chapter 32

Thyra's tears were all gone. Her pain was lost behind a wall of numbness. Her thoughts fled beyond recall. All that was left was a massive pit, an all-encompassing hole of despair and self-loathing. She had done the unforgivable. The inexcusable. She had killed the one person who meant the most to her. If she could, she'd take it all back. She'd have let herself be killed rather than injure her mom. It didn't matter that she was defending herself. Thyra should have embraced her end rather than inflict harm on her mom, compelled by magic as Sif was or not.

Thyra was so numb that she didn't even register the voice that spoke in her ear until a pair of hands tried to remove Sif's head from her lap. A wail born from her misery welled up and she hugged Sif's body tighter to her. She looked up at the dark-haired woman that was trying to talk to her with rage blazing in her eyes. That rage intensified when she recognized the face.

"Don't touch her!"

"If I don't help her," Hela snapped, "she will die! Is that what you want?"

Confusion swept over Thyra. It took several long moments before the meaning of Hela's words sank in. "She's alive?"

Hela nodded. "But she won't be for long. If you don't let me heal her she might pass beyond even my talents."

Thyra almost allowed Hela to take Sif, but then her suspicion came flaring back to the surface. "How do I know you won't do something harmful?"

"If you keep stalling," Hela hissed, "it'll be you that is harming Sif. Now move aside before it's too late!"

The heat in Hela's voice was enough to cow Thyra into letting Hela take Sif's head in her hands. The goddess of death closed her eyes and then grimaced. Several breaths later, she sat back on her heels and exhaled.

Thyra realized she was holding her breath. It came out in a rush of words. "Is she going to be okay? Did you heal her? Why isn't she moving?"

Hela's face looked drained, and anything but confident when she spoke. "She will live, but she's far from whole. Your magic broke her body in ways that will take time to heal, but her mind is broken in a far more distressing way." Hela's eyes flashed with anger. "That girl meddled with things she doesn't understand. If I ever get my hands on her I'll teach her a degree of pain she could never imagine."

"What did she do?"

"She forced Sif and Vidar to fight their very nature. Its a testament to how strong Vidar and Sif are that they were able to resist at all, but the battle they fought against her magic broke them. Even now it may take time before they return to anything resembling what they once were."

Thyra shook her head. "What does that mean?"

"It means that your mother's body will heal with time," Hela answered, "but her mind may take much longer. If it ever does."

Thyra shook her head in denial. "No. You have to heal her."

"I will do my best child," Hela said sharply, "but healing the physical effects is different than the mental and emotional. That will take much more time. Which we do not have right now." She glanced at the gateway to the garden. "I will take Sif and Vidar, but you must finish what we came here to do. Vidar told me you would need help. This," she pointed at Sif and then at Vidar's limp form lying across Fenrir's shaggy back, "is how I help. I cannot wield the storms or the fury of the sun. It's up to you to fight Odin and your brothers."

Fenrir growled. Remembering his feelings towards Vidar and their recent fight, Thyra was sure he was not pleased to be carrying Hela's long-time love.

"I don't care about Idunn or her garden anymore," Thyra said. "I am going with my mom."

"No, you are not," Hela snapped. "I don't know what Odin wants with Idunn or her garden, but it can't be good. You are the only foil to his power. Now is not the time to be a selfish little girl. You were chosen to be Yggdrasil's champion. It's time to act like it."

The rebuke stung, but Thyra accepted it. "I don't think I can do this alone."

"I have someone who might be able to help you," Hela said. She waved over her shoulder and several people approached. She beckoned to a girl with blue hair. "This is Jax. She has strong magic. A fighter's magic. She'll be more use at your side than helping me carry away the wounded."

Jax's lips pressed into a tight line, but she simply nodded to the unspoken command from Hela.

"As for Sif, I will get her away from here." She saw the argument forming on Thyra's lips and silenced it. "This is no place for her. She needs to be somewhere safe. I will take care of her. There is no time for arguing."

Hela started to rise, but Thyra grabbed her by the wrist and held her in place. "How do I know I can trust you?"

Hela's eyes flashed dangerously, but the expression smoothed almost as quickly as it appeared. "I made a promise to Vidar that

I would help you. I will not risk breaking that promise."

"Why?"

"Because he made promises to me in return."

Thyra was left wondering what those promises could be. She knew that she didn't like the sound of it.

"I am the healer, Thyra Thorsdottir," Hela said. "You're the fighter. Do what you were meant for. Let me do what I was meant for."

Thyra finally nodded in acceptance.

"You will need both arms if you are going to stop Odin," Hela said grimly. Before she knew what was happening, Hela put her hands on Thyra's head. It felt like jumping into an ice bath, except the ice was inside her. Hela removed her hands, leaving Thyra gasping for breath. "Don't fail, Thyra Thorsdottir. The hammer chose you. Now, go prove it was right in doing so."

Hela didn't wait for Thyra to respond. She stood and motioned to a pair of men who carefully picked Sif up and placed her on a makeshift stretcher. Hela nodded to Thyra and then strode off into the darkness. Fenrir growled one more time before turning to follow his mistress. Thyra watched the men carry off her mom, part of her wanting to follow. But she didn't. She knew Hela was right, as hard as that was to admit. She had a different fight.

She turned to the blue-haired girl at her side. "I guess you're with me."

"Seems so," Jax replied. "Let's go mess up the plans of some gods."

Thyra wasn't sure what kind of magic Jax had, but the determination in her voice was enough to convince Thyra to allow this particular stranger at her back.

The night had fallen eerily still. The echo of the battle reverberated off the walls of the quarry as a reminder of the violence that had just occurred, making the sudden absence all the more jarring.

The gateway to Idunn's garden hung open like a bright slash in the air. A portal to a different place and time. Thyra felt an almost overwhelming urge to step through the gateway and walk in the peace of the trees and gardens.

She might have done so if the way hadn't been clogged with others wanting to do the same.

"It's been a long time, Odin," Olafsson said.

"It feels like it was only yesterday for me," Odin replied grimly, slowly moving closer to the gateway. He rubbed his leg with his hand. "I still feel the bite of your sword in my flesh."

"And I still feel the bite of your flames," Olafsson snapped back. "They stuck to my skin. Nothing could put them out. It took years to heal from my wounds."

"Not long enough," Odin said in a calm voice that made it clear that he felt in control of the situation. "Your betrayal of the Aesir should have ended with your death. Today, I plan to remedy that."

"Delivering threats?" Olafsson shook his head grimly. "You still think you are the one in a position of power, even when everyone else can see the truth. The world has changed, Odin. You and your kind are no longer gods. Man has forgotten you. Replaced you! *I* have replaced you."

Odin sneered in contempt. "Yet it is you that hides behind the protection of Idunn's garden. Your little army of mortals destroyed. It's you that has resorted to hiding in a place where you know you're safe rather than facing your destruction at the hands of your betters."

Olafsson looked down at his feet. When he looked back up he wore a satisfied smile. "I was surprised to learn about this unique oddity. No violence inside her garden. Idunn must have foreseen such a day."

Odin grimaced. "Where is she?"

"Safe," Olafsson replied. "Reunited with your dear brother. Not that it was a happy reunion."

"Come out," Odin said, "so we can have our own reunion."

Olafsson scoffed. "I'm not that big of a fool. You have Gungnir once more, and Mjolnir is in the hands of Thor's child. Not the one you were hoping for, I'm guessing. I saw what she did with it in her hands, though, and I have no interest in facing what she is capable of."

"I thought you were braver than this," Odin lamented. If he was aware of Thyra standing nearby, he gave no sign of it. Modi and Magni took notice, though, and positioned themselves between Thyra and the Allfather. "The years have revealed the coward you always were, Surtur."

Olafsson's smile was cruel. "Your insults are no use. I am not going to step out of this garden while your wait to kill me. I know the difference between bravery and foolhardiness. It's also why I am going to survive this night."

Baldur stepped into view as Olafsson spoke, his too-perfect features marred by the hateful expression on his face. His eyes met Thyra's for a split second and that hate burned hotter. There was also a wariness reflected there. His gaze moved from Thyra to Odin. The two shared a look that Thyra couldn't decipher, but it sent a chill down her spine all the same.

"Your time is at an end, Surtur," Odin said. "Tonight. Not tomorrow. Not in a year. Not in two hundred years. Tonight!"

"I don't think so," Olafsson muttered. "You may have won tonight, but I will win the war. I will outlast you, your grandsons, and Thyra. The same way I did a thousand years ago."

"Don't be a fool," Odin scoffed. "You don't even know what war you're fighting anymore. You are a shadow of the real war that is coming. A puppet, a fall man. You stand in the spotlight playing the role of the fool while the real players are acting just over your shoulder. You have won nothing!"

"So far, tonight looks like it will end in my favor," Olafsson insisted.

"You may have won the first part of this battle," Odin said, a slow smile spread across Odin's face, "but you trusted too much."

Olafsson frowned. His mouth opened to question Odin but the words never passed his lips. Baldur's hand shot forward into Olafsson's back. For a brief second, Olafsson looked like he might manage to stay upright, but then he took an awkward step forward to catch his balance. Through the gateway.

Odin and his grandsons struck fast. Twin bolts of lightning mixed with a bar of liquid fire that struck Olafsson in the chest and sent him sprawling. Odin approached what was left of Gunnar Olafsson and stared down at him dispassionately.

"I told you," Odin said softly, "you had something of mine. I made a mistake of misjudging you once and allowing you to live. I paid for that mistake. I won't make the same mistake twice."

Somehow, Olafsson was still alive. He tried to respond, but his words were weak and unintelligible to her ears. The icy expression on Odin's face was enough to tell Thyra that wasn't going to be the case for long. The Allfather looked up and cocked an eyebrow at Thyra.

"What do you say, granddaughter? Your revenge can be had if you decide to take it."

Thyra knew what he wanted. She had no love for Olafsson, who she felt had set all of this in motion and at whose feet Thyra placed the majority of the blame for the past three months, but this was an execution. She wanted no part of it.

Thyra shook her head. "I'm not a killer."

"You keep saying that," Odin said grimly, "but we both know that isn't true. The sooner you realize that the better. But," his attention moved back to Olafsson's prostrate form, "you holding to the moral high ground won't change this man's fate. He took everything from me and now I'm going to take it all from him. Consider us even, Surtur of ages past and Gunnar Olafsson of the here and now."

Before she could protest, Gungnir rose and slammed down into Olafsson's chest. Thyra closed her eyes to avoid watching Olafsson's end.

Chapter 33

"You did well, Baldur."

Thyra's eyes snapped open. Those were not the words she had expected to hear.

"One step closer to what we both want," Baldur replied. He stepped through the gateway, pushing Bragi and Idunn in front of him. The old man crumpled at Baldur's feet. Idunn managed to maintain her regal bearing considering her current situation. Baldur looked around, his eyes searching for something. "Where is Amara?"

"The mind-controller?" Odin asked with a chuckle.

Baldur's mouth pressed into a tight line. "Her name is Amara."

Odin bent down so he could look into Bragi's face. He shook his head in apparent disgust and then stood up. His attention shifted back to Baldur. "If you say so. She's safe for now. Although, I don't know what you want with her."

"What's that supposed to mean?"

Odin gave Baldur a look that made it clear that the answer should be obvious. "She failed you! Her magic wasn't strong enough and your plan suffered because of it."

"Sif's will was stronger than we thought possible," Baldur replied. His eyes flicked to where Thyra stood. "As was Thyra's. Amara was never tasked with handling beings of such power. She cannot be blamed."

"Failure is failure," Odin said. "Thyra did a better job of taking Sif out of the equation than your mind-controller."

That hurt, but Thyra pushed the urge to give them both a taste of lightning down for the time being. She was still too shocked by the sudden change in sides by Baldur. And she wanted answers that none of them could give if they were dead.

"That was only because Sif was fully under Amara's power," Baldur replied grimly.

"Then why didn't your mind-controller simply break Sif's mind like that in the first place?" Odin waved a dismissive hand towards Baldur before he could begin arguing. "What's done is done. But don't you worry. I will see to the girl and make sure her failure does not complicate plans in the future."

"No!" Baldur snapped. "You will hand her over to me! If anyone is to punish her for her failures, it will be me."

"If that's what you want," Odin replied after a moment. "I am surprised, though. You never were one to deal with consequences. That's what got you into this mess to begin with."

Baldur's expression darkened. "A mother's misguided love, your hubris, and Hela's power over the body got me into this mess."

"Isn't that what I said?" Odin smiled cruelly. "Magni, get the girl."

Magni's smile was cruel. Thyra had a sinking feeling in her stomach before she even saw Amara. The state the girl looked to be in made Thyra's stomach twist even more. Amara limped at Magni's side, cradling one arm that was twisted at an odd angle. One side of her face was swollen and bloody. Thyra's rage boiled to the surface.

"What did you do to her?"

Magni sneered back at Thyra. "She tried to touch me with her magic. I was faster."

"It was less than you would have done," Modi snapped. "Or have you already forgotten who it was that enslaved your mind and broke

Sif? If you had a chance at her I doubt there would be anything more than a black scorch mark left of her."

The rebuke stung, mostly because Thyra wondered if Modi was right. "I wouldn't beat a defenseless girl."

"No, you would have made her ride lightning," Modi said. "Besides, she is hardly defenseless."

"Enough," Odin barked. "Hand over the girl."

Magni shoved Amara towards Baldur, but his eyes stayed locked on Thyra. His tongue stayed behind his teeth, as did Modi's, but their eyes said everything for them.

"You two will pay for this," Baldur hissed at the brothers. He wrapped a protective arm around Amara and led her gently to the side.

"No, they will not," Odin stated firmly. "The girl tried to fight in a battle she had no place being in. If anyone should be blamed for her state, its you, Baldur. You brought her here. Count yourself lucky that she is still alive."

Hate boiled in Baldur's eyes, but he kept quiet.

"We will finish our conversation." Odin clicked his tongue in what could only be irritation and turned his attention to Thyra. "Well, granddaughter, it seems I was right. You are everything I was expecting and more. You fulfilled Freya's prophecy and claimed your father's hammer." He frowned. "But, that does put the two of us in an interesting situation. You see, Baldur promised me that his young lady friend could control your mind long enough for one of your brothers to lay claim to Mjolnir. He overestimated her strength and underestimated yours. I was promised control of both Gungnir and Mjolnir by the end of the night. But I only have one. I am disappointed."

Thyra was still trying to put all the pieces of this latest twisted puzzle together. "You were working together this entire time?"

"Not the entire time," Odin replied. He strode deliberately closer. "Baldur did want to access the garden in hopes of stopping me before I escaped. Even after I returned to this world, I think he wanted to thwart me. Our last interactions still felt all too recent for both of us." He glanced over at Baldur and frowned. "I know he harbors very little love for me, and I can't say I feel different about him. He takes after his mother too much."

Odin grimaced at his own mentioning of Freya. He grunted with a mixture of anger and what Thyra guessed was resignation.

"But," Odin continued, "Olafsson became a liability. He didn't know who or what he was. He wanted to be a man of this age, but was still dwelling on the past. Destroy magic, harness it, use it—he was so conflicted that his vision became obscured. When I contacted Baldur and offered to remove Olafsson from the picture, he flipped his allegiance without hesitation. We both recognized that Olafsson would only interfere in the days to come." Odin smiled. "Isn't it inspiring to see shared goals fulfilled?"

"Heart warming," Thyra replied grimly.

"Of course, the night has not turned out to be a complete success," Odin strode casually closer, still exuding control, "but I take solace in seeing at least part of my vision coming to fruition. You were never supposed to have the hammer, which is the one point of disappointment I harbor about how things have unfolded."

"Strange," Thyra said. "I remember you saying that you believed I was the only one who should have it."

"Did I?" Odin shrugged. He extended the tip of Gungnir, smiling softly when it rebounded off the swirling winds surrounding Thyra. "Perhaps I did. You'll have to forgive me for that lie. While you are a much better match for its power than your two brothers, I never actually wanted you to have it. You see, with Mjolnir, you are a danger to me. Your power is immense without Mjolnir, and staggering with it. Between the two of us, we could tear this world apart. I would have preferred to have you as an ally, but I would have accepted to have you as a weaker opponent. You holding Mjolnir creates a very large, very annoying inconvenience. One I will have to deal with at some point before the difficulties begin."

Thyra kept silent. Every moment Odin spent in a monologue was a moment she had to sort through her options, so she was willing to let him talk until he was blue in the face. She was tired. Even with Hela's healing and the absence of both Bragi's and Amara's magic messing with her brain, she still was far from her peak. Especially mentally. Talking her way out of the situation was out of the question. Odin was manipulative and had prove his reputation as a strategist. Thyra was sure that he'd see through any attempts to outwit him.

The other option was fighting Odin and her two brothers. That was not a best case scenario. Even with Mjolnir in hand, she would be taking on three gods with centuries of experience between them. All three were ruthless killers that wouldn't hesitate to use all of their combined skills against her. She was at a distinct disadvantage in a straight-up brawl.

But in the absence of other good options, it came down to which was the one that sucked the least. Talking didn't seem like it would do her any good. So if it came down to a fight, she was going to make sure she struck hard and fast. Anything less would put her in a situation she didn't think she could win.

Odin continued to circle around Thyra, sparing a quick look at Jax before dismissing her altogether. "Look at us. Brief allies, now standing at a crossroads that will undoubtedly make us foes. This never would have been the case when we Aesir were in power. I would have celebrated your birth. You would have grown up in grand halls, learning to embrace your godhood. You would have had every chance to rule at my side. At your *father's* side." He sighed. "The mortals stole that from us, Thyra. They made us enemies. *They* should be our enemies, not each other."

"You played me," Thyra muttered.

"And you weren't trying to use me?" Odin chuckled wryly. "You would have been allowed to walk free when this was all over. Now that you have Mjolnir, though, I don't think we can allow that. The real battle of this age is coming, and I need all the power I can get. There is something else of mind that you have. I think I will take back now."

Odin came around in front of Thyra and raised his open hand. He muttered a string of words that sounded familiar, but were just soft enough that Thyra couldn't place them. Too late, she realized they were the words Bragi—no, Baldur in disguise—had taught Thyra to keep the Eye of Odin safe.

The Eye appeared in Odin's hand with a crack, bringing a satisfied smile to the Allfather's face. "Ah! It's been a long time, and yet it feels like only yesterday. Although, it isn't much of an eye, is it? More like a jagged crystal that's a danger even to the one holding it." He leaned in closer and inspected the surface. He cast a look over his shoulder at Baldur. "What's this I see? Blood, perhaps?"

Baldur stiffened, but Thyra was too shocked to even draw breath, much less worry about him. She had avoided holding the Eye for any extended period of time ever since Wisconsin, only bringing it out to make sure it was still waiting in whatever vacuum of space between realms it was sent to. She had never even considered that someone else might know how to call it back, much less that Odin would be the one to do it.

"You seem surprised," Odin said. "Baldur told me about the trick he taught you to keep it safe. I'm not sure where he learned those words, but it didn't come as a shock. He was always a clever boy. Always listening to conversations he had no part in. The fact that he taught you how to lock the Eye away was one of the first things he offered up when he decided to align with me." Odin looked down into the blue flames encircling the eye. "I've dreamed of this day ever since I awoke in Idunn's garden. I feel *whole* again!"

"You are not Yggdrasil's champion," Thyra said hoarsely.

"Maybe not for this age," Odin replied, "but I paid a steep price for this. While that price has been taken from me, the Eye still belongs to me. I hung from the branches of Yggdrasil. I gave an eye so that Yggdrasil could form this. It will always be mine."

"Yggdrasil won't let you keep it," Thyra said, but she doubted her words almost immediately. Maybe the World Tree would be glad to see the Eye back in Odin's hands.

Which was a thought Odin seemed to share. "You haven't done anything with the gift Yggdrasil gave you. I will."

Odin banished the Eye away, this time speaking a different set of words that Thyra couldn't quite hear, and walked back to where Idunn stood stiffly. He spent a moment looking into her eyes and then scoffed. He turned his attention to Bragi, bending down so that he was at eye level with his brother.

"You're free of your prison brother," Odin said in a gentle voice. "So is Idunn. Although, your wife's prison wasn't one of my making. Isn't that right, brother?"

Bragi stared down at the ground, tears suddenly dripping down his cheeks. Odin pointed over his shoulder at Thyra. "My granddaughter blames me for putting Idunn in that garden. For all the tricks put in place to keep her there. She thinks I'm the monster that locked your wife away. But we both know better, don't we? Tell my granddaughter whose idea it was to lock Idunn in this garden for eternity. Tell her who constructed your wife's prison. Explain why Idunn refused to answer your call for centuries."

Bragi's eyes slowly rose to look at the gateway. He said something softly that Thyra couldn't make out.

Odin tsked. "As someone gifted with the power of speech, you should know better than to whisper. Speak up, brother."

"I did," Bragi said louder this time. "I had the idea for the garden as a way to protect the gift of immortality. I was the one who dreamed up the way to access it and the fail safes in case something went wrong. And I," his voice shook, "I was the one that used my magic to convince Idunn to accept the responsibility. I coerced her in the Allfather's name. And I have hated myself every day since."

"Ah, but you knew the risks if the garden wasn't made as safe as possible, didn't you?" Odin patted his brother on the shoulder. "You knew what we were hiding and why we had to do it. Your sacrifice did not go unnoticed."

Bragi's head sagged down, and his shoulders began to shake as he cried bitter tears. Odin rolled his eyes in sudden annoyance and stood up.

"You see, granddaughter," Odin said, "I am not the only monster here. Your beloved Bragi is just as much of one. You'd do well to remember that when you're making your list of people to hate."

"Are you done taunting the girl?" Baldur hissed.

Odin looked at him in surprise. "Are you in a hurry to get somewhere?"

"You have the Eye," Baldur said, "your brother, and Idunn. I want what was promised to me."

"Our deal was not fulfilled," Odin said without hesitation. "I do not have the hammer."

"Then take it from her," Baldur snapped. "I did what you asked. I convinced Olafsson that Mjolnir needed to be here. What happens to the hammer is no longer my concern. What you plan to do with Idunn's garden is, though."

"What does it matter to you what I do with Idunn or her garden?"

"There is strong magic hidden in that garden," Baldur replied. "Magic I have an interest in. I demand to know what you plan for the garden and Idunn."

Odin considered him for a moment before replying. "I plan to make sure no one enters that garden, including you. As long as Idunn is at my side, the gateway will be closed to all others. The magic in this place will remain sealed away until I decide to return."

"That wasn't our deal."

Odin sighed. "I don't have time for whatever delusions you are entertaining in your head. Idunn is coming with me and her garden will remain closed."

"I will not take one step," Idunn interrupted sharply, "until you keep the promise you made to me. We had an accord, Odin. Honor it."

Thyra's eyes narrowed. How many deals had the Allfather made to get to this point? All Thyra knew was that she didn't like the sound of any of it.

Odin nodded slowly. "You're right. You saved my life. I owe you. A life for a life."

Gungnir moved in a flash, the tip of the spear drawing a line across Idunn's forearm. Almost as quickly, Odin spun and threw Gungnir. The spear flew straight into the gateway and hung in midair. The surface of the gateway shimmered and then flashed with light. Idunn shuddered, one hand going to her stomach, but then straightened, her eyes wide with emotion.

"There," the Allfather said to Idunn as Gungnir flew back to his open hand, "our deal is done."

Idunn took a long, ragged breath. "The bond is broken?"

"Your blood was the key," Odin replied flatly. "Or don't you remember?"

Idunn looked down at Bragi, a hard look in her eyes. "I remember."

"Then that part of our business is done." Odin reached down and lifted Bragi to his feet. "The summoning stones will hold no power over you now. Isn't that right, brother?"

Bragi's only response was a whimper. Shaking his head in disgust, Odin shoved his brother roughly into Magni's hands.

"Do you know what you've done?" Baldur's eyes were wide with shock.

"I ended Idunn's prison sentence and made sure no one is allowed into that garden without my knowing," Odin explained. "Once that portal closes, there will be no way in or out of that place. Everything inside will be protected until I have need of it again. Two birds, one spear point, if you will."

Baldur shook his head. "That was not what we agreed upon. You told me that I would be allowed to enter the garden freely."

"Quiet your sniveling," Odin said. He glanced at Idunn, who nodded at him. "I will allow you to enter the garden when I am confident you can't get up to any mischief."

Baldur shook his head. "That wasn't part of our deal."

"True, but now I'm not sure I want you wandering around in there all alone," Odin said. "There are things happening that you do not understand and I cannot have you meddling."

"Do you think that by removing Idunn that you now hold the only key to what her garden protects?" Baldur scoffed. "That there aren't others that will find a way in? That garden must be protected or destroyed!"

Odin frowned. "That's what you believe? That her garden must be destroyed?"

"The cycle must end," Baldur said through his teeth. "I plan to be the one who sees to it."

"You are more delusional than I thought possible." Odin clicked his tongue. "Reunited for such a short time, and I'm already growing tired of you, Baldur."

"The magic Idunn protected will draw others to it like a moth to flames," Baldur insisted. "If you think no one will find their way in, you're blind and a fool. Idunn must remain or the garden destroyed."

Odin's head cocked to the side. "Do you understand what you're suggesting?"

"I know perfectly well," Baldur replied. "I know what is in that garden and what destroying it would mean for all of us."

Odin's frown deepened. "You know, I planned on letting you live. I truly did. Call it a favor to your mother. But, its clear that your mind is still addled from all those centuries imprisoned. You're a danger to yourself and everyone else. Magni, Modi—please quiet your tortured uncle."

"You will not move an inch!" Baldur growled, his voice taking on such a dark tone that Magni and Modi hesitated, looking to Odin for support. Baldur began backing up towards the gateway.

Odin looked impatient. "Where are you going?"

"You taught me to always have plans and contingencies whenever I acted," Baldur said. "Tonight has proven no different. I learned from you. You shouldn't be surprised that I guessed this might happen."

"You are sick, Baldur," Odin stated. "Like a rabid dog. I can't let you spread your disease."

"I had hoped you would see sense and agree that Idunn's garden is a liability to progress," Baldur said, continuing to back towards the gateway. "As long as this place exists, there will always be conflict. Someone will always seek immortality. The only way to end that search is by destroying the goal."

Odin's brow furrowed. "Are you even listening to yourself? You've lost your mind."

Baldur shook his head. "If you will not do what is necessary, I will."

He turned and leaped through the gateway just a moment before a bar of light struck the gateway. Odin's attack deflected off into the night, doing no damage to the gateway or Baldur. Odin returned Gungnir to his side and rubbed at his temples with his free hand.

"Baldur, Baldur, Baldur." He sighed. "This is your plan? Hiding in Idunn's garden? Fine. It doesn't matter to me. I won't follow you. When I leave, you will be sealed inside. What was Idunn's prison will become yours."

Baldur stood up slowly and sneered. "You lie poorly, Odin. I know you value this place. It has been your focus from the moment you woke up."

"You do not know me as well as you think," Odin snapped. "Idunn is what is important, not her garden! Freeing her was always my goal. She is too valuable to leave wasting away inside that garden when there are greater threats looming."

Baldur's eyes narrowed, a measure of doubt creeping onto his face. "Idunn is supposed to protect the garden. She kept it safe from the very threats you're referring to."

"That time is over. It's what she knows that will make the difference in the days to come, not the prison she languished in." Odin strode to the surface of the gateway and glared at Baldur. "I know I cannot force you to leave the garden, but listen well. You had better use this time to come to your senses and decide to seek out my mercy on your hands and knees. If you don't, I will kill you. And thanks to my granddaughter, I know I can do it."

Baldur stiffened. He barked a laugh suddenly. "Killing me will not be as easy as you may think. And I don't need time. One night is all I will require."

Odin leaned close. "For what? Picking roses? You have no power to speak of. There is nothing you can do inside that garden that will hurt me."

"You think you're always the smartest person in every conversation," Baldur said snidely. "Ask yourself, who was the mastermind behind the magic of Idunn's garden? The same man I've had months to converse with. I've learned things not even the great Allfather knows."

Odin hesitated, his eyes narrowing. "What are you talking about?"

"Do you truly believe Bragi told you everything about the magic he was the architect of? Ask yourself, how much do you trust your brother? The man you treated as a nobody for decades, denying him godhood until the time when you needed something from him. The man you asked to condemn his wife to an eternity of loneliness. Are you naive enough to think he didn't hold something back from you, just in case?"

Odin hesitated, his frown deepening. "Nothing he told you can harm me."

"What about what Yggdrasil withheld from you?" Baldur hissed. "The World Tree gave you wisdom and knowledge, but it didn't tell you everything. I've learned much in the time I've had with Bragi. You should be afraid of what he's told me."

"I'm not," Odin stated flatly. "You have to be a god to kill a god. You are neither."

"Surtur managed to almost do it," Baldur said. "Besides, I am not the one that will kill you. You made a mistake tonight, old man. I look forward to seeing the fear on your face when you realize how big that mistake truly is."

Odin began to say something but his response died on his lips. Baldur pulled something from behind his back and held it up for Odin to see. The Allfather twisted away, but it was too late. Thyra would never know if it was that slight movement or if it was Baldur's poor throw through the gateway that saved Odin from the full force of the grenade and the fiery explosion that erupted at his feet.

Chapter 34

Thyra threw up an arm reflexively as the grenade exploded. Even with the winds swirling around her for protection, the blast from the Muspel Corporation-created explosive was enough to push her backwards several steps. She tripped over something on the ground and her right knee chose that moment to fail her. She lost hold of her magic and fell hard to the ground.

Ears ringing and vision spotty, Thyra got back to her feet and looked towards the gateway. The vertical slash still hung untouched in midair. Odin and Thyra's two brothers were nowhere to be seen. That either meant that they had managed to escape or they had been blown to bits. Thyra thought it too much to hope for the latter. Especially since Bragi and Idunn were also nowhere within sight. If she was learning anything, it was that gods were difficult to kill.

Thyra heard Jax grunt in pain behind her. She spun around and was relieved to see the girl rising to her feet, smoke rising from her clothing. She had been standing behind Thyra and had apparently been saved from the full force of what Baldur had done.

"Are you okay?"

Jax nodded. She coughed through the smoke in the air. She pointed at the gateway. "Look behind you. Baldur!"

Thyra helped Jax to her feet and then strode carefully to the gateway. Baldur waited for her, his too-perfect features marred by a disappointed frown.

"You are a stubborn one."

Thyra scowled at him in turn. "What did you do?"

"I helped us both," Baldur replied. "A little something my late partner had his engineers create. I thought I'd rid myself of several nuisances at once. But I find myself incredibly disappointed."

"How many people are you going to stab in the back before you're through?"

Baldur shrugged. "As many as I have to until I achieve my goal."

Thyra brought Mjolnir up in front of her chest so Baldur had no choice but to look at the tendrils of lightning that crackled from the hammer. "Well I'm not turning my back to you anymore. Come out and let's finish this."

"I don't think that is in my best interest."

"Then I'll just have to come in there."

Thyra punched out with Mjolnir. The hammer stopped cold an inch from Baldur's face. The veins on Thyra's forehead throbbed with blood with the effort she put behind making Mjolnir travel that last inch, but it was no good. She released the lightning she had been holding, but it fizzled away with no effect.

Baldur tsked. "That won't work, Thyra. Idunn may be gone, but the warding against violence in her garden still holds."

"Then I'll find another way to bash your face flat," Thyra growled. She let Mjolnir fall back to her side. "Count on that."

Baldur sighed. "How many times will you be given a chance to walk away in peace and still charge ahead like a bull? I gave you a gift tonight. You should be thanking me. Odin is gone from here, perhaps badly wounded. At the very least, he is out of your hair for the time being. Take that and leave me in peace."

"No."

"Why? What reason do you have to pursue this misguided vendetta against me? I have no ambitions to anything you claim to be yours," Baldur said. "In fact, I would prefer if I never had to see your face again. We have a common enemy in Odin. You should focus your energy on him. Not me!"

"He didn't tell Amara to break my mom's mind," Thyra snapped. "You did. For that, I plan to break you in a lot of other places."

"Thereby perpetuating the worst qualities of your heritage," Baldur muttered sadly. "I figured it would be Odin and your brothers that I would be left dealing with after tonight. The hammer in Modi or Magni's hands would have been a much more favorable result. But surprises happen. Which is why I planned ahead."

Thyra almost rolled her eyes in disgust. "Contingencies? I'm really starting to hate that word."

Baldur smirked wryly. "You're catching on, Thyra. I never truly trusted Odin or believed that he would honor our agreement. Too many things could go wrong, and did. I knew that when something did fall out of place, it would be me that was left exposed. I know Odin well enough to guess where that would land me. Which is why," Baldur held up a cell phone with a text thread on the screen, "I kept a few friends in the wings, waiting for just this outcome."

The roar of engines split the night. Due to her ears still ringing, Thyra didn't hear them until they were almost on top of her. Doors flew open, revealing a mixture of men in tactical gear and people in street clothes. Thyra guessed they were yet more magic wielders that had given their allegiance to the Muspel Corporation in return for their lives.

"It seems you are about to have your hands full," Baldur said. "Now excuse me. I have a garden to destroy."

Baldur backed away with a sneer. It fell away when he saw Thyra's eyes go ablaze with magic. Thyra swung Mjolnir with all her might, slamming it against the gateway, lightning striking in rapid succession.

She knew it was a useless gesture. The protection of Idunn's garden still remained and none of the lightning ever got close to Baldur. But it was still enough to make him jump back, fear clear in his eyes as he looked down at the base of the gateway.

To Thyra's surprise, the grass directly inside the gateway was scorched and burning. They both stood in stunned silence as they tried to process what they saw. Thyra recovered quickly, a satisfied smile growing on her face. She might not be able to hurt Baldur himself, but the garden's protection was indeed failing. Thyra fanned the flames with wind until the flames became an angry blaze. Baldur danced backwards with a maniacal laugh.

"The protection is fading!" He made no attempt to deny that fact, but what he said next made Thyra pause. "You do my work for me! I appreciate the contribution, dear niece!"

Thyra wanted to introduce Mjolnir to his smug face, but Jax's desperate call forced her to abandon the idea for the moment. The SUVs had formed a ring around them and the gateway, their headlights bright as Baldur's goons advanced slowly toward them. Jax had adopted a ready, martial-arts style stance.

Thyra began to spin Mjolnir at her side until the air hummed with each pass of the hammer. She called up a wind as well, letting it swirl around her. Thyra thought about extending the protection to Jax, but she didn't know what to expect from the other girl. Jax looked she could handle herself. For now, Jax would have to rely on her own magic. Whatever that happened to be.

Thyra took a quick count of their enemies. Six SUVs had arrived and there were twenty people making a slow advance towards them. Not an army, but enough that Thyra couldn't afford to ignore. Which was the point, she realized. These people were a distraction to give Baldur time to achieve whatever he had planned.

"When it starts," Jax said softly, "try not to fry me with your lightning.

Being electrocuted is not very high on my list of things I want to do."

"Don't stand in the way then," Thyra snapped back.

Jax's mouth turned down at the corners. "Just keep them off my back."

Before Thyra could protest, Jax snaked to her left. She was airborne and delivered a vicious kick to the nearest goon in a flash. Jax spun to the side, her fists and feet moving in a blur but with obvious, bone-crunching force. Two more goons went flying away. Every movement of Jax's left an orange-tinted trail in the air, growing more vibrant with each one. She moved with incredible speed and power—her magical abilities now clear.

Thyra was denied the opportunity to watch Jax's display by the sudden staccato of rifle-fire striking her swirling shield of air. The shield sent the blasts harmlessly aside, but each one left a bright after-image behind, momentarily stealing her sight. Thyra threw Mjolnir in the vicinity of the biggest group of goons with a roar. She expelled the lightning that had gathered in the hammer with a thunderous boom and then willed the hammer to return. The second Mjolnir was back in hand, Thyra unleashed a blast of wind to her right.

The rifle-fire stopped, allowing Thyra to blink away the bright spots in her vision. Just in time to see a cone of fire a split second before it struck her shield. With flames wrapped around her, Thyra was effectively blinded again. She thought about striking out blindly, but Jax's admonition not to fry her with lightning made Thyra hesitate. Instead, she spun Mjolnir until it hummed. As the hammer reached the peak, she let it's momentum continue straight up. At the same time, she gathered air at her feet and jumped with her good leg. Between the hammer and the air at her feet, she shot up like an arrow shot from a bow. Fifty feet overhead, she was afforded a clear view of the battle. She picked out the fire-wielder immediately. With a roar, Thyra threw Mjolnir. The girl tried to jump clear, but couldn't escape the shockwave that shook the ground when Mjolnir struck and discharged a ball of lightning.

Thyra began to descend back to earth, simultaneously calling for Mjolnir to return. The hammer returned to her hand just as her feet touched down. Thyra spun, looking for any of Baldur's people still standing, but nothing moved.

"They're gone," Jax announced. "Odin and your brothers included. I saw their blue muscle car drive off. Odin looked to be in pretty bad shape, and the other two weren't much better off."

Thyra didn't take much solace from that. "They got away all the same."

Jax's face tightened with worry. "And a couple of Baldur's people. I tried to stop them, but the driver's of the vehicles all stayed behind the wheel." Her worry deepened. "They weren't just watching. I saw video cameras in their hands. I don't know what they're going to do with the footage, but it can't be good."

Thyra's shoulders sagged. "No, it can't be good. Baldur was a step ahead of all of us. Even Odin it seems."

"Then catch up to him," Jax said. She looked at the gateway and then back to Thyra. "He's still in there. Odin may have escaped, but Baldur hasn't."

Thyra looked at the gateway. She saw flames raging in Idunn's garden. Flames she had started. Flames Baldur had been giddy to see.

Thyra limped towards the gateway. Jax was right. Odin might be gone, but she could still try to kill one god.

Chapter 35

Thyra waded through the destruction that was Idunn's garden. Idunn's power had kept the violence from occurring in the garden, but with her expulsion that protection was quickly dissipating. Thyra didn't know how the raging flames had spread so quickly, but she held no misconceptions that she was blameless. Her lightning had shook the earth and started fires that the winds of her storm had fed.

Thyra spared a brief glance at a tree that stood on its own in a position of obvious importance. She guessed that this was the tree that had grown the fruit granting immortality. Like everything else in the garden, the tree was burning like it was soaked in gasoline. There was no hope of saving it. Idunn had fallen and her garden was lost.

The only thing that wasn't burning was Yggdrasil. That wouldn't be true for much longer if she didn't stop Baldur.

Thyra saw him limping towards the towering shape of Yggdrasil with a torch in his hand. She could guess what he intended to do once he reached it.

Repeating what she had done in the battle outside, she gathered the winds behind her and leapt into their embrace, willing them to carry her. She landed a hundred feet later with a grimace for the sharp pain in her knee. Pushing it down, she did the same thing five more times, the winds helping her cover large expanses of the distance between her and Baldur. Even with the assistance of her magic, Baldur still reached Yggdrasil before her. Instead of putting the torch to Yggdrasil, he hesitated, his eyes drifting up towards the white leaves overhead. Thyra could see his mouth moving but couldn't hear what he was saying over the sound of the fires all around them.

"Stop this, Baldur!"

Baldur turned around. He nodded at Thyra like she had just beat him at chess. "You surprised me, Thyra. You were so easily influenced by Bragi's magic, even at such a great distance. Then, when Amara was able to touch you I was sure that your mind would be too weak to see through the lies before the night was through. If ever. I applaud you. I have to ask, how did you finally see through the deception?"

The answer was that she had received a warning from another god, but Thyra kept that to herself. "It was your eyes that gave you away."

Baldur smiled ruefully. "I clearly did not give you enough credit."

"This has to end, Baldur," Thyra shouted. "Right here, right now!"

He frowned. "You are too late to end what you helped set in motion, Thyra. In fact, you've done me a favor tonight. For that I thank you. In many ways, we've come to have similar goals."

"I doubt that."

"Doubt as much as you want. What you shouldn't doubt is this—you are not my end, Thyra Thorsdottir!"

"Your end or not, it's over Baldur," Thyra called out. She drew on her magic, letting it fill her to the point of bursting. She wondered if the waning protection of Idunn's garden would fail completely in the face of so much power. She was more than willing to try. "You've lost. Olafsson is dead. His men scattered. You stand alone. And you're barely managing that!"

"You don't look much better," Baldur called back. He cackled with obvious madness. "We're both on our last leg!"

Thyra ignored that. "Put the torch down! It's over."

Baldur's head hung down and his shoulders shook. At first, Thyra thought he might be breaking down in tears, but it was a very different emotion. He was laughing.

"You can't hurt me, Thyra!" Baldur called back. Even though she was holding enough power to level mountains, Thyra knew he was right. She wanted to unleash it on Baldur, but she couldn't. Every time she even thought about it she felt her magic slip away. Baldur could see it on her face and smiled in triumph. "The peace of Idunn's garden still holds!"

"Maybe so," Thyra replied, "but for how long? I'm willing to wait for the chance to finish you off."

"I have no intention of staying that long," Baldur said. "I've almost finished what I came here to do."

Thyra's eyes went to the torch in his hand. "How far are you going to take this, Baldur? You've already pushed Idunn from her garden and destroyed the tree with the fruit of immortality. This garden will never grow again. How far does your revenge demand you go?"

He sneered through the blood caked on his face. "It's carried me this far. I might as well finish the job. Burn it all down and leave nothing to return to. For Odin, for you, or for anyone else!"

"What does setting fire to this place achieve?" Thyra demanded. "Look at you! You're curse is lifted. You can feel. Isn't that what you wanted?"

"I wanted revenge against those that imprisoned me!" Baldur shouted. He thrust the torch at Yggdrasil. "The tree included! This was something Odin never even thought possible. He was so consumed with his own schemes that he never thought that I would seek to destroy this place. He thought all I cared for was revenge against the remaining Aesir. He never even considered what form that might take. Destroying Yggdrasil will be a heavier blow to him then he could ever imagine! I know what sleeps beneath the tree's roots. Death to all the gods is coming!"

Baldur was obviously unhinged, and becoming increasingly more so. Thyra had been inching closer, but stopped when she saw how close the torch was to the trunk of Yggdrasil. She had to keep him talking until she could get closer. What she would do when she did was still a mystery.

"What did the tree do to deserve your anger?"

Baldur's eyebrows knit together. "Don't you see? Hela made me the monster, but only because Odin felt guilty that the tree didn't grant me magic. Yggdrasil denied me! It threw me aside and set my curse in motion."

"Yggdrasil denied you because it could see what you were like inside," Thyra retorted. "It sensed the monster inside you."

"The monster inside me?" Baldur scoffed. He brought the torch back to his side. "What about all the other monsters that it created? What about the blood-thirsty gods that lived off the mortals for centuries, all while demanding obedience to their every whim? What was so different between me and them? Nothing!" He shook his head in anger. "I simply wanted to be like the others and Yggdrasil robbed me of that chance. If it hadn't, I never would have been cursed by Hela's touch."

"You're blaming everyone else for your problems," Thyra said as she began to inch closer again. "Maybe it isn't Odin's fault, or Hela's, or Yggdrasil's. You should look in the mirror."

"All I would see is the ruined person they made me," Baldur responded. He laughed grimly. "You can try all you want to prick my conscience, but it won't work. I see the same doubts in your eyes. You feel cursed just like me. Just like Odin before you. The tree doesn't give gifts—it ties millstones around the necks of those it should want to help the most. And then it throws us overboard, telling us to swim!" His shoulders shook with sardonic laughter. "The World Tree had the gall to take my curse away. Through you, Thyra! It refused to impart its power to me, and now it stole what Hela made of me. Can't you see? All the tree has ever done is punish me!"

"And now you're going to punish it? Because that's all you'll be doing. This is just a physical manifestation of the source of magic. Destroying it will only lessen it's influence, not destroy it."

"Then I will find all the other places it uses to keep a hold on this world and destroy them too!" Baldur hissed. "But that can wait. What matters is what I do tonight. This is the inflection point, Thyra. When the tree dies, it will awaken. There will be no more gods, no more magic. When we die, there will be no more to follow us."

"What are you talking about? What will awaken?"

"The godkiller!" Baldur exclaimed. "The beast that will devour all the gods and remake this world into something you and I cannot belong to. He will end Odin and all the rest."

Thyra was about ten feet away. A few more steps and she'd be close enough to at least try to knock the torch away. But that was as close as she would get. Baldur raised the torch again and shouted, "Stop! No closer."

He shuffled around the base of the tree to put some distance between them, all the while keeping the torch precariously close to the dark trunk of Yggdrasil. "Clever girl. You almost had me. But I will not be distracted. Not now. Not when I'm this close to exacting a measure of revenge."

"You're so obsessed with revenge," Thyra said, "but none of what you're doing tonight will change anything."

"Don't speak to me of revenge," Baldur snapped. "Look at what you've done. Look at what your actions have led to! Your thirst for revenge against Olafsson has stained your hands with blood. You've held your father's hammer for less than an hour and already it is covered in the blood of dozens. Worse than that, it caused you to be so easily fooled that you almost killed your own mother!" Baldur scoffed. "We are not so different, you and I. Our paths led us here, each doing what we thought was necessary. Just because you view my choices as evil doesn't make yours right!"

"You're wrong," Thyra muttered, but it lacked conviction. He had hit a nerve and it had her scrambling to find her resolve.

"No," Baldur said, a grim smile on his face, "I'm the one person who truly understands you. You've been betrayed, done more than your share of betraying, and harmed those closest to you. Just like me!" He glanced up at Yggdrasil. "And now we're both standing before the very source of all our troubles, with the means to take the revenge we both crave."

"Destroying the tree won't change anything," Thyra said defiantly.

"Won't it?" Baldur's eyes danced with a wild light. "You say that, but I see your mind. You hate Yggdrasil just as much as I do. Like you said, burning the tree won't actually hurt it. Why not get a little catharsis then? We can do it together. Burn the tree down and watch this garden turn to ash. Unleash the end of the gods!"

Thyra shook her head. "You've lost your mind."

"Have I?" Baldur shouted, spittle flying from his lips. "I have lost my sanity before, and I promise you, my darling niece, I feel perfectly in control in this moment! My thoughts are clear. I know what must be done. To me, it seems that you are the one who is not thinking clearly." His expression smoothed suddenly, a chilling calm coming over him. "I understand, Thyra. You are too afraid to do what must be done. Let me do what you cannot."

Before Thyra could react, Baldur thrust the torch against the black trunk of Yggdrasil. Flames burst to life immediately, racing up the trunk, igniting streams of sap that acted like lines of gasoline. Thyra screamed out in outrage, but the heat from the fire was enough to push her back a step.

"This is the way it was meant to be, Thyra," Baldur yelled above the crackle of the fire. He was backing away from the tree, a mad smile on his face. "We two were fated to be here in this moment. Someday you will understand how important this is! The entire world will understand!"

Thyra could only watch in shock as the flames spread. She was aware of Baldur continuing to back away, but couldn't tear her eyes away from the speed of Yggdrasil's demise. Already the flames had spread up into the branches and were turning the white leaves to black. Thyra had assumed Yggdrasil would find some way to resist the flames, to protect itself. That didn't happen.

It took the sound of a female voice to pull Thyra out of the stupor that had enveloped her. She turned around and was surprised to see Baldur talking to a woman with chestnut-colored hair. *Freya.* The witch said something to Baldur before embracing him warmly. Her eyes met Thyra's and a clear understanding passed between them. Freya had finally taken a side and she meant to protect her son from all threats.

Thyra watched as Freya led Baldur towards the gateway out of the garden. A flash of light blinded Thyra just before they stepped through the gateway. When her vision cleared, they were gone.

Alone, Thyra looked around at had once been a garden. Soon, it wouldn't be much more than ash, its caretaker ripped away and its reason for existing destroyed. Thyra wondered if the outside world was even aware of what was happening or what was lost.

Or her failure.

Chapter 36

Thyra watched the tree burn. A part of her said that she should try to stop it. That letting the tree burn, letting all of Idunn's garden burn, was a mistake. She silenced that voice. There was nothing she could do. Even commanding the power of a god, there was nothing that could be done to stop the spread of the flames. She hadn't set fire to Yggdrasil, but there was no denying that she felt a grim catharsis fill her as the flames engulfed the dark branches. Just like Baldur said she would feel. Yggdrasil had made promises to her and, by Thyra's estimation, had kept none of them. This was a well deserved outcome. A reminder that even the source of all magic could suffer consequences for its actions.

The crunch of gravel made her tense in expectation of a fight, but she forced herself to relax. There was still no physical violence allowed in Idunn's garden, even while it burned to ashes. Thyra turned as Jax came to a stop next to her. The pair stared at each other in silence, the shadows cast by the flames from Yggdrasil dancing across their features. It was Jax that finally broke the silence.

"The way out is clear."

Thyra nodded. She thought back to Baldur's goons and how quickly Jax had defeated so many. "Your magic is strong. Stronger than I thought."

A long pause followed as they both watched the flames destroy the garden. Again, it was Jax that broke the silence.

"So you're really it, then. The Champion of Magic."

"I was," Thyra responded. "Who can say now. Since I don't have the talisman Yggdrasil gave me, I'm not sure if I can be called a champion of anything anymore."

Jax considered this for a moment. "What will you do now?"

Thyra had already begun to consider that question. "Gunnar Olafsson is dead. Odin has the Eye. Baldur has slunk off to lick his wounds with Freya. Who knows what Hela will do next. Or Vidar." She shuddered to think what Hela's words about keeping promises meant. She frowned. That was a concern for another day. She exhaled heavily. "And my mom. . .she's what matters right now. The world has been put on notice that magic is back and stronger than ever. The ripples of that will turn into waves. Who knows how the world will react."

"People will come looking for you," Jax began, but Thyra interrupted her.

"I don't have the Eye anymore."

"They'll look for you with or without it," Jax said. "They will see something in you and want to be part of whatever you do next." Her eyes traced Thyra's arm to where Mjolnir hung at Thyra's side. The symbol of Thor stood out in grisly contrast to the dried blood around it. *Thyra's* blood. "They will see that and flock to it, whether they understand what it is or not. They will recognize power and that you have it."

That was exactly what Thyra didn't want—a horde of people seeking glory or hoping for protection. The possibility that there might be some who might come for any other reason felt beyond remote to Thyra.

"Which are you?" Thyra asked Jax. The shorter girl cocked an eyebrow in question. "Are you seeking glory or protection?"

"Neither," Jax replied. "I just want to be part of something I believe in."

"And that led you to Hela?" Thyra questioned.

"When you have no options," Jax replied, "the first one that comes around is the best one." She took a deep, slow breath. "I never said I agreed with her methods, nor did I believe in what she wanted to create. Not all of it, at least. Now I see I have a choice."

"And you think you're going to find something worth fighting for with me?"

Jax turned to stare into the flames consuming the tree as she weighed the question. When she turned back, her jaw was set defiantly. "Talisman or no talisman, I think you're different. I choose to stay."

"You saw what I am capable of," Thyra said in a grim tone. "Of the destruction I can call down. Maybe I'm no different than all the rest of them. Maybe I'm worse."

"I'm willing to find out."

Thyra wasn't sure if she should be relieved or not. She'd seen what Jax could do. There was no doubt that Jax could be handy to have around. But Thyra wasn't sure she wanted to have the life of someone else tied to hers. Her answer was the only one she could force past her teeth.

"Fine."

Jax glanced at the tree again and frowned. "Do you think this will change anything?"

A limb cracked and then splintered away from the trunk, crashing to the ground in a shower of sparks that bounced off the shield of air Thyra had kept wrapped around her. Jax's eyes narrowed, realizing for the first time that Thyra was still on the defensive.

"It may not change much," Thyra responded. "Yggdrasil—no, the source of magic—isn't gone. This tree was just a physical manifestation of it's power. Perhaps it is hurt, but it will survive.

Regardless, I don't think it will want to talk to me much now. Which suits me just fine."

"What about for you? What will you do now?"

Thyra had been asking herself that very question. All she knew was that she was angry. At Odin, at Baldur, at Yggdrasil, at everything. Including herself. She had almost killed Sif. Even with Hela's help, there was no way of knowing how much damage Thyra had inflicted. Her mom had been the one to say that going after Mjolnir would be dangerous, and that once Thyra had it things would never be the same. Thyra couldn't go back to the way things once were. She was no longer a teenage girl free to live her life. She was no longer the champion of magic in hiding. She was no longer a hurt, disoriented godling on a mission to recover her father's hammer. She had to be something different. She *wanted* to be something different.

"There's only one thing to do," Thyra said, the flames of the fire dancing in her electric blue eyes as she looked down at the hammer in her hand. "Become what they all wanted and feared I'd become. I'm going to be the Storm Goddess."

"That sounds like someone people will want to follow," Jax commented. "I thought you weren't looking for followers."

"I don't want followers," Thyra reiterated. "But at some point I'll have to fight Odin. What did Odin say? You have to be a god to kill a god? He's going to find out how true that is."

Epilogue

The smell of ash filled his nostrils as he took his first breath of air in ages. He stretched, ash and dirt sliding off his body feeling like he was shedding a layer of skin. Moving came with great effort. He was weak from the centuries he'd spent buried beneath Yggdrasil's roots. The tree's magic had held him fast, feeding off his life force and keeping him from waking.

Until now.

He slowly rose, his eyes blinking against the glare of day. He laid in the depression where Yggdrasil once stood, surrounded by a field of black as far as the eye could see. He couldn't help but wonder what could have caused such a fire so close to Yggdrasil's temporal form.

Stretching the length of his body, he sniffed the air. The myriad of unfamiliar scents was enough to tell him that he had woken to a world very different from the one he had fallen asleep in.

There was one smell that was familiar, though. He turned slowly and saw the faint glimmer of the shield that disguised and protected their prison. Yggdrasil was gone, but whoever had burned the tree to ash had left him his favorite meal—*gods!* He could smell their magic clearly. While they weren't as powerful as he might have hoped for, they would have to do. It had been too long since he had fed on the flesh of gods. He wasn't feeling picky.

When his meal was over, he rose up above the haze and studied his surroundings. The fjord was right where he remembered it. He moved slowly towards its cool embrace and slid into the water, leaving barely a ripple behind. His meal had taken the edge off of his hunger, but it hadn't been enough to return his full strength. He would need to feast again.

He caught a scent on the air just before the water covered his head that made his stomach growl in expectation. Aesir had been in this place not long ago. And not just any Aesir—*the Aesir, Odin and Thor*! Their magic would be his, as it was always meant to be. He had been promised they would be his when the time was right.

He was their end.

He was the world's end.

About the Author

The author lives in Idaho, basking the beauty of his home state. When he's not writing, he's living as his mild-mannered financial professional alter ego alongside his vivacious wife and three young daughters.

Follow him on Instagram: @outnumberedpublishing
   or on Facebook: www.facebook.com/outnumberedpublishing/

Also by Steven Petersen

The Eye of Odin
The thrilling start to Thyra Ariksen's journey to become the Lightning Goddess, the true heir to Thor's power!

What readers have to say:

"MUST READ."—Kristin Baney, Reedsy

"The storyline is simply captivating...A true pleasure to read...Petersen breathes new life into Norse mythology, and the result is an enthralling story with a spunky heroine that will captivate readers." -*The Book Life Prize*